URDESH
THE MAGISTER AND THE MARTYR

More tales from the Sabbat Worlds

• URDESH •
Matthew Farrer

Book 1: THE SERPENT AND THE SAINT
Book 2: THE MAGISTER AND THE MARTYR

THE VINCULA INSURGENCY: GHOST DOSSIER 1
A novel by Dan Abnett

BROTHERS OF THE SNAKE
A novel by Dan Abnett

VOLPONE GLORY
A novel by Nick Kyme

TITANICUS
A novel by Dan Abnett

DOUBLE EAGLE
A novel by Dan Abnett

SABBAT WAR
An anthology by various authors

SABBAT WORLDS
An anthology by various authors

SABBAT CRUSADE
An anthology by various authors

• GAUNT'S GHOSTS •
Dan Abnett

THE FOUNDING

Book 1: FIRST AND ONLY
Book 2: GHOSTMAKER
Book 3: NECROPOLIS

THE SAINT

Book 4: HONOUR GUARD
Book 5: THE GUNS OF TANITH
Book 6: STRAIGHT SILVER
Book 7: SABBAT MARTYR

THE LOST

Book 8: TRAITOR GENERAL
Book 9: HIS LAST COMMAND
Book 10: THE ARMOUR OF CONTEMPT
Book 11: ONLY IN DEATH

THE VICTORY

Book 12: BLOOD PACT
Book 13: SALVATION'S REACH
Book 14: THE WARMASTER
Book 15: ANARCH

URDESH
THE MAGISTER AND THE MARTYR
MATTHEW FARRER

A BLACK LIBRARY PUBLICATION

First published in 2021.
This edition published in Great Britain in 2022 by
Black Library, Games Workshop Ltd., Willow Road,
Nottingham, NG7 2WS, UK.

Represented by: Games Workshop Limited – Irish branch,
Unit 3, Lower Liffey Street, Dublin 1,
D01 K199, Ireland.

10 9 8 7 6 5 4 3 2 1

Produced by Games Workshop in Nottingham.
Cover illustration by Lorenzo Mastroianni.

Urdesh: The Magister and the Martyr © Copyright Games Workshop Limited 2022. Urdesh: The Magister and the Martyr, GW, Games Workshop, Black Library, The Horus Heresy, The Horus Heresy Eye logo, Space Marine, 40K, Warhammer, Warhammer 40,000, the 'Aquila' Double-headed Eagle logo, and all associated logos, illustrations, images, names, creatures, races, vehicles, locations, weapons, characters, and the distinctive likenesses thereof, are either ® or TM, and/or © Games Workshop Limited, variably registered around the world.
All Rights Reserved.

A CIP record for this book is available from the British Library.

ISBN 13: 978-1-80026-145-7

No part of this publication may be reproduced, stored in a retrieval system, or transmitted in any form or by any means, electronic, mechanical, photocopying, recording or otherwise, without the prior permission of the publishers.

This is a work of fiction. All the characters and events portrayed in this book are fictional, and any resemblance to real people or incidents is purely coincidental.

See Black Library on the internet at

blacklibrary.com

Find out more about Games Workshop
and the world of Warhammer 40,000 at

games-workshop.com

Printed and bound by CPI Group (UK) Ltd, Croydon, CR0 4YY

Dedicated with thanks to everyone who was so patient during this story's long, long road to completion.

For more than a hundred centuries the Emperor has sat immobile on the Golden Throne of Earth. He is the Master of Mankind. By the might of His inexhaustible armies a million worlds stand against the dark.

Yet, He is a rotting carcass, the Carrion Lord of the Imperium held in life by marvels from the Dark Age of Technology and the thousand souls sacrificed each day so that His may continue to burn.

To be a man in such times is to be one amongst untold billions. It is to live in the cruellest and most bloody regime imaginable. It is to suffer an eternity of carnage and slaughter. It is to have cries of anguish and sorrow drowned by the thirsting laughter of dark gods.

This is a dark and terrible era where you will find little comfort or hope. Forget the power of technology and science. Forget the promise of progress and advancement. Forget any notion of common humanity or compassion.

There is no peace amongst the stars, for in the grim darkness of the far future,
there is only war.

DRAMATIS PERSONAE

Iron Snakes Adeptus Astartes

Brother-Captain Priad

Techmarine Pyrakmon

Epistolary Hamiskora

Damocles Squad

Brother-Sergeant Xander

Apothecary Khiron

Brother Holofurnace

Brother Aekon

Brother Andromak

Brother Dyognes

Brother Kules

Brother Natus

Brother Pindor

Brother Scyllon

Thunderhawk Pilot Crethon

Erasmos Squad

Brother-Sergeant Symeon

Apothecary Spiridon

Brother Anysios

Brother Demetios

Brother Laukas

Brother Iacchos

Brother Serapion
Brother Agenor
Brother Menoetios

Platonos Squad
Brother-Sergeant Iapetos
Apothecary Kryakos
Brother Adrastes
Brother Panagis
Brother Alekon
Brother Idas
Brother Dardanos
Brother Atymnes
Brother Herodion
Brother Kapis
Thunderhawk Pilot Cepheas

Kalliopi Squad
Brother-Sergeant Kreios
Apothecary Hapexion
Brother Hemaeros
Brother Phaethon
Brother Mathos
Brother Skopelion
Brother Kandax
Brother Coenus
Brother Perdix
Brother Xenagoras

The Legio Invicta

Invictus Antagonistes – Warlord Titan
Princeps Maximus Pietor Gearhart
Moderatus Bernal
Steersman Zophal
Tech-Priest Dajien
Sensori Rakolo

Morbius Sire – Warhound Titan
Princeps Maximilian Filias Orfuls
Moderatus Strakhov
Steersman Paavo
Tech-Priest Zemplin

Lupus Lux – Warhound Titan
Princeps Leyden Krugmal
Moderatus Klyte Beyran
Steerswoman Sola Encantor
Tech-Priest Papagha

Lupus Noctem – Warhound Titan
Princeps Entascha Mereschel
Moderatus Amion
Steersman Bodinel
Tech-Priest Enoq

Raptus Solemnus – Warhound Titan
Princeps Arkaly Creel
Moderatus Torsch

Steersman Maharach
Tech-Priest Inand

The Saint

Saint Sabbat, also called the Beati
Colonel Iovin Mazho, Urdeshi Fourth Light, her military attache
Captain Brey Auerben, Tenth Jovani Vanguard, her tactical advisor
Trooper Brin Milo, Tanith First and Only, her counsel
Sister Yulla Kassine, Adepta Sororitas, her counsel

Astra Militarum

Command

Macaroth, Warmaster of the Sabbat Worlds Crusade
General Illin Grawe-Ash, commander, Ghereppan theatre
Lieutenants Erzien and Oshner, members of her staff
Private Dmorz, an armoured personnel carrier driver
Adept Tschemherr, a wyrdvane psyker
Sergeant Vesherin, Urdeshi Storm Troop

Logistics Echelon, Third Urdeshi Regulars, Ghereppan Army Group

Sergeant Bekt Kellare, a convoy leader
Corporal Verzt, her next in command
Trooper Geizner, her driver
Trooper Kolsh, her gunner

Old Ourezhad expeditionary crew

Zhiery, a submarine pilot

Lyass, a submarine engineer

Forward Observation Point, Encoma Unitae Clade-Tower, Ghereppan Scarp

First Scoper Ottoli

Scoper Dzyne

Scoper Deenagh

Scoper Uzhman

Scoper Stooks

Citizens of the Imperium

Ghelon, a preacher and scratch company leader

Bairet Henztrom, a scratch company lieutenant

Dree, a scratch company watchwoman

Shuura, a scratch company vox-operator

Roboute Frazer, a war refugee

Mikk, a war refugee

Gerreg, a war refugee

Belphos, a war refugee

Tiro, a war refugee

Along with various followers of the Throne, including soldiers, pilgrims, machine-brothers, refugees, et cetera.

The Archenemy

Anakwanar Sek, the Anarch, He Whose Voice Drowns Out All Others

Nautakah, an arnogaur of the Blood Pact

Haliuk, a high sirdar and commander of artillery of the Blood Pact

Verleg Chae, a damogaur of the cult of the Anarch

Mohgun Osh, a sirdar of the Sons of Sek

Engavol the Hunter, a sirdar of the cult of the Anarch

Along with various of the Lost and Damned, including packsons, gore mages, ingeniants, lekts, and sundry beasts, fiends, minions, et cetera.

The events that brought the long and grinding Urdesh campaign to its abrupt tipping point pose a special challenge for historians. The startling events that unfolded simultaneously in the pivotal warzone of Ghereppan and the crusade command at Eltath have been well documented. Even after the inevitable redactions and suppressions, the wealth of primary sources still available to us present remarkably consistent pictures of that strange and tumultuous night.

The same cannot be said for the events that came hard on the heels of the so-called Miracle. While the Astra Militarum after-action reports from the following days are widely available and can be considered broadly reliable, they shed no light on the most vital and puzzling part of the fighting. To this day there remains no officially endorsed explanation – let alone primary or even broadly contemporary accounts – for the Saint's disappearance from Ghereppan with her Iron Snakes bodyguards, or for the act of swift and unnatural destruction that followed hard upon her departure...

– From *A History of the Later Imperial Crusades*

'We have been given a hard road. A road to walk through a galaxy that does not welcome or forgive us, behind one who asks no less of us than He Himself has given up. A road that will lead many of us to bleak and bloody places with nothing but the knowledge of duty done to console us at the end. It is not my work to absolve you of that duty. But He-on-Terra has willed that a light shine in the dark. A sign to lift His people's hearts. Strengthen our stride.

'And I am here.'

– Attributed to the Beati Sabbat at Ghereppan

What Has Gone Before...

Urdesh: The Serpent and the Saint took us to the world of Urdesh, industrial linchpin of the Sabbat Worlds, now battered and weary from the decade-long war of liberation by the Imperial crusade. Through it we witnessed the deeds of the Emperor's Adeptus Astartes, four squads of the Iron Snakes Chapter, as they battled the Blood Pact of Urlock Gaur and the fanatical soldiers of Anakwanar Sek, the Anarch, He Whose Voice Drowns Out All Others.

Kalliopi Squad are immersed in the grinding, bewildering street-to-street war for the heartland city of Ghereppan. This is a prize both sides are bent on taking, and not just for the industrial power of its clade-forges, fabricator shrines and technoarcana libraries. Ghereppan holds one end of the great causeway leading across the straits and over the horizon to its sibling-city, Oureppan, equal in might and the fortress-home of the Anarch himself.

Erasmos Squad has already begun a deadly secret strike against Oureppan, crossing the sea floor to infiltrate an ancient Mechanicus complex in the heart of the volcano known as Old Ourezhad. If they can cripple the ancient geothermal spike that powers Oureppan's defences, they can throw the gates of the Anarch's citadel wide open.

Platonos Squad fights in no one battle zone. Led by Hamiskora the Librarian, they range back and forth across Urdesh hunting the lekts, powerful psykers bonded to the voice of the Anarch. When they intercept and destroy a lekt who was transporting a piece of complex psychic machinery towards Oureppan, they pass on a warning to their commander, Brother-Captain Priad.

Captain Priad is now on a more unusual mission away from the battle lines. Along with his old squad, Damocles, now under the leadership of Brother-Sergeant Xander, Priad has been charged with guarding the Beati, the reincarnated Saint Sabbat herself, who has come to Urdesh hoping to lead the Imperial forces to victory.

But all is not well with the Saint. She chafes at being made a propaganda figurehead, kept from the battle lines. When an enemy infiltration force strikes at her supposedly secret location, enough is enough: she overrules her military advisors and sets off for the battlefront at Ghereppan.

Before she can enter the city proper, the Archenemy strikes at her again. The Anarch's forces set malevolent warpcraft loose in the refugee camps south of the city, creating havoc in the Imperial support lines, while the Blood Pact launch a brutal artillery assault on her position. With Priad gone ahead as envoy to the Imperial commander, Damocles and Kalliopi fight a desperate battle against Sekkite monsters and Blood Pact soldiery. Their final confrontation, with a warband of

Chaos Space Marines led by the deadly Arnogaur Nautakah, is turned by the intervention of the Saint, who scatters the enemy and takes to the skies on wings of green flame.

The Miracle of Ghereppan has begun...

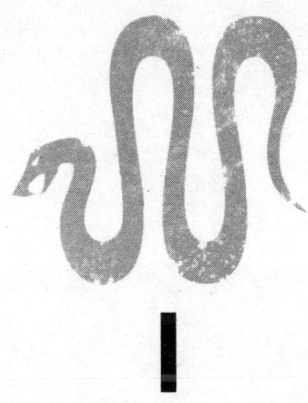

I

THE MIRACLE OF GHEREPPAN

Urdesh was a world of starless nights.

The whole world sweated smoke and steam from its volcanic vents and thermal springs, its atmosphere cataracted over with cloud layers and ash hazes. There was no moon to mirror the sunlight down onto its dark side. When night fell on Urdesh, the sky was blank and dark from horizon to horizon.

Except tonight. Tonight, for the first time, a star hung in the sky over Ghereppan.

Priad
Southern battlefront, Ghereppan

'Did you hear her?'

Priad and the transport driver asked each other in unison, and then they laughed in unison too. The grim mood of the transport of just a minute before was gone.

And grim it had been.

They had made good time out of Grawe-Ash's bunker complex and into the zigzagging secondary streets of the tertiary hab sprawls. The driver had put the transport's vox-pickup onto the internal speaker circuit and Priad had knelt in the rear compartment, eyes closed, matching what he could overhear on the Militarum bands with the random fragments of talk his armour was able to snatch from nearby.

This was nothing like watching glowing runes move in a holotank in among the low voices of staff and the tick and click of servitors. The ever-thickening fighting was coming through to his ears in all its raw, unfiltered desperation. Frantic calls for support. Increasingly urgent reports of Blood Pact contacts, then engagements. Prayers and oaths cast into the vox-band as beleaguered units prepared for their last stands. Scraps of battle cries, pain cries, death cries as those last stands played out. Once or twice he caught a snatch of Pact battle-cant, a hungry snarl of a language with the cadence of a panting carrion-dog.

There was nothing Priad could do about any of it.

None of the transmissions were from Iron Snakes, or about them, and reaching his brothers was his only mission. Once he had rejoined them, and they had vanquished the traitors who assailed them, then this whole vast battlefield would be theirs, to go where they wished, save and slay whom they chose. But for now his mind, reshaped, conditioned and trained for war, simply filtered out the rage, distress and despair from the voices he heard, sieved out locations and force references, fitted them neatly into his mental battle-maps and moved on.

And then, through the middle of it all, they heard her.

54th Urdeshi Armoured
Transduct battle zone, west central Ghereppan

When the green star appeared overhead, the guns on the Third Axial Transduct fell silent. For just a handful of heartbeats, the breeze-swept twenty-four-lane-wide battlefield seemed to hold its breath in the dark.

The Imperial Guard had already been battering their way along the Third Axial for twenty-six hours, advancing by dogged brute force, grinding the enemy down, and back, and back. Vox had become patchier and patchier as the transduct climbed up above the rooftops of the southern belt and started weaving through the Conurb Quinta spire clusters. They had called in status reports, asked for reinforcements, but they could not be certain they had been heard. But their orders were to push forward as far as they could, and so on they pushed, as the spires around them and the streets below them came alive with weapons fire.

The Leman Russ tanks of the 54th Urdeshi Armoured had long since used up the last of their heavy bolter ammunition and the sponsons on their sides had fallen silent. One or two still had a shell or two for the main cannon, hoarded against the chance that they might yet turn a decisive moment. Even their lascannon beams were starting to flicker and stutter as overtaxed and overheated energy systems started to take their toll. The two Griffon mortar carriages that had been so effective at the start of the advance were long out of shells, now only useful as rolling cover for the infantry slogging along behind the armour.

The sole Rhino in the formation, in the scarlet livery of the Order of the Bloody Rose, drove in the last line of tanks, the braziers on each corner of the hull banked down to a dull glow but still bright enough to illuminate the banner of the Emperor Enthroned for the soldiers to lift their eyes and pray to. The Sisters Militant had divided themselves, most of them walking among the leading tanks ready for any enemy counter-assault, a few of them hanging behind with the Militarum troops, singing psalms and saying devotions on behalf of those too used up to raise their own voices.

Their steady advance had left a trail of dead and wounded soldiers and discarded hard-ammo weapons whose magazines were long empty. The dozen armoured gun-servitors from the Xylanter foundry-temple had dismounted and dumped their shoulder-howitzers and grenade tubes somewhere around hour seventeen. After a shouting match with the force's commissar just after hour nineteen, their attendant enginseer had grudgingly allowed them to be hung about with bandoliers and packs so that the exhausted troopers could move a little easier.

It was the servitors who broke the reverie. They jerked as if stimm-jolted, every one simultaneously and then again in sequence, Alpha to Mu, Mu to Alpha. The connectors on their now empty weapon mounts waggled and clicked in the air. Enginseer Onnika's sense-feeds lit up as every one of them suddenly shouted their status across the noospheric link, bright white and green, as fresh as if they had just stepped out of a full refurbishment. Onnika herself had a brief moment of confusion before she fully oriented herself, and then of course it all made sense. Everything was as it should be. Just as the woman in the sky had said it would be.

Everything made sense now. And they had urgent work to do.

The Sky Agora
Ghereppan Universitariate

Bodies choked the gracious water-paths of the Sky Agora, and the flickering lights of war played over the tangles of the dead.

Back before the war, that sky was what the Agora had reflected. The basalt paving was cut back and forth with geometric mandalas of water-channels that filled with the grey of the skies overhead, mellowing into burnished red-gold in the dawn and dusk when the students would gather to talk and court and sing.

They were charnel pits now. Choked with corpses, grimed over with dust and ash, their edges splintered and chewed by weapons fire and tank treads, no water to catch the las-trails, the muzzle flare of the slugthrowers, or the green-white ferocity of photon grenades. They glinted instead off the polished iron of Blood Pact grotesques, off the red wire inlays that made the sneering metal mouths drool blood, and off the brass augmetic fittings of the twice-wrought war beasts at the teeth of the Pact advance.

The beasts were coming again now, galloping on all fours between the crippled and gutted armoured vehicles that littered the Agora's west side, rearing up onto two legs to clamber over wrecks or hurdle waterways, bellying flat for cover behind mounds of corpses left from the savage hand-fighting of two days before. Two of them were clinging to the sides of Jovani tanks that still had living crew, scraping the hulls with their grafted-in talons and clawing at the gun ports while the Pact troopers closed in with krak grenades. Another arched a barbed brass tail from its back whose tip was firing tox-bombs into the Urdeshi and Jovani trying to hold the cloisters and the eastern quadrangles. The three in the vanguard, each gifted with a second pair of arms reaching from behind their bulging, over-muscled shoulders, were grabbing up corpses and flinging them ahead into the dark, pelting the Imperials with friend and enemy alike. The macabre bombardment bowled soldiers over or pinned them under dead weight, knocked crew-served weapons flying, clogged positions and fire lanes with new corpse-piles as the Blood Pact ground forward.

The leading beast, the alpha, panted yellow steam through a riveted-on silver grotesque as it shuffled forward in a simian crouch with half a dozen Death Brigade commandos sheltering behind it. They kept up a steady, staggered suppression fire as the alpha plunged its secondary arms into a rancid waterway and dragged out two corpses, a barrel-chested Pact grenadier missing an arm and a slim Jovani hoisted up by one rotting ankle. It hurled the first corpse forward with a gleeful howl that its human followers echoed, and drew the second back, muscles bunching, ready to whirl the body by its leg and loft it high.

It stopped, the dripping corpse swinging back and forth from its mail-gloved fist. Fire flashed off its etched-brass armour as the commandos opened up with their autoguns to cover it. It didn't notice. It was looking to the sky, mesmerised. Its eyes, deep-set, light brown, jarringly human, reflected something else. A bright green pinpoint high overhead.

A hard round caught the alpha under the chin, cracking the twice-folded bone and lodging in its palate. It fell to its knees, gurgling in rage, but it could not take its eyes off that light above it, so small, so terrible. A fusillade of las-fire charred the side of its neck and set the armour plate grafted into its chest glowing cherry-red. Another hard round punched through the leering silver mask and the mouth behind it. It let the dead Jovani fall from limp fingers and brought the hand around to try and shield its eyes from the green star, but the arm was already peppered with las-wounds and the brain inside the reinforced skull was starting to feel pain mingling with the inexplicable fear.

A commando went down, and then another. The rest of them threw themselves flat among the battle-wreckage and started to crawl backwards. The alpha did not really hear their shouts, or the cries when the Imperial gunfire found them, or the foghorn roars of its siblings as las and bullet slowed them, stopped them and killed them.

The alpha was finally able to tear its gaze from the sky when a chainblade tore through its side between its two left arms. It bayed and swatted the Jovani officer away as a bayonet hamstrung its right leg. It clawed out, felt its fingers close on flesh, felt bones break as it tightened its grip, but gunfire was cratering its torso, bodies were crashing into it, bearing it back. When someone finally rammed the muzzle of a U-90 into the socket of its left eye and gave a burst of .45-calibre slugs, its right eye was still staring upward, catching the light of that single emerald star.

The Saint's voice did not ring out from her own lips, although there were those who would later remember turning to look up at the single green star in the black sky as they heard her speak. It did not spread like a blast-wave or roll over the city like a storm front, although that was how many would try to describe it down the years as the legend grew. And it left no trace of itself in vox-recordings or servitor pickups, no matter the countless hours Imperial adepts would spend combing for evidence of it. All who needed it, heard it. And that was enough.

54th Urdeshi Armoured
Transduct battle zone, west central Ghereppan

The tanks on the Third Axial ground to a halt and idled as if in thought. Then the forward line split itself neatly in two, half of the tanks rolling ahead and the rest reversing. The new front line smoothly rearranged itself into even spacing, the troopers behind them running forward into position around them. The rear line reformed, smoothly wheeled and drove to the transduct's eastern edge, pressing up against the carved rockcrete retaining wall as though they were about to push right through it and into a twenty-one-storey fall to the streets and rooftops below.

Another pause, engines rumbling. A close observer might have noticed their forward lascannons ticking through tiny adjustments and corrections as their crews aligned them to a precise firing solution. And in perfect unison, they let loose.

Their beams struck a point on the wide, windowless flank of a hab-block two hundred metres away. A second salvo opened a second glowing gash in the rockcrete that criss-crossed the first. Then a third.

Another small, breathless pause. Some of the Urdeshi would remember that as the moment they glanced up and first saw the tiny point of emerald light in the heavens. Then the battle cannons spoke.

The first shell hit the weakened rockcrete wall and blasted it inward. The second whistled through the breach and the explosion of the first, exploding the far wall and pulping the Sekkite soldiers who had been assembling to rush the stairwells and ambush the exhausted Guard troopers moving through the tower's south wing. Those troopers were ready for the shell hits, because she had told them to be, and now they were not exhausted any more. The instant the second shell exploded they were in motion, smashing through broken doorways and ruptured walls, trampling and bayoneting the feeble remnants of the enemy as they stormed down the stairwells to the Archenemy enclaves below them.

The element of surprise was complete. Moving at a sprint, firing as fast and accurately as on a well-lit gun range instead of in a dark and half-ruined maze of habs, they ripped through the next floor and out onto the westward walkways and landing-shelves. The Sekkites crewing the autocannon and multi-laser nests along the walks barely had time to turn around before they were gunned down and overrun.

The last gunner's corpse was still plummeting towards the ground far below when the heavy weapons started to fire again, across and down at the broad rooftop plaza that led to the high-domed Administratum complex five hundred metres to the north-west. Now they were firing not on the Urdeshi and Helixid forces they had been suppressing but at the Archenemy positions across the square, lashing out with terrifying timing and precision.

The Imperial siegers who'd been battling for control of that complex for ten days burst into a charge as soon as the suppressing fire from above began. Within minutes they were swarming the dome, breaking in its doors with grenades, weapons or their own bodies, pouring into the serried galleries inside it and raining fire down on the Sekkite command post on the dome floor.

The two Sons of Sek platoons who'd been making ready to depart that command post ended up leading its final stand. They fought with all the discipline and savagery for which the Sons were notorious but still they died there, backed into impossible positions and crushed by the relentless Imperial advance. They had been about to descend to the sublevels under the northern Avenue Solar to intercept and trap a Pragar task force working its way north through the storm-sluice network. That force now had an open road into the Archenemy positions beneath the northern clade-houses and their plasma-pyre shrines, and they knew it. They were already racing forward through the storm-sluices, exultant, jubilant, with the echoes of the Saint's voice in their ears.

Back on the transduct, the retreating Archenemy soldiers had finally shaken off their own exhaustion and moved.

Hounded into a run by their scourgers and led by a dozen Sons of Sek toting hellguns and melta bombs, they came howling from behind their rough rubble barricades. The Sons led the way with their armour-killing charges at the ready, their peon auxiliaries fanning out behind them, making for the gaps in the armoured wall to fall on the infantry beyond.

They met the Imperial counter-charge three-quarters of the way to the tanks. Grim-faced troopers with guns flashing and bayonets fixed, led by a flying wedge of a dozen crimson-armoured Adepta Sororitas swinging adamantine swords and singing a High Gothic canticle in perfect close harmony. The junior-most Sister ran just behind the Sister Superior in the point of the wedge, carrying a stave topped with a bright gold aquila wreathed with red roses sculpted in steel. As they crashed into the enemy the green light that shone on them brightened and seemed to curl and trail around the aquila like a banner, showering the Sisters' wake with rose petals and islumbine blooms.

Mohgun Osh
Fifth Grand Cloister Orbital, west central Ghereppan

Mohgun Osh. A short grunt of a name for a man so massive. Not that many people addressed him by name. 'Scourger' sufficed. Not that many people dared try to speak to him. A submissive lowering of the head sufficed. He wore his lash shackled to his right wrist; its haft had not left his grip since his echelon had been ordered to take and hold the Fifth Grand Cloister Orbital thirty-two days before. Such was the word of Sek, that drowned out all others: that the scourge should not be set down until the Scourger's commander should release the battle-order and permit him to set it down.

Osh was no sadist. The scourge was there to serve the Anarch's purpose, not his own whims, but it had not proven necessary. The Imperials had hurled themselves at the Grand Cloister for thirty-one days now. They had dropped from the sky, stormed up the thick-legged arterial bridges rising from the southern conurbs, tried to creep in at the sublevels and up through the cloister's hundreds of labyrinthine floors, and every time they had been denied. The cloister, its fortified halls, power banks and its commanding position over the city's southern advances, remained firmly in the grip of the Anarch. Not a single Son of Sek under Osh's command had faltered in the fury of the assaults. Not a single one had lost their discipline and gone rushing out from their position to chase down a retreating kill. Not so much as a twitch of the lash had been needed. Osh was proud of that.

And now here they came again, trying to storm across the wreck-littered bridge that linked the cloister's hundred and eighth floor with the 91st Orbital to the south. Did they hate their lives so much, all but begging the Anarch to reach out and take them like this? Were they so hypnotised by the twinkling lights of the battles that had broken out all across the city below them that they wanted to burn again too?

His Sons of Sek had assembled at their ambush points around the portable flakpress barricades spiked into the cloister's beautiful mosaic floor. They loaded ammunition belts, hefted grenade launchers, set themselves along marks sprayed across the multicoloured floor tiles and checked sight lines along the glossy black barrels of lasguns and the thick frames of Urdeshi stubbers. Their brothers were in place in the windows and galleries high above, the snipers with their long-las rifles, the heavy weapon crews preparing to turn the bridge into a foretaste of the hell that the Anarch and his Powers had waiting for the Imperials' souls tonight. Behind him, the peons were scrambling to and fro under the whips of Osh's subordinate scourgers, running trolleys back and forth between the stairs and winching pallets up from the sublevels, bringing ammunition, powercells and grenades. Osh nodded approvingly at the sight of them quailing away from the crack of the whips, ducking their heads to avoid looking at the scourgers' faces. They deserved no better. The vermin of Ghereppan, trapped and captured by the Sekkites' rapid advance, some here in the cloister itself, too broken to resist when the Anarch's handprint was scrawled onto their faces with bayonet-tips and they were lashed into service.

The clatter of rotary stubbers started to echo through the cloister, the high-speed seven-barrelled greaseburners from the northern Ghereppan fabricatories. That meant mostly infantry this time. If they were trying to push to the doorstep with armour again he would be hearing the chug and thump of the krak launchers. Osh walked to the rear of the interleaved barricades, where he could see all of his command with a turn of his head, and thumbed the hellpistol in his left hand to full readiness.

Then the cannons fell silent, and the silence drew out, and out. Osh's nose wrinkled. He could smell something: a sweet, sharp tang to the air that he couldn't place; not the ozone of las-fire or the acrid stink of lubricant scorched into smoke by the rotator guns. From up above him where he should have heard cannon fire he heard instead a sudden burst of cries, and a body slammed into the bridge. Another. He heard the wail of fear as a third plummeted past the bridge and down into the deep rockcrete ravines that were central Ghereppan's streets.

Osh stood up – a breach of doctrine and orders when they were defending a line. He'd have scourged any man in his echelon unconscious for it, and accepted such a scourging as his due in turn. Nevertheless, he stood up, and while he was wondering about that he took a step forward, then another. His right hand was flicking back and forth like a hunting felid's tail, back and forth, the links of the shackle clinking, back and forth, the lash's barbs scratching across the tiles.

Only half-deliberately he clamped his right eye closed, and the monoscope fastened to his helmet over his left eye lit up. Mohgun Osh stopped where he was, paralysed, his breath loud and harsh through the hand-mask that covered his mouth.

The very instant the guns had fallen silent, Urdeshi had rushed the bridge, sprinting towards Osh's line in utter silence. His scope showed him their battleworn uniforms and their gaunt and unshaven faces. These were the same demoralised wretches they'd already driven back time and again; how could they be moving like this after four gruelling weeks when even his own Sons were showing the strain?

Finally a cannon started up again, and Osh snarled in satisfaction. But before he could lift his lash to signal his Sons, the shells started hitting barely two metres from him, smashing apart the barricade to his right. The fire team behind it tried to scatter from the incoming rounds until a burst of las-fire from the charging Urdeshi scythed them down.

The cannon cut off. Too long a burst, barrels overheated, no discipline. The relief from that thought evaporated abruptly when Osh turned his scope upward to see the battered body of one of his sharpshooters pushed out of one of the high galleries to carom off a buttress and shatter against the mosaic floor behind him. He blink-zoomed on the window-arch where the Son had been, the blur of his eyepiece resolving into a cluster of ragged figures staring silently down. He gaped at them, for a moment too astonished to move. The Anarch taught that it was the nature of vermin to cringe and be broken, and once broken to be trampled and drowned out, and once drowned out to be forgotten. His Sons had bested these vermin and broken them. There was nothing in Osh's understanding of the world to explain how it was possible for them to stand up again.

That smell was in his nostrils again, and out of the warm, ashy night air came a clean, cold gust like the wind over a high mountain trail. Osh shouted, turned and fired into the sky, even though he knew she was out of range, out of reach. He knew that even without knowing who the thought referred to.

His right arm jerked. He looked at it, looked down. A las-bolt had severed the shackle that bound his scourge to his arm. He had dropped his lash. The last thing he saw as the gunfire lit him up was three of his black-gloved fingers, welded to its grip.

Priad and Dmorz
Southern battlefront, Ghereppan

'How straight is our way to the passage-point?' Priad asked, because that was what she had told him. New work for him, through the passage-point and then north. He wasn't going to join Damocles and Kalliopi any more.

'Another ten kilometres north on the freightway,' said the driver, whose name Priad now knew was Dmorz. 'Until it crosses the Chromanta Colonnade. There'll be a fight there. Pact are trying to surround the point and break the Pragar tunnelhead, but they won't have managed it by the time we get there.' Because that was what her voice had told him. He was accelerating now, bouncing the transport over rubble, steering it through narrow gaps in buildings and barricades, swerving around buried mines and wheel traps. He didn't question how he could suddenly drive at speed through an unfamiliar battle zone in the pitch dark, or how he knew every metre of the way to the passage-point as if he had driven this route every day of his thirty-eight years. Might as well question *her*. And there was no questioning her.

To Priad, Dmorz was only visible as a shape against the instrument lights. For just an instant it had looked like he had been silhouetted by something else, a gentle green light suffusing the night outside, but then Priad had blinked and the moment was gone.

The engine gunned and they picked up speed again.

Damocles and Kalliopi
Avenue Vertegna, Ghereppan

None of the Blood Pact artillery had escaped, and none had survived. Nor had any of the Blood Pact who had tried to guard them. In the light of the burning Usurper gun-wagons, the Iron Snakes stood guard over their fallen and looked to the north. None of them looked up at the green star, but they didn't need to.

Three of the Traitor Astartes were not accounted for. That gnawed at Kreios. Three of Kalliopi Squad dead, three of the enemy left alive. The symmetry of it seemed like an insult.

Hemaeros and Skopelion were already moving north, bounding one another, scouting a way off the boulevard for when the squad moved. Kandax was standing guard over Hapexion while the Apothecary went to work on their dead brothers. The heavy narthecium housing around Hapexion's left forearm had slid back and the reductor nosed forward, servos thrumming as the spike began to spin.

Looking past him, Kreios saw Khiron standing a little way away with the knot of humans who'd come struggling up to the battle in Damocles' wake. Kreios didn't know what the Saint had told him, or any of them, but he was grateful that the old Apothecary had had the tact to stand clear, letting Hapexion tend to his own.

'We're moving on as soon as we've claimed from them,' he said, walking over. Khiron tilted his helm in acknowledgement. Behind him the three humans were all silent and wide-eyed. The tall one was watching Hapexion at work. The other two, the woman in the tattered Ecclesiarchal shawl and the heavyset Urdeshi officer, were staring skyward. Each lens of the colonel's eyeglasses reflected a tiny point of green light.

'Do you need replenishing?' Khiron asked. 'Our Thunderhawk is under a building down yonder.'

'I saw it go in.'

'She told me our two brothers are unharmed in there. The armoury will be full, too. You need shells? Fuel?'

'Just revenge,' Kreios said curtly. 'But I'm told I shan't have it. At least not straight blood for blood. She tells me I won't cross paths with those traitors again. Other work for us tonight, riding the enemy out of Ghereppan all the way to the Oureppan gate.'

'Worthy work,' Khiron said. 'We're going north-west, into the city's heart, into the Sekkite lines that won't break fast enough without us there. We were aiming to contact the brother-captain, but she's sent him onward already.'

There was a moment while they both considered the conversation they had just had.

'Hard to question her, isn't it?' Khiron said eventually. 'After hearing her. Seeing her.'

'All the same,' Kreios growled. 'I'd have thanked her to keep her divine insights to herself until we'd made three more kills. Keep an eye out for them, Khiron. If you find them, say our brothers' names while you kill them.'

'I will.'

They looked over as the note of the reductor's motor changed. With a single precise movement Hapexion drew it free, and there was a brief and pregnant pause while he tilted it towards his other hand. Something purple-red, the size of a walnut, hard like a cyst, slid into his hand, the blood around it already almost porcelain-hard and crackling around the Apothecary's fingertips. It went into a little steel urn with engraved serpents coiling about its sides, and the reductor's note changed again as it drove into Xenagoras' sternum, drilling through the rock-hard barrel of his fused ribs.

The second procedure took longer than the first. The gene-seed transformation stamped a strong resemblance onto all the Phratry but they were not simple copies, and Xenagoras had been long in the body and lean across the chest. Navigating by feel as much as by the anatomical maps stamped into his memory, Hapexion eased the whirring reductor through leather-tough organ walls and rapid-clotting blood until the haptics in his palm told him he had the second progenoid in his grip. A moment later it was sealed in the urn along with its twin and Hapexion was standing, flushing the blood from his machinery with drops of anticoagulant cleanser and little barks of pressurised steam.

The Iron Snakes held funerals for those of their number

whose bodies could be brought home to Ithaka, and they had battlefield rituals for those whose remains they had to leave behind, when they had the time. But this was the only funeral a Space Marine truly needed, passing on the progenoids that had been growing in his body since his initiation, to seed the transformation in two more initiates in turn. Xenagoras' body had fallen in battle, his soul had gone to the Emperor, his flesh and blood returned to the Phratry. There was no more to it than that.

'The Archenemy owe us for three Ithakan deaths,' Kreios declared over the rising sound of his jets. 'I'm not sure there are enough of them in this city to settle up, but we're going to find out.'

Every Imperial within the borders of Ghereppan, soldier or civilian, Urdeshi or off-worlder, no matter their rank or age, no matter where they were, every one of them heard her. The sleeping, injured or unconscious awoke to her words. Those deep in battle still heard her with utter clarity over the din of combat. The Urdeshi heard her voice in the accent and dialect of their home islands or cities. The Pragar heard her speak in the rhythmic deep-hive argot of their home sublevels, and from that day would laugh and weep at the memory of that night and the memory of home that it brought. The Jovani heard the formal cadences of Old Jovea, the Helixid their own clan-cant. Her voice was soft as snowfall, inexorable as sunrise.

Kellare
Midtract hab zone, southern Ghereppan

'There they are!' Bekt Kellare shouted as the cargo-8 swung off the three-lane freightway and joggled over a double row of tramlines. A crowd of running figures was spilling across the tarmac to intercept them. Kellare felt the ghost of a horrific memory, a split-second flash of the tide of refugees swamping her convoy on the southern roadway and the monster that had been driving them. But no more than a flash, and quickly gone. The soft voice and the clean green light had washed away that memory's power as surely as it had washed away the ringing in her ears and the vile after-images that wouldn't leave her.

This time was different. The figures swarming up into the trucks were all soldiers. Urdeshi regulars, a sprinkling of sappers and storm troopers, a handful of Pragar tunnellers – the remnants of who knew how many days and weeks of vicious street battles deeper in the city. They had been falling back southward, collecting other stragglers, trying to find an Imperial enclave with food and medics and the chance of more than an hour's sleep at a time, too exhausted to think. Until the Saint had lifted them up again.

They were armed and ready. Once they knew Kellare's convoy had changed course and was coming for them, they had spent the wait redistributing powercells and fastening body armour back into place. She knew this the same way they had known precisely when she would arrive, and the way they all knew where they were going next. The Saint had told them.

An enthusiastic banging on the back of the cab signalled that they were full, and Geizner accelerated straight ahead, crashing through the torn chainlink at the back of the storehouse precinct, bouncing over the broken ground beyond. Then *this* way through the tumbled-down particulate silos, *that* way around the labourer barracks still smouldering from the firefight three days ago, now down through side streets and laneways barely wider than the cargo-8s themselves, streets they would have avoided as deathtraps without her words to tell them otherwise.

They came out into the great circular junction exactly at the moment she had said they would, exactly the moment the Blood Pact flanking force was bursting from its positions to assault the Militarum troopers ahead of them. The Pact were caught in the open, wide-eyed and flat-footed, the sudden blaze of headlights turning their metal grotesques from shadowy leers to comical gapes, until Geizner floored the accelerator and ploughed through them. Kolsh was already at the pintle, raking the Pact still behind cover, forcing them back as the other trucks roared out of the laneways and their gunners joined in.

They finished up with the cargo-8 beached on a flight of steps, the blood-slick ram-bar crunched tight against the double doors of the food hall the Pact had used as their base, trapping the last of them inside and cutting off the retreat of the rest. Above them, Kolsh calmly loaded another belt in and kept on firing. The junction was lit from edge to edge with las-shots and flamer bursts as troopers leapt off the trucks in all directions and threw themselves into the fray.

Kellare drew her pistol and kissed the Machina Opus sigil embossed on its top. Geizner had unclipped his bullpup lascarbine from the overhead rack. They grinned at each other.

'The Emperor protects,' he told her.

'Throne light our way,' she answered.

They leapt down onto the steps, into the fire-flickering night.

* * *

Hassard and Voord
Great Obilach Forge, northern Ghereppan clade precinct

'The servitors and menials are working again,' Enginseer Voord observed. 'Unexpected.'

'But positive,' Magos Hassard replied. 'Surely we need no recourse to analytics to agree on that.' The magos-atmotect turned and bowed to the central pillar of the echoing conical vault they stood in. Voord echoed the gesture even though the machine-spirit housed in the gilded column had gone dark when the last of the main power coils under the Great Obilach forge's enormous central ziggurat had blown. There was a single secondary coil operational now, just enough to keep the temple's last vapour-mill running. The munitions lines in the surrounding clade-houses needed that mill, and the war effort needed the munitions, so when the Sons of Sek had finally broken the ziggurat's gates and their ingeniants had begun to violate its systems, the two tech-priests had severed the mill from the surrounding systems and sealed themselves into the control vault to keep it running as long as they could.

That had been three months ago. The forge-temple had been full of the din of battle when they had welded the doors behind them but since then they could only guess at what was going on outside. They had become uncomfortably aware that the menials they had brought in with them had used up their provisions and were starting to fail. The servitors would not be long behind them. Even their own organics were feeling the lack of nourishment. Still, tending to the mill, preserving its Machine-God-given dignity and utility to the end, making sure it would survive them at least by a little while, was as worthy an end as they could hope for.

Until, of course, she had spoken to them. To *all* of them, at once. It was, the two priests agreed, remarkable.

The menials had seemingly forgotten their degraded state and were swarming over the pipes and pressureworks, spinning the mill steadily up to its maximum output. Voord and Hassard watched with equanimity. At any other time they would be outraged, but the menials knew exactly how far to push the machinery now, and the priests knew they knew. It hadn't come from instruments or calculations. It was simply there, the knowledge of exactly which settings and speeds and temperatures they needed. They were even compensating, effortlessly, for the effects of the mill running so long without maintenance, and there should have been no way to know *that* without a week of downtime and rigorous auditing and testing.

The two magi knew what was needed of them, too. Before the ziggurat had fallen they had not been the most amicable of colleagues, but here at last they found they had nothing to disagree on. They bowed to one another and Voord walked to the steps that would take him up into the ductwork while Hassard stepped back and slid his spinal dendrites into the engine hub.

The pipes were shuddering as Voord made his way up through them, but he was undaunted. The menials were cheering and saluting him. Up he climbed, to the spherical chamber that hung beneath the very peak of the vaulted roof. The conduits that fed the vapour up through the ceiling were glowing cherry-red.

He already knew which of the regulators to break, of course, and after hearing her voice he knew exactly when to do it. He had flashed the timing into his most basic cerebral layer. The countdown was as fundamental to him now as his pulse.

He lifted the heavy mag-manipulator and focused it on the regulator ring. He had time for one last delighted thought – what a happy end, compared to the one he had expected! – and he triggered it. The regulator tore open just as Hassard's command threw the mill's entire output into a single super-pressurised pulse.

All through the base level of the ziggurat, the clade-house and the streets beyond, pipes blew open, seals gave way, vents were torn wide. The sudden miasma of white-hot vapour cooked over a thousand Sekkite occupiers alive, reduced twice that number again to staggering, choking wrecks, and blew apart the forge machinery the ingeniants had almost managed to turn to their own works.

The 20th Urdeshi Urban, backed by several hundred Helixid heavy stormers, had been in cover on the clade-house approaches. The Sons of Sek attacking them from the cover of the house and the forge had had them under heavy pressure, but the Urdeshi only needed one chance to reverse the battle. When the vapour-blast blew open the enemy positions right in front of them, they were ready. Because she had told them to be. By morning, the only Archenemy left inside the Great Obilach forge-temple would be corpses.

Wherever her light fell and her voice sounded, pain and fear and fatigue melted away. Soldiers starved of food and sleep in desperate days-long battles felt the fog lift from their thoughts and beautiful vigour course through their limbs. The displacees who had fled the warp-born carnage in the shanty-camps had the terror and despair washed from their minds. All across the vast and many-layered battlefield that was Ghereppan, exhausted stalemates turned into sudden thunderous assaults. Desperate retreats became ferocious counter-attacks. Enemy raiders who had thought they had targeted vulnerable Imperial positions found themselves running into the teeth of alert and zealous Imperial defenders. Pitched battles became routs as Imperial battlegroups struggling in the fog of war suddenly meshed together like perfectly interlocking gears. Exhausted and faltering soldiers now stood immovable in the face of assaults that had seemed unstoppable until the gentle words in their minds had told them just how they could be stopped. They drove into weak points in the Archenemy's lines that they could not have known about until that quiet, miraculous moment.

Invictus Antagonistes
Ghereppan Strait

Moderatus Bernal had heard the Saint's words in the lovely, slow, over-precise diction that the tech-priests used to conduct the Omnissianic Mass on Proximus, coming to him as the ghosts of sounds in his physical ears and as transmissions carried straight up his instrument links from *Invictus Antagonistes'* transcept systems.

His first action, his reflexive response to any change in the Titan's status, was to bring up the vitae readouts for his princeps. For as long as he had done this, it had been with a sick tension in his belly, his rational mind trying to tell him that there would have been an alert if anything had happened, his gut insisting that this would be it, this would be the time he would find the readouts flat and grey and Princeps Gearhart finally, undeniably gone. Bernal realised that he felt none of that this time. Why should he? She had told him to be of good cheer. *Antagonistes* was in good hands, and there was a task to accomplish.

He did not doubt what he had heard. Like everyone else

to whom Sabbat had spoken that night, disbelief simply wasn't in him.

'Closing to the shore, moderatus,' Zophal said. The steersman had already taken them to walking speed, and the pict and pressure sensors on the front carapace were registering the change as a bow-wave built up against the enormous Titan's chest. 'Our full auspex and sensoria array will be clear of the water in moments.'

'Sensori, standing by?' Bernal heard himself ask. He realised he was smiling.

'Aye, moderatus!' came Rakolo's reply. The man was smiling back at him, and actually clapped his hands. Even Dajien got in on it, calling a short binharic hosanna from his shrine behind the Warlord's jaw.

Bernal turned back to his controls. The Warhounds would each have a piece of the picture, but it was *Antagonistes* that was perfectly placed to marshal and direct them. The reignited Battle of Ghereppan would bring the Legio a very specific enemy this night, a powerful and dangerous one, but there was no trepidation in him now. That soft voice and that green light left no room for it.

'Warhounds,' he said into the manifold. 'Stand ready.'

The data-shouts came back in an instant: Orfuls, Krugmal, Mereschel, Creel. Of course they had been ready. He had known they would be, because she had told him they would be.

'Full auspex, moderatus, and the manifold is bright.'

'Invicta,' Bernal said, and his crew shouted it back.

He had put from his mind the enthroned support tank that loomed behind their positions. And for once he wasn't watching its readouts when they began to change, when the oxygen line showed an uptick of indrawn breath, and the figure floating deep in the murky grey amniotic gel began to straighten out of its foetal curl.

The Imperial advance
Albarwise Bridge

Two hours after Saint Sabbat spread her wings over Ghereppan, an Imperial wave came out of the hab-stacks in the mid-south conurb, flooding the streets and smoothly converging into a rolling wall of infantry and armour, closing in on the Albarwise Bridge.

Albarwise was the southernmost bridge arching out from the western headland towards the surrounding islands, formidably protected and fiercely fought over. The Sekkite emplacements around the mainland area of the bridge dominated their surrounds with anti-air emplacements, mortar batteries, lascannons and sniper nests. But not tonight. Tonight the Imperial wave was met with barely more than a sputter of badly aimed gunfire as it crashed forward.

The Archenemy had grown too used to ignoring movement in the tangled reef of wrecked boats that lined the headland's western shore, too complacent about the wretched refugees trapped among the hulks, eking out the days gnawing on seaweed and scrounged provisions, too hungry and broken to be a threat.

Tonight those pallid, hollow-eyed remnants had heard her voice among the lapping of water and the creak of metal shifting on the waves. Silently and solemnly, they had moved. They had crept through the mazes of wreckage, crawling along corroded hulls like lizards and slipping in and out of the water with ease born of practice. With no fear or despair left in them, they ghosted in through openings she had directed them to, blind spots the sentries didn't know they had, up out of the water and into the fortifications while the enemy stared up at the green star overhead and felt the first stir of fear.

Some had blades, some tools, some nothing more than jagged and rusty pieces of scrap they had picked up when they had heard her voice and leapt up from where they had been sitting. But once the sentries were dead, they had guns. Once the mortar crews were dead, they had bombs. And once they started they did not slow or stop, not until the Militarum troopers came vaulting over the trenches, shouting the Saint's name and calling them to come on.

The Imperial surge went racing over the arch of Albarwise Bridge and down on Penekhi Island with a momentum that swept the surprised Sekkites before them, driving them out of their positions and back towards Borlaba Bridge to the north. Within the hour the next island would be burning. Another hour upon that and all the bridge defences would be crumbling, the Archenemy's soldiery lying cold on the streets or swept into the sea.

Engavol the Hunter
East Ghereppan waterfront

Engavol the Hunter could taste his own blood. Maybe from his mouth, maybe his nose, he couldn't tell any more.

It wasn't fighting that had set them bleeding, but his driving. He was hunched forward over the steering grips of the SCU-3 attack trike, peering into the nightvisor that had been fixed to the roll cage at eye level for him to see where he was going. The ingeniants had added another touch: a stamped-metal outline of a hand, so that when he leaned forward into the visor the hand covered his mouth to show the enemy his piety. Whenever the trike bounced over a crater or a chunk of rubble, Engavol's face smacked into it. His lips and nose were bleeding and he'd chipped at least one tooth. He didn't care. He could snuffle out the blood and cry about his lot once he'd led his squadron up the waterfront and safely out into the strait.

Engavol had felt such a rush of relief when the message had come through to flee northward that he'd almost pissed himself. He suspected that made him a coward and he didn't care about that, either. The Sons of Sek whose raids his squadron had escorted down into Imperial territory south-east of the cliffs, they weren't cowards. It'd been beaten out of the big bastards on Gereon and wherever else they'd dragged them in from. That was why they were back somewhere in that mass of flashes and explosions in Engavol's rear mirrors, getting killed.

The eastern Ghereppan docks were a narrow shelf of flat, paved-over shoreline between the sea reaches and the sheer cliffs of the scarp. They had been solidly in Sekkite hands for more than a year, the southward end easily cut off with a line of fortifications from cliff-foot to waterfront that had been incessantly built on. They had all thought those lines unbreachable, until tonight. Engavol still didn't quite understand what had happened, how it *could* happen. The rush that smashed the fortress lines open must have drawn in every warm Imperial body that side of the scarp. That made no sense. Engavol's trikes had scouted that front themselves, and they were good at their job. There was no way an attack like that could have been organised so quickly with so little sign of preparation.

And there was the way they had come on, the tanks and

heavy guns unerringly hammering their hardpoints and defiladed positions, on the move and in the dark, the infantry piling out of the waves of carriers or racing along behind the battle tanks. Engavol had seen some of them when a flare had gone off over his own position. He didn't want to believe how fast they had been running, but he couldn't quite bring himself to call his own eyes liars. If the Imperial commanders had given their assault troops Frenzon... but they had been shooting, too fast and too accurately for that. The laughter and heckling from Engavol's section of the line had died away quick-sharp when they realised what they were seeing. And then the line had caved in.

Then the signal had come through, activating the orders they had all thought were a hypothetical, or a mistake, or a sign that the Anarch they all served and loved really had deserted them, or that his mind had deserted him. And Engavol had wheeled his trike around and left the massacre behind him.

The roadway that ran north along the shore was unobstructed by most severe order to allow just this kind of rapid transit up and down the shore, and the SCU-3s were well placed to make use of it. Engavol swerved back and forth, dodging running pedestrians and slower vehicles, already resolved that he wouldn't be stopping if he heard one of his squadron crash behind him. Not on this insane night.

He almost didn't stop when he heard the echoing boom from up ahead. His first thought was that it was the echo of something massive behind him, an artillery hit or an ammo bunker going up. There had been no flash of detonation ahead. But something was different in the fuzzy yellow image in his visor, and it took him precious seconds to work out what it was.

When he realised, he stamped on the trike's brake and went squealing and fishtailing out to his right, his gunner on the rear step yelling in alarm as he lost his footing and spent several seconds swinging from his harness-straps. The monolithic shape of the cargo container that had just crashed down into the middle of the freightway shot by on his left. Grit and rockcrete chips stung Engavol's face and forearms, and then they were past it. His gunner started to shout a question and then just cried out the Anarch's name, over and over.

Ahead of them, a fifty-metre-long vapour tank plummeted out of the sky. It landed on its end and crumpled downward then tilted over and collapsed onto the docks, taking out a trans-strait hydrofoil and a crowd who'd been milling about, waiting to board it. Engavol sent the trike screaming back to his left as the tank rolled towards him. He thought he heard his second trike smash into it as he accelerated again, but he couldn't be sure because he was weaving like a madman now, avoiding the hexagonal plasteel containers hammering into the ground around him by sheer luck. He had no idea what was in them but the air was suddenly full of an evil alkaline stink. Somewhere up ahead of him tracer fire was climbing up from the dockside, aimed up the cliff, but there was no telling what the gunner had seen. Engavol mumbled an oath through his blood-glued mouth and gunned the engine anyway, heading for the source of the shots. That seemed like as good a place as any to get to an evacuation boat.

He nearly made it. He could see the wharf up ahead, crowded with panicked and scuffling figures, and beyond them the lines of a boat getting ready to move. He lowered his head. He would drive right down that wharf and mow down anyone he had to to be on that boat. He would have them gunned down – the hopper for the rotator cannon mounted over his head was still almost full. He would–

A bound pallet loaded with ceramite sleeper-staves shattered against a buttress just ahead of him and the impact burst the cargo apart with the force of a bomb. A whirling ceramite splinter the length of Engavol's arm struck his gunner's head off from the nose upward. Another crushed in the roll cage and broke Engavol's shoulder just before a third came skimming in to smash the front wheel of the trike away. There was an instant of shock and blur and weightlessness and then Engavol was lying on his back with his ears ringing but empty of sound. He stared up through the wreckage of his trike to the row of enormous freight-lifters that sat with their backs to the cliff. By firelight and flare he saw the yellow-painted girder arm over his head as it ground forward to a new position. The conveyor cable running up its back was already dragging a new container out.

Engavol was too broken to be able to turn his head, but when the container dropped out of sight he heard the crash and the roar and the splatter of water, and realised it had crushed the boat he had been about to escape on. He had had a stroke of luck. Now he would get to bleed out on land in a twisted metal cage with the reek of chemicals in his lungs. He couldn't help but start laughing at that, kept at it even when the laughter was mostly coughing and he was sliding in and out of consciousness. He was dead by the time the next sleeper pallet landed squarely on top of him.

The little scratch company of Imperial partisans had been harrying the operation of the docks for months, but they had not conceived of a strike like this until it came to them in soft words out of a dreamlike green light in the dark. Enough of them had worked on the lifters to know how to get half a dozen of them running again, and enough of them were left over to stand guard outside the lifter cabs and hold off the frantic Archenemy troops for another twenty minutes. In that time they pelted the freightway and docks with containers, clogging the way to the wharf, crushing boats, wrecking defences and killing enemy personnel by the dozen. Eight of them were still alive and fighting when the Imperial wave swept up from the overrun southern lines and carried them with it all the way up the headland. Three of them would even see the sun come up on the reconquered city the next day.

So it went across the city and all its thousands of battles, from the western islands to the eastern docks, the northern shore to the southern hills, from deepest sublevel to spire-tip. The Miracle leapt out like a fire through a tinder-dry forest, ramifying and magnifying itself with every near-spent Imperial who suddenly rose to their feet, and every panicking enemy who was cut down. For that one night the voice of the Anarch was stilled, and it was the soft words of the Saint that filled the silence.

Priad
Municipal passage-point CCS-13997, central Ghereppan

Just outside the fortified passage-point's south-east perimeter the night broke apart in blazing white muzzle-flare and the teeth-rattling staccato of autocannon fire. Three Blood Pact Chimerax carriers tore through the razor wire and clambered over the gravelbag barricades while the dust was still settling. A ripple of explosions preceded them as the infantry advancing behind them lobbed grenades overhead. Then the Chimerax were inside the perimeter, autocannons nosing for warm targets, their ramps dropping and hoarse Pact battle shouts tainting the already filthy air as red-white flares went off overhead.

The commandos spilled out and spread forwards as their support scrambled through the ruins of the perimeter behind them. The flarelight sent hard shadows stalking and dancing between them. The Chimerax engines revved and the cupola motors squealed as the gunners swung their mounts back and forth.

No fire came their way. None of the positions they rushed forward to had Imperial Guard troops lying in wait for them. The advance began to slow as the Pact soldiers became wary, double-checking for booby traps and ambushes. The high sirdar at the tip of the assault shouted back to them, keeping them moving towards the sound of las-fire and grenades from the far side of the point. The Imperials had run. They had thrown their entire weight against the opposite side of the encirclement, running into the guns of the stalk-tanks and Pact infantry rather than let the Death Brigade assault packs get to them. The high sirdar grinned beneath his silver grotesque. They were right to be afraid of his men. And wrong to think there was anything that could help them now.

The Chimerax rolled slowly forward, ready to rip apart the enemy as soon as they came into view. Their engines easily made enough noise to obscure the sound of the cargo transport coming up behind them with its running lights off. Their rearguard only turned at the unmistakable clank of a hatch and something that sounded like oddly heavy running footsteps.

The lightning claw of Damocles punched through the chest and face of the rearmost soldier, hoisted him like hay on a pitchfork and slung him forward. His corpse knocked two more sprawling for the steel-grey giant to crush and cripple as he ran over the top of them without looking down, eyes already on his next kill, his next, his next, a dozen dead Pact behind him now and the rear hatch of the nearest Chimerax yawning open in front. He vanished into it, the whole carrier rocking on its springs with each of his steps, and then finally the Pact were turning, suddenly aware something was badly wrong as the exploding autocannon magazines blew the turret into the sky.

By the time they had turned to look for an enemy, Priad had smashed his way out of the first Chimerax and into the second. By the time two fire teams had started advancing on the stricken second carrier he was killing the third. The passage-point was sinking into darkness as the flares guttered out; the high sirdar was shouting for more when his voice turned into a guttural gurgle and fell silent. The rest of the Pact only saw the giant in glimpses after that, an outline sketched by flickering las-beams, a silhouette briefly painted by flamelight as a stalk-tank exploded somewhere on the perimeter. The glimpses didn't last long; the Pact troops didn't last much longer.

When Priad arrived at the far side of the passage-point, the encirclement had been broken and scattered. The Urdeshi had thrown their full numbers at its weakest point, timing it for the moment that Priad arrived on the far side of their position and a score of Pragar came boiling up through the sublevel vents to enfilade the enemy ahead of them. Their would-be besiegers had been utterly unprepared for the sudden sortie; as he walked in among the milling Urdeshi and Pragar, Priad could not see a single Imperial corpse among the many underfoot.

'Going hunting?' he asked a young Urdeshi captain, who

was reloading his autogun while a medic pressed a dressing into place over a las-burn along his cheek.

'Going warring!' the man said with a grin that had the medic tutting and adjusting the dressing again. 'Enemy's gone from here tonight, she tells us, but there's hot fighting coming up over yonder around Steelwrights' Arch that'll need us.'

'Pick out your best for a vanguard, then,' Priad said, 'and point them back the way I came. Corporal Dmorz has a transport there that'll take a squad in a hurry. He's waiting for you.'

'You're not coming with us, sir?' the medic asked. Priad shook his head.

'My mission takes me onward, tonight.' Priad turned his gaze northward, although there was nothing much to see. He was entering the hyper-dense conurbation of central Ghereppan now, buildings like mountains that could hold tens of thousands and canyoned streets where the roads and rails stacked up twenty high, all of it alive with pitched battle as the Miracle unfolded. Even for an Iron Snake, a journey through that would be a test. He looked across the perimeter to where the mob of Pragar soldiers waited for him around an open vent-lid.

'And she has shown me that the low road tonight is the fast road,' he said with a smile. He looked back when the medic gave a little cough and spoke again.

'You'll know her, I suppose, sir? Course you will. The stories said the Snakes stand at her shoulders. We all like to think we walk with her, but it's not a figure of speech for you, is it? You've looked on her face?'

'I have.'

The medic sighed and nodded.

'Remember us to her, sir, will you? Red Company, Eighth Regulars. We never lost faith in her.'

'Nor she in you,' Priad said, and put his gauntlet on the man's shoulder. 'Throne protect you, Red Company.'

'Aquila watch you, Sir Snake.'

The Urdeshi cheered as he raised his lightning claw in salute and walked away. The Pragar thumped their chests and clattered their battle harnesses as he stepped into the vent opening and vanished, and then went piling down into the dark after him.

Brey Auerben
Imperial command, Ghereppan warzone

The general's command room had fallen still while they all stood listening, but now it was in motion again. Brey Auerben watched it from her position on the hololith platform, smiling a small, wondering smile.

The officers at each tactical station were calling excitedly back and forth, clacking keys and levers and exchanging codes, sending signals and runners up to the hololith, whose display was changing by the moment. Contact markers were flickering into new shapes and shades, and the battle zone demarcations wriggled like snakes as reports of the gains picked up speed.

Not gains and losses. Gains. Every Imperial report coming in was of a victory. Red incursion markers were fading to rust-brown and dragging backward as attack after attack was repelled. Positions that had been given up as overrun were flashing back into existence. Bright gold regimental insignia were touching off like fireworks where scattered and desperate units were suddenly reporting in again. The voices on the vox-links were jubilant, full of determination. But none of them were surprised, none uncomprehending. Everyone knew what had happened. A miracle.

Still smiling, Auerben stepped down off the platform and walked over to the pew where the comm servitors sat. They were sitting as still and serene as the primarchs at prayer in the temple friezes of her home world. Their report tickers were still inching out, but their chorus of alarms had fallen silent.

Auerben picked up one of the trailing streamers. She was curious about something. She held it up to the lamp but there was no need to try to read the tiny, grainy lettering of the timestamps along the top of the paper. She could see it at a glance: the point where the overlapping alert stamps and distress messages had cut out and the steady tick of victory reports had begun. She wanted to see what the servitor had recorded at the moment the Saint had spoken.

It looked like a jumble of code and characters, static on the paper, nothing more. Auerben was about to accept that and return to the platform when she realised what it was, and turned the tape sideways. The collection of symbols formed a rough but definite representation of an islumbine flower.

She dropped the tape and turned at a shout from the hololith.

'Throne be praised! They're running!'

The Enemy
Torcher's Colonnade

The Torcher's Colonnade curved around the northern end of a broad cobbled park east of Ghereppan's central spire cluster. The torchers it memorialised were those who worked with flame, be it gas, laser or plasma, cutting, joining and shaping. Every column was a heat-carved statue of a torcher at their labours, in postures of heroic and devoted toil, faces invisible beneath goggles and shield masks. The delicate illustrated glasswork that had made up the roof had been long since reduced to dusty fragments littering the ground, but the mosaic floor was still intact. Here it showed a torcher on the forge-line sealing the armour plates on a tank, there welding a submarine pipe, there las-cutting the image of the holy aquila into sheet steel for a chapel window. Some passing hands had pulled out and smashed the tiles that made up the aquila's image, but had let the rest of the picture be.

Beyond the colonnade, the cylindrical tower of the Teyozah furnace-forge should have been blazing with light. One of Ghereppan's proudest landmarks, claiming to be the oldest plasma furnace in this hemisphere, it had doused its lights when the Archenemy had captured it months before and had stood dark as a tomb since then. Only the magnetic signature and the dull leak of heat from the crowning minaret hinted that there was still life in the great toroidal plasma chamber deep inside it.

An hour earlier, with no fanfare, the magnetic signature had stopped. It was a blip on the sensors of the Militarum observation posts hidden away in the Archenemy-held streets around it, barely noticed. It was an annoyance to the militia dug in nearby, who suddenly found themselves with auspexes and communications gear throwing odd results as they compensated for interference that was no longer there. From streets away the keen long-range auspex of *Morbius Sire* sniffed out the change, but the Titan's crew had been on the hunt and not interested in such a curiosity. Until the lights came back on.

Suddenly the walls of Teyozah were bathed in gold-white light. The Sekkite troops dug in around it looked about, wondering and blinking, trying to work out what it meant, when their vox and auspex packs suddenly burst into screaming static. A new, monstrous power spike was coming from below the tower.

The gates sealing off the downramp into the furnace-forge's main processional avenue ground open, tearing loose the flakpress fortifications leaning against them, scattering the cursing troops that had been stationed under them. Long sealed, with no engineers to tend their mechanisms, the gates opened halfway and then halted. There was just enough of a pause for the gate guards to start cautiously venturing back, wondering what it was they hadn't been warned about.

Then the deep thrum of a plasma engine and the grind of enormous treads filled the rampway and it came into the light, a great land-crawling whale of fresh-made armour that glittered savagely as the thing's fourfold treads dragged it forward. The top of its hunched back pushed the gates apart and then shattered them, leaving the arched gateway to collapse down onto the ramp in its wake.

A handful of the Sekkite troops recognised the nerve-scraping hum coming from the thing and shouted for their comrades to run. And then its void shields flashed into place, the crack of materialisation knocking troopers sprawling, scorching and blinding the closest, shearing two or three of them apart. In the intricate cagework that ran up the thing's spine, a dazzling stream of plasma was already running down into a launching cage.

The plasmapult had reached street level now. Its prow broke the colonnade and its treads ground the statues and

...ic into gravel as the hulking machine turned itself ...h, towards the strait and the causeway.

The Enemy
Knabanac Magna-Forge, Duodek Shrine Precinct,
northern Ghereppan

The plasmapult that fired up its furnace and voids at the gates of the Knabanac magna-forge was long and low, articulated at the waist, its crawler treads mounted out to each side of it. It had been made that way to fit inside the forge-temple's atrial hall, where the charged copper-filigree roof helped to mask the building work from auspex. Now the thrum of its motor filled the hall from end to end and its ten enormous wheels began to turn. The fabricators who had laboured over its construction shrank back against the walls, raising fists in salute or pressing their foreheads to the floor in obeisance. The ingeniants who had supervised them since the Sons of Sek had conquered the forge stood proud, eyes closed and palms pressed over their mouths.

There was trouble in the avenues outside, bad trouble, a great Imperial surge out of nowhere that the Sons had all rushed to battle stations to repel. When the ceremonial portals in the middle of the hall cracked and swung silently upward in the grip of their maglev mounts, the crews could hear gunfire and distant cries, here and there the explosion of a tank round. None of it mattered now, not to them. Their task was complete and their orders discharged. They had been the instruments of the Anarch's will. It would be hubris to think there was anything more to live for.

They knelt, or cheered, or prayed as the ingeniants took

their leave, filing silently out behind their creation. It was time for the magna-forge to burn.

Raptus Solemnus
Low Mercatory Cluster, north-west Ghereppan

'Not it,' Princeps Arkaly Creel muttered, sparing barely more than a glance through *Raptor Solemnus'* senses to a sudden burst of superheated vapour pluming out of a clade-house to her north-west. That was a sign of something, to be sure, but it wasn't the sign of an enemy that the Saint's voice had told her to prepare for.

'Still not it,' she said when a transmission pulse went flickering across the northern half of the city like heat-lightning on the summer horizon. It was cleverly tuned and compressed, rippling back and forth from many small transmitters rather than a single powerful one. She let *Solemnus* read the signal, cache it and pass it back to Tech-Priest Inand to decrypt while they hunted.

'No,' she said through gritted teeth, as they came prowling around the corner of the Kessowright clade-house and she saw the swirling brawl that was filling the long arterial road ahead of her. According to her maps she should have been passing out of a contested zone into Sekkite territory that the Militarum had been besieging for months. But the troops flooding the arterial for two kilometres ahead were all Imperial, silver-trimmed Helixid battle tanks islands in a sea of running Urdeshi infantry, black-armoured Jovani Sentinels scampering around out of her way as *Solemnus* stepped onto the road and declared itself with a blare of its klaxons. The visual flashes and sensor traces of intense street battle were far ahead, too deep into enemy territory to make sense. And it still wasn't what she was here for.

'Warhounds, stand ready,' Bernal told them over the manifold. Creel mouthed the words *Ready for what?* even as she sent her code-shout back. She took *Solemnus* a full stride onto the arterial, the guns on its arms warming up. Creel shrugged her arms and rolled her head as the movement of the autoloaders and pumping of coolant sent itchy feedback through her neck and shoulders. The dustkickers down around her ankles had better be ready to get their arses out of her way once she found her target.

And then there it was, ahead of her around the curve of the road, almost at the far edge of the enemy zone and into the belt of contested city beyond it, a monstrous power spike the like of which she'd never seen before. Creel could barely process what her Titan's senses were seeing; the nearest she could find to take its measure was a memory of *Solemnus'* from before she had taken the princeps' throne, from before her own birth: a circle of Titans standing in a ring around an open-shielded fusion reactor in the Proximan desert, paying respects to the mysteries of the Collegia Syntik.

After bare moments the energy signature changed, diminished and became coherent in a way Creel's own memory could identify just fine. A powerful void shield had just sprung into being around whatever had blazed up beyond those buildings. Its distinctive tang faded from her senses as its energies were tuned and focused and then turned inward to interlace with each other. Creel bit her lip and scowled into her visual feeds, memorising the shapes of the spires around where she had seen the flare, as if Inand's logisters and the Titan's own cortex hadn't riveted the location into their consciousness.

She held *Raptor Solemnus* in check by main force of will,

letting it do no more than raise a clawed foot and stamp down onto the road. The rolling crowd of Militarum ahead of her got the message, boiling with alarm before they parted for her as neatly as a set of temple curtains.

Creel was leaning forward and panting with adrenaline, and *Solemnus* mimicked her by redirecting its venting systems and jetting a blast of superheated air out through the cruel bronzed-steel gryphon beak sculpted onto its head. The heat in her skull was too intense for words. She gave herself over to the hunt and the Titan's legs sprang into motion, her crew shouting foul-mouthed encouragement as it ran.

Morbius Sire
Grand Northern Transit, central north Ghereppan

Morbius Sire came through the arch and got a thermobaric shell in the face, but that only served to make it angry. The AT-70 that had fired it jittered in place, as though it couldn't decide whether to stay still to try and reload or reverse away as fast as its treads would carry it. A curt cough of plasma from *Morbius Sire*'s blastgun reduced the tank to half a chassis and two fused treads slumping down into a molten crater, and the question became moot.

The Warhound strode forward again, the air around its vulpine metal face still smoking from the shell, its princeps' teeth bared in imitation of the Titan's snarl. In Maximilian Orfuls' conscious mind, that part of it not taxed to the limit with battle inloads, mapping overlays and power calculations, he knew this was a triumph, a miracle, a victory that would tilt the balance of the war over this whole hemisphere. But that was almost drowned out by his hindbrain, his brute emotional consciousness, which the MIU opened up into a cave yawning behind him with *Morbius Sire*'s bestial aggression churning and roaring in the dark. This was not the hunt that the Orfuls/*Sire* coupling wanted. They shifted and growled with the feverish impatience of a hunter who sets out to slay lions and finds nothing but mice.

Mice, ants, targets that Orfuls kept half-instinctually passing over, looking for voids to break and engines to crush, until he made himself concentrate because these fleeing specks of meat and trundling little tanks were all there were for the Legio to hunt. The resistance they tried to put up as *Sire* bore down on them, the little las-bites and missile-scuffs, stung the Titan just enough to infuriate.

'Accelerate, princeps?' Moderatus Strakhov asked. 'Striding speed and we'll plough through them, break them up for the infantry. I'm reading signals from Urdeshi Storm Troop on the clan-house walls and Jovani Vanguard on the second-level arterials. They'll do the job, surely? I wouldn't even ask our own skitarii to waste their time mopping up that rabble.'

'Strak, if Lau could hear you talking about his warriors in that tone he'd take your–' Orfuls bit off the rest of the sentence. He had intended the words as banter but *Morbius Sire*'s battle-rage was saturating his mind, filling his voice with heat, forcing the joke into a threat. 'No,' he said instead. 'We are the mop-up. Keep them running. We're muster-hounds today, not hunting wolves. Any of them that get stuck between us and the Militarum might bed down and make a pocket of resistance. We stay behind them and keep them moving. Just keep your eye out for anything that might be lobbing more of those pressure shells, and warn the others about them too. My ears are still ringing.'

* * *

Lupus Lux
Tyrgos Processional, central Ghereppan

A pair of muzzle-flashes from further along the Tyrgos Processional, and two thermobarics burst against *Lupus Lux*'s voids in deadly synchronisation. The monstrous orange-white fireballs bloomed into a single conflagration that slammed pressure-waves against the Titan's torso and wrapped it in white-hot tornadic winds. The Warhound had been in mid-step when the blasts had gone off and for one stunning moment it actually teetered on one leg as the incandescent air battered at it.

Then its foot boomed down onto the ghost-grey paving of the Processional and *Lupus Lux* strode forward out of the furnace, its silver-white livery seared away, the white silk banners that had spread from its shoulders and hips incinerated. The skeletal frames that had supported them swayed in the air like willow branches, trailing smoke.

'Thermobarics, you say?' Princeps Leyden Krugmal said. 'Thanks for the warning, Max.' His voice was sour but his thoughts and nerves were already racing ahead. He could feel the aftermath of the hit, the crawling scorch like a patch of hot sun moving across his skin followed by a splashing chill as the voids stabilised around *Lux*'s hull and the cooling systems compensated. *Lupus Lux* leaned into another crashing stride as the great machine's walking rhythm came back under control.

'Paint the two little crode-heaps that did that to us, Klyte,' Krugmal ordered, and his moderatus lifted his right hand in assent. The stump of his left forearm was already twitching from the data load pouring through the web of leads that locked into the bright silver collar just above where his wrist had once been.

While Krugmal's lips were still shaping that order he was sending a silent command through *Lux*'s manifold to the tiny shrine-cell behind him. The four-dimensional directive rune lit up in the inload sluice of Tech-Priest Papagha's senses and unfolded into an instruction for a damage audit. Krugmal could feel no alarming sense-analogues flashing in his nerve endings, but then how many soldiers would bull on through a hit without realising they were wounded? Krugmal couldn't be that reckless. It wasn't just his own body at stake. It was his crew's, and the holy war idol he commanded.

<We are blessed by the Cog,> he canted, apropos of that thought. Krugmal was a pious man.

'May it turn forever!' returned his crew. The superstructure around them seemed to thrum and growl in reply, and Krugmal smiled. *Lupus Lux*'s temper was a glowering and brooding thing, smouldering where *Lupus Noctem* and *Raptor Solemnus* blazed, but its patience was not infinite. It needed to strike back. Krugmal pushed his senses out and forward.

The pair of AT-70 Reavers had been crawling backwards along the processional, cannon elevated, waiting for *Lupus Lux* to cross their range as infantry and light carriers poured past them. The Reavers were crude adversaries compared to the elite armour of the Imperial crusade, slow to load and unsteady on firing, but *Lux* was an enormous target closing at a predictable speed and they had lit it up perfectly. Now, as they kept on reversing, they veered apart, the left one slowing and the right one speeding up, trying to spread themselves out so that at least one would survive the Warhound's retaliation. Around them and ahead of them the troops whose retreat they were covering did their best to help, prickling *Lupus Lux*'s voids with small-arms fire. A HET-7 another hundred metres ahead was brave enough to stop and make a slewing turn, scattering running infantry, and conjured a crackling aurora off *Lux*'s shields with a probing yellow las-beam. Even some of the infantry weapon crews were finding cover behind stoops or door-arches and scrambling to load missile tubes or lock and aim tripod-mounted lascannons.

None of it saved the further of the two Reaver tanks, which was gutted by a split-second flicker-shot from *Lux*'s laser destructor that slagged the front third of the vehicle in less time than it took the surrounding troops to blink at the energy flare. A heartbeat after that and thermobarics in the tank's loader cooked off. The fireburst overwhelmed the whole processional with a white blaze before it collapsed and sucked back in on itself. Nearby tanks jolted and stalled. Groundcars and SCU-3 trikes slewed wildly out of control or were just bowled over outright by the searing shockwave. The blast batted running troopers away then remorselessly dragged them back as the fireball sucked in more oxygen, the nearest bodies limp, stunned or dead, the further ones thrashing wildly as they suffocated and then began to burn.

'Forward-left-forward, stately now,' Krugmal instructed, and movement and mapping schematics flashed onto the displays around the bridge as Sola Encantor, his steerswoman, followed the command. The forward visuals were next to useless and even the regular auspex field was full of thermal and particulate churn, but *Lupus Lux*'s hungry mechanical senses were already starting to make out targets beyond the pyre in front of them.

A streak of yellow light burst through the smoke, skated off the starboard angle of voids and punched a crater into the clade-house wall behind the Titan's shoulder. The trail of sensor analytics it left across Krugmal's vision proclaimed it to be a rocket-assisted piercing shell from a 105-mil cannon: the other Reaver shooting blind, switching its load to something it hoped would hurt them.

'Just be patient down there,' Krugmal told it aloud, and let *Lux* give a bellow of its horns to back his words up. 'You won't be left wanting. Just wait.'

'Princeps?'

'I won't approve if you've lost the solution to that second shooter, Klyte, but I won't be too angry. We'll be on them in a moment. I'm taking the laser for it. Double-check the mega-bolter loads so we can sweep the street a little too.'

'I obey, princeps, passing green lights on that arm to your feed. But it's the auspex, sir.'

'Damaged? It's reading clean.'

'Co-ordinates are in the manifold. *Invictus Antagonistes* has given a stand-ready order–'

'I heard that, Klyte, and I responded to it,' Krugmal answered, slightly nettled at the choice of words. He respected Bernal tremendously, but a moderatus did not *order* a princeps.

'Then what shall we do with our new auspex sighting?' Beyran asked, in the punctilious tone that meant he was waiting for Krugmal to catch on to something. The princeps let his pale grey eyes drift closed and drew the full bandwidth of *Lux*'s machine-senses up through the MIU into his own brain. The sensation was like drawing in an endless, enormous breath until the lungs were straining to hold it. A second, two, three, then Krugmal's eyes snapped open and his face lit up in a smile. The energy blooms and void shield signatures scattered through the city ahead of them were now tagged and glowing on every pict-screen across every console. Krugmal's brow became sheened with sympathetic sweat as *Lupus Lux*'s anticipation set the reactor furnace at its heart to boiling.

'I see them!' he called. 'Sola, mark time a moment, turn us on the bearing I've fed you. Now isn't that a damned familiar-looking... Why, yes. *Yes*. Entascha, my love? It seems our little plasma-tossing friend from Perrima Suul was just one of a litter. Look! Siblings!'

The Enemy
The Great Ascent

At long last, dawn was starting to seep up from the horizon. The cloud cover and the waters of the strait out to the east were lightly brushed with grey light, and those in the city's west could look up and see the skyline of the scarp just starting to emerge from the dark.

Except that the Archenemy had brought dawn to Ghereppan a little early.

The plasma cages flew high into the air, each making a little false sunrise in the streets it flew over, too bright to look at directly. One or two came apart in mid-air and dissipated into glowing, churning streamers, but most were made well enough to hit and break.

They struck fires among the clerking-mills and fiduciarate precincts along the western Avenue Solar. They breached the walls of the hulking Zhein-Berek clade-houses and turned those ancient arcologies into blast-furnaces that consumed themselves from the inside. They reduced the iron statuary in the Capitol Akrostoa, untouched by either side since the war had begun, to a molten red stream.

The Knabanac magna-forge was already burning. The plasmapult that it had birthed had orphaned itself immediately, raising and rotating the launch-rail from its hind section and opening its gullet. The firespout that washed over the magna-forge dwarfed the thermobaric blast that had almost toppled *Lupus Lux*. The northern steeple crumpled and fell within minutes, the energies it had contained arcing out and striking the surrounding buildings, earthing itself in the streets. The main dome began to sweat black smoke as the air inside it superheated, and small explosions started to burst around its edges as the internal structures collapsed and the machine-shrines overloaded and blew. The plasmapult crawler was already on its way north, drooling white heat into the walls of the clade-house fabricatories as it passed.

The angular beast that had smashed its way clear of Emptor's Ease was moving parallel with it, rolling down the centre of the Avenue Bastoka as it unfolded the catapult arm from its pointed peak. It stove in the side of a thirty-floor data-mill to its right, and dropped a plasma cage onto a road stack to its left that brought down eight levels of truck- and railways. As it slowed to make the turn onto the Avenue Ybzomen the other two crawlers caught up with it. For a moment there was a scream of clashing energies and the air all around them crawled with stinging discharges and ozone stink. Then their shields attuned and merged, the layers of energy so potent that they were visible as a hazy chromatic blister spanning the avenue, an oil slick curving through the air. Rolling in neat formation, the three plasmapults struck out northward. Ahead of them was the Great Ascent, the sweeping ceremonial ramp-road that rose up and met the Oureppan causeway coming in off the sea. And across the heart of Archenemy-held Ghereppan, their fellows came to meet them.

* * *

URDESH: THE MAGISTER AND THE MARTYR

Raptus Solemnus
Ascent approaches, northern Ghereppan

The domed voids in her killsights shimmered and screamed, but they did not break. Arkaly Creel felt her throat working in a barely audible growl that *Raptus Solemnus'* horns picked up and turned into a bone-buzzing bass rumble. She wasn't going to let the dirty-hulled tread-crawling little bastards beat her. It wasn't fair if Krugmal and Mereschel were the only ones who got to watch one die.

Except this time there wasn't just one, and that was the problem.

Creel fired *Solemnus'* laser destructor again. It was a longer burst than a moving Titan would normally fire, but Creel was a gifted princeps and the beam stayed steady, only shifting infinitesimally as *Solemnus* shifted on its feet like a pugilist sizing up a foe. The beam was barely visible at the weapon muzzle, only shimmering into sight just short of the target where it hit the vapour and smoke swirling around the plasmapult phalanx. As it hit the void blister, though, it spattered off it again in a dazzle of light and heat like a fire-hose jet pointed against a wall. She held the shot, held it until the feedback from the weapon's core was like holding a hot wire in her hand and she could see the amber alerts along the arms of her throne starting to tinge red.

And the voids, spit on their makers' hides, were holding. Someone in the Archenemy fold knew more about the machine-mysteries than any heretek wretch had a right to. They had merged the plasmapults' voids, aligned their structures, meshed their transmissions, mapped them over one another to create a single shield dome stronger than the sum of its parts. Creel had never heard of the technique being applied outside major cult fortresses and certain high ceremonies: it was hard to master, even harder to apply at scale, and of little use to highly mobile engines like Titans. If there were a Legio doctrine on how to break an interlaced void, she was not party to it.

The shield dome was almost lost to normal vision now, so much smoke was being sucked into the air as her laser charred the ground under it and incinerated luckless enemies who had been too close to the path of the beam. Creel felt a snarling cry boiling up from *Solemnus'* consciousness and over into her own, but she throttled it back to a hiss of frustration and took her mental grip off the destructor's trigger. Through gaps in the swirling smoke, she could see the void dome shimmering again as though she had never fired at it. Fists clenched, she dragged her Titan's anima back under control, shouted codes to Steersman Maharach, and together they danced *Raptus Solemnus* back between the blocky, taper-topped skyscrapers of the Lower Circulars. Two plasma cages smashed to the ground where they had stood, and for several seconds the street sloshed and foamed with murderous glare.

Plasma. That was what it would take, she was sure. One blinding punch from the likes of *Invictus Antagonistes*, *Sicarian Faero*, the hellish long-range weapons of *Cour Valant* or even the blastgun on the Reaver *Philopos Manix* would cave those voids in and leave the enemy as naked as their cousin whose scalp *Noctem* and *Lux* had claimed. But *Faero* and *Valant* were leading a Legio task force away along the sea-cliffs to the east, days' walk from Ghereppan by now, the backbone of the Imperial defence to stop the Blood Pact's armoured divisions crossing the straits from the corpse-city of Xavec and crashing into the Ghereppan army's flank.

Worse still, the cunning, craven scrapshunts had made it up onto the Great Ascent. They knew that the kind of firepower to break their shields would bring down the ramp as well, sever the causeway, cut the city's throat. They knew the causeway's worth and they had taken it hostage.

And so Arkaly Creel forced herself back into her command throne, bit down on *Solemnus'* urge to rush forward seeking blood and burning, and tried to think about what they could do.

Gearhart
Invictus Antagonistes, Ghereppan Strait

Pietor Gearhart's ghosts would not speak to him. He had listened to them in the hives and badlands of Orestes, and they had drifted in and out of his dreams in the long voyage-sleeps as the Legio had been carried through the Cabal Salient. He was sure he had heard them at engine-start in the Sehellen Valley landing steps, their voices in his ears as he had listened to *Antagonistes'* great feet crunching the obsidian crust of the volcanic plain. At some level he had known they weren't real. They were phantoms, perhaps echoes in *Antagonistes'* own deep memories, perhaps just the last ephemeral dreams of an old man whose final days were quietly slipping away into the dark. But they had been real to him, realer in the end than the voices of his own Titan's crew, realer even than *Antagonistes'* embrace on his thoughts and senses.

Perhaps that was wrong. He had a nagging sense that it might be. But it was hard to focus on that when the soft sleepiness and the voices of his memories were always there, lulling him, smoothing the edges away from his thoughts. But then even his ghosts had started to fade, their voices harder to make out, their words making less and less sense. And one by one they had fallen silent and left Gearhart to sleep alone in the thick, warm silence of his amniotic tank.

Until tonight. The voice he had heard tonight was not one of the ghosts he remembered, the phantoms of his old friends and companions long gone. He had never heard this woman's voice before, but still he knew it instantly. Her presence had come into his sleep like soft sunlight through a morning window, filling every sense he had. He had registered her in his physical hearing and as sound-analogue input on his cant channel. There had been a lovely, soothing warmth along his skin, dispelling a chill that he had not been conscious he was feeling. And although his nostrils had been sealed shut around filter plugs on the day he was prepared for his tank, for the first time in over a century he caught a scent. It was an astringent flower-scent, bright and lovely. He breathed it in.

Under the membranous visor that held them gently closed, his eyelids twitched. He chuckled at the thought that he had actually tried to blink. For a moment he was sure he was about to pull the mask from his face and take a great gulp of air, the clean air of the mountain trails above the Doctrinopolis on Hagia, crisp and cold with the sweet-sharp scent of islumbine in flower.

He had never been to Hagia. The Legio Invicta had never set foot on the Saint's birth world, her shrine world. But the feel of its mountains were vivid in his mind to the last detail, not fading now but sinking down to the level of cherished memory rather than living experience. And he realised he could feel his actual reality surfacing in his senses again: the slightly bitter air piped into his life-mask, the glutinous semi-buoyancy of his tank, and the low rumble of *Invictus*

Antagonistes' consciousness, growling in his backbrain like a watchful bear. He moved again in his shrouding gel, tilting his head, pushing his shoulders back, hearing the clicks and cracks from his neck and back. Not quite smiling, Pietor Gearhart reached into his Titan's systems and pulled himself back into the world of the living.

Grawe-Ash and Auerben
Imperial command, Ghereppan warzone

General Grawe-Ash's command room was bathed in quiet and green. The angry glare of the hololith alerts had faded fast as the last night of the Battle of Ghereppan took shape in front of them.

The scarp was green from the southern slopes to the cliffs that overlooked the Great Ascent. The strip of docklands looking out to the eastern strait showed a string of markers for engagements resolved and enemies fleeing out to sea. Only the very top of the east side was still a dull orange, and even now it was flecking to grey and to green as more intelligence came in. An emerald wave was washing up through the heartland hab precincts at the western foot of the scarp, and when Brey Auerben leaned in to peer at the shapes of the spires, she could see the tiny threads that laced them together changing colour too as the Imperium retook the soaring skyways and transducts.

There was only one place inside the lith that still flashed red and amber: the elemental savagery of the war engine battle at the foot of the Great Ascent. The cluster of icons for the plasmapults at the foot of the ramp glowed like a litter of cinders while the bronze-and-green emblems for the four Warhounds flitted back and forth through the streets, fading out then flashing back to life as the Titans moved. The battle was turning Ghereppan's northern tip into such an inferno that human observers could barely approach it; auspex and vox were swamped, blinded and swept away by the sheer power rampaging through those streets. They could hear the occasional burst of distorted voices, nothing more.

Every eye in the room was turned to the battle. For now there was little else to do – the Miracle had left little room for generalship when every last Imperial soul on the promontory had been marshalled directly by the Living Saint herself. It would wear off with time (surely it would, surely such euphoria could not last, what simple human could stand the touch of the divine for too long?) and they would be needed again. But for now, all they could do was try to keep up.

'What's that?' Grawe-Ash asked, tapping the side of the hololith. 'Status change. I don't recognise it.' Auerben peered through the lith at the newcomer, an elaborate device hanging over a Titan marker just offshore. 'That's not a tactical marker. Looks like a coat of arms. Heralds? Where're the savants?'

Auerben had already picked it, but it took a moment to speak past the sudden lump in her throat. She didn't see how it could be, but what kind of night was this to question the impossible?

'That, ma'am,' she said, 'is the personal heraldry of the princeps maximus. He has–' She stopped and gulped. 'He has returned. Pietor Gearhart has retaken his command.'

Gearhart and Bernal
Invictus Antagonistes, Ghereppan Strait

'*Invictus Antagonistes*. My warriors. Stand to your orders, stand to your oaths.'

It took Bernal whole seconds to unfreeze, and at first all he could do was gape at the rest of them. Zophal's shoulders were shaking. Rakolo had one hand out to the pict-glass in his control plinth as if to try and touch something he couldn't believe he was seeing. Slowly, the three of them turned in their seats to stare.

Behind them, their princeps hung framed by the silver scrollwork that surrounded the amniotic tank. He had uncurled from his comatose hunch and his aged body was as straight as a young soldier marching on the parade ground. Bernal watched the old man's hands slowly lift to his chest and make the sign of the aquila. And then he couldn't see any more because his eyes had blurred and stung.

'I've been away a long time, Bernal,' the old man said. 'It's good to see you again.' The fatherly kindness in his voice made Bernal want to weep. All the hesitancy, the incomplete words, the dreamy half-coherence was gone. The heart of Legio Invicta was beating again. The princeps was back. *The princeps was back.*

'I'll thank her,' Gearhart said. 'I owe her thanks. But I owe her more than that. Invicta! Legio Invicta! We walk upon Urdesh, we walk upon Ghereppan! The war for this city has been given to us to end!'

All the steel, all the force of will that had made Gearhart the father of the Legio was there in his voice. Bernal could feel *Invictus Antagonistes* quickening around him, see the changes in his feeds. The Titan was coming to full wakefulness. He was no longer clumsily piloting a machine. He was riding in a living god of war. Bernal dashed the tears from his eyes, laughed and shouted and the others joined in.

'Invicta! *Invicta!* INVICTA!'

* * *

The Enemy
Ghereppan City

By the time the eastern sky and sea were brightening to actual sunrise, the abandonment of Ghereppan was on in earnest. Ochre-uniformed soldiers came boiling out of buildings, bunkers and entrenchments, flooding towards the Great Ascent and up onto the causeway. They clambered aboard already loaded cargo drays or clung to the roll-bars of SCU-3s; the lucky ones crammed themselves into the troop compartments of ochre-painted Chimeras or long-bodied Urdeshi CTT-2s. But most just had to get through the canyon-streets of central Ghereppan as best they could on their own feet, labouring up the ramp in the half-light and beginning the long slog away to Oureppan, ready to chance their lives with a leap over the edge and into the water if they came under attack while so excruciatingly exposed.

The Astra Militarum came behind them, fast, and implacable. The power and beauty of the Miracle was still singing in their veins, carrying them forward without tiring, but now it was tinged with something earthier and more human: simple fury. They had fought to the breaking point, not just to drag this city back from the Archenemy's grip but to reclaim it intact. On this new dawning day that reclamation was so close they felt they could touch it, and now it was burning before their eyes.

The Archenemy, their preachers would say, was not an adversary but a mockery, a twisting and mis-making. Turning the plasmapults onto the city they were fleeing, on the grand spires and ancient machines that both sides had understood were indispensably valuable, was the greatest mockery of all, a parting and cowardly insult.

URDESH: THE MAGISTER AND THE MARTYR

The Urdeshi felt it most of all. They threw themselves at the heels of the retreating foe even while plasma cages crashed down among them and burst against building walls overhead. Their savagery was tinged with desperation. They prayed to the Saint, shouted her name as they killed, calling to her and the Emperor who bore her up to not let their city be taken from them. Not now, not like this.

But at the base of the Great Ascent the plasmapults stood firm, their rain of sunfire never letting up. With careful, methodical brutality their crews burned their mark into Ghereppan, a spreading semicircle of gutted and smoking buildings, streets awash in a hot sludge of disintegrating rockcrete and liquefied glass, walling off the path behind them with storms of superheated air.

Priad
Beneath central Ghereppan

Priad couldn't feel the tripwires themselves, but where they had been set particularly tightly and sturdily he could just perceive a split second of resistance before they broke, barely noticeable unless he went through several at once.

The consequence of breaking them, of course, was a little more noticeable. The crack of detonations filled the tunnel and ceramite flechettes and steel pellets spattered against his armour then ricocheted away into the dark. His hearing, superhumanly accurate and resilient to begin with, and protected and enhanced by his auto-senses, recovered almost instantly, so he could hear quite clearly the sound of the Pragar scrambling out of cover back at the intersection and getting ready to follow him. He pushed enough power into his lightning claw for a momentary bluish flare, the all-clear signal they'd settled on each time Priad broke an enemy trap. That same flicker showed him something moving along the tunnel ahead, sight and sound and scent making a fractured kaleidoscope picture of it, not clear yet but that didn't matter. It was something he needed to kill.

'Burning your right!' came a shout from behind him and he sidestepped left, hunching down and half-turning, wedging himself into the curve of the tunnel wall. Two chemical firebombs, the crude but vicious ones the Pragar liked to hand-make themselves, arced past him and shattered against the stonework ahead. Dirty yellow flames billowed across the tunnel, engulfed the moving thing, gave Priad a final couple of seconds to judge its movement and meet its charge with his own.

They smashed into each other, his ceramite thudding on hide and flesh rather than clashing on armour. Even after only a few steps Priad had built up enough speed that he bulldozed the thing backwards barely slower than his running pace. He could hear metal scraping along stone as it tried to dig in and resist him, and some kind of limb was locked around his helmet collar trying to break the seal and prise the helmet free. Priad hunched lower and drove harder, pulling his left arm back and pistoning it forward, feeling the lightning claw flare and buzz as it sank through flesh.

Then they were in mid-air, tumbling out of the tunnel mouth into one of the high-ceilinged junction chambers that Ghereppan's builders had been so in love with, crashing down into shallow, filthy water. Whatever Priad was fighting was on top of him now, wrestling his arms with surprising strength as clawed lower limbs scrabbled to try and wound his legs. The face that it pushed into his own was a featureless mask of tarnished copper and silver, riveted to the front of its skull.

It pinned Priad's left arm down under the water with what felt like some kind of pincer-limb, then another one, and when it shifted its weight onto its two right hands Priad swept his own right around and clubbed the back of its head with his bolter, smashing its ugly metallic dish of a face into his own faceplate, then again, his bolter wet with its blood now as well as the water, something neon-yellow oozing from under the mask and onto him. It had a second left hand as well as a right and that jammed its buzzing tip up inside Priad's pauldron, some kind of shrill oscillating blade or spike feeling for an armour seam. He drove his left knee up into it, tilting it off-balance for the moment it took for him to get his left foot flat on the floor and push himself up, still feeling the maddening mosquito-buzz of that spike trying to drill into his armpit, raking the points of the lightning claw up his attacker's thigh and hip and finally skewering its flank a second time. The sizzle of scorching meat filled the air as Priad flashed full power into the claw and twisted his fist back and forth, ploughing up and cauterising the thing's torso.

Its aggressive clawing turned to panicked thrashing, and Priad punched it up off him. He could see its shoulders and head silhouetted in the last of the firebomb flames from the tunnel mouth above, and separated them with a twisting strike of his claw and an actinic blue lightning-crack. Even as its body went limp its pincer-hands were still tightening their grip on his armour, and it took three more slashing clawstrokes before he was finally free of them.

He got his legs under him, but as he started to stand he heard bad sounds over the splash and scrape of his own movements: the grind of a heavy mechanised joint and the buzz of small motors, the size that might be found in a weapon mount. There was no time to try anything fancy:

Priad launched himself into a long dive, crashing down flat into the water again as a lascannon flashed up a puff of steam from where he had been crouching a moment before.

Priad's reactor pack stopped him from shoving himself cleanly over onto his back but he managed to roll up onto his side and fire two quick, wild, one-handed bolter shots up and behind him. The first detonated in among the stalk-tank's legs, and the second caromed off its canopy, then again off the press-block wall above it and exploded in mid-air. The flash lit up a towering tangle of hooked metal limbs and glowering armaglass faces.

Priad pushed up into a crouch, waited until he saw the stalk-tank's cannon swing to bear on him again. He could make out no movement behind the canopy but he could see the odd temperature flashes as coolant pumped and then heated around the weapon mount, and he sprang away again as the beam triggered, firing a third round in return. It ploughed into the side of the lascannon casing and blew it apart, and the tank shuddered as the inside of its pilot bubble was spattered with spalling armourplas and jets of coolant.

The Pragar troopers came pouring through the tunnel entrance, moving with the easy speed of hiveborn for whom climbing was as natural as walking and a discipline ingrained by long, brutal, claustrophobic battles beneath the cities of Ashek II, Balhaut and Urdesh. Their dirty grey camo turned them into shadows among shadows. Their helmets were full-face, no two alike, visages like dogs, rats, insects, snouted and bulbous with hearing-protection baffles and emergency oxygen caches. At a warning shout from their sergeant they grabbed and braced, and two more firebombs burst against the pile of tanks that filled the far side of the chamber.

The *pile* of tanks. The Archenemy must have been more pressed and desperate than Priad could have hoped for. There was an access well behind that tangle of machinery, and to block it from the advancing Pragar the retreating foe had simply dumped a mob of stalk-tanks down it as their rearguard, scrabbling atop one other like crustaceans in a bucket. In the light of the firebombs Priad could see the gleam of razor wire festooning their bodies and legs. An attempt to protect them from a close assault, along with whatever that thing had–

The second kill-construct came hurtling down from its hiding spot high in the heap of machines. Priad managed a shot as it fell, winging it but no more. He ran forward as it splashed down in a crouch among the Pragar, taking in a long curve of emaciated torso and two arms of obscenely uneven lengths –one a fat trunk of muscle whose hand was a ring of stitched-on human fingers and metal hooks, the other a too-long segmented thing of severed human arms bound by gleaming brass joints. Its face, its whole head and neck, were invisible inside a heavy iron basket that seemed to be jammed directly into the weeping flesh of its shoulders. From inside the basket came a constant, liquid panting sound.

Its long arm was tipped with a bundle of short-barrelled flechette guns that went off in tight sequence. Several Pragar on that side of it had already thrown themselves down, but two more of them were caught and shredded, flopping lifelessly down into water that instantly bloomed crimson around them. Its other arm shot forward as the creature lunged, grabbing the Pragar sergeant by the collar and dragging her in. She got off two wild hellgun shots, one scorching the thing's thigh and the second going into its belly, before she suddenly convulsed once, twice, thrice and a pistoning motion from that trunk-thick arm sent her flying. Her front was wet and red; inside the mismatched ring of fingers a spring-spike slid in and out of its mounting like an eager tongue.

A salvo of las-shots struck puffs of cauterised flesh off the thing, and then openings like quivering gill-slits gaped down its flanks and breathed out a billowing, sickly fog that filled the bottom of the well, milky and blinding. Priad's vision danced and refocused as his helmet systems searched for the right settings to compensate for it, but there was no time to wait until he could see again. Those same systems and his hyper-conditioned brain had made a millimetre-precise map of this battlefield without his conscious prompting. The white fog was full of noise now: the chatter of the flechettes, the crackle and bang of las-fire and hard rounds as the Pragar tried to bracket and kill their attacker, and that hot, foul panting.

There was a hoarse wail of agony from in front of him and a Pragar trooper appeared out of the fog, left arm gone and left shoulder a gory crater, helmet visor cracked. Priad half-turned to let him fall, concentrating all his efforts on his hearing and smell, and when he heard the whoop of something heavy swinging through the air and the almost supersonic squeak of badly lubricated brass joints he shot his hand out flicker-fast, grabbing the strung-together gun-arm, cursing as it bounced back out of his grasp, then catching it again, locking his fingers so tightly around it that his armour protested the actuator strain with red pinpricks in his vision. Sweating skin split in his grip and the panting accelerated in pace as yellow blood slicked his hand.

Priad yanked the thing towards him, so hard that the metal joint tore half-free. It lurched out of the fog towards him, easily visible in preysight now: the thing's flesh was fever-hot. Priad severed the gun-limb with a claw-stroke, dropped it into the water and punched through the basket where the thing's head should have been. He felt no resistance, as though whatever was in there were fragile as paper or even missing completely, but the creature hung on, caught on his fist, scrabbling to get away. Then a wide-bore stubber bellowed beside him and the thing dropped to its knees. Another two shots sent flesh and bright golden fluid pluming out of the creature's back and it flopped into the water, dead.

Priad was moving again before it had finished falling. The fog lit up as a lascannon beam sizzled through it, then two more, firing at crazy angles as the stalk-tank gunners aimed as best they could. One had some kind of small-calibre coaxial mount that was banging off hard rounds and sending ricochets singing. He needed to close in before one of them got a lucky hit. That last beast had done them a backhanded favour with its fog, but already it was starting to thin out and settle in an opalescent scum on the water. They wouldn't have cover for long.

Two strides took him to the tank at the base of the pile, borne down to its knees by the weight above it. It tried to drag its cannons up to bear on him but he sidestepped and the beam hissed past him to carve a glowing rut in the well wall. Priad gouged a criss-cross of claw-wounds into the front of its canopy and then smashed the weakened armourplas in with his boot, leaned in and tore the head off the figure strapped into the cockpit. Human or servitor, he couldn't tell through the muck, scars and darkness. He picked his bolter out of the water, mag-clamped it to the side of his pack and began to climb.

He was too close and too careful for any of them to be

able to aim their cannons at him. One fired at him with an auxiliary stubber barely bigger than a handgun tucked in under its chin, and three rounds it fired actually struck chips off his faceplate before he answered them with a bolt-shell that pulverised the tank's innards. He pulled himself up over that one's wreck and made a claw-stroke that severed the cable-train under the next tank's belly, and stilled it in a shower of orange sparks.

The one above that seemed inert, from the fall or the Pragars' shooting or both. Priad had braced himself to tear away the garlands of razor wire to clear a way for the Guard troops to follow him when suddenly it jerked into life and fired the double grenade launchers that stuck out of its canopy like spider mandibles. One grenade rang off his helm, then off the wall and fell past him, the other exploded against his plastron and almost knocked him loose from his handhold. He roared down a warning moments before the second grenade went off beneath him, for whatever good that would do for humans unarmoured against the confined pressure blast, and then dragged himself up one-handed. The tank's frame was groaning and deforming under his weight and the whole stack of them had started shifting ominously. Priad grabbed one of the grenade tubes and tore it away, bringing the guts of its motorised mounting with it.

He had just tossed the tangle of machinery aside when a stunning blow to the back of his helmet sent him toppling forward with his vision flaring amber. Had he been a second slower he'd have crashed all the way back to the foot of the well, but he managed to twist and grab the limb that had hit him, the hoofed and hooked foreleg of the topmost tank that was now kicking its other legs against the walls and huffing hot, yellow bursts of promethium flame from its thorax mounts. Above it he could see the thick bars of the grille-gate up into the open air, and when he listened he could feel great shuddering concussions from above ground, getting louder, getting closer. *Almost there. Not much time.*

He kicked loose from his footholds and hung for a moment, reaching up. The tank pawed at him with a second limb, trying to dislodge him, and he grabbed that leg in turn and hauled himself up.

That brought him face to face with the pilot. Wide brown eyes stared at him from a bony, sweat-soaked face over a filthy bandana bearing a handprint insignia. Priad leaned back and then slammed the brow of his helmet into the canopy, sending the man jerking back in shock. The flamers triggered again. The angle was bad but the space was so tight up at the tip of the conical well that Priad was spattered with burning promethium gel. He grimaced at the dancing telltales in his faceplate display and cocked his arm back for a killing stroke with the lightning claw, but before he could land it the tank had started to tilt. The bank of legs on its opposite side pushed themselves straight and the whole machine teetered over to trap Priad against the wall. Cursing, he tried to find the leverage to push the tank away with his arms or legs but he could barely shift its weight. The pilot was still gawping at him from less than half a metre away, eyes reflecting the red light of his instruments, the Anarch's emblem over his mouth billowing in and out with his terrified breathing. He didn't seem to know what to do next.

Then he flinched, a whole-body convulsion, as a burst of hard rounds cracked against the other side of the canopy. The lead Pragar troopers had climbed high enough to see what was going on and open fire. The Sekkite's shaved head started whipping back and forth in panic as a second salvo crazed the glass even further. The red instrument lights that bathed his face brightened and began flashing, and the tank started to rotate itself, grinding Priad against the wall like grain under a millstone. The flamers triggered again but the motion of the tank had pushed their mounts the wrong way. One sprayed into the wall, the other billowed up through the grille overhead.

Finally Priad was able to move. He got his feet against the well wall and used his whole body to push the tank outward, then braced his legs against it and shoved it hard across the well. With his hands behind him he slowly pushed his legs straight, pinning the stalk-tank as it had pinned him. Feedback from his armour systems scrolled in his vision and tingled in the haptics around his thighs and hips, but he kept the pressure on. The tank's hull began to buckle. One flamer mount was already crushed to scrap. The pilot had succumbed to panic now, scrabbling around in the little coffin-shaped cockpit for a weapon or an escape. It was a weak, undignified ending even for a suicide post and a point-blank bolt shot through the damaged canopy put an end to it.

The Pragar came swarming up around Priad with blasé underhiver agility, shouting and signalling to one another. Their instincts, training and lack of enveloping armour gave them a keen sense for balance and stability that Priad found it hard to match, and he watched in frank admiration as trooper after trooper zigzagged up the stalk-tank scrapheap, compensating effortlessly for the sway and shake of their makeshift ladder even as it started to slide away under them.

Priad looked up. The whole well was vibrating. Those booming impacts up above ground were close enough to shake the walls, and when the walls shook, the pile of wrecked stalk-tanks shook with them. When the tanks had been dumped down the well they must have filled it almost to the street, but as they had died they had crumpled, the shocks from above had tumbled them down further, and now there was a three-metre gap up into the mouth of the well. The access ladder had been torn away, the walls were smooth. There was no way up.

'Grapple-line! Somebody top-heap bust out a grapple-line!' It was a broad-shouldered Pragar with a rank badge Priad didn't recognise, hanging casually off the wreck that the Iron Snake was still pinning to the well wall with his feet. 'One of you ugly-arse beetles better have a line!'

The impacts from the street were thunderous now. Priad could hear voices below, but it only took a few seconds to lose his patience.

'Moving!' he shouted. 'Brace!' The Pragar troopers went for handholds and solid positions with pleasing alacrity. Priad twisted his body, flooded the tines of his lightning claw with crackling energy and drove it into the wall. Smoke coiled around the blades and tiny specks of cauterised rock-crete pinged off his armour. There was no time for more warnings or countdowns. He pulled his feet up and as the stalk-tank slumped down onto the pile he pulled the claw out and drove it in higher, pulling himself up again as though the claw were a piton. Feedback blared in his wrist and knuckles – his weapon had not been made to take a load like this. He forced it to anyway, lifting himself up on his claw arm then stabbing the wall again. A damage icon lit off as he dragged himself higher, one of the blade mountings giving out under the strain. Letting out an angry roar, Priad shot his other hand up and grabbed the access grille. The metal creaked in his grip but did not break.

'Climb!' he shouted, and again when they didn't move. 'Battle won't wait for you! *Climb!*'

The man with the rank-badge was the first to obey, leaping up to grab Priad's ankle and clawing his way up the reactor pack, hissing as he brushed against one of the hot conduits, then planting his feet on the helmet and pauldron and squeezing through the grille bars. Two more came after that, the second one trailing a grapple-line. Then two more, and then a trio hard on one another's heels. Someone found the slider door in the grille and rolled it away, and then there was a clear square overhead that the Pragar could clamber through two at a time, some silent and some laughing at the sheer and delirious audacity of what they were doing.

Priad came out of the well next to last, pulling himself one-handed, the very last escapee an injured Pragar clinging to his leg as the pile of dead stalk-tanks finally gave way and tumbled out from under their feet. The man's squad-mates rushed to help him, lifting him up and bundling him towards the edge of the street. They were shouting to Priad as well, pointing to the colossal shape that was bearing down on them out of the dark, the source of the shuddering impacts that had come to them underground.

Priad rolled to one knee, looked up and grinned. He had made it in time after all.

The Warhound Titan took another thunderous stride, passing completely over them, its bulk and noise blotting out everything for a moment before it took another step and another and suddenly seemed distant again even though its tread still shook the street underfoot. Its gait was proud and aggressive, the livery on its armour and the tattered black banners that fluttered from each shoulder that of the Legio Invicta.

Priad sent a subvocal command to his helmet vox-systems, instructing them to search for a very specific band on which to talk. And then he ran, ran as hard as his armour systems and his own inhuman muscles could carry him, sprinting along the corpse-littered avenue at *Lupus Noctem*'s heels.

Legio Invicta
Northern Ghereppan advance

'LEGIO INVICTA!'

Maximilian Orfuls bellowed it in vox and code, and *Morbius Sire* took up the shout. As the crew of *Raptus Solemnus* whooped and drummed their hands on their consoles, Arkaly Creel leaned her machine to one side and fired the inferno cannon up into the sky, bathing the plaza she was standing in in orange-gold light and challenging for a moment the growing dawn and the plasmapult shots alike. Leyden Krugmal lifted the gilded-steel Machina Opus seal that hung at his chest, murmured a choked prayer of thanks into it and pressed it to his cheek before he opened his eyes and hailed his betrothed.

'Entascha? *Lupus Noctem*! Affirm your location! The princeps, Entascha, did you hear him? Did you hear?'

'Closing,' Mereschel told him curtly, and fell silent again. All her concentration was on guiding *Noctem* through the maze of Ghereppan's innermost spires, pushing its stride into a run. She felt every flare of the reactor furnace that pushed power to her enormous adamantine limbs, felt the great mechanisms in her waist and hips pushed to insane tolerances as they handled the weight, the speed, the impact of each stride, the balance and strain of each turn. She saw through the pict feed and the auspex, watched the milling people and vehicles, used the lightest of touches on *Noctem*'s superconductive carbon nerves to place each crushing footfall in a clear spot. Amion and Bodinel were hard at work at their stations but there was only so much they could do, and the work was stretching her mind to the limit.

But there was still that tiny peripheral awareness of something new, a little speck of weight on *Lupus Noctem*'s right shoulder, the barest pinpricking itch of a magnetic field where something had locked on to her hull. It was the reason she had slowed in the first place, fallen behind the others as they moved to the Great Ascent. The reason she was speeding now.

There would be time later, she promised herself. She had never heard Pietor Gearhart's voice directly. The old man had already fallen into his slumber when she had brought *Noctem* to walk upon Urdesh with her new Legio. There would be time, later, to think about what it meant to hear him now, like this. Just... not...

Noctem's foot skidded and embedded itself in the foot of a mercatory tower, and the Titan's shoulder and arm caved the front of the building inward before Mereschel could calm its howling distress and bring it back on balance.

Just not yet, she finished the thought. She had done as the woman in the sky had bade her, but she wasn't done yet.

She had adopted what Amion called her 'battle mien', eyes closed, head pushed forward from her shoulders, teeth clenched. There were times after combat that her muscles were locked so fast she couldn't open her mouth.

<Lupus Noctem!> Orfuls' cant-voice. <Affirm! Join your formation, Mereschel! The princeps is awake! We need you here! What delayed you?>

'What delayed me?' Mereschel answered him, a little indistinctly. Amion and Bodinel both winced at the loud cracks from her jaw hinges as they loosened with her smile. 'As it happens, Max,' she said, 'I had to collect a passenger.'

Priad
Legio Invicta advance, northern Ghereppan

From his perch mag-clamped on to *Lupus Noctem*'s shoulder, Priad could only track the engine battle by glimpses. They would hurdle a drift of rubble and he would catch sight of a salvo of plasma cages dropping out of their ballistic arcs, and a moment later see a roaring curtain of heat go up from beyond a jagged roofline or around a looming spire. They would race across a broad basalt-flagged park or around a Cult Mechanicus monument, and over the sound of *Noctem*'s footsteps far below him he would make out the angry bellow of klaxons as the Legio traded shots with the plasmapult phalanx or were forced back by a concentrated barrage. The sheer walls of the avenues turned the clamour of the battle into a clamour of echo and counter-echo that grew louder with every stride.

His armour could sense the sudden feverish traffic in code-shouts to and from the giant machine he was clinging to, but it was couched in an esoteric Mechanicus dialect that his systems couldn't parse. He put it from his mind. He had followed her words and they had brought him here just as she had promised. He still had his task to do. He put his faith in that.

Invictus Antagonistes
North Ghereppan waterfront

The foreshores around the Great Ascent were edged with sweeping, open concourses, built to allow everything from daily waterfront traffic to ceremonial parades hundreds of thousands strong, to mighty Mechanicus load-crawlers carrying enormous prefabricated works from the spire foundries. They were among the few structures in the city rugged enough to take the tread of a Warlord Titan without crumbling. It was on the waterfront east of the Great Ascent, beneath a cluster of slender volcanic-glass obelisks, that Gearhart brought *Invictus Antagonistes* to shore.

The Warlord Titan rose up out of the sea like a released kraken, brushing aside broken ships, trailing wreaths and cables of seaweed, water cascading from its carapace and flooding across the concourse ahead of it. With both feet planted on the shore it stood silent, surveying its new domain. Its auspex pings rippled through the towers and streets, setting diamond-glass to thrumming in spire windows and sending strange squealing echoes out across the water, as though the cetacean species that Urdesh's shallow seas had never evolved had finally appeared in them. Its voids hissed softly in the humid coastal air and flared into strange, crooning aurorae as they brushed against the stone underfoot.

Gearhart looked at the obelisks ahead of him. Their needle-points had once supported ten-ton prayer wheels whirling on magnetic bearings, but those were long gone. The sacred code adorning their sides was still there, though, the titanium inlay covered in soot and grime but readable to the senses he shared with his Titan. The verse that caught his gaze was a psalm to the Emperor upon His throne, the union of will made flesh and will made machine. Gearhart nodded in approval. A good omen. A good omen for a good day.

<Ease yourselves,> he said. <Stand back.>

<They are wounding the city, lord!> Orfuls cried back, hearing his own cant but barely believing he was meeting the return of the father of the Legio with backtalk.

<And they will pay,> Gearhart told him calmly. <Let me show you how. Rakolo is about to exload a firing solution. I want it perfectly inloaded, Orfuls. No static from struck voids. No high-energy weapon-wash. Inloaded and followed, on my command. Perfectly. Affirm.>

<So affirmed.>

Morbius Sire backed away, sidestepped and went prowling at a crouch through a loading-yard that had collapsed into its sublevel, behind a row of storehouses that blocked it from the plasmapults' fire. *Lupus Lux* made an elegant one-heeled turn and raced into the aisle between two bomb-battered ceramite forges. One of the pults was sharp enough to anticipate the sudden rush and put a shot into its path, the heat of the bursting cage denting the voids over *Lux*'s shoulder and setting the generators screaming. *Raptus Solemnus* backed away like a defiant hound, head lowered, snarling over every vox-channel it had. Four plasmapult shots converged on it at once, merging just over its head and exploding in mid-air, the surrounding buildings shuddering and igniting in the blast, but when the sunburst finally cleared the Warhound was gone, vanished in among the buildings.

Invictus Antagonistes began to walk, with a regal lack of haste, towards the Ascent. Somewhere under the dome of yowling energy one of the plasmapult crews realised something had changed, and crude mechanical senses swung out across the concourse. The pack of crawlers stirred like a pod of ambulls sensing the approach of a challenger. The ones highest up the Ascent tried to edge their way further up. The ones closest to the Warlord's approach began backing and filling, trying to bring their catapults to bear on the new menace. Gearhart chuckled as he saw the shield dome ripple and distort. Whatever passed for an enginseer in among the enemy was struggling to keep the shields meshed. Poor upstarts.

He felt the data exload go out. He needed no visual cue or word from Rakolo. His union with *Antagonistes* was total. He simply knew it had gone.

<Affirm inload.>

<Affirm!> from Maximilian Orfuls. *Morbius Sire* was sprinting through the high rhyolite arches around the Grand Tsirka to his firing vantage.

<Affirm!> from Arkaly Creel, full of relish as she prowled forward, turbolaser mount already glowing with power.

<Affirm,> Krugmal sent as *Lupus Lux* marched up the tiered slope of the Demipalatine amphitheatre, leaving ragged footprint craters in the stone. He listened for his lover's cant-tone, and didn't hear it. <Entascha, do you have a firing solution?>

<Not for me, dear one,> she answered. <You're going to beat upon the shields. I'm going to deliver the dagger.>

Lupus Noctem
Great Ascent approach, northern foreshore, Ghereppan

There was no point left in stealth, and everything to gain from bravado. Entascha Mereschel let *Lupus Noctem* howl through its klaxons once more, and she and Amion added their own voices. Bodinel was hunched forward in his seat, breathing hard. Six more steps and they would be in the open, walking face-first into the plasmapult barrage.

'This isn't goodbye, 'Tascha,' Krugmal told her. 'Ride in power. We've got you.'

Five more steps. Bodinel opened the Warhound's stride a little further.

<Semper Invicta!> Max Orfuls canted.

Four, three more steps. The weapon arms were cool and numb: Entascha had withdrawn her senses from them along with all the power they could yield up. Tech-Priest Enoq had pushed spare power into the voids, tuning them finer and finer until they were throbbing like drums. Entascha felt the power coursing through the Titan's hips and legs. Her own muscles jerked in sympathy and she breathed deep, sinking deeper into the bond, re-establishing control.

<Semper Invicta,> Pietor Gearhart echoed. <Wheel and Throne. The Saint is watching.>

A heatwave rose up in their auspex. A concerted bombardment, at least half the plasmapult formation by the feel of it. Recharging would take them several seconds. Their opening.

Two steps, one.

Lupus Noctem came around onto the Ascent approach leaning hard into the turn, twisting at the waist to keep its snarling metal snout pointed at the shimmering blur of heat and void ahead of it. It straightened into a loping stride and now it was running in enormous, earth-shaking, actuator-straining bounds, its own voids a sizzling, almost visible prow in front of its muzzle. It howled again, an air-shattering cry edged with sharp metallic distortion from the voids and the energy backwash that filled the Ascent approach.

Her three companions had burst from their own cover and had opened fire. Their turbolaser beams struck the very tip of the void dome and held there, churning the curtain of energy into a fury. Then *Invictus Antagonistes'* volcano cannon spoke, the shot hitting just below where the lasers intersected, bowing the dome downward before it splintered into whirling superheated pyrotechnics that briefly dimmed the dawn.

Mereschel was leaning forward in the princeps' throne, head down and eyes closed, concentrating on feeling each crashing step of *Noctem*'s feet. White heat splashed onto her right shoulder and the side of her neck as a plasmapult cage burst against the voids outside, and she growled and twisted her head from side to side. There was no time to slow or swerve, shift the Warhound's body to distort the voids and shrug the plasma off. Closing the distance was all that mattered.

Lupus Noctem was almost at the base of the Ascent by the time the plasmapults retrained on it. The first shot went wild, rippling the voids over its hunched shoulders then falling to skitter across the approach, melting a trench into the road before it finally broke apart into a sunburst. The second went off too soon and too low, splashed off *Noctem*'s waist and left a trail of foaming light in its wake. The third hit square in the prow of its voids and the fourth finally fractured them, only for a moment but for long enough.

The temperature in the control cabin was soaring. Mereschel could feel the heat in her control plugs, and hear the whine of the cooling hood as it tried to stop the metal interfaces in her neck and skull from cooking her nerves. Sweat was pouring from Bodinel's face and splattering on the console. Amion was gulping and panting as he worked his controls.

'All that can slow us down,' she declared, 'is that we care that we burn. And the answer to that is...' She bore down with her mind and drove the Titan's howling spirit even faster.

Priad and Noctem
Causeway approaches, northern Ghereppan

Priad, clinging to *Lupus Noctem*'s upper arm, was barely aware of the final rush up the causeway approach. Even while the voids had stayed up he could feel the heat soaking through them in the seams and joins in his armour as he struggled to hold his position against the sway and slam of the Titan's gait. Worse was the sensory assault, the plasma bursts, the noise of the shields struggling to throw them back, the dazzling discharges of light and static that left his hardened organic senses battered into nothing.

His vision lit up with alert runes as another burst sizzled around him and he fought the urge to let go or to try and swing about to a more sheltered position behind the Warhound's shoulder. The slightest error would cost him his grip, and then he would be under *Noctem*'s feet, out in the open, dead before it could close, leaving its sacrifice hollow.

A shot burst on the ground in front of them, and *Lupus Noctem* was moving too fast to pull up. It ran through the flowering of heat, as the paving was incinerated out from under it, and its voids buckled and crazed. Priad was yanked back and forth as the gun-limb he clung to spasmed so hard that his mag-locked boots almost pulled free from the armour plate. He couldn't tell whether they had stopped, fallen or arrived; the fury of the energies around him had left him almost blind and deaf, and even if the princeps was trying to talk to him there was no way her transmission could reach him through that.

Another shot broke over the Warhound's back and *Noctem* staggered under the strain, voids burned down to the barest breath of energy. Smoke was streaming from the collar behind its head and Priad sensed more than heard the impact as its left arm fell limp and swung into the arc of its striding leg. Sizzling light spattered his helmet and shoulders, triggering another flashing cluster of warning runes. He wondered if the bolt ammunition he was carrying might cook off and detonate, and then found himself wondering if it had already done so and he simply hadn't felt it.

'I just need to know the moment,' he said aloud, not knowing who could hear him or even who he was talking to. 'Please, just help me to know the moment.'

As if in answer, *Lupus Noctem*'s shoulder plate tilted under his feet and the Titan set foot on the Great Ascent, swaying and staggering like a blood-blinded pugilist but barely slowing. Priad closed his eyes, counted strides. In four more of the Warhound's steps, its mission would be done and it would be on his shoulders instead. Three strides. The charge, the battle, the war for the city, the war for the world, for the Saint. Two strides. And then, just for a few minutes, it would be on him alone.

There was not a trace of fear in his mind. This was his element; he inhabited the moment utterly.

The mag-locks opened and Priad tilted off the edge of the Titan's shoulder, dropping away and vanishing in the storm of blaze and void.

Lupus Noctem
The Great Ascent

Neither turning nor slowing, wrapped in sunfire from snout to toe, *Lupus Noctem* staggered up the Great Ascent on nothing more than momentum and willpower. It had not deviated by so much as a tenth of a degree from the course Mereschel and Bodinel had set for it, its tread passing within metres of the flapping edge of the void dome. It ran blindly now, neither seeing nor caring what was around it. One foot in front of the other, and again, and again. Around it the air itself was burning.

Noctem was above the plasmapult battery and almost at the top of the Ascent when its run took it over the edge. Its legs were still trying to move as it toppled into the air and plunged. The sound of it hitting the sea was almost lost in the madness of the energy bombardments behind it, but the plume of water and pillar of steam that marked its fall could be seen halfway back across Ghereppan, rising into the dawn sky as the Titan boiled the sea in which it lay. It did not move as the waters of the strait closed over it.

Priad
The Great Ascent

Priad half-lay, half-knelt in the crater he had made on the Great Ascent. He could feel the burning at every armour seam, at his collar, elbows, the backs of his knees and around his waist. His nose and mouth had scalded and blistered where a puff of the furnace air around him had made it through his rebreather. Red environmental alarms ringed his helm display, making a flashing tunnel of his vision.

Down that tunnel he looked up at the plasmapult phalanx. The turbolaser and volcano shots were still beating down on the top of the dome but the individual impacts were barely visible through the riot of concentrated energy and bucking shields. Ahead of him he could see the ragged lower edge of the void shield, billowing like a jellyfish skirt under the strain, shrivelling upward each time the other Titans renewed their furious assault. He had to move.

He managed to half-stand and force himself a few paces forward before the voids fluttered again and a crackling arc of energy earthed itself in the side of his helmet. His vision went black and his ears filled with the scream of his armour.

The actuators around his hips and legs jerked and locked, and he fell onto his face until his systems managed to regain control and let him drag himself to the edge of the dome.

He was reaching through it when the voids firmed and their edge came down like a guillotine. Priad pulled his hand back but armour damage made the motion sluggish, and three of his fingertips sizzled and went numb. He froze there, glanding away the pain and watching the energy haze fluttering in front of him, forcing himself not to think of what would happen if the Legio's bombardment fell silent now.

It did not. The air overhead ignited once again, a fusillade that would have reduced an unarmoured human soldier to ash, and the voids in front of Priad withered and lifted as the hits overhead drew up their power. With a wordless shout he propelled himself through the gap on all fours.

Under the void dome was madness, a furnace, a fever-dream. No horizon around him, no sky overhead, just flat depthless light, dimming to yellow or flaring to agonising blue-white, squealing and snapping, rippling and bulging as if a pack of great beasts outside were trying to force their way through to the great beasts within.

Which was exactly what was happening. Past time for him to move.

Pushing through the shrieking sensory feedback of the voids as if it were a physical miasma, Priad fetched up against an enormous steel tread that jutted out of the corner of some misshapen steel beast whose ridged back mounted the spined cylinder of its magnetic catapult. White light flashed between those spines now as the thing lobbed another shot away. Targeting a Titan or simply wreaking spiteful havoc on the city they had lost, Priad had no way to tell.

He cocked his arm, the tines of his lightning claw sliding

into place and igniting, putting his other palm against the crawler's hull and sagging there for a moment, looking up and around for the target he needed and not seeing it.

Keep moving. No time to waste. Find another pult where the kill would be easier. He pushed himself away from the first crawler and staggered onward. The motile systems in his left hip and thigh were seizing up, and he had to use his own strength to force the armour joints to bend. The damaged tine of his lightning claw had gone dead, hanging in its mounting like a loose tooth waiting to be pulled.

The next pult was a better target, a long low thing with a nose and cab like an overblown cargo truck, more chance of its vitals being within easy reach. Priad couldn't make out movement inside the armaglass cab windows but someone in there saw him, and when he was halfway to it the crawler jerked into motion, rolling forward to try and run him down. Priad staggered to his right, saw the crawler's wheels turn to match his motion, and pushed himself over onto his non-responding left leg and crashed to the ground. The crawler ground to a halt, unable to turn tightly enough to flatten him in his new position, and backed up to come at him again as Priad fought his way back onto his feet and faced it.

This time it came at him fast, the ram-bar level with his face and the windscreen glittering in the light of the plasma shots. Priad went to jump up but again his damaged leg systems betrayed him, turning the jump into an ungainly stumble forward. His forehead smashed into the ram-bar and he vanished under the crawler's advance.

The plasmapult sat there, neither firing nor moving, for almost a minute. Then finally it began to reverse again, turning itself, preparing to grind the Space Marine into the surface of the Ascent with its metal wheels.

Then Priad reappeared, pulling himself up one-handed with his lightning claw raised. The tips of the tines skated off the armaglass then found purchase and started driving through it like hot metal pressed against ice. The glass around each claw-tip started to deform and discolour.

Priad felt the crunch but didn't hear it. All he knew at first was that he had been knocked loose from his handhold but hadn't fallen, until he looked around. The crawler he had bypassed had reversed, pinning him against the nose of the second with the back of its hull. A magnetic cage was loaded into the base of its catapult, and now white fire was boiling out of the plasma nozzles to fill it. It was barely arm's length from him. Close enough to cripple him, maybe kill him just with its radiant heat once its plasma load was complete.

He hacked at the cab window in front of him with his claw as tingling pain began to nest in the small of his back – the overload on his armour systems spilling through the biomechanical link into his own body. He was out of time. He beat at the cab front with fist and claw and finally tore it open, twisted one shoulder through and began smashing at the instrument panels.

He hit some kind of control connection, but the wrong one. The cab surged forward, grinding him even harder into the back of the pult behind him. In the hellish glare coming over his shoulders he could see the Sons of Sek crewmen scrabbling back from the smashed windscreen with their hands over the tinted visors of their helmets.

Priad reached up and grabbed the top sill of the cab window. It only took a second of dragging for it to deform and tear in his grip but that was enough to pull him half a metre upward, and that was enough to free his right leg, kick backward and boost himself up onto the pult's roof. He clung there, trying to get his bearings, while smoke burst from the shattered window underneath him as the control cab caught fire. If there were screams, he didn't hear them.

From here he could see down the crawler's long body to the catapult rising from its rear. It must have had its own control room because he could see it moving and re-aiming, trying to get an angle low enough to fire at him directly. The conduits leading down inside the hull were crackling and glowing as it prepared a shot.

Priad didn't care, because he had found what he needed.

Halfway down the hull, tucked in among some irregular protrusions from the roof designed to disguise it, was a dorsal ridge of grey metal that somehow seemed out of focus no matter how hard Priad looked at it. He bear-crawled towards it, ceramite plate clanging against the hull, left leg scraping limply behind him.

Three metres behind his new target a hatch ground open and two ungainly ochre shapes pushed their way up. Humans, probably, unrecognisable in visored protective hoods, lifting weapons in clumsy gloved hands. Fat armour-piercing hard rounds punched at Priad's pauldron and faceplate. The left side of his vision flickered as a bullet cracked his helm's eyepiece. A hellgun round scored the armour seam at his collar and ploughed a hot scar through the mouth grille of his helm. Priad rolled onto his left side to put the metal ridge between them and dragged himself forward again while they wrestled and pushed, trying to get a clear shot at him.

They never did. Priad reached the midpoint of the hull, pushed himself up on his knees in front of the metal fin. He could see the components in its mounting now, impossible to disguise, the distinctive coils and vanes that fed the raw energy in and drew the transformed energy out, feeding it up into the roiling dome overhead.

He struck.

The backwash shattered out the circuitry in his claw. Two of the tines blew clear of their mountings and spun away. The flash sent Priad's hand numb and locked his gauntlet's fist closed. His vision blurred and filled with random runes and markers.

The haze of power around the void shield projector flickered, flashed red then black, then vanished. For just a heartbeat the metal crawled with brilliant sapphire sparks like an infestation of iridescent beetles, then it split apart with a crack of parting metal. The feedback wave echoed up and out of it into the void dome, tearing the delicate interlock of merged shields apart from the inside, the void collapse accelerating and cascading, sending the shields' energies arcing back down to their sources.

In a series of hard, flat concussions all the other void generators went the way of the first. There was a roar of wrenched air as the insane heat that had built up outside the void dome reacted to the cooler air pocket inside, and the two Sons who had shot at Priad vanished, dragged out of their hatch or crushed back down into it. Priad got a grip on the now jagged edge of the generator fin and pulled himself half-up. He had to move. He knew exactly how little time the plasmapults had left.

He had hit the ground and was stagger-running down the Ascent when all four surviving Titans opened fire.

The Saint
Avenue Vertegna, Ghereppan

Full morning had come to Ghereppan, the sun over the scarp and shining on the western city, by the time the rubble over Damocles Squad's Thunderhawk groaned and shifted and finally parted in a shower of dust and grit. A servo-arm reached up through the gap and tapped about until it found a good clawhold, and Pyrakmon came clambering up through the hole. The copper eye on the brow of his helm caught the morning sun.

'Nobody about,' he said over his shoulder, and lowered his servo-arm back into the hole to hoist up Crethon. Together they skidded and dropped down the collapsed heap of building that was now their gunship's funeral cairn, and were standing on the road looking about. The streets around them seemed silent and empty. Peaceful. It took them several moments to register that they had company.

Saint Sabbat was sitting on a chunk of broken rockcrete, kicking her heels as she looked up at the sky. She looked around and smiled as the two Iron Snakes walked over to her.

'Are you alone, mamzel?' Crethon asked her.

'I've been praying.' Apparently she was happy for that to be her answer, because she turned and looked at the sky again.

'Are Damocles Squad–' Pyrakmon began after a while.

'Gone north,' she told him cheerfully. 'I think we lost touch during the night. But.' She smiled again. 'The two of you are Damocles, at least here and now. So the squad is here, really, still standing by me. Your word is good.'

Crethon bridled a little at that, but Pyrakmon bowed to her.

'It is good to see you so hale, my lady. Can we take you now to the general, or–'

'We're going north too,' she said, sliding forward and dropping to the ground. 'Keshriy clade-house. That's where I'll be tonight. My people are waiting for me there. Milo found us. I thought he might. He's already led the others onward. And you'll meet your people again there too, I think.'

'Ma'am,' Crethon said after a half-second of flicking through hypno-briefings, 'Keshriy is in the heart of occupied Ghereppan, now we–'

'There is no "occupied Ghereppan" any more, Brother Crethon.' She spread her hands. 'Can't you feel it?'

'I know that during the night–' Crethon began uncertainly.

'During the night. That was when it happened.' Suddenly the Beati seemed uncertain too. 'I remember flames. Green flames. Red teeth. A constellation.' She shook her head. 'Ghereppan belongs to our Emperor now. That's the point.'

'Aye, mamzel.' Crethon bowed as Pyrakmon had.

'So will you walk with me?' she asked. 'Northward to Keshriy? The night is over but the day will be busy.'

The three of them turned and walked away, and for a time the street was silent again. When sound returned it was faint, too faint for anyone but a keen observer who knew to listen for it. A rustling coming out of the cracked pavement.

The vines grew with dreamlike speed, like sped-up footage of themselves. Their tendrils coiled up around the piece of rubble where the Saint had sat, thickening in moments into tough, bark-wrapped cables as thick as a human thumb. Sprays of slender, dark green leaves unfolded from the twisting vines. Finally the blooms opened, wide and white, with a very particular sweet, astringent scent.

In the empty street, the islumbine blooms turned up towards the sun.

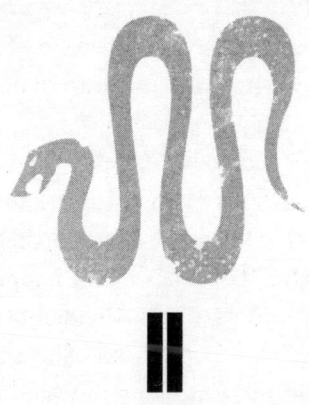

II

THE VOICE THAT DROWNS OUT ALL OTHERS

Oureppan. Ghereppan's sibling city at the far end of its causeway, the pair between them forming a centre of power around which everything in that whole quarter of the planet was defined. The two enormous cities matched and complemented one another as light and dark, or land and sea.

Ghereppan crowded onto its little ridge-backed promontory and loomed out into the water, reaching out over its bridges for the high-sided islands along its eastern flank. Oureppan was defined by the grand circular sweep of its bay, the curve of some aeons-dead volcanic crater that had spread its arms out into the strait. Ghereppan was a vertical island of rockcrete and carved stone that climbed towards the sky and cut off with startling suddenness at its southern boundary where the weedlands began. Beyond the ridge of the crater-rim that rose from the water, Oureppan was a horizontal sprawl stretching from the shore away over the horizon, wearing its lacework of transitways like a mystic's tattoo. Barely a tower broke the flat plain of roads and low rooftops until the eye settled on the upswept lines of Pinnacle Spire, dead in the centre of the innermost ring of driver silos, the electroplated steeple at its summit reflecting the grey sky.

Ghereppan was a city of forges, artisans, mastercrafters and coders, the home of manufactoria as old as Imperial settlement and Mechanicus libraries full of lore that was even older. Oureppan made almost nothing but moved almost everything, from the manufactoria across the strait and the refineries in the northern flatlands, down from orbit onto the vast fields of landing docks and gravitic pads, and back into the sky from the mass driver silos whose shafts drove deep into the ground.

And where Ghereppan had been a battle zone almost since the campaign's beginning, Oureppan had remained an Archenemy fortress, untouched, some thought untakeable. Old Ourezhad, the looming, smoking volcano at the city's eastern fringes, housed the geothermal spike that let Oureppan's defence grid and strategic voids spend power like water. The city sat at the bottom of a well of airspace dominated by its laser and driver silos. The flatlands and the western coast had been fortified over the years of the Urdesh war into a deathtrap for infantry and armour alike. Assault from the east would have to pick its way along Ourezhad's sulphur-hot flanks, exposed and unstable. The weapon batteries arrayed around the ridged curve of the bay could obliterate anything coming from the south by sea, and marching down the open causeway into the maw of the city's heaviest defences was suicide.

Except that now there had been a miracle, and all the old certainties were gone.

The Saint
The Primary Highwork, Keshriy Clade-House, Ghereppan

In daylight and clear weather, the Oureppan causeway would have been a straight white slash against the grey waters of the strait, cutting the sea in two all the way to the horizon. In peacetime it would have been swarming and glittering with traffic. Mountainous hauler-trains, gleaming groundcars and motor-sulkies all swarming the centre lanes, and whirring railcars speeding along the underslung lines on each side. Even the raised pedestrian walkways that overhung the road would have been full, with off-shift workers from the city taking the sea air and footsore pilgrims showing their devotion by carrying icons and statuettes back and forth between the Ghereppan tech-shrines and the great Ecclesiarchal altar at the heart of Oureppan's Pinnacle Spire.

This day, the causeway was a blood- and soot-stained

scratch across a strait scummed over with ash, slicked with fuel and studded with half-sunken wrecks. Much of it was lost to sight completely behind the palls of smoke from the burning vessels beneath it and the burning vehicles scattered along it. *Invictus Antagonistes* stood at the base of the ascent, staring inscrutably out through the smoke and wind, oblivious to the bustle around its ankles as Militarum crews laboured to drag away the corpses of the plasmapults and the litter of smaller wrecks that jammed the Ascent below them. Every so often, as the breeze stirred the waters below the Ascent's western side, the upper edge of *Lupus Noctem*'s carapace would briefly break the surface.

The transmechanic standing on the roof of the Keshriy clade-house was indifferent to the visual panorama below him: he was utterly immersed in the electromagnetic one above him. Antennae extended from beneath the scarlet hood of his magos' robe, three silvery-bright flowers of metal and carbon lace which completely obscured the face that had housed them. Through them he was speaking to the high-gain communication array that had been inelegantly but sturdily fixed to the carved basalt steeple overhead. The heraldic steel sculpture that had once capped it – a cloud coiled around a crossed drill-bit and lightning bolt – was long gone, but enough of its fastenings were still there to hold the makeshift uplink mast nicely in place.

The transmechanic ran a light virtual touch through the uplink's transmission pattern, listening to its song, studying the jolt and spike of the encryption protocols and finding them good. Shaping his hands in the sign of the cog, he slipped his code-self free of the meat and metal that his robe enclosed and submerged it in the rush and flow, his entire mind the gateway for the bright blast of information. Above him, the tight-beam signal stabbed into the sky to the first of the orbiting ships that would send it on over the horizon towards Eltath. The few remaining organic parts of his body were quivering with strain and religious ecstasy.

Beneath him, the mast's receivers dumped into the shielded data-sluice cables that ran into the upper levels of the clade-house, dropping through ventilation shafts and snaking along corridors under the watchful eye of armed Mechanicus servitors and Militarum guards. Down from the roost apartments that had housed the clade's seniormost families, they cascaded down the ceremonial stair to feed the hololith in the centre of the Primary Highwork.

The Highwork was the clade's grandest ceremonial space, a vaulted hall which ran from the great stair out to an enormous archway that framed a grand sweep of the docks, the causeway and the strait. Built spacious enough to hold a thousand clade elders and their retinues, its cavernous space swallowed up the officers and adepts assembling in it.

They came trickling in in ones and twos, still battered and dirty from the long and frantic night, speaking mostly in murmurs. The soaring devotion that had carried them through that night like the upward surge of a gravity lift was now taking on the feel of a dream. *Am I remembering this truly?* The question had crossed all of their minds, and they could see it in one another's faces. *Did I really feel those things, do those things? Could it have happened the way I remember? Am I mad? Or was it last night that the madness was lifted?*

Some had mourned the loss of that feeling, frightened that they might never recapture such purity of sensation again. Some welcomed its departure, frightened of what that intensity might have done to them if it had lasted. Some had wanted nothing more than to collapse into sleep as it left them, others had been left twitching with energy, pacing and muttering and wanting to hurry on to whatever was next. But gradually they all gathered around the hololith, squinting into its bilious green light, wincing at the almost inaudible keening squeal of the power unit and jumping in unison at the occasional loud crack of interference.

There was a soft rumble of machinery from the end of the Highwork, and the view of the city and the sea began to narrow as interlocking layers of blast shutters began to slide into place. The smudgy grey daylight shrank to an aisle down the middle of the hall, then to a path, then a line. Then the shutters boomed closed, the internal lamps fizzled on, the processional doors creaked open, and the Saint walked in.

She was still dressed in simple fatigues and her herder's cloak. Armoured Iron Snakes loomed on either side of her, Kules on the left and Xander on the right, although all the humans saw were two giants whose armour was so scorched and pitted that its livery was barely discernible any more. Sister Kassine and Trooper Milo came behind them. Kassine bore a banner-staff onto which the helmet from one of the snuffed-out wirewolves had been mounted and then garlanded with islumbine blooms. Milo was empty-handed, his camo-cloak making a patch of odd, depthless blur as it swung back from his shoulders. And alongside them...

There was a stir. Brother-Captain Priad was unarmoured, dressed only in a grey chiton and a broad hide belt that held his combat blade. His hair was oiled and bound back again, his face expressionless. Few of those gathered at the hololith had ever seen Space Marines close up, but the armoured forms flanking the Saint at least called to mind the monumental statues and devotional art that had been the furniture of their lives. Priad's unarmoured bulk, the huge proportions of his face and hands, the not-quite-human patterns of muscle in his bare arms, the interface membranes and plug-sockets that covered much of his exposed skin: he was a stranger and more intimidating sight than his comrades with their battle-beaten power armour and giant bolters. With shortened steps Priad kept position with the two humans, making a point of ignoring the eyes on him.

'It's almost ready,' Sabbat said, looking at the hololith. 'That gives us time. Will you all pray with me?' There was a murmur and a downturning of eyes. Two dozen pairs of hands crossed in the sign of the aquila. There was even the tiniest sound of motors as Xander and Kules tilted their helms in respect.

The Saint made no sound beyond the tiniest breath through her moving lips. The silence that had fallen over the group seemed to intensify for a moment, and then the moment was gone.

'Thank you,' she said, straightening up, and then smiled. The hololith had gone from drifting green-white blankness to a depthless black to a sign of the aquila, and now was showing a new image: a cannon shell enclosed by a wreath, in turn surmounted by a sickle-shaped constellation surrounding a single bright star – a map of the space around Balhaut.

Another stir went through the group as they realised what they were looking at. The personal comm-seal of Warmaster Macaroth. The man with the weight of a crusade of billions on his shoulders. The one they said had hidden himself away in some bolthole in his command post at Eltath and gone quietly mad under the strain of command. Macaroth? Talking to them, now?

'Welcome back, Warmaster,' Saint Sabbat said. 'May we hear your voice again?'

'Thank you for the welcome, mamzel,' came a voice from the hololith's plinth. The visual transmission was poor, just hints of forms and faces that dissolved into odd angles and smears of green light whenever their owners moved. The sound, though, brought Macaroth's voice across perfectly. It was a light tenor voice, quick and precise as though it couldn't wait to dart on to the end of the sentence, retaining the clipped and skipping Arvinx accent even after decades on campaign. *'Who is with you? Oerzhan had the promontory approaches and Grawe-Ash had the battle zone itself. Are either of them there?'*

The Beati looked around her, caught Mazho's eye and tilted her head towards the hololith.

'Marshal Oerzhan was killed in action on the western advances two months ago,' he said, stepping forward. 'General Grawe-Ash was at the waterside staging positions when this audience was called. We are informed that she's on her way now.'

'I don't know that voice. Identify yourself.'

'Colonel Mazho, Warmaster. Urdeshi Fourth Light Urban.'

'The Cinder Storm!' came Macaroth's voice, to Mazho's visible surprise. *'I used you on Sapiencia. And you were invaluable on Enothis, smoking out the last of the strongholds the Anarch left behind. Good, good. Who else? I want to know who's carrying my banners over there.'* That pause again, everyone's eyes on the Saint, until she gave a smile and the tiniest motion of her head, and then they stepped forward one by one. The Urdeshi went first: Storm Troop, Heavy Infantry, Siegers, Regulars. Then the Pragar in their baggy grime-grey fatigues. Jovani Armoured Cav and Special Assault. A lone Helixid officer in red-and-silver carapace. A couple of the senior Munitorum officials and a junior Magos Fetial from the Adeptus Mechanicus.

'Priad. Iron Snakes Adeptus Astartes.'

'*Ah!*' exclaimed the voice from the hololith. '*Yes, even with this miserable transmission quality you aren't hard to pick out, brother-captain. Although... are you standing back from the rest? Come forward, sir. Your shape is a little odd... Ah, you're out of your armour, that's it.*'

'My wargear was badly damaged at the end of the last engagement, Warmaster,' Priad said. 'It is being attended to. The Saint has two of Damocles here with her in full armour, if that's your concern.'

'*It isn't, brother-captain, don't be troubled. I don't doubt the tenacity with which you are guarding our precious companion. I didn't when I personally gave you that task, and I haven't since. Hmm.*' The hololith fell briefly silent. '*Have I? I think I would have recorded it. No. I didn't, so I haven't. You have nothing but my admiration for your work, you and your Snakes.*'

'Thank you, Warmaster.'

'*Although...*'

'Although?' The conversation had Priad smiling slightly, but there was a strange edge underneath it all that he couldn't quite make out.

'*Did you try to keep her out of Ghereppan, Priad?*'

Ah, there it was.

'No.'

'*I had had it very much in mind to keep her behind the lines, captain. I think I even had the conversation with you as we orbited in. You were wearing your warplate then. Hmm. Well, keeping her behind the lines in any literal sense is out of the question. The entirety of Urdesh is a warzone. Any talk of clear-cut lines a joke. But there's the matter of taking her from a pocket of quiet where the fighting has been sparse for over a year and straight into the teeth of one of the half a dozen bitterest battle zones on the planet, on the doorstep of probably the most redoubtable Archenemy fortress in the system. It's the difference between making the enemy come and find her on our terms, and delivering her to the enemy on theirs. You see my point, Priad.'*

'I see it plainly, Warmaster.'

There was a pause. Presumably Macaroth was waiting for him to go on. Priad hadn't raised his voice nor shifted his posture, but nevertheless he noticed that the nearest officers and adepts seemed to have drifted a couple of paces further away from him.

'Did you make that point to her?' Macaroth asked after a moment more.

'No.'

A babble of several muffled voices came through the hololith's connection, and when the image briefly managed to flicker into coherence Priad saw the Warmaster was partly turned away to the staff behind him. It was enough of a glance to make Priad wonder at some of the whispers that had come out from the Militarum command about the state of the man. His uniform looked rumpled and hastily thrown on, his hair was unkempt and his face haggard and unshaven.

'Say that again,' he heard Macaroth telling someone, but in reply to what he couldn't tell. Priad's hearing was as inhumanly sharp as the rest of his senses, but the mechanical ears half a planet away at Eltath weren't passing along anything more than an inchoate buzz. *'...along nine and six. And make sure Urienz knows too.'* The Warmaster's voice grew louder again, and another blink of clear transmission left a bright print of his face looking out from the display. As worn as his expression was, his gaze was still clean and sharp as the whetted blade at Priad's hip. *'I believe my command laboured the point repeatedly with the Beati,'* he went on. *'The importance*

of keeping her safe. Did my ranking officers there emphasise that importance too?'

'I did, Warmaster,' Mazho put in. 'Before we came north and into Ghereppan.'

'You did? Singular? So Priad really didn't take your side?'

'He said he would march his squad into the sea.' The sweating colonel seemed to get a little satisfaction out of imparting that.

'The sea? Was that a mis-transmission just then? Priad, is this some kind of old Ithakan metaphor that'll need explaining?'

'No and no,' Priad answered him, 'and nor was that precisely what I said.'

'But yet,' Macaroth said, *'you brought her to Ghereppan.'*

'Again, Warmaster – no.'

'What?'

'I did not bring the Beati here. Nor did the colonel, nor any of the officers in this room or the ones outside here still organising the advance. The decision to come here was made by the one who was authorised and qualified to make it. That person is with us now, Warmaster. You greeted her personally. If we all adore and revere her as much as we keep telling one another we do, then perhaps it's time to stop speaking about her as though she's not here, and put your question to her directly?'

There was a long pause. The hololith gave off a long susurration of static and then went blank. Priad wondered if the Warmaster had severed the connection in a fit of pique. He had heard accounts of volatile human commanders doing such things and more, but Macaroth had seemed far more in control of his faculties than the officers' talk had credited him with.

Sabbat walked past him, put her slender hands on the railing around the hololith, and stared into it. When Macaroth's face reappeared, he was closer too, magnified until he filled the projection space, his face twice human size and above hers.

'It was not my decision,' she said. 'It was willed that I be in Ghereppan. I had already stayed away for too long because I had been persuaded to doubt myself. Blameless men and women had to die to open my eyes.' Behind her, Mazho's face jerked as if he'd been stabbed. Priad found a moment to pity him.

'This isn't still about Marrow Harbour, is it?' Macaroth asked. *'You and I had that out at some length at the time.'*

'No,' she said. 'A botched, spiteful little raid on Rhole Cliffs while I was based there because of pressure from your command that I not get any closer to the fighting. But He-on-Terra used the loss of those lives, because all of our lives are His to use. Mourning for loss leaves a space for Him. It lightens us so that we can rise above mortal desires and be touched by His purposes. You and I have spoken about this before.' She waited, watching the hololith display attentively, but no answer came back. 'Once I knew, what was left to do but come here? Once I was where He needed me to be, His will was free to work as it would. And am I not vindicated now?' She spread her arms, looked around her. A smile transformed her usually sombre face. 'His will, our faith, our hands in His. Victory at Ghereppan!'

The soldiers and adepts around her answered with aquila signs, upraised fists, applause and a chorus of shouts. *Victory at Ghereppan! The Saint! The Saint of Hagia! Eagle and Throne!* Even Priad smiled.

'Get those people out,' came Macaroth's voice through a shivering haze of broken image. The burst of exuberance in the room didn't seem to have carried across the link to him.

'These people?' Sabbat spread her arms again. 'The officers from your army? Didn't we arrange this meeting so that we could strategise?'

'Out!' Macaroth snapped. *'If we manage to get back to discussing strategy over theology then call them back in. Make sure they don't go beyond messenger's reach of the doors.'* The blurry image of the Warmaster squinted past her, trying to make out the room. *'Or whatever you have there.'*

Nobody was moving. The assembled officers were looking at the Saint, not the hololith. Finally she looked around at them again and gave a small shrug and a glance towards the stairs, standing with her eyes downcast until the last of them had passed around the curve of the stair and disappeared from view.

'You're not alone,' Macaroth growled. *'I can still see people behind you.'*

'I've dismissed the officers, as you asked. Kassine and Milo are part of my personal retinue. Brothers Xander and Kules are my honour guard. Brother-Captain Priad is their commander and my champion. All of them will remain. Who is accompanying you, Warmaster?'

'As soon as those doors close I'll be alone but for one of my tacticians and the enginseer who's tending to this holotank.' He directed some words away behind him that none of them quite caught, then spun back to glare out at them again.

'What the hell has just happened?' he demanded. *'I'm quite sure that when I lay down to sleep last night Ghereppan was still the grinding-machine it's been for fifteen months. A war unto itself, of a magnitude that's drawn every other conflict all around the strait into its orbit. The reports I've been given make no sense. What kind of victory are you talking about there? What's the state of the fighting?'*

'The fighting is over, Warmaster,' she said. 'Ghereppan is in the hands of the Imperium. Where the Archenemy has not been routed, they have been destroyed.'

There was a long pause.

'How...' said Macaroth at the end of it. *'No. Wait. Priad, are you, yes, there you are. Pardon the impiety of the question, but is our Beati perhaps speaking metaphorically? Or is she... let me see, how shall I... is she being carried by her fervour and perhaps conveying something she would not otherwise mean to?'*

'I am not the one to judge your piety or otherwise,' Priad said, stepping forward. 'But the Beati has been utterly truthful with you. She has retaken Ghereppan for you. There is no need for you to doubt her word. Let alone to openly question it in front of her.' He gave a small nod to Sabbat, and when she returned it he stepped back again.

'All right,' Macaroth said flatly. *'All right, you've taken the city. Absolute pacification and compliance. Tell me how such a megalopolis was conquered in a night. I'm not blustering, madam, I honestly want to know. I can't see how it is possible. What miracle did you employ?'* He stopped. The hololith was quick enough to catch the change in the Warmaster's expression as he processed his own words.

'Ah,' he said. *'I see.'*

'So you do, when you simply take a moment to look,' Sabbat said. 'I told you. He wanted Ghereppan to be His again. He has made me His instrument before, and in this case He decided to do so again.' She placed a hand over her own heart. 'When I came to the place He needed me to be, His plan was able to unfold.' The hand on her chest stretched out, the fingers fanning and the thumb against the palm, in devotional imitation of an aquila's wing.

Another pause. Priad fancied he could see Macaroth's jaw

silently working, but perhaps it was just an artefact of the hololith's image drift.

'How complete is your control of the city?' he asked eventually.

'Total,' Sabbat answered without missing a beat.

'How can you know? The city is enormous. How are you securing it against partisans and locating pockets of resistance?'

'There are none to locate. They were all destroyed. The city is ours. We know.'

'Mamzel, that is...' Macaroth rubbed a hand over his eyes. It left a green-white trail of unresolved image when he removed it. *'You haven't physically combed the city. You just know you have it to yourselves now.'*

'Yes, Warmaster.'

'Because of the Miracle.'

'That is so.'

'This is providing a new perspective on some of those reports, certainly,' Macaroth said. He appeared to be looking down at his steepled hands. Sabbat's posture hadn't changed at all.

'The ones that didn't make sense?' she asked.

'They still don't make sense,' Macaroth said, *'but now I'm a little more hopeful that they might start to.'* His eyes narrowed. *'Your miracle. Did it extend to Eltath? Did you do anything to chase off the assault we just saw off here?'*

'I did nothing, Warmaster,' Sabbat said, with a gently coaxing tone as if she were reminding a child of its lessons. 'What happened here was done through me, not by me.' She thought for a moment. 'If it's His will that I come to Eltath at some point then He has not revealed that to me yet. But I will pray for guidance this afternoon.'

'Are there particular things you can ask about? We need to know about movements between Eltath and Zarakppan, and exactly what's massing at the Eshom Way channel, or–'

'No, Warmaster.' It was Sabbat's turn to cut Macaroth off. 'It doesn't work that way. If you want me to know those things, pray to Him and ask that they be revealed to me. Or to you. But you don't get to decide what comes of that, or how. He does. Only Him.'

'Could you repeat what you just did if I put you on the Zarakppan approaches?'

'I just answered that question, my lord.'

'How about Uxel Caldera? There's a Commandery of one of your Sisterhoods on the front line at the basilica there. Would that make it more amenable?'

The Saint just tilted her head and shrugged.

'You aren't making it very easy for me to strategise around you, madam,' Macaroth said.

'Are you the servant of the Emperor, Warmaster?' Sabbat answered with perceptible chill in her voice. 'Or do you presume to claim that He is yours? I didn't think I would have to explain any of this to you, after all this time.'

'I was attempting levity, my lady.' Priad didn't think he had heard much of an attempt in the Warmaster's tone. *'My apologies.'*

'Accepted, with thanks.' Sabbat stepped back from the hololith and ran a hand over her close-cropped scalp. 'Was there more you wished to discuss?'

'Your own movements now that Ghereppan is secure.' Macaroth was still saying the words as though he didn't quite believe them. *'Are you attaching yourself to General Grawe-Ash's command? Or do you feel guided to be about other work?'*

'Ghereppan will be my home for now. Displacees are already flooding back in, in huge numbers. They'll need to be cared for, fed and led. Ghereppan was sorely wounded in the last hours of the battle but it doesn't have to be a ruin like Toloppan or a tomb like Xavec, not if we decide we won't let it.'

'You'll pardon me for still considering you a military asset at this point, madam. I suggest that the Missionaria Galaxia and the Officio Prefectus are both quite capable of getting the civilian mob under–'

'No.'

'No. I see.' The Warmaster's face was stony-still to the point where Priad found himself wondering if the hololith were malfunctioning. Then he clapped his hands, making Kassine jump.

'Surviving Archenemy forces have fled back along the causeway to Oureppan, correct?'

'And across the straits,' Sabbat said. 'They took most of the working vessels and crippled what they couldn't take. We took a good toll on the sea retreat but we couldn't get them all.'

'And you're keeping the momentum going? The Oureppan defences are formidable. Even riding the enemy's own heels in through its defences, this is going to be a monster.'

'Priad's people will tell you a monster can be slain if the lance is thrust true,' Sabbat said with a smile. 'Have faith, Warmaster, it can be done.'

'Good,' Macaroth declared. *'Call your officers back in. Let's get to it.'*

The Imperial vanguard
Oureppan Causeway

The causeway came in between the horns of Oureppan's crater bay, bisected the circular lagoon and went ashore beneath the six high arches of the Espylean Parade. They were called the Gates of Oureppan, ancient defences erected by long-lost cabals of Mechanicus priests. Urdeshi still told one another breathless folk tales of the strange devices with which the towers in the arch supports had once crushed would-be attackers. Whatever those weapons had been they were long gone now, but each archway could still grav-lift great adamantine slabs up through the causeway to seal it off, lace the space between with voids and lash out at anything that tried to overfly them or bypass them with batteries of lascannon and storms of vicious hypervelocity ceramic flak.

They had not been built for what had happened to them that night, nor had the gate commanders been ready for it. They had been ready for a fast but disciplined flight, an orderly exercise done on the Anarch's own orders and terms. Not the tide of battered, scorched and terrified humanity that had clogged the causeway for hours, fighting to push ahead faster, clambering onto and over vehicles that themselves were crushing the careless or unlucky underheel.

Before long it wasn't just the fleeing forces of the Anarch filling the parade, but if any of the overwhelmed gate garrisons realised that the Imperial Guard were coming in on the tide their alerts were lost in the bedlam. The frantic rearguard battle had spilled through the first two arches before it even slowed down. It was through the third before the machinery of the gates themselves began to power up. The outermost gate never even started to move, the towers broken in by ferocious assaults from the Urdeshi stormers and the garrisons wiped out to the last. The second arch managed to lift a slab into place and block a third of the causeway but only raised the second a handful of metres before its towers fell in turn. By the time the slabs started to rise and the crackling curtains of void shield materialised between them, the Six

Gates of Oureppan were hopelessly compromised, the towers filled with savage face-to-face melees and the point-blank firefights on the causeway broken into pieces.

A handful of exultant Guard units even managed to spill off the end of the causeway and into the teeth of the Oureppan urban defences. The pursuit from Ghereppan, that would be the stuff of legends, songs and plays for generations of Urdeshi to come, had finally ground to a halt. The fleeing Sekkite soldiery began filling up trenchworks and redoubts that had stood ready and empty for them, and the sunrise brought them some courage after the horror and confusion of the night before. More voids started going up over the most vital points of the fortifications, and the artillery batteries embedded around the head of the causeway started to find their ranges. The Guard, for their part, would not be denied the foothold they had claimed in the Archenemy's most feared citadel. Not on the day of the Miracle, not with the Saint watching over them.

Somehow, the deadlock had to break. The Militarum's own heavy artillery was still struggling onto the causeway and their flying strength had been drained to nothing by the air battle for the Warmaster's own command at Eltath. General Grawe-Ash could not hammer Oureppan's defences with shells or bombs, so she hammered them with Iron Snakes and Titans instead, and for the enemy the results were no less catastrophic.

Legio Invicta
Oureppan Causeway

The causeway would not carry the massive *Invictus Antagonistes*, so the Legio Invicta's three Warhounds were once again hunting on their own. The Titans were achingly exposed with little room to manoeuvre, and the weapon emplacements around the curve of the bay to each side were determined to punish them for venturing so close. They were already being battered from a hundred angles.

Lupus Lux was the first to answer, with a sky-cracking succession of shots from its turbolaser destructor cutting the air over the causeway and clipping neat pieces out of the fortifications rising up from the shore. Half a dozen shots in, it was rewarded not with the distant heat-flare of a cannon hit but the sensor-squalling haze of a void shield. Rather than move on to seek a softer target *Lupus Lux* planted its feet, locked in the firing solution and hammered it with all the power it could spare as its own shields were taxed with the rain of beams and missiles from the shore.

Morbius Sire danced past its sibling and raced further forward still, Princeps Orfuls gritting his teeth at the thudding impact of rocket-rounds and the hot scrape of las-beams as his rush brought him into range of more and more of the weaponry clustered around the Six Gates. That was where the true engine-killing guns lay in wait. The Espylean Parade had been created as a deathtrap for machines like his.

It was a trap he had no intention of entering. *Morbius Sire* skidded from a stride to a walk, hunching down against the incoming fire as a real hound would against a gale, and fired a string of wild shots from its blastgun, barely bothering to stabilise itself to steady its aim. A moment later *Raptus Solemnus* was by its side, its destructor burning a white trail down the dead centre of the causeway and striking the outermost void shield that the gate arches had managed to erect.

That was as far into Oureppan as any of the Legio Invicta made it that day. As more and more emplacements around the bay fired up and found their range, the Warhounds' own voids started to buckle. Krugmal jerked in the grip of blinding feedback as *Lux*'s void generator reached overload and his crew worked frantically to stabilise his inputs and back-pedal the Titan out of the firing line. *Morbius Sire* went stamping after it, its carapace now cratered and deformed from a shell burst that had found its way through the buckling shields. *Raptus Solemnus* brought up the rear, walking backwards, its destructor beam still flickering out and fencing with the shore batteries while its inferno cannon filled the air with defiant bellows of flame.

To the Archenemy gun crews, it felt like the first victory of the new day. Some even cheered at the sight of the Titans beleaguered and forced back. None of the three had come close to setting foot on the Oureppan shore. But none of them had been trying to.

Kalliopi
Over Oureppan Bay

Cepheas had brought the Thunderhawk in low and slow, weaving between the causeway pylons and using the bridge itself as cover, barely an arm's length between the gunship's tail and the stone. He was tracking the immense energies being discharged over his head – he barely needed the auspex, the storm of vox-interference alone told him what he needed – and brought the gunship twisting out from under the causeway and up past the Six Gates as the duel between the gates and the Titans hit its crescendo. With their instruments struggling to make sense of the miasma of heat-haze and screaming shield-wash, the defenders had no idea the Thunderhawk was coming until it had already passed over their heads. By the time a handful of energy beams and flak missiles reached up after its trail it was a vanishing speck speeding away over the strait.

A second later, the five armoured figures tumbling down through the sky from it sparked their jets into life.

Sergeant Kreios was in the centre of the loose line of Snakes, plummeting through the rushing air head down, feet up, body utterly relaxed. It was pleasing to see how sloppy the Oureppan defenders had become about disguising their positions. The defences underneath him were as clearly readable as if he had been looking down at a map.

Here, a double row of armoured vehicles incompetently camouflaged. There, unusual numbers of personnel milling about outside a compound that should have been allowed to look deserted. Over there, a haze in his heat vision where a powerful generator was leaking heat out of the building it was hidden in. He spotted and tagged the quick hot churn of air left by high-energy weapons fire, and puffs of heat and shock as cannons fired solid shells out of their concealed emplacements. He could see half a dozen targets in his landing window that seemed to be weapons big enough to threaten the Legio Titans. Once those were gone they were free to tear the Archenemy lines apart however they wished.

'Kandax, the two missile trucks in that cul-de-sac,' he voxed. 'Got my marker?'

'Affirm.' There was a flash of blue light and a sudden gap in the straggling line of falling Snakes as Kandax fired himself onto a new trajectory.

'Hemaeros. Those two minarets off the inner gate spitting las.'

'I see them. The dome behind them's warm, bet that's where they're powering from.'

'Kill it.'

'Affirm.'

'Skopelion, see the heat churn around the base of that freight-lifter?'

'*Affirm. Heavy plasma shot.*' Skopelion amped up his suspensors and vanished upwards, somersaulting in the air to re-aim himself.

'Hapexion. That truckport way back from the fortifications with the rear ramp full of people and vehicles. I think that's a command post. Let's find out.'

They were feathering their suspensors now, just enough to let their thrusters turn them, curving out of their vertical plunge. Barely seconds left now. They were low enough that small-arms fire from the tarnished metal roofs could have hit them, but the rooftops around their target were deserted and no fire came.

The truckport did have roof guards, a trio in shabby yellow uniforms crouched around a tripod stubber on the straitward edge. They were all staring at the dot in the distance that was *Morbius Sire*, barely visible through smoke and the distorting smudges in the air where its voids were dumping off the energy of another hit. The two Snakes dropped in fast and silent, and the sentries never realised there were enemies above them.

Kreios and Hapexion ignored the humans in turn. With only metres left Kreios slammed his suspensors and thrusters to maximum, turning his drop into a swoop across the rooftop barely an arm's length above the metal. He came down on the far side of the building, back to the rockcrete, bolt pistol already blazing, enemy troops panicking and scattering as explosions littered the marshalling yard. Hapexion followed him, barely bothering to slow his fall as he crashed feet first into a groundcar that had just been coming through the yard's rear gate. The car's body crumpled in around him, almost smashed in two, and Hapexion fanned his hand flamer around the wreck before he kicked his way clear of it. The fuel went up around him as he tore his way out of the blaze.

The depot's rear door was too small for an armoured Adeptus Astartes, and Kreios had to waste a couple of seconds smashing the frame wider with shoulders and elbows before he stepped through. Stub-rounds spanged off his chest and faceplate. He took a couple of strides into the space beyond, a set of corrals made from flakboard partitions, a central broad table scratched and scrawled with crude maps and dispatch slips. Somewhere a vox-unit was crackling and squealing with interference from the energy discharges closer to the lines. With a quick blink signal his helmet took an image of it, then Kreios shredded table, papers and bodies alike with bolt-shells.

It took the two of them less than ninety seconds to plough through the command post, leaving the whole space ablaze from wall to wall as they tore the front curtain-doors open and broke out into daylight. In the next street a booming shockwave threw smoke and fragments high into the air and they ignited their packs in unison, hurtling up and out of the smoke and towards the source of the blast.

They landed among a gaggle of enemy who were milling, shouting and firing shots at a ball of black smoke and dirty yellow flame that had been an AT-70 battle tank a moment earlier. Kandax came roaring out of that smoke in a flat trajectory barely above head height, rolling in the air to catch the nearest two enemy with a single sweeping melta shot. Both burst in mid-stride as their body fluids explosively vaporised from the heat. Their panicked companions redoubled their fire at Kandax, and by the time the arrival of more Space Marines behind them had penetrated their adrenaline-fuelled tunnel vision it was too late. Six seconds, and the Iron Snakes were alone in the street.

'Missile trucks dead,' Kandax confirmed as he landed next to them, 'but some kind of overpowered las-shot killed my pistol. Magazine went off right on my hip.' There was a pitted scar on the ceramite where his bolt pistol had been anchored, the armour up that side scorched and stippled, and Kandax's left arm was moving stiffly and a fraction of a second behind his right.

'Damage is to my armour's movement,' he said, anticipating Kreios' question. 'I can compensate. I'm not injured.'

'Save your melta reserve,' Kreios told him. 'Armour kills only from now on.'

'Affirm. Speaking of which, hear that?'

The rev of engines was echoing off the walls around them, bigger than an attack trike but too light for a battle tank. SteG-4s, HET-7s perhaps, in numbers.

'All right, let's not wait for them to box us in,' Kreios said. 'In towards the causeway road and we'll cut the sinews on those big voids.'

'Where's Skopelion?' Kandax asked as he took second spot in line. A jump took them back down the transitway and a few running steps brought them into a laneway choked with litter. A corpse, far enough gone that not even its sex was recognisable any more, swung by its ankles from an access stair. 'I only had the target you sent me and I–'

A scream of released energy filled the air ahead of them and the laneway mouth was bathed in a shimmering wash of heated air. Jogging to its end, they looked out to see the freight elevator collapsing into the melting wreckage that was all that was left of its foundation level. Crumpling steel roared like a dying beast and threads of plasma stretched up to dance and twist in the heat-contorted air before they cooled and vanished.

'I withdraw the question,' Kandax said, and then barked 'Prey!' A HET-7 was nosing its way around a corner two blocks away.

'One high and down,' Kreios said, and launched himself in a backward arc over their heads, up towards the fire stair with its carrion ornament. The grillework immediately began to deform under his weight, rivets pinging loose as it started to tear away from the wall. Before it could collapse completely Kreios smashed in the door and lintel and squeezed through. The floor creaked and cracked under him each time he took a step, but he ignored it.

The HET-7 was fully in the street by now, followed by an open-topped transport with a handful of helmeted soldiers in it and half a dozen more jogging behind. The footsloggers had all turned to gawp at the freight elevator coming down but one of the truck riders had kept their head about them, and spotted Kreios in the upper window.

Too late and too slow. In the time it took the rest of them to look around at their companion's yell there was a bolt-shell on the way down, and in the seconds it took them to find their wits after their squadmate exploded in their midst Kreios had landed in amongst them, crashing the truck violently down on its suspension. He fired another shell down to scatter the foot squad, aiming mostly by memory and peripheral vision, as chainsword strokes scattered bodies all around him.

The HET had surged forward and away from him, turning to

bring the lascannon sponson to bear. Its flank was to the laneway where the others waited, and its crew's attention was all on Kreios as he butchered their companions on the truck and in the road. They almost certainly never saw Hapexion step out into the road and aim his bolter. Kandax was already in the air when the Apothecary fired, the shells passing under him to wreck the HET's middle and rear wheels. Kandax landed with his melta's muzzle almost to the armour, the angle already carefully chosen, and fired. A patch of metal skin the size of his palm flashed straight through red to white-hot, and the HET shuddered and died as the heat beam skewered through it and burst the bank of powercells inside.

And without further word or pause, they were on the move again.

Verleg Chae
Oureppan foreshore

Verleg Chae was no Son of Sek. He was slightly built, crooked in one ankle and *old*, fifteen years older than most of the others wearing the Anarch's colours alongside him. But the Sons thought enough of the way he ran his motley little collection of armour that they had made use of him in the aftermath of the horrifying, humiliating retreat from Ghereppan.

Not that that retreat had left him with much. They hadn't been much to start with, but they'd had their pride, fixing the image of the Anarch's hand over their mouths and claiming every kill they'd made in the name of the Voice That Drowns Out All Others. But now he was down to his own battered SteG-4 and a single HET-7 lascarrier, and barely the people to run them. And he was lucky to have that much, after the

Imperial Titans had run them down on the causeway and the mad giants in the grey armour had dropped on them out of the sky.

But Verleg Chae had survived it all, and made it to Oureppan with a hatch still over his head, and now here he was, trusted enough to park himself behind a rubble barricade out on the long rockcrete finger of the docks with orders to kill anything that came in.

Anything. And that extended to the pair of little harbour-workers' runabouts that they had been watching for the last few minutes as they struggled out from under the monolithic protective bulk of the causeway and towards the dock where he sat peering out of the forward hatch of his SteG.

'Voi esh mertokah,' he told the crew below him without lowering his magnoculars. *'Chyet tshek!'* The 40-mil autocannon in the turret above and behind him began battering the air, the shock of each shot like open hands slapping the back of Verleg's head in the rhythm of applause. Its bursts stippled the high prow of the nearest boat, walked up it to rake the crew cabin and up again to the pilot's position. Someone appeared along one of the side walkways, waving their arms frantically for the shooting to stop, then convulsed oddly as a shell passed through their sternum as effortlessly as if flesh and bone were air. By the time they dropped to the deck the gun had raked back down the boat again.

The second boat's pilot was undaunted by the fate of their sister ship. Or, more likely, wasn't properly processing it with a mind still reeling from the previous night's insanity. It made no difference. A beam from the HET-7 carved the cabin in half along a neat diagonal, ascending left to right, letting the structure collapse in on itself in a welter of smoke. A second later the beam reached out again and slid through the runabout's thin hull. Something it found in there touched off, and suddenly a boil of dirty orange flame erupted from the vessel's hatches and from the wounds in her hull. A pair of flailing, burning human shapes staggered to the gunwale, pitched over into the water and were lost to sight.

Several more survivors had made it into the water from the lead vessel, which was now listing and smoking behind them, already more hulk than boat. One or two were visibly in trouble, weighed down by injuries or kit. Most had had to tear off the iron grotesques that were pulling their heads too low in the water. One or two of the stronger ones were closing on the wharf with their faces still covered. Verleg watched them disappear from view beneath the wharf's edge where the ladders were. He gave no more firing orders; his crews had done their part.

Half a dozen Sons of Sek came jogging past him, vaulting or leaping over the chunks of rockcrete piled in front of him without breaking stride, toting heavy, long-barrelled lasrifles as though they were toys. They spread out along the wharf, lining up like an honour guard on parade. Verleg heard cries coming up from the water, but he couldn't hear whether they were curses or pleas for aid. As one, the Sons took aim and started shooting. The first shots went almost straight down – the leading Blood Pact survivors must have been very nearly at the ladder.

'Sko vai etshka!' crackled the warning in his ear-loop and Verleg lifted his eyes to see a third vessel coming in along the wake of the first two. It was larger, a rattletrap relic that had been a cross-strait ferry in quieter days, moving almost fast enough for its hydrofoils to deploy. Verleg was no mariner but it was obvious in a moment that this one would not be able to stop at the wharf even if it wanted to.

The HET-7's lascannon jabbed into the ferry's rump, raising a puff of smoke but nothing more. The Sons' rifles swung up and a fusillade of las-fire crackled across the bridge windows. The shots were frighteningly precise, cratering and melting one window after another, but the boat bore down regardless, shouldering aside the crippled runabouts. The Sons had time for one more volley before they had to scramble back out of the ferry's way. The last one was barely clear when hull met wharf with a long, shrieking grind of steel on rockcrete.

When the terrible racket of the collision was over and the ferry lay gutted and stalled across the wharf, Verleg raised his magnoculars again. There was no point in spending ammo and power on a dead craft. If anyone was actually in there still they would find themselves targets soon en–

Three of the Sons exploded, one after the other but so close together the detonations seemed simultaneous. Verleg's stunned eye lifted from the three showers of gore, following three straight trails of black smoke to the grey-and-gold shape squatting in the ferry's prow. The bolter braced against its armoured barrel-chest cracked and flared, and Verleg ran his gaze back down two new smoke trails to see the remnants of two more Sons scattering onto the rough grey 'crete. The last was spinning to run from a nightmare that was bearing down on him.

From top to toe it was the same clotted red as the uniforms of the Blood Pact they had just murdered, chased with glints of brass and bone and overlaid with soot and grime and rockcrete dust. Barbed iron hooks lined the oversized pauldrons on its armour; wrinkled and colourless ribbons fluttered from them. One upswept helmet antler had been chewed half to shapelessness by who knew how many battles' worth of gunfire. The other was gone completely, leaving an ugly brass stump jutting from the helmet's left side. One immense gauntleted hand gripped a bolt pistol that Verleg could barely have lifted, but the monster wasn't bothering to use it. It caught up to the sprinting Son in a handful of strides and took him apart at the waist with one stroke of the buzzing chainaxe in its other fist. A backhanded swing with the flat of the enormous blade swatted the two halves away into the water. With weird, slow-motion clarity Verleg was sure he saw the Son turning his head, looking around as he fell to try and work out what had happened to him.

A black line scored across the rockcrete behind the thing's pounding feet, skidded off the side of the wharf and sliced up a line of steam from the placid water beyond it. The HET-7 crew had tried a shot with their lascannon and hadn't allowed for the charging thing's insane speed. Verleg took a breath, ready to scream into his headset for them to cease fire, thinking with the delirious logic of terror that if they sat silent the nightmare would pass them by.

That was stupid, of course, and he realised it a heartbeat later as he saw the great shape reach the end of the wharf and turn its cinder-glowing red eyes on them. Pivoting faster than anything so massive should have been able to – still with that adrenaline clarity, Verleg saw one armoured boot carve a divot into the rockcrete as it skidded a little on the turn – it raced for the HET.

'Tshek tiil, tshek uzket!' he shouted, but only his own crew paid attention and another round of detonations whacked at him from above as the SteG's cannon tried to knock the thing down. He saw the rounds kick up dust from the rockcrete behind it, gritted his teeth and moaned as he tried to force the gun to traverse faster with sheer will, and howled in despair when the HET jerked backward, trying to reverse away from its attacker, and its final lascannon shot went wild.

And then the thing was on it. A bolt-shell exploded against the HET's little half-turret and the chainaxe went up for a swing. Verleg dropped down and pulled the hatch closed, pulling the ear-loop off so he didn't have to hear his other crew dying. His own people were silent, drawn with fear, but they were still feeding magazines and keeping the engines at readiness. None of them panicked or babbled. He had a good crew. Verleg reached for the scope handles, framing his next order.

Something stove in their front armour, and after a moment of blackness Verleg came back to consciousness on his back in the middle of the compartment. His eyes were full of blood and his ears full of noise. Someone trod on him. He couldn't hear what was going on. Shaking his head, he turned himself over and started to crawl for the back of the tank, thinking blindly of the rear hatch and its quick-blow release. The tank took another hit, on the side this time, rocking it back and forth on its suspension until it came to rest at a bad, broken lean. Someone fell on him and squashed him to the floor, then pinned his arm under their boot as they scrambled up. Ahead, the bolts on the rear hatch triggered with a bang that Verleg felt as much as heard, and gloomy grey daylight poured in. His blurry eyes saw a silhouette in the square of light as one of the crew led them out, then someone else got their arm around him and helped him move.

Head hanging, Verleg greyed out again until the gritty pavement smacked him in the face. Gasping with shock, he jerked back into consciousness and managed to get on his hands and knees before he looked up.

Toek the motorman was the one who'd dragged him out. Shket was the one who'd gone out ahead of them. Two-thirds of Toek lay motionless a metre away from him, the body simply absent from the chest up. Shket was on his knees, one hand clamped to his face, the other stretched beseechingly out to the clanking, squelching mass of plate and chain that loomed over him. Kneeling, the little gunner barely reached the figure's thigh. It looked at him for a long time and then, rather stiffly, unclamped its left hand from the barrel of its bolter. The last two fingers were fused together and grown into a long bone hook which flicked out and opened Shket's throat. His death spasms were barely more violent than his terrified shuddering had been, but eventually they ended and it was just Verleg. The muzzle of the giant's bolter was a black eye that he could not look away from.

'Wait,' said a voice from behind him. 'Not this one.' And a crimson-and-brass gauntlet hoisted Verleg Chae up by the scruff of his neck.

Priad
North gallery, Keshriy Clade-House, Ghereppan

'Tense your right leg.'

Priad obliged, closing his eyes and concentrating on the feel of each muscle from hip to toes, locking each in turn, feeling the slick black second skin beneath the armour's surface knot and move with him. He could sense as much as hear the flex and tick of actuators. There was a tiny movement under the arch of his foot as his boot got ready to respond to a step.

'Ease off. Let the muscles go limp.' Pyrakmon was kneeling by Priad's hip, head bowed. A gleaming braid of fibre optics ran from the back of the Techmarine's hand up into the receptor panel set into the top of the thigh. Pyrakmon could feel the slightest twitch of the armour components as though they were his own muscles and nerves.

'Tilt your weight from the hips again, side to side.' Underneath his instructions, Priad could hear the soft code-songs as the machines Pyrakmon wore spoke to Priad's own. 'Now from the knees. Side to side. Now from the ankles. Lock your boots. Unlock.' Priad couldn't help trying to listen for some variation in the sounds, although he wouldn't have known how to interpret a pattern if he had discerned one.

He turned his attention instead to the two sets of footsteps coming up the long, shallow steps to the arched belvedere over the shore where Pyrakmon had set up shop. One set of soft soles, squeaking slightly against the basalt floor, half drowned out by the heavy clanks of the ceramite boots that they were trotting to keep up with. They reached the top of the steps, turned, came to a halt four metres away, outside Priad's eyeline.

'This is the one, sir.' The voice of one of the stewards from General Grawe-Ash's staff, whose name Priad didn't know. 'I shall go forward and announce you.'

'Unnecessary. You aren't needed now.' Priad nodded slightly to himself. He knew the walking rhythm of every member of Damocles as well as he did their names. He hadn't recognised these steps, but he did know the voice.

'Come on up, brother,' he called, and listened to the other Space Marine's heavy tread across the floor of the belvedere until he came into view.

Like Priad, Holofurnace was armoured in the simple steel-grey of the Phratry. He was bareheaded, his face the same bronze-brown, his hair the same glossy black although it made a cap of tight ringlets where Priad's fell straight. His jaw was narrow, his eyes deep-set, dark and watchful beneath a high brow.

'Please pardon my not turning to greet you,' Priad said. 'As you see...' He pointed his chin down at Pyrakmon still at work on his armour. 'But it's good to see a face we'd thought lost on the tide the last ten years. We're glad to have you back.'

The other Space Marine didn't reply. He stared at Priad, then out over the city and the sea. The belvedere was a broad, roofed gallery running around Keshriy clade-house's waist, its elegant arches framing the same panorama that the Highwork doors did many levels above them. They were low enough that Priad had been able to watch the Militarum swarming at the waterfront, hunting for wrecked boats they could make seaworthy again, and pouring up the Great Ascent onto the causeway. As Macaroth had put it, the Imperium were riding the enemy's heels through the gates of Oureppan.

Priad had plans for it soon. Kreios had led his brothers up and over the hulks of the plasmapults while they still glowed cherry-red in the dawn, chasing down the terrified rabble ahead of them and reaping brutal revenge for their brothers. And Platonos Squad had answered Priad's summons, arriving from the west halfway through the morning, Thunderhawk above and the twin speeders below, drawing a neat line across the Archenemy's rearguard like a scalpel across a windpipe. The Platonos Thunderhawk was now on a landing shelf high on the Keshriy house's south face. Priad had plans for it soon.

Holofurnace finished surveying the smoke- and wreck-scarred panorama below them, and looked back at his two brothers. He had the air of someone deeply angry, but at a loss for what to be angry about.

Priad thought he knew.

'You heard, then,' he said. Holofurnace nodded. 'Did they tell you when you landed?'

'No. All I asked was where my brothers were and that ended up with me being brought here. Then when we were in flight I tried to instruct the pilot to take me to whichever front Andreos Squad was on. That confused them. They kept telling me they were bringing me to the rest of you, and mentioning Kalliopi and Damocles over and over. Finally one of them realised.' He looked back out through the arch. Some of the tension seemed to go out of him.

'Did they tell you any details?'

'Not many. They didn't have many to give.'

'We'll be able to help you there. We were all in the vanguard in the Ghentethi landings. We'll have enough for you to build a declaration of deeds when we're home.'

'Good.'

'In the meantime, you'll come under my banner. You'll be part of Damocles until this undertaking is done. I welcome you, Kater. I'll embrace you, once I'm allowed to move again.' Holofurnace stared out through the arch again. His jaw worked for a few moments.

'So none of them left, then,' he said neutrally. 'None of Andreos Squad left at all.'

'Yes, there is. You.'

'You know what I meant!' Holofurnace snapped. 'There was an Andreos Squad at our foundation. There has been an Andreos Squad in our ranks in every generation since. If I had fallen on my last mission then it would have been Andreos who lost a brother. I landed on Urdesh as a warrior of Andreos!' He stopped short.

'And then you found there was no Andreos to rejoin,' Priad said quietly. 'I am sorry you had to find out the way you did. Pyrakmon, are you close to done on the armour?'

'Done...' There was a succession of mechanical clicks

and the sounds of armoured fingers on armoured plate. '...now.' The Techmarine stood up and stepped back. 'For now, anyway. I want to keep watch on how everything's integrating as you move.'

'Can you leave us for a few minutes?' Pyrakmon looked back and forth between his two brothers, then tilted his helm and grunted.

'I'll go and look over Dyognes' power connection,' he said. His servo-arm unfolded itself from the back of his pack and plucked up a thick stub of cable from a sill behind him. 'See if he's managed to avoid setting it up to incinerate the back of his skull when the reactor properly ignites. We're not done yet, though, Priad. Walk around in that armour for a while. I want to watch for any irregularities that prolonged movement is going to bring out before you start running or fighting in it.' He indicated a little bronze-and-steel amulet that hung from the still-open panel at the top of Priad's thigh. 'That will keep the record for me. Don't dislodge it.' He made a slight bow to them both, muttered a short blessing in a throaty Ithakan mountain dialect and another in binharic, and left them to it.

Gingerly, bracing for resistance from his newly reassembled leg armour, Priad stepped forward and extended his hand. Holofurnace clasped it unenthusiastically, and fell in beside Priad as he began a stately walking pace down the belvedere. For a minute or two the only sound apart from their footsteps was the soft scritching and ticking from Priad's hip as the amulet wrote its records.

'Why here?' Holofurnace demanded eventually, pointing through the arch and out over the city and the water. 'We're in plain view. There's not even glass in the arches. The simplest scopes would pick us out. You're here with your armour open and under repair and your squad's battlegear all around you.' He swept a hand around at the narrow stone benches that Pyrakmon had dragged together to use as work surfaces. Every one was filled edge to edge with carefully laid out tools, icons, gun components and polished grey pieces of warplate. 'What do you think a single shell from a half-competent gunner could do?'

'I took a risk,' Priad agreed. 'Not a large one, in my assessment. I chose to accept it.' The belvedere narrowed as it followed the clade-house's sharp corner around to the building's east side, and Holofurnace paused so Priad could walk through without breaking his step.

'Why?' he asked when they were side by side again, unwilling to let the point go. 'I saw Damocles' lightning claw on one of these benches next to where you were standing. Your weapon of office. Disassembled.'

'That's one way of putting it.'

'Disassembled and sitting on the arch sill with the cuff casing open. Even a grenade blast could knock it free. That doesn't give you pause? Our ship touched down in Eltath. That city is the headquarters not just of the planet but of the entire Sabbat Worlds Crusade. Warmaster Macaroth is there in person.'

'I'm familiar with our disposition here, Kater.'

'And even that place is rotten with infiltrators and partisans! I was there barely a day and in that time I know of three different contacts all around the city, all with Imperial casualties. Every street is strung with anti-sniper bunting and riddled with checkpoints, but you don't even have that here.' He gestured out to the broad avenues that stepped down from the north face of the scarp to the water, the great grey blocks and domes of the clade-houses giving way to the slenderer, more elegant spires of the accounteries and envoy compounds. Out in this direction, the view was a fine one. Half-close the eyes and one could almost forget what a bitter warzone it had been until the previous night.

'We have all fought through exactly what you're describing in Eltath,' Priad said. 'But Ghereppan is... Ghereppan has been through something very singular. Things are not the same here.'

'Can you explain?'

Out of the corner of his eye, Priad could see Holofurnace staring at him. He thought the question over for a moment.

'No,' he said as they reached the end of the colonnade. There were four human-scale steps rising up from it; the two Iron Snakes each took them with a single stride and walked out onto a circular platform that jutted from the centre of the western wall, roofless and ringed with the snapped-off stumps of flag masts. 'No, not yet. I don't know how easy it will ever be to explain to someone who wasn't here for it, to experience it. I did experience it. Part of its aftermath is that I don't believe that this is a position of active threat. And...'

His voice tailed off in thought as they lapped the platform. The rumble of engines drifted up from the interlacing roadways below them as convoys of Urdeshi and Jovani armour rolled towards the causeway.

'The Archenemy had this city in their grip for far too long,' he said eventually. 'Now they've been expunged from it. Utterly. And so when I needed to choose a place for us, somewhere near the Beati, I chose this, because, well.' He gestured out over the city as Holofurnace had done. 'Partly because it's the closest thing I've found in a long time to home. A place to walk in the breezes high up over the sea. And anywhere else, in any other circumstance, it would be risky. Madly risky. But here, now, on this day in Ghereppan, it isn't, and so by standing here we're picking up that fact and throwing it in the Archenemy's face. That's important. It's like raising a banner.'

'You've been spending a lot of time among them, haven't you? You're thinking like them.'

'Possibly,' Priad said mildly. He didn't need to ask to whom Holofurnace was referring. 'As a matter of fact I was talking with Xander about the same sort of thing not long before we came here.'

'You like your symposia in Damocles, do you?'

'It's a way of thinking. It's another edge along which we can sharpen ourselves. You never know when that's going to be the edge that you have to bring to bear. Was this not the custom in Andreos?'

'Not in the way you mean.' Holofurnace sighed. 'Ephoris, though, and Thalio, they had a way about them. They knew the histories, and they could bring out passages of them, or the accounts of some event, and between them they could make a wonder of it.'

'I know they spoke of Thalio as a great loss,' Priad said. 'Although I didn't know him well. Ephoris I knew, although I never heard him tell the histories. I wish I had, now. But he fought with Platonos Squad when Andreos was all but gone. Perhaps when we see Platonos again they'll be able to talk about him with you.'

'Was he the last?'

'No.'

'Who was the last?' Holofurnace flicked a hand pre-emptively. 'Apart from me.'

'Xenagoras joined Kalliopi Squad after Moschion fell in the Cowden Ash.'

'The place means nothing to me. Is that where Xenagoras died too?'

'No.' Priad suddenly found it difficult to reach for words. 'Here, just before the Miracle. Traitor Astartes in amongst the enemy. Kreios tells me he led the way to them. The first to fight them, and to take a kill.'

'Of course he was. He was the most hot-blooded of us. Always telling the rest of us we were too heavy-footed.'

'Kreios gave him the chance to lighten his feet. I think he took to it.'

'Kalliopi always had that reputation. I remember their arrowhead assaults at the Grand Justiary on Balhaut. Was Damocles there for that?'

'We were caught in the void fighting further out-system,' Priad said. 'We didn't catch up with you and Kalliopi and Andreos for weeks. But I heard the stories. Rushing like madmen, never letting up. They drove their Razorbacks so ragged they almost emptied the Hephaestium of its stocks keeping them running.' The two Snakes found they were sharing a small smile at the memory.

'And do they still?' Holofurnace asked. 'Or have they emptied the forge out completely now?'

'They took to jump packs for the Ghentethi atolls, and never took them off again. Kreios has a talent for the air. I think Xenagoras had it too.'

They were both silent as they finished their second circuit of the platform and descended the steps, Priad consciously extending his stride now to step back down into the colonnade with a heavy *chank* of boot on stone. There was the hint of a nagging stiffness in the armour's knee, but for all he knew he was imagining it because he had been preparing to feel something. He watched Holofurnace looking out over the dull sunlight on the war-soiled sea.

'I'm not inflexible,' he said. 'The final decision would be

Kreios' but if you wanted to take Xenagoras' place in Kalliopi Squad I would hand down the word, and I don't think he would go against it. Nor would I take insult–'

'You should. Damocles are one of the Notables. Turning my back on you for Kalliopi, no, I wouldn't do that to either of us. Thank you, though,' Holofurnace added as an afterthought. 'You were willing to humble yourself and your squad to allow me my head, for the sake of Xen's memory. I understand the weight of that, but…' He broke off, thinking through his words. 'But it's not about any individual one of us. It's about Andreos Squad, coming to an end. Andreos is…' His hands made fists as he looked for the words.

'We don't have the same relationship to death as the humans,' Priad said. 'Our minds get changed as much as our bodies do, and we get made so that it's harder for us to grieve the same way it's harder for us to bleed. One of the ways that works is that we are taught to connect ourselves to other things. Our squad, our Phratry. The Golden Throne itself, I suppose.'

'I understand how it works, brother.' Holofurnace gave a humourless little twist of his mouth and corrected himself. 'Brother-*captain*. You're right. War takes us, one way or another. I've seen it happen to brother after brother and I know it will happen to me. And to you.' He shook his head hard. 'This isn't the same.'

'No, it isn't. That was my point. Each of us was made for war. Or remade, if you prefer, from what we were. War taking one of our brothers is a hurt we know about, and the wound seals and we march on. War taking many of us can be a bad pain but it's still a pain we know. Then war takes something bigger. The name of a squad. Its lineage from the founding at Ithaka until now, its place among the lots on Karybdis…'

Holofurnace's eyes were closed and his hands in fists again. 'And the lineage of our squad is the first thing we're given to hold on to, as something that will endure even if every one of its members falls. So now we have a different kind of loss that none of our remaking against grief has been designed to cope with. It's a kind of loss that uses those very defences against us.'

'*We* have a loss? I appreciate you're trying to be kind with all this talk, Priad, but it isn't Damocles who ceased to exist when you turned your back.'

'What does it mean for a squad to cease to exist?' Priad asked, shifting tack. They had rounded the corner and were almost back at their starting point in the belvedere. Priad slowed his pacing as much as he could and tried to meet Holofurnace's eyes.

'What kind of question is that to ask?' There was audible heat in the other Snake's tone now.

'Look at the armour laid out on those benches,' Priad said, indicating them with an outswept arm as he walked back past them. 'Every piece there is older than we are. I am marching up and down like this because I'm bedding new components into mine. They're from Brother Lekos, of Platonos Squad, who was lost to us last year. A tank shell and a close assault by four Sons of Sek as Platonos was breaking the lines at Ulethppan. Pyrakmon has had them in his stores ever since. That plastron there. Look at it, please. That was Pindor's. My oldest squad member, one of the most quietly steadfast warriors I've ever fought with. Phaethon's armour will be rebuilt around it so he can catch up with his brothers in the Oureppan assault. Mathos too. His armour will be repaired with that pauldron and armplate at the end. Those were Xenagoras'.'

'The Hephaestium picking our brothers' battle-gear over for spoils,' snapped Holofurnace, 'is no consolation for–'

'You're not listening,' Priad cut him off. 'Or you're not thinking, which is worse. Every one of us goes to battle in a suit of warplate that will have been broken apart, lost pieces of itself, and been rebuilt into something new. Every piece of armour, every mechanism and component, has been recombined time after time. My armour has pieces in it now that came from another's, but it is no less my armour than it was before it was damaged. The armour I wore when we arrived in Ghereppan has many components that weren't there when I was first fitted with it. But still, it's my battle-gear. I look to it and revere it and it protects me. Do you understand what I'm trying to say?'

'Sophistry.'

'No. After Ganahedarak, all that was left of Gorgion Squad was its Apothecary and a new petitioner who wasn't even far enough along for his body to accept its armour connections. Remember that? Old Hierax and Agattis. They went and served with Phobor's own retinue until Hierax could raise up half a dozen more petitioners and take Gorgion to war again. There are four whole squads with gaps of years in their lineage after the undertaking to Ophyon. Two of them were refounded within our own lifetimes. Broken and rebuilt, like armour.' Priad whistled through his teeth in frustration. 'I need Khiron here. He'd be better for this.'

'You needn't call him here on my account,' Holofurnace said. 'I understand your parable of the armour. And I meant what I said about my respect for Damocles. We can spare the old man's time.'

'The reason I mentioned Khiron,' Priad said, his patience abruptly draining away, 'is not just because he has a knack for setting these problems in a pithy phrase that's easy to carry away with you. I wanted him because he came to me in nearly identical circumstances to you, Holofurnace, except that they were worse. He was the last survivor of Ridates Squad. He was brought home in disgrace and thrown into a cell for fratricide because of the tricks of a piece of warp-filth that could have poisoned who knows how many of us if Khiron hadn't been able to pass on a warning. He asked for death in the trial of Oethenor and he very nearly got it before he was exonerated. Don't even try to tell me you don't remember.'

'I wasn't there for it. Andreos Squad was on an undertaking to Sorenum.'

'Fine. It doesn't matter. What matters is that Khiron knows the same loss you do, and he went through worse because of it. And he came to Damocles with grace and humility that I have never stopped admiring. He'd be better for this because I can only name those qualities to you. He can show you what they look like so you can learn a little of them. You've been through a great loss, Holofurnace, but here in this conversation you've about reached the end of what that loss will excuse.'

Holofurnace didn't reply, but he did stop, wait until Priad had wheeled around at the far end of the belvedere, and bow his head. That was good enough for the moment.

'Very well,' Priad said. 'Your third task as a brother of Damocles Squad is to ask Khiron, as privately as you wish, whether he will talk of these matters with you, for the reasons I've given. Your second, though, will be to first have him do as complete an assay on you as he has time for before we strike out from here. You're one of his to tend to now. He'll need to know you.'

'Yes, brother-captain. And my first task?'

'Go find Pyrakmon and ask him politely if he needs anything more from me or if I can stop parading up and down like... I don't know like what, just go.'

'When I see Apothecary Khiron I shall ask him to suggest a simile,' said Holofurnace. 'A pithy one.' He turned on his heel and disappeared down the internal steps.

Priad had to wait until he was sure the other Space Marine was gone before he let the laugh out.

Platonos
Oureppan foreshore

The hydrofoil ferry was still beached across the rockcrete wharf that Verleg Chae had been given to guard. No one had come to investigate it, or to replace the little garrison that should have been watching this stretch of the waterfront. The hulk of the HET-7 was still burning. The human wreckage along the wharf and around the torn-open SteG-4 had gone cool.

Nobody was there to see the splintered and battered fibreplas container, a demountable bulk carrier doubtless knocked clear of one of the wrecks further out in the strait, come drifting slowly in towards the shore. Nobody scanned it, reported it, or noted it as another piece of war detritus cast onto the waters. Nobody was there to notice that its gentle bobbing progress was actually at right angles to the breeze, or to realise that its apparently undirected movements were deftly steering it around the broken ships in its path. Nobody watched it come around the stern of the gutted ferry. Nobody was there to realise that the empty bit of flotsam was in fact hanging half a metre above the water.

And so nobody raised the alarm at the series of explosive bangs as four carefully placed grenades blew the tank to pieces. The space where it had been was a crazed lens of bent light and reflections, surrounding a tight blue spark of light that blazed like a plasma torch. An eye that could have looked at that spark without blinking would have seen that the spark was a double-bitted axe-head, held high at the end of a long haft by a blue-armoured fist.

A split second later Hamiskora released the compacted shell of psychic force that had held the tank in place, sending it forward as a pressure wave like the blast of a cyclone hitting land. The blue-grey shock-front slammed waves against the seawall, tossing the handful of floating Blood Pact corpses into the air amid the spray, and boomed across the wharf, shaking the two wrecked tanks and tumbling the bodies of Chae's crew along the ground. In its wake came Platonos Squad's two speeders, grav engines keening as they vaulted the seawall and sped towards the line of buildings.

Swift as they were, the speeders were not moving with their usual hell-for-leather rush of arcing leaps and joint-wrenching turns. Today they had the rest of Platonos hanging off clamp-grips on the speeders' rear cowling, their battle-brothers hunching inward trying to minimise drag and the speeders wallowing and yawing from the extra load.

For a few excruciating moments they were exposed, relying on speed and surprise to be their armour, then they were through to the buildings and in cover again, weaving between collapsing mounds of corroded containers, then through a chainlink fence laced with razor wire and booby-trapped with frag grenades. Platonos didn't even slow down for it. The two loaded speeders tore through the sagging wire and dragged ragged shawls of it after them, barely even registering the grenade detonations. A dozen metres later the remnants tore loose and flopped to the ground behind them.

'That was it?' Alekon asked, risking a quick lean back from his handholds to crane around at the buildings flicking past them. They were already at the base of the crater-ridge and starting to climb up the steep, zigzagging streets to its crest. 'That was the dire and dreadful battle we were going to fight to break into Oureppan? Are we at least coming up on a second line?'

'Shut up,' Herodion barked back at him, 'and hold your position. When you swing yourself around like a loon you throw off my balance. Pull yourself back in...' He bit the conversation off while he wrestled the loaded speeder through an ungainly banking turn that brought an imminent-overheat warning rune from the grav plates '...and be the nice quiet ballast you're supposed to be. Closing on the ridge top, contact ahead. Get ready.'

They fell silent, letting their armour's senses look through the speeder's eyes as they skated through the air on the final corner, hurtled through a rail junction and gunned hard for the rockcrete hardpoint blocking the way onto the broad avenue that ran along the ridge crest.

Dardanos was accelerating again, stuttering the grav field to make his speeder list from side to side, turning the clumsiness of the extra weight into an asset to make his trajectory even more unpredictable. Heat-sight was striped this way and that with shining red-tinged trails as the hardpoint gunners tried to zero in with small-arms and emplaced multi-lasers. Coming in on Dardanos' left stern, Herodion gritted his teeth and held his course as a burst of stub-rounds spanked off the speeder's sloping front and a las-shot cut a black scorch mark along the side of his helm. He was about to curse Kapis' overscrupulous aiming and jink away when the heavy bolter coughed out a quick burst. Three almost simultaneous explosions walked up the hardpoint's front and then the firing slot at the top lit up as the fourth shell slipped neatly through it and detonated against something inside.

Dardanos thinned out his speeder's repulsor pad and opened the engines to full, dropping so low that the ventral fins almost clipped the rail lines. Las and hard rounds started to fire sporadically from the hardpoint's secondary compartments but none of them came close, and then the lead speeder was in range and Atymnes opened fire. The heat-flash filled the Snakes' vision as they passed through the superheated tunnel of air, then shredded and fell away behind them as the beam cut out. Kapis had been waiting for his moment and fired another handful of bursts the instant his sight line was clear. He read the patterns in the heat-glow across the sloping bunker wall with trained, inhuman ease and his shells hit just where the melta had weakened the armour the most. One wing of the hardpoint exploded, a steel hatch flying up from its roof as the blast punched upward.

The two speeders split apart, pushed themselves just high enough to hurdle the lines of tank traps and sandbags, and whipped past the hardpoint on either side. Smoke began to seep from the firing slit of the central bunker. There had been no further shots.

Then they were up on the avenue, accelerating westward around the curve of the ridge. Away to their left the terraced streets dropped away to Oureppan Bay, the great grey plain of the city stretching to the horizon on their right. The distant shape of Pinnacle Spire was a dagger stabbing up from the horizon, and the brooding cone of Old Ourezhad dominated the sky ahead of them. Framed by the volcano's dark, distant bulk was a pair of slender pylons and a fat white minaret: one of the procession of power hubs that studded the top of the crater ridge all the way around the bay like molars in a jaw. Those pylons sank roots down into the fulgeducts that brought the electricity flows from Old Ourezhad, drawing it up to power Oureppan's defences.

Hamiskora, hanging off the lead speeder just by Dardanos' elbow, felt a chill between his shoulder blades at the sight. He had seen its echo in the dissolving memories of the lekt they had killed on the street of that little nameless town an ocean away, and it had appeared to him again in the oneiric trance he had put himself into as the Thunderhawk had brought them across to Ghereppan. His directions to Sergeant Iapetos had been correct. This was a place that meant something.

Hamiskora wondered if he were going to die here. He suspected he might. He put the thought from his head, closed his eyes and let all his thoughts rest inside the cool crystal matrix of his force axe. Whatever happened, he needed to be ready.

Nautakah
Bayside approaches, Oureppan

It had been easy to stop the SCU-3 trike that came beetling around the curve of the street towards them: they simply walked out and stood in front of it. The Tusk panted and clanked into the street first, then the grey-armoured Space Marine who wouldn't tell Nautakah his name, then the arnogaur himself at the point of the triangle. As an afterthought he'd held Verleg Chae out in front of him. There was no way the little tank captain would pass for alive any more, not even at a glance, but he managed to be useful one last time by distracting the trike's driver so that he spent his final seconds trying to make sense of the corpse being waved at him instead of calling in the contact. Then a bolt-shell from the Tusk punched through his head and exploded in the midriff of one of the excubitors on the footplate behind him. The other one wailed some Sekkite gibberish as the out-of-control trike slewed and shot between Nautakah and his grey-gold companion. The other Space Marine reached out to pluck the last survivor off the footplate but, unthinking, did it with the augmetic arm that had been broken off him in the fight against the Saint, so the wailing dopplered past them and only stopped when the trike struck the kerb and vaulted over onto its side. Then it changed to an agonised moaning, given a weird metallic edge by the excubitor's voice box.

'Sloppy,' Nautakah said. The grey Space Marine stared at him, then raised the combi-bolter he held in his surviving broomstick limb. There was a chug and a boom as the grenade blast consumed the trike and its last surviving crewmember.

'Also sloppy,' Nautakah said as he tossed Chae's remains over his shoulder and walked over to the dead excubitor. 'Explosions might be investigated.' But there was no rancour to it. He was about ready for word to get out and for them to come and find him. The memories that had come bobbing up amongst his own once Chae's brains had slid down his gullet had been instructive.

There had been an order. There had been a *plan*. The Anarch had told his Sons and his serfs to stand ready to abandon Ghereppan. To let the Blood Pact think that they were launching a mighty joint assault, filling their ten-year schism with a mountain of Imperial dead upon which the lightless sun of the Ruinous Powers would smile forever. And to let the Pact dash themselves against the Imperium while the children of Sek laughed from the Oureppan redoubts.

That part had been very clear. The thought of it woke the machine in Nautakah's skull, set it scratching and scraping at the back of his mind like a cat at a door.

There had been a plan, but the plan had not survived the night. That had been obvious even to the three Chaos Space Marines as they dragged themselves out from under that accursed green starlight and slipped away northward. Something had happened all across the city, something that neither the Gaur's nor the Anarch's followers had been prepared for or even fully understood. Sek had hollowed out the mighty Oureppan garrison to lend its strength to the Ghereppan front, but Nautakah doubted the Anarch had brought even a quarter of it back across the strait to safety.

Safety. His lip curled at the thought as his helm came free of its seals. The most fundamental duty of an arnogaur was to punish treachery. If the Sekkite rabble thought there was any safety anywhere in this life for them after last night then he had a lesson to teach them.

Partition 510
Old Ourezhad

The repair crew rode a cable-tram into the upper level of Partition 510 and straight away when the doors opened they knew things were bad. The whole partition, a two-hundred-metre-deep well whose walls were lined with pipes, valves and access ladders, was hazy with volcanic waste and forge exhaust.

The carriage was full of hot, foul-smelling fumes almost before the doors were fully open and every surface of the transit dock they stepped out into was caked with hot, ashy grit.

There should have been a warning klaxon going off, but for once the crew were glad for how the systems all through the enormous volcanic warrens under Old Ourezhad were starting to get ragged about the edges. This work promised to be uncomfortable enough without its howling mechanical voice beating at their ears. The heavy work-hoods would stop the gas from crackling the skin off their bodies (for all that they all felt like they were cooking inside already) and the masks would keep the worst of the grit out of their eyes and lungs, but it did nothing to stop the noise.

Awkward in their hoods and gloves, they clambered down ladder after ladder, down and away from the yellow lights of the carriage platform and into the red of the emergency-lit piping levels. The haze around them thickened.

And of course, the damn pipe-breach was at the very lowest level. So down they climbed, and down.

The crew all knew what the machinery in the partition was for, even if they didn't know every last detail of its engineering. Skewering down through the main vent of the monstrous volcano like the metal stopper in a vast basalt bottle was the Adeptus Mechanicus thermovoltaic spike, soaking up the heat from the magma chambers beneath it and pushing it back out as raw power. Power enough to run the entire vastness of the city of Oureppan, with plenty left over for the layered forges and mills inside Old Ourezhad itself and for the chain of fortifications that joined the two.

The spike itself was a sovereign Adeptus Mechanicus shrine. None of the repair crew had ever been in there, not before the mountain had been overrun by the Archenemy and certainly not now. Outside its sealed doors and elevated promenades the priesthood's territory ended and the world of Urdesh began again.

Outside the shrine's perimeter there were more generatoria, cruder, locally built machines to siphon more power from the heat and pressure of the volcanic vents. Piezoelectrics kept the giant volcanic city powered, and great turbines spun by the volcano's gases fed both electrical energy and raw mechanical motion to the machines dug into every slope. Once the gases had done their duty by the vast ceramite turbine blades, they were vented off through the great maze-like refinery chambers, filtered and processed so that every useful mineral and chemical could be stripped out of them and piped on to the small city of processing plants that permeated the mountain itself and spilled out and down onto the plain. Finally, the last of the residues, still carrying the killing heat and pressure of the volcano, were shunted out of the central chambers and out through the long pipeshafts that carried them out of the volcano entirely, burying them in the sea floor, letting the seaweed plantations in the artificial coastal lagoons draw whatever they could from the warmth and the last remnants of the ash and dust.

That was where something had gone wrong. The crew were close enough to hear it more clearly now: a series of thumps and clangs from further up the pipe, and then a great boom of pressure and a hiss of rushing, ash-laden gas as the hot residue came blasting into the pipe and then out of it again, through some breach or broken seal, to send a choking tide of hot grey silt up through the partition. The crew tried to keep climbing for a moment, then abandoned the effort, signalling to one another to stay put with shouts up and down the line that fought against the noise of the leaking gas and the muffling of their hoods. They hung in place while the miasma swirled and burned around them, and then, when the choking pall had thinned and settled as much as they thought it was going to, they reluctantly started moving again.

The leak shouldn't have happened, but it wasn't itself crippling. What bothered the partition wardens back in their control roost was what would happen next. If something went wrong with the vent then the high-pressure blasts of waste would start backing up, pressurising further, choking the valves higher up the system, pouring heat and strain on parts of the system not built to the right tolerances. From there, the damage and the failures would cascade. Vital systems would start to collapse.

Too much depended on Old Ourezhad's great geothermal heart continuing to beat. Their masters depended on it. And the crews had learned, early and scarringly hard, that the displeasure of their new masters was far, far worse than the displeasure of their old.

The crew were almost at the foot of the well, now, down among the drifts of powdered ash and stifling air. The smell was starting to leak through their filters and the seams of their suits, and the steps, rungs and rails were blisteringly hot, enough to warm their hands and feet through glove-palms and boot-soles.

There was another rapid-fire sequence of mechanical crashes and the leak boomed again, sending a roaring torrent of furnace-hot air churning around the bottom of the well and shoving up past them, plucking at their clothes and shivering the ladder they were hanging from. But they were close enough that even through the smoke and the dimness the source was visible.

It wasn't a leak. The hatch was open.

The maintenance hatches were on the undersides of the pipes, so they could be dropped down, rolled away on their mounting rails and machinery could be lifted up into the pipe from a platform. Stumbling off the lowest ladder and down the steps to the partition floor, they stared up at it, each trying not to be the one standing closest to it. If the hatch had blown off its mountings and fallen to the floor, they would have to rummage round directly under the opening, in the downblasts of scorching ash, to find it, then lift it up and time the remounting and closing to avoid being caught and cooked.

The clumsy, hood-shrouded shapes looked at one another silently in the hot murk. Any hopes they had had that all twelve of them would be climbing back up the partition after this job were vanishing. They could tell that this was not a job they had been assigned to; it was a job they were being expended on. But the same thought came to them all: dying in the heat down here among their fellows was better than what they had seen happen uplevel to workers who failed their posts.

They looked at each other, and each one spread their hands in resignation, then turned to the great pipe that bridged the partition from wall to wall above them. At least when something had gone wrong, it had gone wrong where they could get at it easily. Beyond this point the pipe started its kilometres-long journey through solid rock out to the fortified coastal venting station; this was the last exit point on its journey down to the sea.

What none of them really thought of – why would they have? – was that it was also the first exit point for anything coming up.

The crew chief was the first to start shuffling towards the pipe, and Sergeant Symeon came out of the dark along the partition wall, met him and cut him into three with a quick back-and-forth stroke of Akanthe. He killed the next two as well, as they stood gaping at the pieces of their chief dropping into the ash. The third had just enough time to raise her hands in front of her before the sergeant ended her.

Around him the rest of Erasmos Squad were about the same work. Not a weapon was fired, but the Karybdis-pattern Astartes knives, each as long as its wielder's forearm and heavy enough that a human would have had to lift it two-handed, were as mercifully quick in the heat and confusion as bolt-shells would have been. A handful of seconds and the Iron Snakes were once again alone on the partition floor.

'Close that,' Symeon voxed. There was a crack and a thump as the clamps that had supported their descent lines disengaged from the hatch-rails, and then a squealing of grit-fouled rails and a clang as the hatch automatically rolled back into position and mag-sealed itself back into its socket. And just in time – a rushing thrum from the pipe meant that the next blast of gas and ash was back on its proper way again.

Symeon peered upward. The top of the partition was only visible as a faint yellowish glow through the settling ash, but with a thought and a careful series of eye gestures he brought up the schematics he had inloaded in the briefing. The green and white lines matched what he could see of the ladders and stairs. Nothing seemed to have been re-engineered. The rail-carriage would be waiting at the top, ready to carry them deeper into the volcano's mazes. And from there, well, they would see.

He sent a blink-quick flare of power down Akanthe's blade, crisping off the blood that had stuck to it, and clipped the sword back into place at his waist.

'Let's climb,' he said, and led the way to the stairs.

* * *

Erasmos
Partition 510 transport station, Old Ourezhad

The cable-tram line went along the tops of the venting partitions and terminated at a junction in the guts of some utility hub up ahead. As targets went that was low enough priority to almost fall off the list. They needed to get off the rail line and go higher.

Symeon had been toying with a couple of different plans for the tram as they had clambered up from the bottom of Partition 510: packing it with explosives and sending it on down the line as a diversion, or getting the same effect with greater economy by simply accelerating it to lethal speed to plough through whatever got in its way. Their briefings about the machinery they could expect to find had been thorough, and Symeon did not anticipate having any difficulty with the carriage controls, or finding any safeguards built into it this far beneath the complex.

In the end, they simply got in it. One look at the banged-up old machine made it obvious that it wasn't actually capable of going fast enough to use as a weapon, and after the climb Symeon was anxious to keep moving, prizing forward momentum over clever stratagems. Symeon took the controls himself and the others packed into the carriage as best they could, oversized armoured bodies clinking and scraping against each other as they embarked. There was a brief and ugly sound from near the doors as someone tore a pair of bench seats out of their mountings and tossed them through the doors to make room. The carriage swayed and creaked on its overhead mounting. Iacchos cursed as his elbow knocked a plexglass pane out of a window and his shoulder bowed out the carriage's chassis.

'What the hell is this thing built of? Tree bark and foil?'

'It must be rated for cargo,' Anysios said from the platform, waiting with Laukas and Serapion as the rest of them made space. Another torn-out bench seat flew past him and clattered onto the platform. 'They have to bring machinery along these lines, don't they? And it wouldn't make sense to have some cars for loads and others for passengers. They must be designed for all kinds of uses. Anything else is just stupid. In you get.' Laukas stepped past him and took his place in the carriage, trying not to notice that the floor had been crushed down into an uneven mess by the pressure of armoured boots. The carriage juddered as Symeon started the motors. One yellow forward lamp came on; the other had blown. The doors tried to slide across and banged repeatedly into Agenor's reactor pack until he got fed up and kicked them out of their mountings. The movement rocked the carriage from side to side.

'Are we set to move?' Symeon asked over the vox.

'Hold off a minute,' came Anysios' voice. 'How sure are you that that motor's even going to move us?'

'Weren't you the one telling us that this must obviously be able to carry a load?' Symeon snapped, but he moved the drive lever forward anyway, to test. There was a squealing groan from above them. A smell of burning lubricant and hot metal drifted down to them, strengthening as the carriage laboured forward a couple of metres.

'I counsel that...' Anysios began, but Serapion was already pushing his way onto the carriage. Something overhead squealed again and then came the rapid *tunk-tunk-tunk* of parting metal joints. The set of grips that held the carriage to the right-hand rail popped apart and tore loose, the left-hand grips followed a second later and the carriage crashed down onto the bed of the tunnel. Anysios watched pungent blue smoke curl up from the motor mounts along the roof.

'For what it's worth,' he said, strolling to the front of the carriage as Symeon kicked out the forward-facing windows and tore the struts apart so he could climb out, 'there was no way that thing would have carried us faster than we can run, anyway.'

'For what it's *worth*,' Symeon shot back at him, 'this isn't as funny as you seem to think. Running armour echoing down the tunnel is going to send out a fanfare that we're on our way. Perhaps you could turn your mind to dealing with that instead.' Behind him more metal tore as the squad disentangled themselves from the wreck.

'We forget the air scrubber wells we were heading for,' Anysios said. 'Too much tunnel travel on foot now we know we can't reliably use their own vehicles. The next load depot is three stations down. It links the levels and passes through the refinery complexes to lift out the heavy stuff they can't pipe out. I counsel we go through the refineries, follow the power conduits through to the forges. That puts us back on our original run, from the forges over the top of the turbine houses and into the Mechanicus spike.'

'Consider your briefings, all of you,' Symeon said. 'Has anyone anything to add to Anysios?'

'Support him,' Laukas said. 'The run to that third station should be easy. Even if they've missed the crew by now, they won't know why.'

'We'll be fighting hard by the refineries,' Iacchos said, inspecting the belled-out nozzle of his flamer. 'They'll be good ground for us, natural advantages.' He tilted his helmeted head back to the ash-filled Partition 510 to illustrate his meaning.

'And any man smart enough not to get aboard that rickety little bucket is worth listening to,' added Apothecary Spiridon. 'Sergeant?'

'So ordered,' said Symeon. 'Run hard.'

Erasmos
Partition Transduct, Old Ourezhad

Erasmos Squad looked hopelessly encumbered, each of them bundled about with breaching charges, demolition packs and magazines, but none of it was apparent in their gait. They came down the tunnel with a deafening clamour of armour on rock that echoed out in front of them and reverberated after they had passed. They passed through the dark spread out in a zigzag line that would make it harder for a surprise attack or pitfall to claim all of them; when the dirty orange lights of the platform started to show ahead of them they sped up even more, packed together, and raced through the little patch of visible track so fast that anyone watching would barely have had the time to process what they were seeing before the Space Marines were gone again.

The second station was another partition like the one they had ascended through, and the overhead rails continued right over the pit and away down the other side. Erasmos didn't miss a beat, going over the drop in pairs, hand over hand along the overhead rails with their weapons slammed into magnetic hold points on their armour or packs. Still they had seen no one, heard no alert, drawn no fire. That changed.

'Too early for the station,' Symeon voxed as light came pouring around the curve of the tunnel ahead of them. ''Ware and ready.' Agenor moved up beside him, flamer raised, and

Erasmos fanned out behind them into a gun line. They ran through the curve and into the lights.

It was a haulage platform, an open flatbed hanging from the rails with a control cage instead of an enclosed cab. The lights were its running lights. The driver hadn't bothered to turn the headlights on. He hadn't thought there was anything around the tunnel he'd need to see.

He just had time to register the sound, gawp at the moving shapes rushing at him, and then was reaching for the headlight trigger when Akanthe was thrust through the front panel of the control cage and through his heart. He jerked once and died before he even had the chance to hear Agenor saying, 'Where were you when we needed you?' as the Iron Snakes leapt up and onto the flatbed.

Even built like it was, it creaked under the load. The truck bed was scattered with chemical drums and equipment cases, sloppily dumped on it any which way, and as Symeon tore the rest of the cage free and dumped it onto the tracks on top of the dead driver, the rest of Erasmos began stacking the trunks along the back and right side of the flatbed, high enough they could half-crouch behind them and not be seen from the platform.

'You're right, Anysios,' Agenor said. 'All the railcars would need to be built the same, wouldn't they? After all, it would be stupid to make different kinds.'

'Gentle and forgiving humour is most becoming in a battle-brother,' Anysios answered him, hefting a case into position. 'And it's a fine honour to a warrior to have his squad appreciate his qualities.'

'Are you getting yourselves ready to chatter, or to shoot?' demanded Demetios from the truck's front corner.

'The God-Emperor, in His grace, has blessed us with a design capable of both,' Agenor told him. The lights of the station were washing over the front of the hauler now, and a moment later they were in the open space of the freight hub. There were voices from the other side of the wall of cases, questions shouted, confused and irritated, not yet angry.

'Case in point,' Agenor said. 'Observe.' And he reared up, kicked a hole in the stacked barricade of cases and stepped through it, flamer blasting an incandescent cloud through the air in front of him.

Hauler Grey-347
West-Three freight hangar, Old Ourezhad

The hauler servitor was alone in the freight hangar.

There were not many servitors left in the lower levels of the mountain. Most of them had been seized as the battlefront drew closer, and put to work hauling munitions onto the docks or wired into gun emplacements or crude improvised fighting machines. Many of the ones that were left had shut down and died, of mechanical failure, malnutrition or infections to their organics that should have been easily preventable. But a lot of the people who had known how to properly look after servitors were gone too. Some might be using their skills on those repurposed battle servitors, but mostly they had just come up unlucky in the regular lots the controllers made them draw, dragged up to the surface to put on an ochre bandana, given a second-rate lasgun to grip and put on a boat for the front.

There was talk that some were sent deeper into the mountain, instead of out to the war. The talk did not tend to speculate on what that might be for.

The servitor was there to drag this level's refinery products to the central lift. It could read serial numbers and match letter strings to destination codes. It could tell an empty drum or case from one that was full of chemical distillates or mineral bricks. It could run for hours off a handful of carefully worded commands from one of its authorised instructors.

It sat on its four stubby steel legs in a side passage that led to the ablutories and bunk rooms. Its head was tilted slightly forward and its bony torso slumped, the pallid skin sagging. Its organic arms, cut off at the forearm and spliced into bundles of cables that controlled its cargo-grips, hung by its sides. Its mouth hung open, although its dry white tongue didn't taste the smoke in the air. It awaited instructions.

Two of its authorised instructors lay burning in the mouth of the passage. The servitor had heard them shouting, but their demands to know what was going on and then their dying screams were not part of its auditory lexicon and it had ignored them. It had registered metallic crashes and associated them with its accident-response routines, but those did not compel it to action at an incident unless it were within five metres, and the sound of cases and drums being kicked off a flatbed by ceramite-armoured boots were further away than that. It had no frame of reference to understand the sounds of gunfire, or the detonation of bolt-shells inside hangar system components or human bodies. Amid the racket it had heard one of its authorised instructors crying for help, and had awaited further context or instruction, but none had come.

Now the only noises it could hear were odd, hard sounds with a rhythm like footsteps. The smoke seemed to be thickening. Somewhere a particulate alarm went off. A shutdown siren joined it as some damaged piece of machinery or other announced its intention to power down before it broke itself. The servitor waited to see if anyone would tell it to assist them.

In the span of perhaps a second, a little intangible tendril of will reached down out of the hangar's wires and wormed through the cerebrospinal plug at the back of the servitor's head, and into its brain.

The head snapped up. Its organic eye was bleary and cataracted but the monocular in its other socket lit up bright and true. The red, swollen flesh around the respirator sealed over its mouth and nose twitched. With a jerk of its organic body it began clanking along the passage, stepping over the corpses of its authorised instructors without looking down.

It had timed protocols for dealing with fires and accident casualties if it had no other orders within sixty seconds of seeing them, but it was no longer under its own control. The wriggling, niggling little touch inside the back of its skull goaded it onward, turning its back on the flatbed hanging at the rail-tunnel platform and the kicked-over cases littered in front of it, moving it over the tangle of corpses on the floor, the burning tunnel-buggies, the shattered and blood-mottled freight-control cubicle, the shot-out surveillor pods. The sounds were coming from off the tunnel platform, in the nearest of the heavy-duty cargo lifts.

The servitor picked its way forward. Its own programs did not record the image, but the mind pushing it on noticed the idol as it passed. It had been a crude human face hacked and beaten into a drum casing, a safety glove resin-glued in place to stop its mouth. Now it was barely recognisable, viciously cut and scorched by a powerblade and then stamped down by a heavy boot.

The servitor clink-clanked its way past the idol and round the corner into the freight-house and lift bay. It was a tall space, brightly lit by caged incandescent bars, blocked out by great stacks of crates and drums. All the broad lift doors were closed, bar the nearest.

The monocular buzzed and zoomed. It saw the white light spilling out of the lift, shining off the steel-grey armour and the snake symbol on curving pauldrons. It met the gaze of the pitiless red optics of the Iron Snakes' helms.

Light glinted off a gun barrel.

'No,' a voice said. 'Servitor. Don't waste a round.' The closest of the enormous figures strode forward, filling the flesh-machine's vision. One gauntleted punch pulped its skull and sent the raddled little organic body limp. The mind's eye went dark: the pict units in the bay had all been destroyed. Half of them hadn't worked in months to begin with.

It didn't matter.

For several seconds after the lift departed, the lights fluttered and the sirens stuttered in what might almost have been laughter. And then light and sound shut down and the only break in the dark and quiet was the flicker and crackle of the fires.

Kalliopi
Southern shorelands, Oureppan

Half a kilometre beyond the wreckage of the freight-lifter they found Skopelion lying unmoving in the wreckage of the ash-brick outbuilding he had crashed into. The rounded lines of Astartes armour were designed to deny incoming fire a clean flat surface to hit, but the missile seemed to have caught the tiny overhang at Skopelion's waist and detonated under the rim of his plastron. Cracks ran across his warplate, and the ugly gouge under his ribs was filled with glossy flash-clotted blood.

Kreios was the first to reach him, but he didn't stop. He flashed a waypoint tag to Hapexion over the squad band and then sped onward, jets open on full, suspensors flicking off and on to add extra unpredictability to his flight. Kandax, perched in cover on a raised weighbridge, watched for signs of another shot, and when none came he sent a signal of his own and leapt after his sergeant. Hapexion vaulted the loading dock he had been sheltering behind and landed on one knee beside Skopelion, the heavy armoured housing on his left forearm already opening and sliding back.

The lower edge of the smashed plastron was too damaged for the narthecium's augmetic probes to work on, but Hapexion found an intact keypoint under the plate at his brother's sternum and clicked the probe home. The plate disengaged with a grind and a hiss, but the damage and Skopelion's posture would not let it come away clean. Hapexion was wrestling him into a better position when he heard Kandax shouting a movement warning and position, followed immediately by the coughing ignition of three rocket exhausts: Kreios' and Kandax's jump jets, and a second krak missile. He pulled the plastron partially open, accompanied by the crunch of splintering ceramite and Kreios roaring in pain and anger. Gunfire barked back and forth around him as he found undamaged contact plugs in the ridged black carapace over Skopelion's chest and pushed the probes home.

The shaped blast had punched into Skopelion's side, driving through the fused barrel of his ribs and pulping the surrounding flesh. The flash-clotting that had saved his life was now in Hapexion's way as the inhumanly fast tissue knitting kept trying to fight off the Apothecary's attentions and weld his side shut in a way that would cripple him. The combined neural feedback from the pain of the wound and broken armour connections had left Skopelion dazed and barely conscious. Had the shooters reached him in this state he would be dead by now.

The hormones and drugs that Space Marines could call up from their synthetic glands were astonishingly powerful, but also crude. Hapexion set the narthecium to work again. A connection to his own combat glands drew out an adrenaline derivative and fed it into the narthecium's micromachinery. There it was refined and spun into something subtler and more complex, something that could muffle the broken connectors screaming into Skopelion's nervous system and clear the stunned fog from his head. The other Space Marine's double heartbeat was still steady, and it only took moments for the drug to reach his brain once Hapexion had pushed it through the chest port.

Skopelion stirred and the rhythm of his breathing changed as Hapexion turned his attention to the wound itself. A scalpel-thin combination tool slid into the carapace and through Skopelion's skin, pushing out an agent to suppress the flash-clot, and with that done Hapexion cut and then tore the hand's-length, glass-hard scab loose and tossed it aside. A probe jabbed into the wound and unfolded into a set of spider-limbs that moved flicker-fast as they spun synthetic fibres across the gouge in Skopelion's flesh. They threaded fibres through the torn tissue, laying down bridges and armatures for the regenerating flesh to grow back along.

As they worked, another tool slid from the base of Hapexion's wrist to pluck blood and tissue from the wound. He tasted it with his augmetic senses, compared it against the bio-assay he had taken of every one of his brothers, and corrected for metabolic changes from combat and wounding. Hapexion felt tiny insectile movements up his arm as the narthecium's machines retooled themselves to adjust the formula they were producing. A dozen seconds later he was able to start coating the edges of the wound with a new gel coded not only to Skopelion's own tissue but to the exact nature of his injury, that nourished the wrecked flesh to grow and then goaded it to grow even faster.

This was the stage Hapexion hated, the wait amid the sounds of battle, to be sure the healing was under way, to know whether his brother would fight again. His nerves always drew taut in a way that Astartes deep conditioning and Apothecarion training between them had never managed to take away. Although, he thought, here and now the sounds of battle seemed to have–

'Elak eshet khou! Var tezhoi!'

The shout came from close by, off to the right where Hapexion couldn't quite see over the broken wall. He didn't know the words but the tone betrayed surprise, not aggression. He could hear booted feet scrambling through the tumbled brickwork.

He shifted his body to put himself between Skopelion and the new enemy, just in time for las-shots to score his back and shoulder. Scattered, glancing, badly aimed, but the second volley stippled the back of his leg, one striking smoke from the gap in the back of his knee. A frag grenade clinked off his pauldron and bounced down on a neat path right into Skopelion's wound. Hapexion caught it in his right hand, crunched it in his fist before it could detonate, then threw the remains away and drew his hand flamer. Without turning around he hosed fire around his whole right flank and back again, listening to the shouts become screams. Then he made a thought-quick adjustment through his armour link for a heavier mix and narrower nozzle and opened up again, tilting the weapon so the stream of fire arced over the wall to saturate whatever ground had remained sheltered from the first pass.

There were no more shots. Hapexion checked the wound again, grunted, spooled out and tore off a sheet of dressing that bound itself to skin and carapace alike and set hard. He pushed Skopelion's plastron back into place, seating the cracked and broken side of the plate as best he could. There was a quick double bang from the flames behind him as some sort of ordnance lit off. Hapexion left the flamer where it was and reached for his bolter.

Not rising above a crouch, he circled away from Skopelion and around the corner of the broken building. Two heavy forms lay motionless on the paving, the fire already eating them down to the bone in places. Another was sliding down from where it had been propped against the wall, thrashing at the flames that enveloped its legs. One had escaped the flames almost entirely and was pushing up to the broken wall again with a short-barrelled Urdeshi hard-round cannon up to his shoulder. He heard Hapexion coming and turned in time to get the bolt-shell in his chest instead of his back. The cannon clattered into the rubble with his wet remains showering around it.

The last survivor stopped beating at the flames on his legs and rolled sideways, trying to get to the cannon. Hapexion straightened and crossed to him in three strides, the narthecium unfolding from its casing again. The reductor drill was designed to punch through ceramite armour and rock-hard Adeptus Astartes bone to reach the progenoid glands buried deep in each Space Marine's body. It went through the soldier's ochre helmet and the back of his skull with barely more trouble than a steel chisel punching through an egg.

Hapexion revved the drill to its highest speed, let it spin in the man's brainpan for a count of three, then withdrew it and went back to his patient.

Skopelion was conscious and most of the way to sitting up when Kreios and Kandax rejoined him. They had Hemaeros with them, his armour scorched to black down almost the whole right side but otherwise unharmed and apparently in high good humour.

'They'd cut a slot along the back wall of some long damn building,' he was telling Kreios, 'and there was a battery of lascannons running the whole length of it. Big ones, I didn't recognise the pattern but at least the size of what our gunship carries. Real armour-killers. Nine of them, each with its own auspex, crew shields, servo cradles. Big, powerful ventilators, back of the room stacked high with drums of fresh coolant. There was a power stack out back that looked specially built, going down into the city fulgeducts with a strongbox constructed around it. Great stacks of spare cells in back of the building for if it dropped out, with pallet trucks ready to start running them in.'

'Do you need ammo?' Hapexion asked. 'Sounds like you had plenty of work to do.'

'I'm fine,' Hemaeros said. 'That's the thing. It was barely crewed. There were enough people there to run two of the cannons. The others weren't even powered up. I did most of it by hand. The Guard element was next to nothing, and I only saw a trickle of reinforcements coming in after I was well away to meet up with you.'

'Sko?' Kreios asked. 'You?'

'Almost the same.' There was clear strain in Skopelion's voice but he was in control of it. 'It was a proper plasma cannon, not those cage-catapults we met in Ghereppan.

Looked like an Urdeshi make, more like the Eotine patterns we saw after planetfall.'

'Images,' Kreios instructed, and grunted at the still picts from Skopelion's eyepieces that flickered past his vision for a moment. 'Monster of a thing, but it's as undercrewed as that las emplacement we just heard about. Am I assessing it right?'

'Yes, brother-sergeant. I saw auspex vanes but no display, they were using basic glass sights. Only Sekkite mass militia in the bunker, no Sons in the crew or on guard. I killed an ingeniant who seemed to be in charge of the furnace machinery but that whole section of the weapon was overheating and badly unstable before I got in there. I don't think it would have coped with even the low-level barrage it was firing, let alone full battle conditions.'

'I will observe,' Hapexion put in, 'that we've been hunkered down here since I arrived at Sko's side. Are we moving on, Kreios?'

'Thinking the same thing,' Kandax put in from his vantage on the weighbridge. 'We've escaped being boxed in once. We're weak enough to get crawled over once this location gets called in and they move in on us in strength.'

'Except, have you noticed?' Hemaeros asked. 'What strength? This entire seafront is supposed to be one of the most impregnable fortress lines on the planet. Never mind the enemy closing in on us if we wait too long. We should be in a pitched battle every single time we touch down. Where are they all?'

'Waiting for us to come and kill them,' Kandax answered. 'Armour moving but none of it close. I've seen no foot troops since you finished off that last nest. Some high-energy shots coming out of here towards the causeway, but mostly what look like batteries of smaller las and missiles. I've tagged two heat sources that seem to correspond to super-heavy energy shots like the ones we came hunting, but I've seen no actual output so far.'

'We move,' Kreios declared. 'Skopelion, on your feet. Condition?'

'I can walk and jump. Movement up that side is bad, I'll be clumsy in close.'

'Take Hapexion's bolter, give him your sword. You'll stand off and anchor the column, Hapexion, centre with me. Hemaeros, lead us.' He pointed with his sword. 'We're making for that pylon over the water there. Don't stop to engage.'

'That's almost at the causeway,' Kandax said. 'Are we withdrawing?'

'We are here to hunt,' Kreios growled at him, drifting up off the ground as his suspensors took his weight and his jump jets ignited again. 'But something's wrong with this damn place. I want to get close enough to get a good transmission to someone that can send it back along the causeway. I want Priad to know.'

'Then?' Hapexion asked.

'Then if he tells us to scout some more, we'll scout some more. But until then, we are going to scour this waterfront from end to end and show these incompetent slugs what a mistake they're making each time they fail to catch us. Move.'

With a chug and a whoosh of jets, the scorched husk of the little blockhouse was left empty.

Nautakah
Ninepoint Juncture power hub, Oureppan

'V-voi shet?' The voice from the bunker didn't quite dare finish its sentence once its owner got a proper look at whom she was addressing.

'Etoi vhar eshko boluch,' Nautakah said as amiably as he could. The back of his mind was sizzling like an egg on a hotplate as the machine scented the chance at bloodshed.

Once again he was at the head of a triangle of Chaos legionaries, the Tusk behind his left shoulder and the grey renegade behind his right. Cradled in his left arm was a limp body in a scorched and bloody ochre longcoat. The excubitor's remains were just recognisable enough to make the defenders hesitate and wonder. In most circumstances Nautakah would have considered such a trick thoroughly beneath him, but it seemed to have helped with the trike, and anyway, these enemies were thoroughly beneath him as well.

The three of them came walking across the piazza towards the trenchworks. The climb up the serried streets from the bay had been uneventful, disquietingly so even though Nautakah now knew why the city was so empty. But here, finally, were proper fortifications, ringed around a pair of pylons that framed a white minaret. The excubitor's memories had been scrambled and foul-tasting but the impression of the power hubs was clear and vivid, the routes the patrols had travelled between them carefully laid out. The hubs meant something to the Anarch's plan. And so that meant they meant something to the arnogaur's, too.

I know why you're here, Nautakah thought, looking at the ochre-uniformed shapes who were popping up to look at him. *Do you? I doubt it. You don't even know whether I'm supposed to be here. You don't think I am, but you're not certain. And you're going to die wondering. Which is no better than you deserve.*

His stolen knowledge told him about an armoured shutter-door, facing north-east around the curve of the wall, but that would be too much trouble to force. The porticoed double doors ahead would be easier. They just had these fortifications in front of them, that was all. They had been well put together: flakboard, gravelbags, razor wire, tank-teeth, defilades and gun nests, bunkers and soldiers, ringing the hub and extending away down the street to each side.

Trivial.

Agitated voices from the nearest hardpoint told him the trick had about run its course. He wound his arm back to throw the corpse in among the soldiers but the back of its coat tore in his grip and it flopped onto the road at his heels. With a mental shrug, Nautakah broke into a run as the Tusk's bolter opened up behind him and bodies started to explode ahead.

Nautakah
Ninepoint Juncture power hub, Oureppan

The doors to the power hub had been well secured; it took Nautakah three kicks to break them wide enough open for his armoured bulk to fit through. He was wet from chin to knee now and the chain of his axe puffed foul-smelling smoke where a dozen humans' blood was cooking off it. He hadn't bothered to waste shells ploughing through the trenchworks, but whatever was so valuable in here would be sure to have better protection.

He stopped, sniffed the air, found the smell of machinery, gun-oil and human sweat. He was right. This facility was live, the air was being circulated, there were other defenders here. He stalked forward into the gloom, sweet hot pain still throbbing in his brain, the Nails' appetite barely blunted.

'What is here?' The grey Space Marine's voice was a rush of echoing air that barely managed to be words. Whatever the warp had done to him, the mouth and throat behind that grey-and-gold faceplate were clearly as transformed as the Tusk's. 'What will we kill next?'

Nautakah looked around. The legionary's combi-bolter was nearly empty and he had clamped it at his back. In its place he carried a U-107 cannon he had ripped out of one of the trench hardpoints, a fat high-speed stubber with a swollen drum magazine hanging off its belly. As comically spidery as his surviving golden limb was, it was strong, and held the weapon out without a tremor. Just as well the Space Marine no longer had his own arms, Nautakah thought. The nine slender fingers grasped the weapon easily where an Adeptus Astartes gauntlet would have fumbled with the human-proportioned grip and trigger.

'Whatever it is–' Nautakah began, and then a grenade ricocheted around the curve of the hallway and went off almost in his ear. The smoke and blast smashed the air in the hall apart, but the Space Marines' senses recovered in a heartbeat and Nautakah was already sprinting around with his axe running hot. A burst of cannon rounds went past his ear and punched through the first two Sons of Sek before they'd had time to straighten up from the grenade, and then Nautakah swatted their bodies aside and plunged into the rest of the squad. He took two heads before the rest scattered, hurling themselves flat under the sweep of his axe and firing up at him. He shook off a shotcannon blast to his faceplate as he would a swarm of midges and exploded the cannoneer with a bolt-shell. Pain jabbed in under his right shoulder and through his left hip, and the barbs in his brain screamed at the insult, their bright pulse racing along his nerves, his body moving so fast that for a moment Nautakah himself lost track of it.

'There are more!' he bellowed, standing in the marsh of

bloody flesh that he had created. 'There are.' He breathed hard, brought his voice under control. 'There are more. I can hear them *deeper in.*' He was roaring again, shouting over the scream of his axe-chain. Another breath. 'I can hear them deeper in the building. And…' He closed his eyes. 'And I know what we will kill. *Who* we will kill. Aah. Who we will kill.' The shrilling of the Nails was abating, making way for a new goad. The collar around his neck was growing warm, the warmth crawling into his flesh, quickening his hearts and slicking his throat with the taste of hot brass. Nautakah grinned, panted, forced his thoughts into focus. Witchwork in the air. He had been right. This was more than a humble power station. He smelt lekts. Somewhere ahead in these passageways the Anarch had hidden some of his pet psykers for Nautakah to find.

He looked at his two companions, still standing and watching him. The grey helm tilted to indicate something. Nautakah followed its gaze and saw a crusted ridge down the side of his plastron where one of the Sons had got a bullet up under his arm and through a gap in his ancient warplate.

'It's nothing,' he said, forbearing to comment on the stump of arm that jutted out from the other Space Marine's pauldron. 'There will be a price for that, I assure you.'

'I thought that Khorne cared not from whence the blood flows?'

Nautakah stared for a moment, trying to parse whether he had been mocked, then shrugged it off.

'He doesn't,' he said. 'Nor should I. But there are times when my pride gets the better of my piety. I confess it, I am an imperfect servant.' He turned away, brain twitching at the twin goads from the lace in his skull and the collar at his throat. 'No more talk, now. Come with me.'

* * *

Platonos
Ninepoint Juncture approaches, Oureppan

The broad ring road around the power hub had been torn up and turned into a maze of trenchworks and hardpoints. Kapis peered at it through the magnification of his weapon's eye as Herodion closed the range. The fortifications were solid but they were not hardened like the ones around the Six Gates – he saw no heat-glow from powerful energy systems, no void signatures. What he did see was odd. Uniformed figures were swarming around the trenches but they seemed unaware of the speeder's approach. He saw no Sons of Sek, but militia officers and excubitors were running among the gravelbags and emplacements, seeming to argue. Some of them were dragging crewed weapons out of position and around the building. Kapis noticed several of the figures were bloody, some moving badly, clearly injured. As more of the ring road came into view he started to see some of the south-facing fortifications were damaged, barricades smashed, corpses draped over the edges of gun nests. Smoke rose up from several places. He could still see no sign that they had spotted the incoming speeder.

The code-bark came in: Dardanos' speeder had made its way forward through the twisting secondary streets and had eyes on the target. Kapis opened fire. Within seconds the trenchworks were smothered in smoke, dust and flying gravel and rockcrete chips, shot through with yellow flashes of explosions as more shells struck home. He let up just in time for the other speeder to go barrelling across the ring road, the white point of Hamiskora's force axe leaving a distorted track across the machine-eye. With a boom halfway between the thunder of a great ocean storm and the crash of a great wave, a surge of power burst from the head of the force axe, rolling back over the trenchworks, surging like water and flaring like fire, forming itself into whirlpools and thunderclouds and the jaws and coils of great ocean-snakes before it dissipated. Enemy soldiers dissolved, exploded, were tossed through the air. At the fringes of the blast they dropped their weapons and clutched their heads, staggered blinded and deafened, or fell to their knees trying to vomit phantom water out of their lungs. Then Herodion's speeder closed the last of the distance, wisps of strange energy coiling about it and trailing from its fins, Kapis breaking the surviving defenders with surgical single and double shots. As they reached the heart of the fortification lines Sergeant Iapetos barked an order and he, Alekon and Idas disengaged their grip and sprang clear.

'Rearguard away,' Herodion announced as he kicked his speeder forward. The sudden airy lightness and nimbleness was exhilarating. 'Beginning my sweep. Auspex sharp.'

'Good hunting, brother!' Dardanos called back. 'Fling yourself on the kill!' Herodion gave a bark into the vox that might have been an acknowledgement or might have been just a snort, and shot away.

Platonos
Ninepoint Juncture power hub, Oureppan

Like a man having to strain further and further down to reach the water in an emptying barrel, Hamiskora could feel the increase in effort it took to draw up another thunderhead of psychic force. The energy of the immaterium welled up inside him constantly, ready to burst into reality at the touch of a thought, like a powerful electrical charge leaping between two contact points. But two major battle-conjurations so close together would take a toll. Much more exertion at this level, and anything more than the most trivial psyk-work would force him to leave off waiting for the power to seep in. He would have to reach out into the warp to seize it and drag it out. Doing that would have... implications. To be an Iron Snake was to live shoulder to shoulder with mortal risk, but that only made needless and foolish risks an even greater crime. He would have to be careful.

He drew the power around him now, inhaled it with his mind, teased it out and rewove it until thought and power were moulded to one another. The glow of the crystal matrix in his axe-head lit his mind's eye and dimmed his simpler senses down to barely more than human level.

The white glow of the axe was joined by a red one as Atymnes poured power to the multi-melta, loading the firing circuits until alert runes danced in the corners of his vision. As the speeder careened almost side-on around the base of the minaret the great armoured shutter came into view, riveted closed with its base piled with sandbags. Nothing moved ahead of them – any defenders around this quadrant of the hub had fled for their lives.

Dardanos squelched the leading edge of the repulsor pad and let the speeder skid forward through the air almost standing on its nose, and Atymnes finally let the carefully nurtured artificial power surge loose. Normal doctrine was to focus tightly on as small a spot of the target armour as possible, to use the multi-melta's penetrating power to its deadliest effect, but this time he fanned the beam over the centre of the door. Instead of a head-sized hole melted almost instantaneously through the shutter, he created a rough oval of softening and deforming metal almost two metres high, glowing a blistering orange-red.

Hamiskora had borne down on the power still in him until it was compressed to a knife-point. Now he framed a ritual code in his thoughts and it burst out again, focusing through his axe like light through a lens. The psychic ram bowed the door inward then reversed itself like a tide, tearing the weakened shutter apart.

In the moment the metal parted Dardanos reared the speeder savagely back onto its tail. Through the controls he felt the resistance to the repulsor pad as the almost vertical speeder flew at the doors belly first, and then the sudden lightening as his battle-brothers dropped clear. Instantly Dardanos slammed the field to maximum gain. The speeder catapulted backwards into the air as though an anti-tank mine had gone off underneath it, making a complete nose-over-tail turn before it landed on the buzzing blur of energy, repulsors and suspensors squealing and heating in protest but their systems holding strong. As Dardanos wrestled his charge about and set it fishtailing wildly away around the curve of the building, the rest of Platonos Squad had slipped through the glowing wound in the shutter and were inside.

Platonos
Ninepoint Juncture power hub, Oureppan

Iapetos wasn't bothering to spend his shells. His broad-headed sea-lance was enough as he methodically and brutally mopped up the trenchworks. He drove it forward now, in a perfect fleche along the top of a trench, shattering the pintle-mounted lascannon with enough reach left over for the tip to go a hand's length into the belly of the frantic gunner. Iapetos dragged the lance back as the woman doubled soundlessly over, the quarter-turn of his body positioning him perfectly for a backhanded swing. The gun's other crewman was halfway through throwing a grenade at a spot half a dozen metres away where Iapetos had been two strides and less than a second ago. The swing lopped his arm off at the elbow, a spray of his own blood coating his face and blinding him. He was just starting to shriek from shock and pain when the grenade in his severed hand went off at his feet, blowing flesh and metal alike out of the nest to shower into the trenchworks around them.

'Las nest out, Alekon. Going to show myself, eyes to me. Ready?'

'Readying...' From somewhere in fortworks behind him Iapetos heard two quick consecutive bolter shots and then the squeal and crash of metal being torn and trampled. *'Ready,'* Alekon confirmed. With a grunt, Iapetos dragged part of the gun nest's sandbag parapet down into the trench and clambered up through the gap, letting his head and shoulders bob above the level of the fortworks, drawing fire for Alekon to spot. Some sort of mid-calibre stub gun cracked out a shot a dozen metres away, and two infantry-level lasweapons scrawled hot lines through the smoke and dust. Nothing came close to hitting him. That was all.

'No more crewed weapons,' Iapetos said. 'Make for those portico doors.'

'We can't rule out carried weapons,' Alekon put in as he spotted his sergeant across the ruined defences and increased his pace to catch up with him. 'We haven't confirmed clearance on all the trench lines, not even close.'

'Our objective was the hub,' Iapetos said. 'To weaken the fulgeduct grid and bleed power from the gate defences. And because this is where Hamiskora guided us. We can be satisfied there's not enough strength left here to trap us inside, so they cease to be a priority. We're not here to mop up every useless twitching bit of meat so the Militarum can just sleep-walk through to Pinnacle Spire. Idas, are you catching us up?'

'Affirm. Had a heat signature I had to check.'

'Anything?'

'Nothing. Ammo crate for a missile tube emplacement. Already hit and exploded, I'd spotted the burning propellant.'

'I don't remember seeing anything like that go up,' Alekon said.

'No.' Iapetos pointed his lance forward to the smashed defences, littered corpses and kicked-in doors ahead of them. 'And I certainly don't remember us doing that. Something is wrong here.' Iapetos stared around him, echoing the same unease that Kalliopi Squad were voicing in the bayside streets somewhere below. 'Little pockets of scrawny devotee militia. Defences half-empty or already in flames. Where are the beasts we were sent to kill?'

The answer to his question almost cut off the last words of it. The echo came bouncing around the ring road, off the building fronts: weapons fire and the wail of gravitic engines pushed to their limits. Shouting came over the squad band, abraded by interference from the power hub but recognisable as the voices of their two pilots.

'The far gates,' said Iapetos, and the three of them were moving at a sprint.

Platonos
Ninepoint Juncture power hub, Oureppan

'Leman Russ,' Panagis said. *'Dead.'*

'Fine,' Kryakos said. 'Keep moving. What are the others?'

'Front rank? One more Russ. Annihilator pattern, Sekkite livery.

And an AT-70 Reaver on the end. All cold, no movement.' Panagis turned sideways and sidle-shuffled between the Reaver's chassis and the entryway wall. His helmet optics were at close to maximum gain, showing him the blocky shapes filling the space ahead of them. He could see a shimmer of heat moving among them, the rising plume from Adrastes' plasma gun.

'One SteG-4 in the second rank,' Adrastes said. *'All the rest are those PTV-5 troop-trucks. No actual enemy so far. We've broken into an empty hangar.'*

'I don't believe that,' Kryakos said. 'We got shot at coming in. The power stack is still ahead. It's insane to think there's no opposition here. Epistolary?'

'There is an undercurrent of life here,' Hamiskora said. 'A feeling... but...' He swung up his axe-head as though he were looking into its soft glow for answers. 'It is *idiot* life.'

No one tried to joke about the word.

'Find what you can,' Kryakos told him, 'but we can't slow. Adrastes, cripple the fighting vehicles as efficiently as you can. Panagis, vanguard.'

Lights began to break up the murk. A clammy, ghostly glow came seeping through the air from no particular direction as Hamiskora let his psyker's senses drift more and more out of his body, and a thick dew began to form on the Iron Snakes' armour and the flanks of the machines around them. Through that came quick stutters of bright white glare as Adrastes triggered tiny microshots, as twitch-quick as the plasma gun's mechanism would allow, just enough to weld axles and sever tank-treads.

'Blood in the currents,' Hamiskora said. 'The smell of it. Not just spilled. Not battle-bloodshed. Something greater behind it. *Appetite.*'

'Keep looking,' Kryakos said as he moved past the motionless

Librarian and into the gloom. 'We need to know what's wrong here, because something is.'

The moment the words were out of Kryakos' mouth a sharp burst of wordless code on the squad's priority band brought a dark orange warning rune flashing in his vision, and his body reflexively snapped into firing posture. Up ahead, Panagis had found the Sons of Sek.

Platonos
Ninepoint Juncture power hub, Oureppan

'Corpses,' Adrastes said, stepping over the tangle of dead limbs and down into the circuit hall. 'But not our work. Is it? Who else of ours is here?'

The hall curved away to each side of them, wrapping around the power stack's shaft in which the flywheels whirled and the capacitors thrummed. The lights were on, although many of the overhead panels were dim and flickering. The hatch-doors around the outer wall all looked to have been sealed shut. There was only one hatch-door on the outer wall in this quadrant of the hall, the one the Iron Snakes had come through from the entry hangar. A handful of Sons of Sek had been trying to pull it open when they had died.

They had died together. Looking at the charnel mess plastered against the walls and floor, Kryakos judged that the last of these men had been extinguished before the remains of the first had finished falling. Not a single body was whole; some were barely recognisable. But the damage that had been done to them was recognisable, chillingly so. Kryakos knew exactly what kinds of weapons killed like this. He had wielded them himself. He was carrying one now.

'Bolt-shells and chainblades,' he said aloud. 'Astartes work.

I understood Platonos was supposed to be alone on this front...'

'...but we are not,' Hamiskora finished, coming down the steps after him. He was not bothering to tread clear of the dead Sons of Sek and flesh and bone crunched and squelched under his feet. His axe-head flickered like lightning off black water in a midnight ocean storm.

+We are not,+ he repeated, in a transmitted thought this time, and in echo of his treading feet, Hamiskora's psychic speech carried the ooze of blood and the splinter of bone.

Platonos
Ninepoint Juncture ring road, Oureppan

+Death is ahead of us.+

This close to the power hub, the raw current running through the fulgeducts leaked into the vox-band and jumbled it almost to uselessness. Dardanos and Herodion could barely make out their squadmates' voices as they circled the ring road, but the Epistolary's psychic call came through clean and sharp as a lash. With it came a flurry of images that arrived in their memories without passing through their senses. Empty defences that should have been full of the enemy. A curving corridor littered with fresh charnel that had once been the Sons of Sek. A mental ache, a ghostly reflection of something perceived with senses they did not share, a hot, sour psychic mirage, deserting the hub and fleeing northward...

...straight into their path.

Ignoring their auspex and letting the strange phantom certainty of Hamiskora's transmitted thoughts guide them, Dardanos and Herodion banked and spun their speeders around and inward. They skated through the air over a stormwater canal, vaulted clear of it using a little footbridge as a contact point for their repulsor fields, and then shot low across a patch of open paving dotted with the dusty hulks of cargo drays. Ahead of them, an ash-dump, rows of grey, dusty dunes and hillocks, pushed up here by long-vanished street crews who had never come back to clear them out again. Beyond that, the jungle-grove of girder and cable that was the power hub's northside switching station.

Herodion was first over the ash-dump, deliberately clipping the dune tops with the speeder's lower fins and then slowing and skidding in the air, pumping the repulsor field to kick a rolling cloud of ash and pumice out ahead of them for cover. Dardanos overshot him, dived into the cloud and came bulleting out of its cover and head first into the enemy.

He killed a Son of Sek, absent-mindedly and almost instantly, jinking the speeder to one side and clipping the man's chest and shoulder with the starboard fin. A second Son had brought his lasrifle up as he ran towards the ash cloud and got a shot off on reflex, then he was behind them. Dardanos and Atymnes both ignored him, left him for their comrades. Dardanos had a bare glimpse of the fence around the switching station, its gates pushed open, a Son of Sek on each side, half-turned, weapons pointing back inside. Then he was jinking again, slewing the tail about, finding a clear line across the open ground and away into cover and aiming the speeder along it. He hesitated for a split second, heard the *thud-hiss* of the multi-melta and instantly accelerated them away.

It was their comrades following behind who saw the lekt emerge from the station. A shirtless scarecrow of a figure with jutting ribs and one augmetic leg, he craned back over his shoulder to stare at something behind him. When he turned his head back, Kapis, in a blink-quick zoom through his weapon's eye, saw blood streaming from the man's eyes and nostrils, running down over the livid hand-shaped scar over his mouth that badged him for the Anarch. That mouth opened to speak.

There was no audible word, not even the psychic word-print that Hamiskora's sendings made. This was a scouring *gap* in thinking, an ash-storm sweeping the earth clean of tracks, a wave that drowned out and swept away the message Hamiskora had left them with. As Herodion and Kapis wrestled with the sudden static in their minds the lekt and his two bodyguards were boosted forward as if on a blast wave, three pairs of feet making comical running motions in the air before they stumbled to the ground more than a dozen metres on. A burst of las struck smoke from the speeder's angular nose: the Son that Dardanos had missed had dropped to one knee and was firing on them. Two more came running through the gates as Herodion brought the speeder about.

Herodion was coldly aware of how exposed they were, out in the open and slowed to a human's running pace. If any of the Sons were carrying a heavy weapon they were in danger. He dug the speeder's nose down, funnelled power to the rear suspensors and let the suddenly weightless tail whip around, reversing them in barely more than their own length and bringing Kapis around to face the Sons. Heavy bolt-shells obliterated the two men at the gate and punched the shooter off the ground before they exploded him.

When the heavy bolter came to bear on the lekt the burst simply stuttered out, and the shells that would have passed closest to him curved away into empty air.

Herodion snarled, and his hands and feet bore down on

the speeder's physical controls as his mental commands bore down through the interface link. Every scrap of his pilot's instinct and training was ringing like a klaxon: get moving, accelerate out of this position *right now*. The suspensors evened out, the repulsor flashed steady and the speeder turned smoothly, as if it had been on rails. The lekt was dead ahead of them. The way out was simple. The speeder's engines screamed as it cut through the air like a lance-head.

The lekt's mouth opened impossibly wide, the flesh at the corners splitting, two of his teeth exploding. Herodion felt the hot sandblasting of his thoughts again, but now he was prepared for it. A bubble of sound and distorted air welled from the broken-open mouth, and in a fraction of a moment had expanded into a dome like the first microseconds of a nuclear blast. The speeder's prow hit it and the whole vehicle was flipped upward in the shockwave, its systems dead, Herodion and Kapis blind, deaf and numb as the auto-senses in their speeder and their armour cut out. The speeder sailed high into the air, standing on its tail as though it were ready for an orbital launch, before it cleared what was now a whirling column of energy and arced back down. It hit with a heavy crunch of armour on paving and lay motionless at the centre of a web of cracked and pulverised asphalt.

Behind them the lekt was invisible inside the vortex of foaming, buzzing un-light. The power he had dragged out of his words in his raw terror had dissolved his two guards and was eating away at the air around him and the ground beneath him. The flick of a thought would have sent it out to eat away the speeder and the Iron Snakes trapped in it. What saved Herodion and Kapis was that they were not the ones the lekt was in true terror of.

* * *

Nautakah
Northside exit, Ninepoint Juncture power hub, Oureppan

The other two legionaries were somewhere behind him in the circuit hall. Precisely where, and doing what, Nautakah didn't care. At that moment he had forgotten that his misbegotten allies-of-circumstance even existed.

He came out through the minaret's hindgate at an easy lope that ate up distance at a terrifying rate. His bolt pistol was back at his hip and his axe held before him in both hands. The path through the switching station's thickets of pylon and cable was narrow and jagged but every muscle and nerve was singing in chorus with the machine in his skull and he travelled with an eerie, unthinking grace that was all the more terrifying for his hulking size. As he came in sight of the gate he saw the lekt in vibrant, feverish colour even as the rest of his vision washed out into drab hints of shapes and movements. The man was running empty-handed, carrying no weapon, and Nautakah's gut churned with the offence of it. The lekt shot a look back over his shoulder and the blistered handprint of scar tissue over his mouth moved and gaped.

Nautakah had his own scars of allegiance. They ridged across each hand, where he had gashed his palms against Urlock Gaur's armour to seal the Blood Pact. They circled his body, too, in a rope of tiny, careful cuts, from a far older ritual before an older and greater master, one he had loved and hated both at once and in equal measure. But he carried a third sign of allegiance too, to the oldest, the greatest, the most loved and hated master of all. The lekt had already had one taste of it through the rat-snivelling witch-gifts of his worthless owner, and had fled in terror as he felt it closing on him. Good. Well he might.

Facing him now, still not admitting he had been brought

to bay, the warpstained little runt went floating backward, drawing the whirlwind of energy inward like a shy coquette pulling scraps around his nakedness. Nautakah did not slow as his charge knocked the cage-gates off their hinges and sent them clattering off to either side. The lekt spat blood and began to speak, to give voice, not voice but Voice, calling down the Voice That Drowned Out All Others to echo through him and speak reality into a different shape. The vortex that surrounded him flattened into a whirling ring, crackling with the sound of a million tongues declaiming a million blasphemies. It came at Nautakah like a bolt of colourless lightning. The air boiled around it and the ground shattered beneath it.

It stopped. Like an electrical circuit hitting earth, it stopped. The lekt, stripped of every last trace of warp power, flopped backwards onto the asphalt, wailing and gurgling, fresh blood at his eyes, nose and ears just as when his mind had first brushed against Nautakah's presence beneath the circuit hall. Strutting arrogance and a skull full of tricks and witch-reek, broken in an instant by the touch of the brazen collar.

Nautakah walked over to him, every breath heavy with silver pain interleaved with the rhythm of his double heartbeat and the answering pulse from the metal lace in his brain. For a moment there was a deeper, slower beat in counterpoint, like a monstrous kettledrum, vibrating up into his senses from the eight brass links riveted into the collar of his armour. Then it faded. His arm was already turned out from his body, axe tilted away, ready for a short beheading stroke.

'Nothing more?' he asked. He could hear the jaggedness in his voice, the Nails trying to push him into screaming, and controlled himself. There was no satisfaction of conquest in this, just the itching need to expunge the insult in front of him and have done with it. 'No weapon to draw? Not even a fist to make? Are you so degenerate that you've left every instrument of the warrior's trade behind, in favour of a skull full of tainted smoke?'

With each word it took less of an effort to keep his voice smooth. He studied the lekt's face but there was nothing to read in it.

'There is only one worthy use for such a skull,' he said. The teeth of his axe bit home.

He let the breath out from all three of his lungs. Colour swam back out to the corners of his vision. The gouge and burn in his brain faded to a hot scratching. His mind began to move more freely, like a locked muscle warming and unknotting, letting him think again. Before this vermin had commandeered his attention he had been on his way inward, through the Sekkite lines. That journey wasn't close to being over. There was still an account to settle.

His head snapped around at a shot from behind him: the distinctive chug-scream of the Tusk legionary's boltgun. Nautakah's companion had planted his glistening bulk in the gateway behind him and taken aim at something away to their left. The Nails realised what it was before Nautakah's conscious mind did, and suddenly his body and mind were lit again, lit with a glorious, agonising fury. It was a speeder. An Adeptus Astartes speeder, crashed and immobile, and inside its cockpit he could see two Imperial Space Marines, one apparently motionless but one, deliciously, struggling to climb free.

Nautakah and Platonos
Ninepoint Juncture ring road, Oureppan

Kapis could hear his own breathing in his helmet as he levered himself up. Every system in the speeder seemed to be dead, their animas snuffed out by whatever obscene warp breath the lekt had conjured up. Even his armour was sluggish, its senses murky. He was aware of its weight and chill, even as it promised him through every feedback channel they shared that it was undamaged. His right-side helmet optics were almost out – he had ministered to them on the flight over from the Perrochyne hinterlands where they had been damaged, but now the maddening flicker was back in his vision, the world through that eye a stuttering blur.

Next to him Herodion was still working the physical controls, punctuated by momentary, motionless reveries that meant he was trying to send directly through his link. But the speeder was still inert and they were still grounded, unmoving. They couldn't afford to be unmoving. Kapis felt no fear, but there was a bright urgency flaring behind his methodical thoughts like lightning through a cloud layer.

The Tusk's bolt-shell struck the curved peak of his left pauldron, caromed upward and detonated against the side of his helmet. Kapis reeled away from the impact, biological and mechanical senses all ringing and useless, and only the fact that he was still partly coupled into the speeder seat stopped him from toppling over on top of Herodion. Steel-grey ceramite chips scattered around him. The side of his helm had been laid open to expose its adamantium bones and the precious circuitry of the Hephaestium smiths.

But as he sagged over to his right, his left arm was still lifting his bolt pistol. Stunned and half-conscious he might be, but reflexes deep-conditioned and battle-hardened for over a century kept him moving without a pause. On pure instinct Kapis reacted to the feedback from his armour's mechanisms about the point and direction of the impact and the microsecond before it when he had heard the whistle of a shell.

By the time his superhuman metabolism had kicked into overdrive, he had already sent a salvo of his own back along the line of the shot.

One ploughed into the pavement in front of the Tusk as it trudged forward a step. One skated off the side of its armoured thigh and detonated in the air behind it. One flew past it and blew a bundle of cables apart in a shower of brilliant sparks. The last one punched into the dead centre of its belly, where its armour was a wet lacework of rusted metal bands and ceramite scraps.

There was a dull thud as the shell detonated. A spray of greasy black fluid burst through the cracked armour at the small of its back and splatted onto the paving behind it. The Tusk rocked back, rocked forward and looked down at the wound. From its faceplate grille came a soft grunt, but it was impossible to say what emotion had just been voiced. Without looking up it fired, and fired again. The first shell hit Kapis' extended hand, blowing apart the bolt pistol and pulverising his fingers. The second hit his hip, splintering the armour, destroying the last of the connectors that held him inside the speeder and knocking him off-balance again as Nautakah came in for the kill.

Not a sound passed the arnogaur's lips, his only war cry the scream of his chainaxe. A great overhand arc took Kapis' left arm off at the elbow, blood painting Nautakah's faceplate and plastron before flash-clotting sealed the stump. Nautakah carried the swing through, twisting his massive body for another blow. Kapis was leaning forward, trying to get his other hand to the heavy bolter grips, but his wounds had made him clumsy, too slow. Another swing of the axe hacked away his damaged pauldron, another drove deep into his shoulder, the buzzing teeth spraying a mist of flesh and blood down his side and into the air.

And then there was a squeal of released energy from beneath them, a thump of displaced air and the speeder had leapt off the ground, the axe almost wrenched from Nautakah's hand before he could drag it free and stagger backward. Now he gave voice, screaming his blood god's name as a defiant curse, and Herodion answered him by whirling the speeder on its centre, smashing its armoured flank into the berserker's chest and face and sending him sprawling on his back. The movement almost dislodged the barely conscious Kapis, and for a moment as the speeder lifted itself higher it was tilted in the air, off-balance and drifting as Herodion grabbed his brother's arm, a slow and easy target. The Tusk raised its bolter for a more careful shot, sighting in on a line that in a second's time would lead into Herodion's right eye. A single hit there would be a kill-shot, but there was enough left in its magazine for a volley. It grunted again, and its half-dissolved hand moved on the trigger. Its hearing was full of the keening of gravitic drives, louder and louder, too loud, two sets of engines, not one, but the realisation came too late.

Atymnes' multi-melta blast obliterated the Tusk from the collarbone up, the armour cracking and flying apart as the flesh inside boiled away. The armour sagged but it had been locked into firing posture and there it stood, with a rising pall of toxic steam where its head had been, one arm coming away at the shoulder and sagging down to hang from the bolter by the hand that had not released its grip on the barrel. Dardanos' speeder whipped past a second later, engines screaming, already banked over almost onto its side and starting to come around.

Still sprawled on his back, Nautakah had snatched his bolt pistol from his side. Two shots burst against the flank of the speeder staggering in the air above him. A third punched into its belly and the cry of its gravitics suddenly became hoarser, discordant, but now a rune was flaring in Nautakah's vision and his palm and thumb were needling with alert feedback: one round left in the magazine. Snarling, he rolled up onto one knee and took his final shot just as the speeder tilted and spun again. The shell missed the open wound that was Kapis' shoulder, passed a finger's width in front of his faceplate and smacked into the vambrace on Herodion's left arm, punching home hard enough to crush the muscle underneath and dislodge his grip. The speeder suddenly bounced high into the air and Kapis toppled out of the cockpit and crashed head first to the paving.

Raving, Nautakah was on him. The axe was a blur, striking off his other arm, his leg, splitting the helm once and twice, gouging the plastron open from throat to belly.

'Blood!' Nautakah roared, standing in a mist of it, the Butcher's Nails turning every impulse of his nerves into sunfire and screams. 'Blood for the Blood God!' Everything was in slow motion. The wounded speeder was circling him, sinking lower and bleeding smoke but still flying. The heavy bolter in front of the now empty gunner seat was wriggling on its mount as the pilot connected himself to it. His peripheral vision filled with white, the other speeder sending up a blizzard of powdery ash from the dump dunes as it ricocheted off them to orient itself on him.

He launched himself forward. In the ecstasy of the Nails every movement felt as slick and frictionless as liquid mercury. He leapt, closed with the speeder, grabbed the leading edge of its canopy. The damaged armour deformed and splintered in his grip as he pulled himself up one-handed and began chopping at the pilot, hacking the front of the speeder fairing, gouging the control banks, sending the speeder on a dizzy zigzag through the air as it tried to buck him off. The heavy bolter stuttered out a quick burst, one shell kissing the curve of his helm and ringing his skull, another clipping off one of the curling horn-like vanes on his reactor pack. Nautakah swung his axe, batted the muzzle away, swung it back edge-on and struck the bolter bodily from its pintle mount. Before it had hit the ground he had levered one leg up and onto the speeder's front cowl, the mag-clamps in his boot buzzing as they looked for metal to lock on to. Everything around them was a spinning blur. Nautakah had no idea how in control the pilot was any more. It didn't matter. The Snake wouldn't get his pistol out in time. Another skull taken from the ranks of the throne of gold, to place at the foot of the throne of brass.

A blinding, choking heat flashed through his body. He could feel his flesh blister. His armour systems locked and his vision turned crimson. A crawling, drumming sensation ran from his shoulder blades to his hips, haptic feedback from the frantic efforts of his reactor pack to stay running as the blast slammed through it. The stink of scorched ceramite filled his breathing but he couldn't tell if it was coming from inside his helm, or outside, or both.

He lashed out again, half-blindly, and then there was a crash and a screech of abrading armour, his senses spiky with alert runes and haptic jabs, crushing pressure and external damage. The speeder had dived nose first into Nautakah and was pinning him down, bulldozing him along, using him to plough a furrow along the road's paving. The nerve-stretching rapture of the Nails was now a curdled fog of rage and pain.

His vision went blank, sounds almost vanished. There was a hiss as his armour began routing internal air stocks to him. With the clamour of the Nails filling his thoughts it took Nautakah a moment to realise what had happened. He had been driven right across the open paving and into the ash-dump, and buried in a collapsing dune of old volcanic soot and pumice.

His double heartbeat roared in his ears, driving at him to rise up out of the ash like a beast from the depths, cry out his god's name, plunge into the killing until his blood too was finally made welcome. He fought against it, caught his limbs already trying to move and froze them. His hearing was still muffled by the ash, but clear enough to hear the shrill song of gravitics pass over him then fade. The other speeder had overshot him. His reprieve would last for as long as it took for it to slow, turn and make its next pass. The multi-melta had scored the barest of brushing hits but he would not be so fortunate the next time it caught him.

He burst out of the dune, throwing up a swirling grey fog of foul-smelling powdered ash, half-prepared for another instant of searing heat and then oblivion. Then his head snapped around at the sound of more voices, powerful ones, the product of inhumanly oversized lungs, with the tinny overlay of helmet amplifiers. As the static fields in his eyepieces shook away the ash that had clotted them he saw movement at the ruined gates, where the corpse of the Tusk still stood beneath its column of smoke and steam. His grey-armoured companion came back-pedalling out of the gates, moving faster backward than the Sons of Sek had managed at a forward sprint, his remaining skeletal gold-plated arm extended to its full two-metre reach. The clatter of his looted stub cannon filled the air. A bolt-shell exploded against his plastron in answer, knocking his run into a stagger. Nautakah ground his iron teeth together and tried to gauge the distance from himself to the other traitor, from there to cover in the power station, listening for the speeder engines, calculating strides and seconds.

Then his erstwhile companion's cannon clicked empty and the twiglike golden fingers released it and plucked the combi-bolter from its clamp. Shells struck his thigh and knee but his armour held, and he only staggered a little as he fired a grenade back into the cable forest. Suddenly his pursuers' path was blocked by buckling supports and cables that sizzled and spat lethal current through the air as the Traitor Astartes ran past the still-standing remains of the Tusk and the keening of grav engines filled the air again. Only the one speeder, the accursed multi-melta carrier that had almost murdered him, riding in high over the ash dunes looking to finish the job, until they saw the new enemy standing there in the open, calmly raising his weapon at them.

The traitor's method was exquisite. He had read the movements of the speeder perfectly, predicted its trajectory, understood that its pilot wanted to stay high, out of reach of their quarry's chainaxe, knew that they knew that he was now the greater threat. It was a duel of anticipation and reaction measured in microseconds, and the traitor won it.

He took a graceful step forward and outward, under Dardanos' flight path, forced him to twitch the speeder's course to port so he could roll it down for Atymnes to take his shot. He fired his second-last bolt-shell into the speeder's path to force Dardanos to respond again, giving himself a precious fragment of time in which the speeder's movement was constrained, taking another step in under the multi-melta's lowest traverse as its beam drilled a crater in the road behind him, firing his last shell up into the speeder's chin as it passed over him.

The hit was not clean. Dardanos was better than the grey traitor had given him credit for and had jolted the speeder a handsbreadth to port as he turned, enough for the shell to miss the target point where it would have wrecked the melta's power feeds. But the detonation punched up through the speeder's fairing into the mounting rail, jamming the weapon in place and flooding Atymnes' senses with a squall of feedback while he struggled to physically yank his connectors free. The speeder yawed and spun, weaving a mad drunken pattern in the air over the ring road as the grey legionary let his combi-weapon drop to the road. His duel with the speeder had played out in less time than it took the empty gun to fall.

A bolt-shell smashed into the collar ring below the stern, gold-crested grey helm. The nameless traitor swayed backward, his one spindly golden arm clawing the air, before he dragged himself back on balance to face the three Iron Snakes sprinting around the outside of the power hub, two of them aiming bolters, the third rushing ahead with weapon raised. The grey traitor lunged forward, trying to close the distance to the Snakes sergeant and foul the others' aim. But he wasn't their target any more. They were taking aim at the figure hurtling at them from the dunes, trailing a comet's tail of ash and dust.

Nautakah had been running before he even realised he was going to move. Iron Snakes. Loyalists. *Enemy*. He was growling, in pain and with aching longing, the grip on his axe shudderingly tight. The lead Snake, the one in the sergeant's colours, carried a harpoon-like weapon whose piercing head stretched back into a cleaving edge. An enemy to be bested hand to hand and blade to blade. Hot metallic screams filled Nautakah's thoughts at the sight of it.

His pistol spoke and the furthest Snake had to twist and brace as the shell cratered his plastron, costing him his chance to fire as Nautakah closed the distance, unstoppable as a pyroclastic wave. The other managed two shots, the first shattering against the arnogaur's armoured flank and the second, by the grace of the Nails and the Brazen God himself, swatted aside by the flat of the chainaxe before it could burst in his faceplate.

Iapetos heard firing from behind him but no shots came past – this one would be his kill alone. He cast his lance when he and the grey-and-gold warrior were barely paces apart, hurling it at the precise instant his quarry was in a fully extended stride and unable to swerve or shift his weight. The spidery gold hand came up to bat the lance away or even catch it, but the warrior had misjudged its weight and keenness, the force of the cast, and the lance sliced through the augmetics, took away his first two fingers, smashed into the grey faceplate, bit into the ceramite and lodged there. A heartbeat later the two armoured giants crashed together.

Half-blind and disoriented, the warrior had still pivoted to take Iapetos' charge on his pauldron while the remains of his hand scrabbled at the lance now jutting from his face. He got his grip on it just fractionally faster than Iapetos managed, and yanked it away from the sergeant's hand, letting himself be knocked staggering, back towards the ruin of the switching station gates where the wreckage might yield him advantage or escape. A backward swing of the stolen lance tore a gash in the high fence and then he dropped into a crouch to put all his weight and the power of his legs behind the return sweep.

But Iapetos was too close behind him, already inside the swing. He kicked out, his boot hitting the lance-haft below the cleaving head, the impact jolting it out of the mutilated metal hand. Iapetos shot a hand out without looking and caught it by the head as his other fist crashed into the grey helm, knocking it inward along the seam his lance-head had already cut, punching it inward again, cracks in the ceramite now leaking an oily, heavy black vapour, and now he had tossed the lance into the air between them, caught it in his other hand, whirled it over his head to smash down through the ruined helm and the skull and brain beneath it. When he yanked it free it came away slicked with a thick white-gold fluid that puffed away into vapour and whispers as Iapetos turned to his second enemy.

Alekon had thought to feint the World Eater, taking a deep sidestep and reaching around his hip as if reaching for a new magazine, presenting his head as a target the chainaxe would not be able to resist when the creature thought his bolter was empty. Then a one-handed point-blank burst or an upward swipe with the combat blade his hand was actually going for, whichever presented itself the best. Alekon liked having options.

And Nautakah, who even in his killing fever had read the movement like a diagram drawn out upon a wall, feinted him in turn, opening his stride wide to invite a blade into the seam at his thigh, lifting his axe high to present the gap beneath his arm for a bolter shot, priming Alekon for the kill then sweeping the axe down early, ignoring the kill-stroke the Snake was trying to lure him into, hacking Alekon's boltgun in half and then crashing into him, running straight over him, bearing down on Idas, firing his pistol back behind him on pure unthinking memory. His shell exploded between Alekon's pauldron and collar as Idas' shot cratered the arnogaur's gorget.

Nautakah gave a retching laugh and swung the axe up to bat the bolter muzzle away; Idas tilted the weapon aside and back again, triggering his next shot as the axe came down, fast, too fast, the shell exploding in the barrel as the chainteeth tore through the weapon and drove it downward. Idas pivoted, trying to let Nautakah carom off him and stumble, but he caught too much of the arnogaur's momentum and went over onto his back, pulling his leg up and stamping at the side of Nautakah's knee, a kick with enough power to dent tank armour, to snap the joint had it landed squarely. But Nautakah had dropped his stance to ready a skull-taking backhand sweep and the kick caught his hip, knocking him staggering, the decapitation stroke changing its arc mid-swing to hook the chainaxe-head under Idas' leg and drag the screaming weapon forward, the spray of smoke and ceramite chips abruptly becoming a spray of flash-clotted blood flakes and bone shards as the leg came apart at the knee.

And then the head of Iapetos' sea-lance chopped a deep groove across the brow of Nautakah's helmet, knocking him backwards, the sergeant whirling his weapon to readdress and launch a killing thrust at the World Eater's broken gorget.

The lance-tip crunched home, dead-centre in the bolt crater, and stopped abruptly. Nautakah's left gauntlet was gripping the lance-haft so tightly that the metal was creaking beneath his fingers. The sound made a beautiful chord with the metallic squeal that the Nails raked from his nerves. Iapetos tried to pull the lance free, could not, could not even move it. The steel began to deform in Nautakah's grip. Pavement cracked and ground under Iapetos' feet as he dug in and bent all his body into driving the lance forward. Nautakah shouted for his god and swung his axe around.

The world vanished. Everything was a churn of weightless grey, as if Nautakah had been caught and tumbled by a monstrous storm-wave. Flying chips of pavement and gravel crackled off his armour. He was twisting and kicking in the air, orienting himself and halfway around to landing on his feet, when he crashed against the wall and then to the ground.

He sank down there, body and mind both dull and leaden, until a bright flash from the Nails scrubbed his thoughts clean like a wire pad on metal. He was on his knees, then his feet, pistol gone but axe already in front of him and criss-crossing the air.

He had been thrown clear across the ring road, into the side of the curved building terrace on its far side. The spot where he had stood with the Snake's weapon at his throat was now a waist-deep crater where a point of conjured force had detonated under the road and flung him backward. Around it were three armoured bodies, the Snakes he had just battled, one on all fours, head hanging, blood and smoke leaking from his collar and shoulder, one scuttling on two arms and the stump of a leg towards the bolter his brother had dropped, and the sergeant, only just starting to use his lance as a crutch to drag himself to his feet. There was a vicious, ragged gash running from his shoulder to his midriff – Nautakah's axe had made its mark before they were separated. The World Eater took in barely any of it, even the kill he had been denied. Another sight had consumed all his attention and thought.

A torrent of raw energy had come sluicing through the switching station, lifting the fallen struts and cables and shoving them aside, bursting the gates and flattening the fence. It flashed like lightning and glowed blue-grey like moonlit water, foaming around the figure that walked through it and out of the broken gates with its lightning-wrapped axe raised in its hand.

Nautakah's rage was choking him. Another one. Another psyker to kill.

The chainaxe howled in his hands. The edges of his vision were purple-red, scarlet and yellow veins pulsing across his eyes. The migrainous song of the Butcher's Nails filled his backbrain, and the only thing clear in his vision was the white outline of the force axe as the Librarian raised it. Pointed it directly at him. And around him, more enemy, more loyalists. More Snakes. Their eyes on him.

They took aim with bolters. One was unlimbering a plasma gun that glowed in his heat-sight – the flask was at least three-quarters full. Somewhere, the engines of the other speeder were finally growing louder again.

Too many. Too many, now. He had survived one charge across the ring road. He would not survive another.

Nautakah took a step forward. He couldn't help it. His foot dragged and scraped on the ground but it moved. He whirled his axe around him, bayed the name of his god.

But he took no second step.

The scene in front of him seemed to diminish, to recede and be overlaid by the ghost of another. A moment from the oceanic trenches of his deep memory, a scene he knew at once, had relived many times before, could not seem to forget. A city at the fall of dark, the lethal ice already forming across the distorted buildings and madly curling streets as daylight fled. The yellow tongue of a flamer jet licking out against the purple-black dusk under the double moon, even as the metal at the top of his spine sent flames into the dark of his mind. Into all of their minds.

The enemy still lives, their champion had told them as he took the flamer. Perhaps he had said more after that. Nautakah couldn't remember. He remembered there had been no words later, deep in the insanity of the night when he had found them again and there had been no friend or foe, just the work of axe and flame, blood and skulls.

But they had not all lost themselves. And not all of those who had managed to remain their own master had fallen to the betrayer that night.

He was more than this. He was no beast, no puppet. Sometimes a servant, but never a slave. He was the law of the Blood Pact made flesh and iron. He was an arnogaur.

Nautakah threw back his head and screamed in rage, frustration and pain. The drilling goad of the Nails, the beating rage of the throne of brass and skulls, his own furious soul rode the sound. It crashed and rolled out from him and echoed away through the empty streets. Time thickened and slowed. Droplets of blood precipitated out of the air and rained down all around him.

He threw himself backward through the broken wall and vanished into the building behind him.

Platonos
Ninepoint Juncture ring road, Oureppan

'Both.' Kryakos spat the words, and Iapetos felt an ugly chill in his gut.

'Both damaged? Neither reparable?' Iapetos asked, although he knew the answer already. If there had been anything to salvage then Kryakos would be at work now, cracking the armour and cutting out the progenoid glands that had nestled in Kapis' chest and throat. But the abomination's chainaxe had ripped their brother apart too completely, the gene-seeds destroyed beyond the Apothecary's ability to recover. The lifeline the primarch had passed down the generations to him had been severed. There would be no more initiates transformed into full brothers of the Phratry in Kapis' memory.

Iapetos looked over at the ruin that had once been a warrior of Platonos, now laid out in Herodion's broken speeder. The speeder's basic lifters were still working but the thrusters and directional repulsors were gone, and it could no longer move under its own power. Herodion would have to walk behind it pushing it along. It made a fitting catafalque. They could not bear their brother home just yet, but they would not just leave him where he had fallen.

Iapetos opened his vial. There was not much left in it, but enough for a drop of Ithaka's ocean to fall on the spot where Kapis had died and one to anoint the cloven and bloody helmet. It beggared belief that the creature could have done such butchery in such a short moment as it had had – but then, butchery that defied belief was the blood-and-brass traitors' stock in trade.

Iapetos opened his vox as Herodion took his gunner's remains away.

'Have we found it?'

'They report no contact,' said Panagis, who'd moved out to the edge of the ring road to try to keep vox contact with Dardanos as the other speeder went hunting for revenge. Adrastes was covering him with the plasma gun in case the bastard creature had hidden nearby to strike at them again, but Iapetos thought not. He thought it was gone.

'Hamiskora,' he said.

'Went back inside,' said Herodion.

'Did he sense resistance?' Iapetos found himself hoping they would find some living Sons still in the bunker ready to fight them. He knew that was the thinking of some hot-blooded neophyte, not a sergeant, but he had had enough of corpse-choked halls and traps run by machines and carrion. Platonos had been handed a loss that he was keen to hand on in turn.

'He found machinery,' Adrastes voxed back, and Iapetos couldn't stop himself from sneering inside his helmet. Of course he had. 'Void shielding.'

'Not a surprise,' Iapetos growled. 'This is a strategic target. We know why it would have its own voids. And now we know why the shields weren't turned on. Archenemy traitors did the work before we got here.'

'That's the thing, though,' Adrastes said. 'Hamiskora says he thinks it's not a shield generator any more.'

'This is about that creation we found under the assembly-house, isn't it?'

'Hamiskora can be a little hard to understand when he gets... outside of himself,' Adrastes said. 'But he says that the machinery that's been grafted into the power hub is cousin to what we caught the lekt trying to smuggle on that highway, and the hub's voids have been cabled into it too. It's not a shield generator any more. He doesn't know quite what it is, but–'

'Go on,' Iapetos said. He was passing his lance from hand to hand, taking comfort in the weight.

'Hamiskora said we'd find one of the Archenemy psykers here, and we did, but for the fact that that foulness beat us to him. Hamiskora said that was because the machine would need someone like the lekt to speak to it.' Iapetos felt that chill in his gut again.

'Has Hamiskora tried speaking to it?' he asked.

'No. But he says he's pretty sure that it's trying to speak to him.'

Nautakah
Hab precinct, central Oureppan

It was an hour before Nautakah came to rest, far out in the deserted urban waste of the Oureppan plain between the crater-ridge and Pinnacle Spire. He crouched his gargantuan form into a dirty little box of a ground-floor tenement, bending his head under the sagging ceiling and oblivious to the gouges his shoulder spikes had torn into the walls. He kicked the furniture away into splinters and knelt in the centre of the room, locking his armour in place and beginning the auto-hypnotic drills to bring his body to rest within it so his tortured metabolism could finally begin to properly repair itself.

He had made the right choice. The Snakes' numbers, their weapons. The plasma gun. Even the speeder's melta, damaged as it was. Had he run at them there would be no more skulls to his tally. All the battles of the rest of eternity would unfold without him.

He could frame these thoughts and know them to be true, but it did not blunt the jagged teeth that the engine in his skull was sinking into him, did not appease it for a thousandth of an instant. All that the Nails knew was that blood had gone unshed.

'No,' the arnogaur said aloud. He spoke softly but the augmented grate of his voice still filled the apartment, although there was no one to hear. 'No.'

Memories crowded in again. The madness of the nightfall,

hearing his brothers lose the power of words as the Nails ate their minds, hearing their voices become barely distinguishable from the warpscreams of their adversaries, rushing through winds that froze onto their armour in the wake of the betrayer's flames.

Not like that. He had sworn it to himself that night and never recanted. He would not become like that.

'I know you will welcome my blood,' he told his god. 'But you will not have mine until I have given you theirs. This is an oath I have sworn to you before. You should know by now that I mean it.'

His voice fell silent. The eyepieces of his helmet went dark. For a time he could have been a statue in a strange little temple, kneeling there in some long-gone stranger's empty, shabby home.

Erasmos
Outer foundry chambers, Old Ourezhad

'Demetios,' said Sergeant Symeon. 'Catch an image for me. Don't be seen to look or aim. There.' He moved his head and eyes, letting his helmet system tag the little speck of movement hanging high in his vision. With a quick set of eye gestures and direct neural commands, he had his armour feed the target to Demetios', whispering a quick blessing to both sets of systems for their sharpness. Throughout it all he kept moving forward in smooth, even steps, ash waste gritting beneath his boots, and Erasmos Squad followed suit. Dissembling was not central to the Iron Snakes' nature, but they were capable enough warriors to know how to act oblivious to fool a spy or an ambusher.

They were moving through the mountain-forge's foundry

layer, picking their way among the towering silo stacks like little armoured beetles scurrying about the feet of a Dreadnought. The mazes of pipework that fed millions of litres of chemicals into and out of the silos were mostly far overhead, lost in clouds of steam or particulate haze. Even the Iron Snakes' auto-senses could only pick them out occasionally, and then usually by the dim orange halo where some of the lights were still working. The mountain's workforce must have been hollowed out too much by the war outside to be able to maintain the silo chambers fully – the floors were drifted with dust and leakage that scuffed up into little clouds behind the Snakes and made dunes and slopes against the silos' sides.

The crunch of ash underfoot did more than get on the nerves. It provided just enough white noise in their hearing to blur the sound from above them. It had taken Symeon and Anysios several minutes to agree that the sound was actually there, and several more to properly pinpoint the source of it. As soon as he realised they were under observation, Symeon changed the squad's direction, moving away from their actual objective, slowing them down, trying to give the impression they were lost, or at least in no hurry.

Fifth in the formation, Demetios shifted his posture and the angle at which he cradled his bolter, so that the snout of its muzzle and the eye of its enhanced optical scope pointed up at the movement. There was no need to raise it and look through it like a human trooper looking through a sight; the scope fed through the bolter and into Demetios' helmet display. He waited until he had a good, focused image of the thing, captured it and passed it back to his sergeant, again without breaking stride.

Symeon studied their watcher, in all its unlovely glory. Too small to reliably tag with a bolt-shell, even for a marksman like Demetios. Possibly light enough to jink aside once it saw muzzle flash. Too high to grasp, of course. But hanging low enough for something else to work. Symeon knew their presence must be known by now, but that was no reason to let this thing just hang over them and keep watch.

Anyway, just looking at it, he just wanted it dead.

'Iacchos. Agenor.' He fed the picture and the positional data to his two squad-brothers. 'Quietly, so it doesn't bob up and away from us. We'll bear right. You outrig.' Affirmation signals flickered green in his display.

Erasmos Squad bore right, around a little headland of ash caked solid by some long-ago liquid leak. Iacchos and Agenor allowed themselves to be shuffled out to the left flank, under their observer as it kept pace above them, too primitive to realise the two Space Marines with flamers had taken positions under it, or too blasé to care. Agenor's 'Now' showed not a hint of emotion. The thing hung in the criss-crossing yellow-white flame clouds from his and Iacchos' weapons, then dropped soundlessly to the floor between them, sending up a little puff of ash.

Symeon walked over to it, entrusted an image of its remains to his armour's keeping, then ground what was left down into the ash and moved on, leaving nothing recognisable lying there. But as he led Erasmos around and back towards their real objective he brooded on the image Demetios had sent him.

The spy had flown on three tilting propellors run by tiny, buzzing motors, the source of the sound that had alerted the Iron Snakes in the first place. The eyes, glossy black and insectile, hung in a semicircle rig beneath it on hastily soldered brass armatures and poorly fastened wires. A little tail of matt-grey metal had hung down behind it, probably a transmitter vane. The frame that all of this was fastened to was a human jawbone, most of the teeth yanked out but one or two still sticking out of their sockets at bad angles. Scraps of bloody tissue clung to the bone and hung from the broken joints at each end.

There had been words between the squad leaders before Erasmos had been chosen for the mission to enter Old Ourezhad. Iapetos and Xander had both said it would surely take the expertise of a Martian-trained machine-priest to cripple such an edifice enough to deny it to the enemy, but leave it intact enough that it could be brought back to the Omnissiah with greatest speed. And yet with Argys fighting with Brother-Captain Cules, and Steropion still caught in transit through the warp-tides at the Cabal Salient, Pyrakmon was the one fully fledged Techmarine the Iron Snakes had on Urdesh. Could they risk the one man on the planet who could properly tend the machines of the Phratry's three other squads? In the end Pyrakmon had remained with Damocles Squad. Symeon, a veteran of many ship-to-ship actions in the Reef Stars, whose experience with entering and crippling enemy systems was well known, had sworn to Priad when he had taken the mission that he was equal to the job not only of breaching the ancient volcano's defences but of cutting its sinews.

That little machine, though. Servitors and augmetics were one thing, but there was a brutally heathen, effigy-like quality to that machine that troubled him. Who would go to the trouble of adding a piece of a human to such a device? The Techmarines might at least have encountered this before, or learned of such beliefs in their studies in the locked libraries of Mars. Symeon had long since outgrown the proud hot-headedness of youth. He disliked novelty in his battlefields. He still hadn't quite succeeded in putting the little grotesquerie out of his mind when they reached the silo cluster and it was time to climb.

Erasmos
Inner silo complex, Old Ourezhad

In among the pipework now, Erasmos Squad waded through drifts of hot ash up to their knees, in gloom so deep that they kept pace and formation by the shuffle and crackle of their steps, not sight. The silos and pipes gave off a scalding heat that filled their heat-sight with glare, and the dust and shadows distorted the light-intensifier filters to the point that they were a supplemental sense, nothing more.

That heat was their shield and concealment for the next stage of their mission, intense enough to mask the signature of an Adeptus Astartes reactor pack and lethal enough that no fragile human guard could fight in it. Unarmoured, it would have given the Iron Snakes some trouble, but inside their steel-grey warplate the only sign of it was the warning prickle through their neural links, the sensation their armour used to warn them when external conditions passed particular thresholds. Above them were chemical refineries, metal forges and enormous geothermal arrays drawing the heat from the volcano's core and turning it into the lifeblood of all the mountain's machines. That was their target, and here was their ladder.

Laukas and Agenor led the way, weapons stowed, each trailing a climbing-line behind them. With quick, sure movements they swarmed up through the gantries and pipes, using split second mag-locks of their boots to stabilise themselves or cling while they shifted position, ignoring the pulsing amber runes in their vision displays that warned them they were pushing the tolerances of their armoured gauntlets as they grabbed for handholds of scorching hot metal. There were no catwalks or platforms this far down, but the two Iron Snakes climbed until they found broad pipes or strut supports that they could lock on to and secure a line from, then readied their weapons and guarded the position while their brothers came up the lines after them. Menoetios and Serapion climbed past them, their own climbing lines ready, and kept moving steadily upward while Laukas and Agenor guarded the anchor point.

Anysios was in the lead when the explosions started. As with the little flying spy, he heard the thing before he saw it. It was a little ridged metal cylinder, wrapped and nested in twitching, wire-fine limbs, tap-tap-clinking towards him through a face-level gap in a tangle of pipes and conduits. Then he registered what it actually was, and he jerked back from the gap and was shouting a warning into the vox when the grenade blew.

It was a frag –not a very big one, nor powerful, but the slap of its shockwave and the lacerating hail of plastic flechettes were enough to knock Anysios off his balance and send him swinging out over a hundred-and-twenty-metre drop, cursing, his left eyelid twitching madly in reflexive response to the flechette that had ricocheted directly off his helm's eyepiece. Iacchos, clambering up a zigzag steel waste-flume three metres to Anysios' right, wordlessly found handholds, mag-locked his boots to the flume, and stood out from it at a comical right angle to gravity, bolt pistol nosing the air for the source of the attack.

Something rattled and scrabbled in among the pipes and

then a bizarre little thing with a fat, round, metal body and powerful rear legs like a locust's leapt out from the silo, caromed off Anysios' pauldron and detonated in the air between them, sending Anysios swinging and scrabbling for purchase again. It didn't hurt Iacchos in the slightest, but it ruptured the flume he was anchored to, which had already been groaning under the weight of an armoured Snake suddenly concentrated through just the soles of his feet. With a wrenching squeal the outermost side of the flume peeled away, Iacchos still anchored to it. He did not cry out, but Anysios heard a single gulp of alarm over the vox as he dropped out of sight. A babble of commands came from below him as the rest of the squad grabbed for handholds and made fast, and a second after that came an echoing clang as Iacchos was caught by his climbing line and swung in against the silo superstructure.

'Advancing.' There was no time to wait while more of the little grenade-bugs rained down on them; they needed to somehow gain height and disrupt their source. Anysios matched action to word, spider-scampering sideways along the pipework and then upward, trying to get above and aflank of wherever the things were coming from. For a heart-stopping moment he almost lost his grip when a corroded support came apart in his fist, and then he was back on balance, perched on a bundle of rattling, steaming pipes, bolter back in his hands, peering about him.

Through the pipes came a squeak of metal on metal. Anysios locked his boots to the piping and risked a lean around the vertical strut he was concealed behind. It only took a second to pick the fine metal thread lowering down through a gap in the works, something twitching and wriggling at its tip like live bait on a fishing lure. A blinked command brought it into magnified focus: a clumsy bundle of body scraps and metal fragments wrapped around another grenade. As he watched, the thread stopped and jolted, setting the thing free: it had been anchored to the grenade's pin. The ugly little fetish dropped half a metre and then suddenly unfurled four rattling insectile wings, which immediately fouled one another. Within seconds one was knocked loose and limp and one broke off completely. The thing dropped out of sight just before the grenade that made its abdomen went off. Shrapnel whickered and chimed all around him.

'They're lowering on lines and releasing,' he reported. 'That one was in a gap in the outer right quadrant. Brother-sergeant?'

'Ride them,' Symeon told him. Take the vanguard, keep the momentum, rock the enemy back for the rest of the squad to catch up and exterminate. Anysios grabbed the strut, swung around it and walked forward down a square conduit casing just as the next bug came down.

This one had a thick circular body with a small curving handgrip jutting from its back, some kind of melta bomb or krak charge designed to be planted by hand. Human fingers had been stuck around the edge of it, hanging down like spider legs or medusoid tendrils. Two of them fell off as Anysios grabbed the thing's line and severed it with a quick sawing stroke of his combat blade. He twisted and flung the bomb-spider backhand, sending it arcing out past where he had just been hanging, spinning blur-quick to grab the dangling end of the line before it could retract. In the cavernous space outside the silo superstructure, he heard the hissing thud of a detonation and a brief yellow light shone off the metal around him. *Melta, then,* he thought absently as he slammed the blade back into its scabbard and grabbed his bolter off its mag-clamp in the return motion. The whole operation had taken less than two heartbeats.

He pointed his bolter upward, one-handed, keeping his grip on the lowering-line. He was standing under a shaft created by a coincidence of spaces in the layers above him, their metal angles vanishing into the gloom even to magnification. He didn't risk standing under there, simply sent a shell speeding up along the line of the metal cord. The instant he heard it hit and explode overhead he stepped away again, dragging the line with him, feeling with satisfaction a moment of resistance before it tore free of whatever was holding it. There was a slithering sound as more of it fell past him through the gantrywork, and then its anchor point came clanging and bouncing down to finish its descent by his feet. It was a quick-release motorised winch, nothing unusual at all, the other end of the line threaded through the spindle at its centre and locked in. One end was scorched and deformed from where his bolt-shell had blown it loose of its mounting.

Anysios paused and looked again. Strips of human skin had been wound around each end of the winch spindle and tied into neat, ornamental bows. One strip was a shade darker than the Iron Snakes' own deep olive complexions, the other was pallid and rough with light brown hair.

Clink-clink-clang from above, and a thrashing starfish of jointed plastic and ceramite arms came scampering through the pipes above, a red light winking at its centre where a shaped mining charge nestled in a ring of wires and actuators. It weaved as it came, seeming unsure of where Anysios actually was, so he put an end to its doubts by hurling the broken winch into it, then stepping into a striding kick that sent the thing bouncing away through the silos with its front limbs smashed in. It detonated somewhere out of his vision, at the same time as another frag grenade went off not far over his head, peppering the back of his helm, some of the shrapnel hitting hard enough to trigger amber flickers in his vision and warning twinges through the haptic link. Faint noises from above him told of more on the way.

Enough of this. Anysios half-crouched and launched himself in a bounding stride to grip a stanchion, swarming up it to a raft of pipes and leaping from those to the domed top of a suspended chem tank where he balanced for just long enough to haul himself up into a V-shaped rockcrete pillar. As he went up his next two would-be attackers shot down past him, taken by surprise by his speed. First, a rattling centipede-analogue whose segmented body was a mix of frag grenades and human vertebrae with the gristle still wet on them, its uneven legs barely keeping their grip and rhythm; second a scorpion-thing whose triangular body was a shoulder blade, a krak grenade clenched in its wire claws, the little propeller in its tail struggling to hold it aloft. As Anysios began climbing again it lurched in the air, broke its propeller against a support and fell, wriggling, onto a gas pipe. There was the diaphragm-jolting implosive report of a krak charge, and suddenly Anysios was engulfed in an expanding white fog of superheated steam.

'Advancing.' Anysios was already fairly confident that the enemy's senses were less keen than his own, and this was too good an opportunity to miss. Navigating on memory and on-the-fly triangulation, he zigzagged up through the silo again, circling around the chute as more creations swarmed down it. He could hear detonations beneath him and all around him as the grenade-bugs came faster and faster, the shrill metallic notes of frag ricochets, the heavy thud of kraks and meltas. Twice the steam cloud he was climbing in turned dazzling white from a flare, and once was shot through with hot, grainy puffs of black when a thing made of a blind grenade lashed to a steel frame with strands of human hair spied him and raced to detonate before he could climb past it.

And then with no warning he was there. The maze of pipes and valves was beneath him; he stood up into a clear space surrounded by the peaks and shoulders of the chemical silos, laced about with walkways, stairs, control platforms and access ladders. Finally he had reached the level made for the human workforce.

There were no humans left any more. Just their enemy. Anysios had his bolter in his hands before he had even stood up, and was taking aim even as he stepped forward onto a steel-mesh walkway that creaked and dented beneath the weight of his tread.

'In sights.' The confirmation from Symeon was blurred by static but Anysios hadn't waited for it. His first shell was already in the air.

It flew at the pyramid of mutilated flesh and misshapen metal that crouched on a pallet truck in the centre of the lowest viewing platform. The front of the pyramid was made of two corpses, headless sacks of carrion in torn and blood-saturated menials' overalls, held up by metal girders rammed through their torsos from neck-hole to rectum. Beneath them was a bizarre tangle of whirring machine parts, mazes of glass tubes and retorts churning with sickly fluids, and twitching fragments of more human bodies. Twitching and *working*. In that assembly, hands gripped and turned and manipulated, in concert with bundles of awkward mechanical claws. Neon-yellow fluid pumped through transparent lines between them. A rack of eyeballs of half a dozen sizes and colours, kept moist by a constant mist of water from overhead nozzles, turned back and forth to watch the hands and the claws and the work they were doing. A mechanical eyepiece glowed green at the pyramid's peak and an auspex dish wobbled back and forth on a mast above it.

Some of the flesh was already dead, some of the metal was lifeless and broken. Some of it looked as though it had never been functional at all, but was simply crammed into the construction from the sheer glee of ornamentation. But the two cranes that extended out over the edge of the platform lowering their cargo on fine metal cords were working, and a scorched wound on the obscene thing's chassis showed where Anysios' shot had blasted off a third. In the cavity of its innards, in among the wriggling of fingers and twirling of dendrites, two more little bomb-bugs could be seen taking shape.

The first bolt-shell ploughed into the floor of that cavity and blew it into a crater. The whole edifice rocked and shuddered and the pallet truck's engine coughed into life, but before its thick rubber treads could start to move, Anysios' second shot whipped through the hole the first one had made and obliterated the drive cell. His third and fourth shots blew the top off the pyramid and then made wreckage of its centre. The structure started to fall in on itself as fragments of meat, bone and machinery pattered onto the platform around it. Rivulets of bright yellow blood began to drip over the edges of the platform.

Once he judged the thing to be fatally ruined, Anysios loaded a full magazine and moved to a safer spot at the corner of its platform, where the floor didn't give under each step and he could keep all the walkway approaches in his vision at the same time. He wanted nothing more than to kick over the little cart he could see hitched to the back of the pallet truck, paw through the spilled mound of grenades and munitions the thing had been using as its raw materials, and find enough meltas and incendiaries to reduce the thing to a puddle of bubbling fat and molten slag. He didn't, of course, because his brothers were trusting him to hold the lead point and be alert for more enemy while they climbed up to join him. He murmured trigger phrases to himself in ceremonial Ithakan, and let his conditioned thoughts settle into the smooth, unconscious flow of alertness until finally, finally the rest of Erasmos Squad came climbing up alongside him.

Erasmos
Foundry control platform, Old Ourezhad

'Has anyone else across the front reported anything like this?' Agenor asked. He was standing where the obscenity had sat on its truck until a minute before. Symeon, as repulsed by the thing as Anysios had been but unwilling to spend flamer fuel on incinerating it, had Menoetios and Serapion pick the truck up and throw it bodily over the platform's edge, down to the distant rock floor.

'Nobody else on Urdesh, so far as we've been told. Let's go.' Symeon unsheathed Akanthe and pointed up through the lattice of stairs and platforms to where a cluster of boxy personnel modules clung around the top of a rockcrete support pillar, spreading out as they climbed towards the ceiling in an inverted ziggurat of steel walls and dirty glass windows.

'So these are new,' Agenor went on doggedly, taking his position in the column. The walkways could take two humans abreast, which meant one Iron Snake. They were spread out, moving metres apart, trying to minimise their vulnerability if they were caught on the walkways where they couldn't manoeuvre. 'How long have we been fighting for Urdesh, now?'

'Since our own last landing?' Anysios asked, giving the superstructure behind them one more searching sweep before he fell in as the column's rearguard. 'Or since Slaydo brought his army into Newfound Trailing? Or are you going to go back as far as–'

'Give it over, Anysios,' Symeon told him, pausing at the foot of a long metal ramp to look about for more traps or spies. 'And Agenor, get to your point.'

'If these things, these…'

'*Things* is fine,' Anysios said. 'We all know what we saw.'

'I don't think the Archenemy brought these *things* in with them when they took Old Ourezhad,' Agenor said. 'They're new. Completely new, I think they've barely fought outside this mountain, if they've even been outside this mountain at all. I think this place is making more than just fabricatory jobs and refined chem and power for the island strings. I think it's been given over to making…' He trailed off again.

'Monsters,' Anysios said, and the vox carried a ripple of softly hummed agreements, the voxed equivalent of nodding. 'The forge levels are making monsters.' He turned as he walked, scanning behind them again as if the very word had conjured something into their trail, but there was nothing. 'I agree with you, Agenor.'

'Thank you, both,' said Symeon, 'for giving us all something to think on. I trust your instincts, Anysios, but all of you remember. Nothing changes. We came here to silence the forges and break the power feeds. Whatever else is going on here doesn't matter to us. We will do what we came to do. There is no more to the matter than this.'

'Aye,' Anysios replied, accepting the ending of the discussion, and clashed a fist against his plastron. 'Ithaka.'

The air rang as the rest of the squad repeated the gesture, and then Symeon led them up the ramp.

Damocles and the Saint
Keshriy Clade-House, Ghereppan

They had made her a hanging palanquin high above the street, so that she could look down upon the columns marching towards Oureppan and say her blessings, and they could look up and see her watching over them as they once again went to war. It swung on creaking cables from one of the clade-house's flying buttresses, salvaged devotional statues sitting awkwardly and not quite symmetrically at each end, the whole thing wreathed in paper islumbine blooms. Militarum and Ecclesiarchy banners hung from the whole length of it, undulating in a soft sea breeze and from the exhaust updraught of the rumbling engines below.

It was empty, of course. The Beati was down amongst her soldiers.

'They still don't seem to really know her, do they?' Priad asked aloud, then waved away Xander's curious response and led the way down from the doors.

They found her in the crowd by finding Natus. His battle-brother's massive grey-armoured shoulders loomed out of the throng of purple-and-black Jovani uniforms like an iceberg rising from a wine-dark sea. Priad and Xander threaded their way to him through the milling humans, moving with elaborate care. These women and men were about to go across the causeway to war, and none of them deserved to be crippled at the eleventh hour by the careless sweep of an Adeptus

Astartes hand, or an unthinking crush between a pauldron and a tank hull. Natus acknowledged Priad's hail over the squad band without turning around.

'Down there, between the two Chimeras. Right in front of Aekon.'

In among a knot of Jovani devotees, the Beati was invisible until Priad was almost on top of her. She stood with her back to Aekon, the wings of the aquila on his plastron seeming to rise up from her own shoulders. A long garland of islumbine looped many times around her neck, hanging down over her chest. The wind was at his back, thick with promethium exhaust and the faint tang of volcanic sulphur that seemed to be everywhere on Urdesh, but still Priad was certain he was catching the scent of the flowers each time he took a breath. Soldiers mobbed about them, calling to her, straining to catch her glance, the closest reaching out to touch her, some of the luckiest being given a leaf or a petal plucked from her garland. The ones who had already seen her and heard her blessing lingered on at the edges, reluctant to break from the moment and climb aboard their mounts. Disciplined though they were, the memory of her Miracle and the knowledge that they might never set eyes on her again were not easy to shrug off.

She saw him, and nodded. Priad halted and waited as abruptly as if she had spoken to him, and found himself wondering whether or not she actually had. Then he realised that although he had come down here to find her with the very clear message that he had been sent for, he could not remember being brought the message. For all his words to Xander about the strangeness of the war this was something that he had only become fully aware of since they had arrived in Ghereppan. The way the sureties of the world seemed to dissolve slightly in her presence. Hard reality. Cause and effect. The workings of senses he was accustomed to trusting utterly. As though she were a rogue planet quietly moving into an ordered system, subtly bending the trajectory of everything that came into contact with her. He caught himself wondering what it must be like for people like Milo and Kassine, who were with her almost every waking hour. What was real for them? Neither of them, he noticed, were here now.

'Carry His blessings,' she was saying. 'Walk in the light of the Throne, sister. Victory in Oureppan.' Every utterance carried her simple and total conviction, as if it were the first time she had ever said it. They repeated her words back to her, saluted, made the sign of the aquila. Priad saw tears on many faces. But gradually they moved away, thinned out. Tank engines were revving, and hatches slamming closed. The last two Jovani knelt in front of her, and Sabbat put a hand on each of their shoulders and bowed her head before she sent them on their way. The look she gave Priad then was haunted, her face drawn and eyes wide. Like many Adeptus Astartes, Priad had trouble with the nuances of human faces, but his combat perceptions were sharp, and his first thought upon seeing her face was that Sabbat had sustained an injury.

Then she gave him a tilt of her head and led the way between the tanks and off the roadway, back towards the north-eastern doors. Aekon went ahead of them, Natus hung behind. Priad walked immediately behind the Saint, blocking her from view, feeling somehow that the troops shouldn't have to see their Saint turn her back and walk away from them.

The high-vaulted rotunda inside the entrance doors was full of bustle, Militarum and Munitorum uniforms swarming around the checkpoints that led deeper into the building. An instant, respectful circle of empty floor opened up around them, but she still looked about her with an expression of dismay until she spotted the stairs up to the gallery that ran around the inner wall. It was empty but for half a dozen Guard sentries, but at a gesture from Xander they gave nervous salutes and hurried down the far stairs.

'I am troubled,' she said without further ceremony as soon as they had the gallery to themselves. Priad nodded as the other three made up a triangle around them, facing outward. He didn't press her, just waited.

'Dreams,' she said, and immediately shook her head. 'No, not dreams. Waking dreams. Visions.' She shook her head again. 'The same vision, each time.'

'Do your Sisters know? Does the Warmaster? You didn't speak of this to him at the Highwork.'

'They hadn't come to me then,' she said, with a strained little smile. 'I am... I'm not accustomed to this. When He has a purpose for me it comes in different ways. It is a knowledge. Simply there. I don't hear a voice talking to me. Sometimes He shows a portent which...' She made a cupping gesture, looking for words. 'My new knowledge might crystallise around it. But visions are so rare. So rare.' Her voice trailed off.

'Until today,' Priad said.

'Until now,' she said. 'This afternoon. Here, with those soldiers.' Her hands began to work against each other and she knotted her fingers together to keep them still. 'At prayer. Every time I prayed with them, I saw the same thing again.'

'Did they see anything too?'

'No. We said our prayers and they went with my blessing. I think I would have known if they had seen what I did.'

She fell silent again, and there was nothing else for it but to ask.

'What did you see, mamzel?'

'The Pinnacle Spire at Oureppan,' she said immediately – she had been waiting to be asked. 'In the highest cloister where the statues stand.'

'I don't know it.'

'Four statues look out through the four colonnades in the centre of Pinnacle Spire,' she said. 'The Soldier, the Labourer, the Magos and the Pilgrim. But I see the statues gone and the mosaics on the floor blotted out with blood. Then I am outside, walking the streets of Oureppan. Lost in them. The city is empty of life except for me, and as I look around me the buildings crumble to the ground and the earth begins to open.'

'And then?'

'The visions end when the prayers do. They have not shown me anything more.'

'What do you think they mean?' Priad was conscious of the rumble of engines outside, the troops moving, his brothers fighting through the city across the strait and perhaps dying even now. But he was also conscious of with whom he was speaking. The slight figure before him was the fulcrum across which unimaginable weights were being moved. He listened to her the way he listened to his own Chapter's Librarians when they told him things from beyond any realm his own mortal senses could operate in. He studied the changes in her skin temperature and breathing, the tiny adjustments in her musculature as she shifted from foot to foot.

'I think they mean there is nothing for me in Oureppan,' she said finally. 'I cannot think of anything else it could mean. And I've been trying.' She managed another smile. 'The weak, vain little part of me doesn't want to remain in Ghereppan now, brother-captain. It wants to carry my banner across the strait and raise it at Pinnacle Spire. Lead the triumphal march through the city. Be there to run the Archenemy to ground in some fastness out there and then burn it clean.'

'You're a warrior, my lady,' Priad suggested. 'I don't see the shame in a warrior wanting to go to war.'

'It's a fine joke, isn't it?' she said. 'Can you imagine trying to explain this to Macaroth after the conversation we had? But now I can't be certain. That is what eats at me. Listen, Priad. I knew that He had work for me in Ghereppan, but I let them persuade me that I didn't know that after all. And then when my eyes were opened and I came here, then His work unfolded as it should have. And once I was here I had such a sure sense that I had come to rest where I was needed. The advance would go on to Oureppan without me, and that was as He intended for me. But now the battle has begun, and I came out to see His soldiers who needed me, and I find myself doubting. *Wanting* to doubt, because suddenly the thought of watching them disappear down the causeway, and then just turning my back, climbing the stairs and sitting down to a meal is more than I can bear. I start to want to march with them... and then these visions come in my prayers. An empty city falling to pieces around me. I want it to mean something else. I want to find a way to think of it as calling me to battle. And I'm ashamed, because of all the times to become uncertain of His purpose, of all the times to suddenly want to lift my wishes up over His...'

'Have you discussed this with Sister Kassine?' Priad asked.

'I sent Kassine back up into the clade-house on another matter,' she said, and shifted her eyes and feet back and forth. Even Priad could pick up the evasiveness in her, although he was at a loss for how to respond to it – she had been the one human he had come to believe had no tricks or guile in her. He watched her, and found that he had nothing to say.

'What do you counsel?' she asked finally.

'The first thought that comes to me when you ask that,' Priad said carefully, 'is that I would rather listen to you than counsel you.'

'No.' She shook his answer off, something Priad wasn't used to from humans a third his size. 'I mean, all right, thank you, Priad, there is true respect in those words and I don't dismiss it. But I'm looking for signs of His will here. Do you understand? Imagine yourself scouting a battlefield, trying to spy out your course of action in the tiniest, most trivial-seeming clues.'

'Am I part of the battlefield?' Priad asked. 'A foe to be measured up?' He spread his hands when her eyes widened. 'You haven't angered me, mamzel, I'm honestly trying to follow.'

'You are part of...' She ran out of words again, sighed, and with no self-consciousness at all dropped down to sit cross-legged on the floor. Priad, feeling like an adult stooping over a doll, got down on one knee in front of her.

'Prayer is a connection to Him,' she said. 'The Adepta Sororitas lead lives built around devotions that bring them closer to Him, so when I am with Kassine and her Sisters He is present there, in another way. This city is a work devoted to Him because it was made over centuries by millions of humans in His service, so being among the people here is to be with Him in another way again. His presence infuses every human undertaking, whether the humans are aware of it or not. I believe that absolutely. The greater the venture, the easier the patterns of His presence are to see.' She looked up and around her at the walls and domed ceiling, as if she could see the Emperor's own hand in the las-scarred rockcrete. Perhaps she could. 'The machines that adorn this planet come from Him by a different hand, for which He wears a different guise and speaks to a different priesthood who venerate Him in their own way.'

'You're talking about the Adeptus Mechanicus.'

'And then,' she said with a nod, 'I have you. Your connection to Him is unlike any of these others. You were remade under His stamp. Your bones and blood carry designs He laid down. You are one of the ways He is present with me. I can't ignore that.'

'I think that our Epistolary Hamiskora–'

'No,' she said with absolute certainty. 'You.'

The two of them made a brief, silent tableau.

'All right,' Priad said. 'I still won't counsel you. But I'll speak my mind to you, frankly, as a war leader whose brothers are in battle there now.'

'Good. Go on.'

'Something seems wrong about the Oureppan assault. From the first messages back from Platonos and Kalliopi, what they are finding there is nothing like what we expected. The defences are token and brittle at most. At their least, they're just phantasms. None of the information that's coming back across the strait makes sense to me yet. Oureppan was set in stone in everyone's mind as the most formidable citadel in the system, but that truth turned out to be written in sand instead. That's the conclusion I want to jump to, but I can't quite make myself believe that it's that easy yet. We're missing something and I don't know what.'

'So you're in the same straits as me, brother-captain,' the Beati said, finally forcing a smile. 'We are both looking over the northern horizon and seeing a riddle there. What will you do?'

'I would stand my Phratry shoulder to shoulder by any other warrior in the Imperium,' Priad answered. 'The Adeptus Astartes were made to win over odds that look like madness to anyone else. I have faith that when they meet the enemy in Oureppan they will destroy them. When they find that riddle you talk about, they will drag it out and pull it apart and we'll have our answer to it. Then I'll form my judgement and command as I need to. Until then, I have my mission here with you.' He thought for a moment. 'That's really all.'

'Be patient. Await clarity. Have faith that it will come.' Her smile was genuine now. 'Thank you, my captain. See what I meant?'

'I think so,' he began, but stopped when she suddenly sat upright and shot a look over her shoulder as though someone had entered the room.

'The Thirty-Third Urdeshi Regulars will be passing us very soon,' she said. 'I want to be out there to greet them, and I will pray again before I go out. Priad, your brothers can remain with me, but I believe there is word from your Librarian across the strait that you will want to hear. We'll speak again soon.'

Without further word she shifted into a kneeling position and dropped her eyes. Priad watched as her muscles stilled and her breathing slowed to almost a sleeper's pace. Her lips moved slightly, but watching them to read what she was saying seemed disrespectful. Priad walked away instead.

'I think you're going to have to explain–' Xander began over the vox, but Priad hushed him. As they walked along the gallery the bustle below them grew in his hearing, as though sound had been damped down while he was close to her.

A man was waiting for them at the end of the gallery, shifting from foot to foot. His bony face, clumsily shaven hair and baggy Administratum tunic were barely differentiated shades of pallid grey. The shimmering green sash across his torso was a startling contrast, the elaborate gold brooch that pinned it at the shoulder even more so. A winged eye of gleaming sapphire beneath an Imperial aquila, the bird's claws clutching a staff and its blind right-hand head raised. The man was on an errand for the Scholastia Psykana.

'Brother-Captain Priad, you are asked into the Sanctum for communique receipt, s-s-sfragismen Karybd-tria-viridd.' The hoarse voice stumbled slightly over the unfamiliar words and fell silent, then the old man jerked, blinked and cringed back. Reciting the message had broken the trance he had entered when it had been planted in his memory. He had obviously not expected to come out of his sleeprunner's state to find two armoured Space Marines towering over him.

'Have you other assignments,' Priad asked the shaking figure as kindly as he was able, 'or can you perhaps show us the way?' The man gulped and nodded, and backed a full half-dozen paces away before he risked turning around to lead them.

Priad turned the code words over in his mind. Hamiskora. He noted his own lack of surprise, both at the message and at the fact that the Beati had known it was coming before he did. But for all her talk of clarity, patience and faith, his unease was deepening. He couldn't shake the feeling of being caught in an ocean current that shouldn't have been there, drawing him towards a storm whose force he could sense but whose size and nature he could not see.

He turned to look back just before they passed from the gallery. She had taken the posture he had held while they were talking, on one knee with her head bowed. Her right hand hung down, fingertips lightly against the floor, and her left was against her chest, gripping the islumbine garland. That sight brought into focus a thought that had been nagging at the back of Priad's mind ever since he had met her on the avenue. He had watched her plucking leaves, blossoms, whole sprigs from it to hand to the men and women around her, enough to strip the garland bare. But when he looked back now, he could not see a single leaf or petal missing.

Then they rounded the corner of the gallery and she was lost to sight.

Psykana roost
Keshriy Clade-House, Ghereppan

'The message came upon Adept Tschemherr,' the old woman in the flowing black told them, champing and chewing the name through creamy-yellow dentures. 'He wasn't ready for it, and the force of it wounded him a little, but he's still holding one end of the thread.' She peered up at him. 'Can you fit in there without breaking the archway? There's a necessary level of tranquillity that–'

'Thank you,' said Priad a little curtly, and sent the woman shuffling back out of his way as he stepped forward and stooped down.

The Psykana enclave attached to Grawe-Ash's command had set up their roost in the private templum that had served the clade's most senior families, commandeering it out from under the noses of the general's scandalised Ecclesiarchal party. They had made the most of the maze of alcoves, side chapels and meditation cells, filling the dim space with incense smoke and rows of tinkling chimes which Priad supposed were meant to be soothing. The incense seemed cloying and sickly to him, utterly unlike the sharp scents the

Phratry's Librarians used, and the chimes seemed to shiver and ring in erratic non-rhythms even in the still air. It had set his teeth on edge as they had picked their painstaking way through to where Adept Tschemherr was waiting for them.

The psyker was young, but his face was already taking on that sunken, half-consumed look as the rigours of his calling took their toll. Crossed black feathers were tattooed over his sealed-shut eyelids. Blind as he was, his hands moved with utter surety across the low table in front of him. It was laid out with thin plaques of black volcanic glass, blank of any design that Priad could see, arranged in a twisting line on an embroidered royal-blue cloth. Tschemherr kept the cards in constant motion, stroking them, tracing their outlines, tweaking them into slightly different positions.

'The Imperial Tarot,' Xander observed, peering through the arch as Priad hunkered down almost into a sitting position and carefully manoeuvred himself as far into the little den as he could. 'Are we here to hear a message or attend a soothsaying?'

'You would be surprised,' said the boy at the table in a lilting little whisper of a voice, 'at how that distinction can dissolve when you look it full in the face.' His head was still lowered, his sealed-shut eyes resting on a point midway between his cards and his visitors. His voice never rose above a murmur, but his diction was clinically perfect. 'As it is without, so within. The shapes we make within our minds cast shadows in the immaterium. The dreams of the immaterium are answered by what grows within us. The Tarot gives us a vocabulary of icons, dreams and archetypes. It mediates between the dreams in our minds and the dream that is the warp. The smell of seawater.'

'Clarify,' Priad said, catching himself in time to keep his

voice down. Whatever he had been expecting when they had entered the Psykana roost it had not been this.

'The smell of the sea is important to you. That was easy to see even without the two.'

'The two?'

The boy smiled and the tip of one slender finger brushed across a glass plate. For a moment Priad saw a movement in the glass that was not a reflection, something as quick and insubstantial as an after-image in the corner of the eye.

'Two of Seas,' the adept said, and tilted his head and nodded as though he had heard an actual reply. 'The major arcana are always the same. Some of us work with universal houses for the minor arcana also. I find more clarity when the minor arcana speak for their world. The Urdeshic Tarot is Sea, Ash, Hammer and Cog.' He touched a card again, and this time there was no mistaking it. The image of rippling waves formed in it, and then rose up from the surface of the glass in ghostly miniature. Priad even thought he could hear them. Then the boy made a pass of his fingers and the plaque was just slick, blank black glass again.

'You're a saltwater people, you Iron Snakes,' Tschemherr breathed. 'Seawater in your veins. You share it, blood and water both. Six of Cogs.' Another flick of the hand and there was the briefest hint of motion over another plaque, iron wheels locked and turning. 'The sea is so... fundamental to you, even as you're separated from it, placed on another sea that is so foreign to you.' Suddenly the cold tang of Ithakan sea air was in Priad's nostrils, and he gasped aloud at the vividness of the sense-shadow and the chord it struck deep inside him. 'Not as important as it is to him,' the boy said.

'To Hamiskora?'

'Holofurnace. The scent of the sea will come to mean much

more to him soon.' Pale fingers darted, pointed. 'Nine of Seas. Two of Hammers. The Throne.'

'Is this usual?' Priad asked the woman. 'To be bringing other... matters into it like this?'

'It's not another matter,' Tschemherr whispered. 'Your oceans are what make you, aren't they? The snake on your shoulder swims in the ocean. Five of Seas. The Kraken. The Space Hulk, inverted.' Glass clicked against glass. 'The first touch I felt from Hamiskora's mind was the touch of the sea. Cold, cold but exhilarating. It stung. Urdesh's seas are warm, warm and full of ash and silt. So I'm told.'

'Can you tell me what that touch brought you?' Priad asked, and the old woman stepped around him and bent stiffly forward. Priad noticed that she kept her hands scrupulously clear of the Tarot plaques, even though it would have been easier to lean on the table. He followed her example, tried to rearrange his posture to make more space between himself and the cards, but he was already hunched over and in on himself as much as his armour would permit, and acutely conscious of the warnings they had given him not to clash or scrape his great numb bulk against the walls and arches.

Tschemherr's breathing had sped up and sounded deeper, harder than it had. The black feathers on his face twitched as though the eyelids beneath them were trying to blink. His hands remained in tight, weaving motions, the pattern of the plaques changing with every flicker of his fingers. With another twinge of alarm Priad realised that the adept had arranged them into a familiar pattern. *The snake on your shoulder*, he had said, although he had had no way of seeing Priad's armour to know what his Chapter symbol looked like. But he had still named it, and now his cards were laid out end to end, the line weaving back and forth across the cloth, reproducing the Iron Snake of Ithaka in shimmering black glass.

Tschemherr gulped.

'The choir, adept,' his handler told him. 'Feel for the choir. Ease your grip on the symbols, feel for their minds. Can you centre your breathing?'

'I have it, mamzel.'

'The choir are burning Balhaut bloomgrass and ghente-salt. Can you smell the censers?'

'Yes, mamzel.'

'Describe the scent.'

'Perfumed, sweet white, white and red.' The boy's nostrils flared, but the perfume from the censers wasn't coming to him through his own breath. It was coming into his mind from the senses of the chorister psykers sitting in rings around the altar in the main chapel, as their etheric song surrounded Tschemherr's mind, meshed with it and made him stronger. Priad noticed tiny movements and responses in his armour systems. The ambient temperature had dropped four degrees, and its proprioceptor systems were convinced that there was something wrong with his posture and balance although Priad himself could sense nothing.

'Are you still connected with Hamiskora?' Priad asked. 'Can you speak with him now?'

'Give him time, sir,' the old woman put in. She had managed to squeeze through the arch behind Priad and had fitted herself into one of the den's dim corners. 'Our adepts' minds trail out into the warp like a net hanging out of a boat. Every one of them has their own way of sifting through what the net drags in to draw out the treasure from the flotsam. Talking is one of the ways.'

'Thank you,' Priad answered her, ignoring a non-verbal code from Xander that prickled into his senses through the armour link: *Hamiskora doesn't flap his mouth like this.* 'You know whereof you speak, of course. So please understand that I know the same when I tell you that I have battle-brothers, brave Iron Snakes, important to our war, who are trying to reach us through your adept here. You sent a runner with our Librarian's cipher to show us how important it was. We currently have no other way of communicating with his squad. I want to know what he's saying. Can you at least tell me,' he went on when she didn't respond, 'how long ago he first hailed you?'

She shrugged.

'The question may not apply,' she said. 'The deeper you venture in, the further you go from any meaningful relationship to time. Hmm. This message only went through the shallows. Not far enough for the dislocation to be profound.' She sniffed. 'Probably. My own educated estimate would be probably not more than an hour each way.'

'Each way?'

'Your Librarian's first hail struck Tschemherr just over half an hour ago. He might have first framed and sent it up to an hour before that, or we might have caught the pre-echo and the actual message is being sent as we speak. Or he might not know that he's going to send a message at all yet, but will find himself needing to send it in the next half hour or so. It would explain the effect it had.'

'Clarify,' Priad said. It was starting to take an effort to keep his voice down.

'There was a lot of storming around the contact when it was made. A lot of...' She broke off and looked for words.

'Churn,' Tschemherr put in. 'Blizzarding. Whirlwind, vortex. Shredding, razor wire. Broken mirror shards. Cacophony.

Harp strings breaking one after the other. Sparks settling on the skin. Cold.' His voice was starting to shake and the movements of his hands were becoming jerky, as if he were feeling a string of shocks to his nerves. The surfaces of the cards had clouded over with condensation. 'Cold as seawater. Drowning. The voice that drowns out all others. Listen for the other voices. He can hear me. Three of Seas, inverted, Nine of Ashes, the Harlequin.' The boy yanked a hand up from his cards and scrubbed hard at his scalp and face, grinding the heel of his palm into the sealed skin over his eye sockets. 'Corpses in the hall, corpses at the engine. Enemies. All right. I know, I know– aaah.' One shaking hand made a fist over the plaques, and they rustled and clicked together of their own accord.

'Queen of Cogs. Luna. The Inquisitor. One of Seas. Twelve of Seas, inverted. P-P-P-*Priad*.'

Priad almost physically started. The young adept's whispering voice had become Hamiskora's. It was slightly tinny, distorted just as if he were hearing it through a battlefield vox, but still unmistakable.

'Brother Epistolary. Speak.'

'There are psyker emplacements built into the Oureppan defences. We have broken one we found hidden under the minaret at Ninepoint Juncture, inside another bolthole in turn that concealed reserves for a counter-attack. It matches the wreckage from the highway, but a little more sophisticated and there are elements to the machines similar to the holding and sluicing designs the Librarium uses. Another component is a salvaged void shield generator, small, armour or Knight scale, that has been rebuilt into the larger engine. It had two of the Archenemy's lekts shackled to it.'

Priad's conditioning had kicked in and he could feel his

brain grabbing for each new piece of information, slamming it into his memory with eidetic force that was almost physically palpable, gulping after new data to create a tactical picture. The sensation was familiar and comforting, but under it he could hear something else. Even though the adept's mouth was forming words in that eerie twin to Hamiskora's voice, he could hear the boy's own voice speaking in whispering counterpoint, even though there was nothing to physically make the sound.

'The Lightning Tower. Seven of Hammers, Knave of Cogs inverted, Thirteen of Seas, His voice drowns out all others. One of Ashes, Thirteen of Seas repeating, may the Throne preserve me, may...'

Priad looked over at the corner. The old woman was watching attentively over Tschemherr's shoulder, her eyes on his glass Tarot and the images that flickered across the cards. She gave no sign of seeing or hearing anything untoward.

'Hamiskora–' he began.

'The lekts are dead. We think a third is fleeing to the surface levels. Intend to pursue. We believe this emplacement is a node in a network. Priad, have our brothers break open hardened locations that seem empty. The machines need normal power as well as psyker will to function. Look near power hubs, they will use the interference from the stations to drown out all others.'

Priad felt his skin chill.

'Hamiskora, repeat. Repeat last.'

'They will use the interference from the stations to obscure the power signature from the engines. Auspex may not be enough.'

'Confirm that you made no reference to drowning.'

'Drowning?' Tschemherr repeated the word in a voice that

dragged Hamiskora's voice simultaneously up and down out of its range. 'Drroowwninngg?'

('The Beast,' his own voice kept whispering below it, 'First of Hammers, Queen of Ashes. Please let me speak. The Astropath. Five of Hammers. The Despoiler.')

Suddenly the adept gave a sharp, barking cough. Priad smelt blood, saw the red flecks on the boy's lips. One of the glass cards flipped into the air, landed on its edge and ricocheted off the table. Several others were flickering as if there were firelight inside them.

'Bring the choir back down, *now!*' The old woman had lifted her medallion to her mouth and was speaking into a vox-pickup built into its face. 'Vitifers to stations, weapons unshrouded. Bring me a hood.'

'How long can he hold?' Priad asked, voice tight.

'Tschemherr? He's strong. He's meshed into a strong choir, the cards will buttress him a little further. He's not new to opening his mind in a warzone, so...' She shook her head. A few strands of white hair came loose from her black gauze veil and Priad saw they were damp with fear sweat. Her birthmark seemed to grow more livid as her face paled.

'How *long?*' How could she not understand the question?

'Three, four more minutes, one way or the other. He's had shadows fall on him out there before, but you never know how strong a given attack can be. If he can't break his trance in that time we do it for him. You may need to if the infestation spreads to the choir and the vitifers have their hands full.' She said it without a trace of hesitation, although she couldn't meet his eyes. Tschemherr showed no sign he had heard them at all.

'Infestation?' Priad shook his head. 'No. I don't believe this is just another phantasm that condensed out of the aether as a human mind passed it by. Didn't you hear the words he used? The phrases?' She stared at him with wide eyes. Between them, one of the glass Tarot plaques cracked in half.

'Priad?' Tschemherr was still speaking with the Epistolary's voice, but it was growing fainter, blurred, muddy somehow. 'Brother-captain! Be advised I will break the trance if I must, the connection is–'

'...*drowned*,' said Tschemherr in his own voice, 'drowned out with all others... all other...'

The lower half of the young adept's face had grown flushed, and then bright red as if from sunburn. Now it was as vivid as the birthmark on the old dam behind him. The skin around his mouth was starting to rise in blisters and veins of scarring.

'–before they can fix our location,' came Hamiskora's voice again. 'Priad, I feel that someone has hold of the connection.'

'Oh,' said another voice, coming out of the adept's mouth hard on the heels of Hamiskora's. 'Oh yes.' The skin around the young psyker's mouth was a churned mass of wounding and scar tissue now. Scarring that made a shape. The print of a hand had branded itself onto that smooth skin, a hand that stopped his mouth. The ritual sign of Magister Anakwanar Sek.

'Oh yes,' boomed the voice, and the old woman shrieked as half a dozen cards scattered through the air and burst into glass splinters against the walls. It was an unstoppable voice, rolling, resonant, hearty and amused. 'Oh yes, I think *someone* has.'

Psykana roost
Keshriy Clade-House, Ghereppan

'Nothing to say!' the voice exclaimed, Tschemherr's mouth making such exaggerated movements to shape the booming words that his jaw-hinges cracked and his lips tore at the corners. The rest of his face was utterly expressionless even as his body spasmed back and forth. 'Of course! Of course! You are here to listen. Your place is to listen.' A Tarot plaque spun up into the air and hung there, and for a moment the voice came from it as well as from the adept's throat, as if they were matching vox-casters, 'Your place is to listen to *me*.'

The old woman was crumpled far back into the stone corner as if shoved there. She had her medallion to her mouth again and was trying to speak into it. Her chest hitched and heaved as she tried to gather breath and shout, but all that came out was a hoarse and garbled whisper overlaid with a keening sound, sharp as tinnitus, that her throat should not have been able to make.

'Hamiskora.' Priad slid himself forward, still in his crouch, staring intently into the adept's face and keeping his voice rigidly level. 'Hamiskora, answer me. Status. Hamiskora. The connection is still open. Your mind is still there.' Outside in the main templum there were shouts, curses, gabbled entreaties to the Emperor, the strange half-nonsense of the Telepathica catechisms. A metallic clatter. A burst of screams. A small rune at the bottom of his helmet display changed colour as Xander signalled he was going to full combat readiness.

'Little girl, little girl.' The voice crashed through the side chapel and filled their hearing like an engulfing wave, thick with unconscious power and vibrating with merriment. 'Why such a temper, now? Has the thrill from your pretty little performance worn off so soon? Did your grand guiding star on His gilded chair not appreciate it? Did He shrug you off, you lovely, you brave, you fierce little thing? Shrug you off like the peevish, selfish old corpse that He is?' The great voice gave a rueful chuckle that reverberated in Priad's chest like the beat of a monstrous kettledrum. 'How shameful!'

'Xander,' Priad voxed. 'What's going on out there? Is anyone from the Psykana coming to aid us?'

'Choir is in disarray. One of them's been shot. One of the censers burst up, hell of a lot of flame, now it's putting out more smoke than a blind grenade. Smoke and some light distortion in the way. I can still see movement in there but it looks like the choir isn't completely out of control yet. Armed retainers at three other side chapels. One of the others has lights coming out of it.'

Priad thought he said something else, but the vox-connection was crushed to static as that hellishly jolly voice came out of Tschemherr's mouth like an avalanche.

'What an imagination you have, you dear slip of a thing! Is that it? Do you imagine yourself powerful? Do you imagine yourself to be His favourite daughter? Do you imagine a hand stirring from where it has clutched the arm of that golden throne for ten thousand years, finally reaching out to pat your pretty head?'

The old dam was shaking her head back and forth, her veil fallen half off now, more wild straggles of white hair hanging down in front of her face. Her eyes were wide and bruised-looking shadows were forming around them. She was pointing at Priad.

'Break it!' she hissed, and Priad realised that it was anger that had her as much as fear. 'End him and break it! The channel is tearing wider every second! His mind is anchoring one end of it! Kill him and kick it loose!'

'My Librarian has the other end of that connection,' Priad barked at her. 'What will it do to him? I will end my brother's life if I have to, but I will *know*. Will he surv–'

'Ah, but you aren't answering *my* question, though, are

you?' Tschemherr's stolen mouth thundered. The adept's body was tilted sideways at an impossible angle. He was gripping a cracked Tarot plaque in his hand, and smoke seeped from the fracture in it. A patch of grimy yellow-red frost had formed on the wall where it was closest to his shaven head. 'What do you imagine you've seen? What might you have truly seen? You're no different, little one. You're no different to every other carrion-puppet tramping in step on the road to the same end that your lifeless husk of a god has gone to before you. You think you've been raised up to the Throne's right hand, don't you? But all that's happened, sweet little Saint, is that you clawed your way up onto the backs of those around you and even that tiny change in altitude has addled you, poor precious pet.'

'Priad, I have a signal through from Holofurnace, bounced up from Aekon at the road. The Saint has bolted from her station at the street and she's coming up through the building. They're keeping pace as best they can. Whatever's wrong goes further than just the shelter.'

'Damn your bloody-mindedness,' the dam was yelling at him at the same time. 'One punch from you will do it, just d–'

'What a clever sprite you are!' the voice rolled out, and her words were lost. 'But not clever enough. I understand the body I disrupt better than you shall ever be allowed to, little girl. It is the river that breaks its banks that is feared, not the meek thing that lets itself be tamed with locks and dams. You hollowed out everything in yourself that was yourself, and handed what was left over to that shrivelled mummy on Terra to use as it wished. What a tragedy! To have been taught to hate yourself so!'

Teeth bared behind his faceplate, Priad leaned forward.

His gauntleted hand effortlessly encircled the boy's neck. A single motion would do it. But the choir was still coherent, and the vitifers still vigilant. What could be salvaged here? If he clenched his grip and pulled the head loose, what would he find left of his Librarian across the strait? Was he saving Hamiskora or damning him?

'Sabbat,' he murmured. 'Lady Saint, will you help m–'

'Oh, now!' the torn mouth boomed. The blind face was staring past his shoulder, through the wall, into some unimaginable distance. 'Oh, now, little one, but you *do*. They have sunk you so deep in self-hate that you think the only way to worthiness is to deny yourself so that you can be another. Twice! Twice, little girl, little *girls*. Sabbat denied herself to become a vessel for her dead god. Sanian denied herself to be a vessel for Sabbat. What did they tell you? That you were being uplifted by something greater than yourself? To be humble and let yourself be used? I grieve for you, poor girl, and I don't lie now, I *grieve*.'

'Priad!' Xander on the vox. *'Something's coming. Something–'*

'Humility is self-murder.' Priad could *feel* the voice thrumming in his armour as he held the psyker's throat. 'I would not murder myself, Sabbat, even with you entreating me to in your sweet, trembling little voice. And what a voice you *could* have! But you disguise it. Veil it. Slave it to a chorus with all the other pitiful cases, speaking into the dirt with your faces pressed into the ground because your *humility* tells you that's where you belong. If only you had had the chance to learn from me, rather than *Him*. I could have taught you to murder self-murder. To never quiet yourself because you were *told*.'

Light was coming through the arch behind him. Green light, growing brighter.

'I could have shown you what it means to exert your power

for yourself. To make your voice a voice which drowns out all others.'

The light was all around him now. Flickering around him like emerald firelight, beautiful beyond bearing. A breeze swirled around the chapel, chilly and clean as high mountain air, and the surviving plaques swirled along with it as if they were no heavier than leaves. Priad saw that the plaque Tschemherr had been gripping was gone. An islumbine bloom sat on the adept's palm in its place.

The Saint was standing beside him.

'*There* you are!' the voice guffawed in delight. And then she reached a slender arm out alongside Priad's great armoured one, placed her hand on the back of his. Priad watched his gauntlet open and release Tschemherr's neck, watched the cruel handprint stigmata across the boy's face fade and heal until the skin was as unblemished as before. The frost on the wall vanished. The voices outside were stilled. Tschemherr's body seemed to sigh as something was taken out of it.

'He's gone,' the Beati said. 'Be at rest. He's gone.'

She stepped back, and Priad moved with her as best he could. They both watched Tschemherr as he slumped back down behind the cloth-covered stand. The boy was shaking with exhaustion.

'Brother-captain,' the old woman croaked, still slumped where the force of the voice had pushed her. 'Lady Beati. Please. Once the rot is in there it can't just be slipped off. We're not safe. Finish it. We're not safe until you finish it.'

'He's gone, madam,' Sabbat told her. 'It's done. Your adept is a strong and brave young man. He has much more to give his God-Emperor. I won't let that filthy creature cost us a spirit as brave as his.'

'Xander,' Priad voxed.

'*Choir are at rest, far as I can tell. Their lead adepts are back in control. Some of the main psykers are coming out of the chapels but I don't see any sign of trouble, no taint. Smoke's gone. Those bad lights are gone. Aekon, Natus and Holofurnace are here. Khiron and Andromak are outside.*'

'Take the lead out there for now. Talk to whoever's in charge for the Psykana and do what they need you to do until I'm out.'

'Affirm.' Ceramite clinked and actuators hummed as Xander straightened up and moved away. Priad returned his attention to the scene in front of him.

Tschemherr was clutching fistfuls of his robes and rocking to and fro, his blind gaze once again fixed on the scattering of surviving Tarot plaques. His mouth opened and closed, but he was making no attempt to speak. The old woman was holding her winged-eye medallion up in front of her as though it were a shield. The Beati was standing motionless, hands open, controlling her breathing. She was looking at the same thing the adept was.

Eight of the volcanic-glass Tarot cards had survived the ordeal, snatched up and scattered again in the dying moments of the stolen connection. They had not landed randomly, but in a pattern as precise as though an engineer with a measuring laser had laid them out. Four cards closest to the Beati and Priad, a row of three behind it. The third row just a single card, perfectly centred.

'Eagle stones,' Tschemherr said in his own tiny, whispering voice, and pitched over sideways in a dead faint.

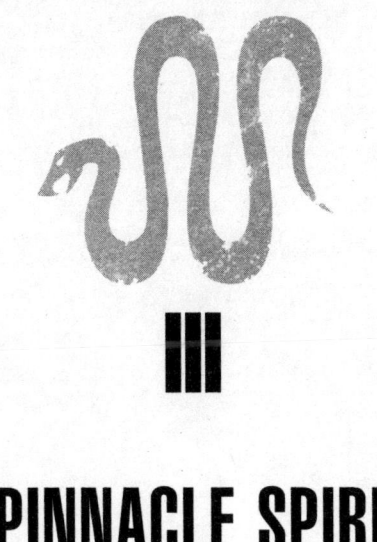

PINNACLE SPIRE

The Saint
Below Keshriy Clade-House, Ghereppan

It was Natus' turn to stand directly behind the Beati while she spoke with the Urdeshi 33rd, looking over her head for threats, and so it was Aekon, four metres away and facing them, who was the first to see her stand straight and then onto tiptoe like a marionette being pulled almost clear of the stage. Her eyes were wide in shock. Her mouth was open, but for one long, bad moment Aekon was sure her respiration had stopped.

He barked three short syllables of battle-cant for *alert, look to the objective* and *check injury*, then began swinging his head, then his head and shoulders, back and forth, all auto-senses on maximum gain, trying to see. Las-shot? Hard shot? Venomed dart, a blade? Had she seen an incoming attacker they had missed? A ripple of alarm rolled out through the soldiers around him. He scanned them again, trying to find a movement out of place in the crowd of camo grey.

While he was looking, Natus was listening. When the greenskins had ruined his eyes on Ganahedarak he had fought on in the dark, dragging his audio inputs to their highest gain and mapping the raging melee around him by sound alone. Even after his body had accepted the burnished bronze augmetic eyes the Hephaestium had crafted for him, his hearing was still the sense that he trusted the most. With a finesse born of decades of self-training he sieved through the cascade of sound. The rumble of engines receded to form a dim, looming wall at the edge of his hearing. The shuffle and tread of boot heels sank down and spread under him, the shift of cloth and clink of battle harnesses counterpointed the mass of breaths and worried voices that rolled over the top of it. He ignored the words, focused on the patterns. He could hear the whine and thrum of actuators as Aekon looked about him for an enemy and the burst of movement and voices from around him as the human troopers reacted.

But from in front of him, where the Beati was standing, there was nothing. Just silence.

As though her voice had been drowned out.

Damocles
Keshriy Clade-House, Ghereppan

'*Don't hurt anyone!*' Aekon kept shouting into the vox. '*I can keep pace with her!*'

'So you think,' Natus' growl came back at him. 'Damn and break you, *move!*'

The shout worked. Amplified by his faceplate grille, it hit the soldiers in front of him like a slap to the backs of their heads. They flinched, started, looked around, and finally began parting enough for him to pick his way between them. Natus had the brief urge to simply start ploughing forward, shoving and throwing them out of the way, so strong it felt like he had started doing it, and was instantly ashamed. He vented that shame by roaring at them again instead.

'Out of the way! Feet out from under mine if you don't want them smeared onto the road! Out of the way! Part, damn you, part!'

'Wipe your boots when you get to the top of the steps, Natus,' Aekon voxed him back. *'Can't be tracking bits of them up the nice clean halls.'*

'You had better have caught up with her if you're up to making jokes,' Natus snapped as he finally got clear of the press of soldiers and broke into a run up the steps.

'I'm a step behind her on the Way of Stations, we're just coming to the switchback with all the empty pedestals. Don't wait for the lifts, cut through the utility keep and up to the ramp from the south landing shelves and you should just about intercept us.'

'How did she get such a lead on us?'

'Can't begin to answer you. By the time I saw her moving she was halfway to the doors. Can you hear that?'

'Hear what? You almost faded out for a second there. I'm in the rampshaft now, should be on you in about fifteen.'

'Dial your transmission up and listen to my background. She's talking again.'

Damocles
Keshriy Clade-House, Ghereppan

Aekon had heard her speaking as she sped through the entrance vault and through into the pillared feeder passages beyond it. He was aware, as he went crashing and pounding along, that she barely seemed to be running at all – she was moving in long, balletic strides that seemed to carry her along in barest contact with the floor, like a slender insect skating across the water. He decided not to think about that, but to concentrate on her, on closing the distance to her, watching as best he could for harm to either of them, and hoping to the Throne that nobody came wandering out of a doorway right in front of him.

'Begone from here,' was what she had said as the giant doors at the top of the clade-house steps had flown open in front of her. Aekon had triggered a set of auto-hypnotic commands and memorised the words, just in case. 'You are banished from this place. You are excommunicated from it. It is closed to you in the name of Him-on-Terra. Remove your filthy touch. *Begone!*'

As they weaved among the statuary beneath the chandelier-vaulted Way of Stations, he got close enough to hear her again.

'Shame? If you had a scrap of understanding of what shame is you would have ended your own life a lifetime ago. You would have begged on your knees. Begged in tears. Pleaded for your last words of repentance to be heard as you stoked the pyre to throw yourself on.'

She wasn't carrying a vox, she almost never did. She wasn't addressing anyone they passed, or anyone he could see ahead of her. Her head was still up. There was very definitely a fixed point she was looking at up there, some place above them whose location she was exactly, intuitively sure of.

He had to slow to round the turn into the Way's upper ascent, putting out a hand to shove himself clear of the basalt pedestals where the statues of the saints and primarchs had once stood. She gained ground on him then, and as he closed it again he noticed her image had started to waver, as though she were leaving a wake behind her in the air. A wake that foamed with faint green light.

Damocles
Keshriy Clade-House, Ghereppan

'Just ahead,' Khiron said, jogging awkwardly sideways with his hands on Holofurnace's shoulder. 'In the hall.'

'What's she doing there?' Holofurnace was moving clumsily too, holding his plastron closed and his pauldron in place.

'Running up it, as far as I can tell.'

'Are we here to stop her?'

'No, brother, we are not going to stop her. Stopping her from doing things is very *explicitly* not what we're about. Concentrate! A little less haste won't be a disaster. Once it's locked we can put on the pace then.'

Holofurnace's frustrated grimace didn't abate when he felt the interleaving plates around his shoulder slide over one another and lock, nor when the opening down his side finally sealed with a hiss and a click. The feel of his pauldron finally anchoring itself back to him was what did it. He felt as if his body had been reassembled, not just the plate that enclosed it. Shrugging and rolling proper movement back into his shoulder, he drew his bolt pistol as they ran out into the Way.

Holofurnace had been a little concerned that he might not recognise the Beati when he finally did meet her. He kept hearing she was an ordinary young woman, who dressed so as to pass for any other such, and now he was entering an active situation with no one to point her out to him. How would he know her?

The question immediately became ridiculous.

There was a thunderhead coming up the Way, a boiling storm cloud of power whose lightning flashes were emerald instead of electric blue and whose thunder was a clear, pure voice raised in song. It paralysed him for a moment, his body resting limp inside a suit of armour that seemed locked to the floor, until he gulped a breath and blinked and suddenly it was a young human woman, just as he had heard, sprinting towards him with startling speed, Aekon racing along behind her and Natus a length behind him.

'I don't expect you to understand,' she said as she bore down on him. 'A cancer cell doesn't understand the healthy body it disrupts with its uncontrollable upstart ravening. We do not reason with those. We cut and burn until they are gone. And I have a blade and flames to bring you, you tumour of a thing.'

He came within an eye-blink of aiming at her then, until he realised she wasn't speaking to him. She barely seemed to have registered him there except as another obstacle to veer around. He turned and started to run as she passed him, leading what was now a quartet of Iron Snakes running in her wake. Soldiers and staff scattered out of their way with cries and exclamations.

'Where are we headed?' Khiron asked.

'No idea!' said Aekon. 'She's talking, but not to us. Natus reckons the old templum chambers, that's the psyker eyrie now.'

'Andromak! Hear that? Meet us there! Flask hot!'

'Affirm!' came the answer over the vox. *'Almost there.'*

'So are we,' said Khiron. 'Another few seconds.'

'It is not myself I feel hate for,' Saint Sabbat declared ahead of them as they charged up a ceremonial stair beneath a scorched-black stained-glass window. 'Soon enough you'll learn where my hate is directed.'

'That sounded bad,' Khiron muttered. 'Ready, everyone.'

'What for?' Natus asked as they bore down on the templum doors. Of the Ministorum devotees Priad had walked past minutes before, most had fled. A handful were slumped against the walls, apparently dazed by whatever they had seen beyond the doors, or had flown into hysterics, gabbling prayers and psalms, pressing their faces against reliquary boxes or aquila medallions. The Saint marched through the middle of them looking neither left or right. She no longer moved in those strange far-gliding steps, but walked with her head lowered and clenched fists swinging at her sides, the gait of a pugilist walking out to settle a grudge. As she walked past the psyker nests and the choir stall, tendrils of corposant floated through the air towards her and wrapped her as she passed them, tangling around her like seaweed. As they did they changed, each growing brighter and becoming suffused with a rich green that flickered like firelight. The sight of that glow filling the templum and spilling into the hall sent the devotees around them into new ecstasies.

'Do we follow her in?' Natus asked.

'Whose charge is she right now?' Khiron responded.

'Mine and Aekon's.'

'Then you two go in with her. Holofurnace, you too. I'll stand at the door and wait for Andromak. Hurry! Xander's on the vox. Wherever he is, I'll wager that's where she's bound. Andromak!'

The stocky Space Marine had made the top of the stair and was advancing on them. His plasma gun was live – Khiron's auto-senses registered the heat cloud from the muzzle and flask and the electromagnetic fuzz of the containment fields.

He was holding it just below ready position, prepared in an instant to send a plasma shot past them into the templum.

'I've been getting Xander's hails,' he said. 'What's happening in there?'

In the instant he asked the question, the green light that had been flooding past them went out.

'Whatever it is, it just ended,' Andromak went on. 'Sorry.'

'Don't apologise too soon,' Khiron told him. 'And keep the gun lit for a little while longer. This doesn't feel like an ending to me. Not yet.'

The Saint
Keshriy Clade-House, Ghereppan

'Bring–' she said, then shook her head, turned and walked out of the side chapel, down the very centre of the central aisle of the templum hall, and out through the doors. The astropathic choir seemed to sigh and almost drowse in her wake. The devotees still clustered at the doors made no attempt to push past the Iron Snakes, who made an aisle for her to walk down, but wept and called out hosannas to her as she passed by.

'Bring–' she started to say again on the templum landing foyer, as an ashen-faced Sister Kassine hurried forward with two juniors of her order in tow. But then there were more people all around her, a jumble that seemed to contain every uniform the clade-house fortress did, all wide-eyed with nerves and clutching weapons.

'Are you going to make way for the Saint?' Priad asked the little crowd, after several seconds in which it appeared they were not.

'Standing emergency protocol, sir,' said one of the men at

the front of the group. He was a sergeant in the fatigues of the elite Urdeshi Second Storm Troop, in full helmet and combat mask and a fast-cycle hellgun in his hands. One of General Grawe-Ash's personal guard. Looking past him, Priad saw another half a dozen of them behind him in the crowd. 'At any kind of disturbance in the command psyker enclave, all able-bodied personnel nearby are to arm and move to assist in quarantine while the rest of HQ goes into lockdown. The all-clear hasn't been given yet. Sir.'

Priad thought the Beati was going to argue, then she shot a look over her shoulder, nodded her assent and retreated. A wave of muttering went through the impromptu blockade as the seven burly storm troopers moved to form its front rank and took up firing positions. The flat red gaze of their mask eyepieces followed the Saint as she and Kassine retreated towards the templum doors. When they stopped to speak, Priad made a gesture and five of his Iron Snakes stepped in and wheeled about in perfect sync to enclose them in a protective ring. The Saint beckoned him through it to join them.

'Bring my banner,' she said. 'And my weapons. As soon as this is lifted and you can do it without a clash of orders. Bring them to my...' She stopped and scrubbed a hand over her eyes, a mundane gesture loaded with exhaustion and frustration. 'No, not to my cell. Priad, which landing shelf is your Thunderhawk on?'

'Stationed for lift-off on South-East Two-Gamma,' Priad replied promptly, a moment before it occurred to him to wonder why she was asking.

'To there, then. Priad. Have your pilot wait.'

'My lady, this gunship is–'

'Priad.'

The bare whisper of his name was enough to stop him

cold. He watched her while he sent the signal, but she didn't return his gaze.

'Cepheas is now holding his departure upon you, my lady.'

'Upon *us*. Ask Damocles Squad to assemble and board.' She let out a long breath. 'We won't be in the air for very long before we'll be over the fighting. I'd best armour myself before we take off.' She smiled at Kassine. 'You too, Yulla, I'm sorry. And will you please pass the word to the others? Once you're allowed to pass. I want Brin with us. That's important. Ghelon, and some people he trusts. And we owe it to the colonel.'

'What destination do I instruct Cepheas to be ready for?' Priad asked her. She was about to speak it, then looked between the encircling Snakes to where the white-haired Psykana dam was walking past them. She bowed her head and mouthed the answer instead. Priad passed it on with no surprise. He had known it even as he asked the question.

'All clear!' The storm troop sergeant's mask filters turned his shout into a harsh inorganic clack. 'By authority of the enclave warden, we declare all clear. Stand down from quarantine override orders, repeat, stand down and return to your duties.' The old woman was standing next to him, staring back at the Saint through a gap between Khiron and Aekon and fastidiously adjusting her veil. She remained there as the sergeant left her side and walked over to them.

'Madam,' he said. Through the mask's distortion it was hard to tell if any deference had managed to creep into his tone, but at least he now had his hellgun lowered.

'Sergeant...' She looked at him carefully. 'Sergeant Vesherin. Thank you for taking the lead in implementing the quarantine order. This has been a bad day for our comrades in service.'

'Yes, ma'am,' Vesherin said expressionlessly. 'The same

orders require a full report to command HQ with most urgent despatch. I have the warden's report but the general will be requesting a direct report from yourself. Will you accompany me, please?'

The Saint's eyes narrowed. Her expression became almost sly.

'There was a manifestation in the Psykana roost. It is possible I may have helped end it, but I was only present for its end. Do you not have the warden's word?'

'Mamzel, we–'

'Battle-Brother Xander was present in the roost for the entire manifestation,' Priad put in. 'He will accompany you and can make a full report to the general. I will make myself available to add to it if I am required to. I am sure the lady Beati will do the same.'

'Priad?' came Xander's voice on the squad band. 'Did you just–'

'Listen, all of you,' he cut his brother off, bringing the rest of Damocles in on the conversation. 'Disperse from here, go back to our quarters. Arm up, load up, full readiness. Khiron, your medicae stocks?'

'Ready.'

'Scyllon's leg?'

'The full augmetic isn't fitted but he's got one he can move on.'

'Natus, Aekon. You're staying with her, do you need to be brought anything?'

'Grenades, for both of us,' Aekon said.

'Reactor pack fuel,' Natus added, 'but the 'hawk has enough reserves for me to feed it once we're airborne.'

'And I'm staying here to talk to the general?' Xander asked incredulously.

'You're talking to the general, but you're not staying behind.

So work out your words and get them in order before you get to her so you can excuse yourself and join us.'

'What am I supposed to tell them?' Xander asked. 'How am I supposed to make sense of all those questions and discussions that don't have anything to do with us?'

'Start by briefing them exactly as you'd brief me. Answer questions as economically as you can. Don't try and dissemble. Don't bat an eye at telling them you don't have an answer. Don't make guesses if you're uncertain, just let them tell you what they need from you.'

'Will that work?' Xander's voice was dubious.

'You now have all the wisdom your brother-captain has distilled from his work with our loyal allies,' Priad said. 'You're as equipped as I am.'

'And remember,' Holofurnace put in, 'if they press you then they are being insolent. Answer them as such. You owe them nothing.'

'Thank you, brother,' Priad said flatly. 'That will do. Xander? Off you go. Join us at the Thunderhawk. We'll share the water before we take off.'

'Affirm. If I tweak some officer's nose and get thrown in a cell I'll have someone send word.'

'It is insolence, though, isn't it?' Holofurnace asked as Xander strode away. 'In true war, in the wars that come down to us in the Karybdiad and our declarations of deeds, how many verses do you remember about how the great notables of the past sat hunched over a table and haggled?'

'How many verses are there about how the great notables of the past had to stop to work a jammed shell loose from their bolter?' Khiron answered him. 'In your magnificent, legendary war, every single shell would fire true with every shot we took. But here we are, mortals in a flawed and mortal war, and so we have to know how to unjam a weapon even though the murals don't show our glorious bygone brothers fiddling with the action of their guns. This is a skill the war requires of us, and so we develop it.'

'I don't think your analogy holds up,' Holofurnace said, 'but now isn't the time. For now, you talk to me about anything I need to know from that assay you took before we fight. And once we're done with this next slice of our war, I'll talk to you about martial philosophy.'

'Agreed. Let's move!'

The straggle of devotees and sundry onlookers hadn't heard the vox exchange. They scattered with cries of alarm as the knot of Iron Snakes burst into motion and crashed through their midst. Even then, many of them couldn't quite bring themselves to turn their backs and walk away from their Saint. Priad was conscious of nervous, hovering figures in the periphery of his vision as he turned back to her. Kneeling down next to her, he broke the seal and lifted his helmet away so that he could whisper to her.

'If you want to be aboard and battle-ready before the general or any of her staff have the chance to countermand you, then you have until Xander reaches her and tells her where you're going.'

She nodded, face tight.

'Our journey out from Ghereppan mirrors our journey to it, doesn't it?' she said. 'Equal and opposite. Identical but reversed. We left there in secret so the enemy would think we had remained. Here we're going to hide our movement from our own. We left Rhole Cliffs because I knew that His place for me was here, whatever the Militarum command willed. Now it's command who wanted me to follow the fighting, but...'

Her voice had suddenly grown strained, and now it tailed off entirely.

'But?' Priad asked.

'It's the *insult*,' she hissed, and Priad realised it was not fear or exhaustion that had put the strain in her voice, but an ice-blooded fury that he had never seen in her before. 'The *stain*. We won this place through an act of grace and beauty that He-on-Terra saw fit to grant us and now it's... it's befouled, it's *stained*. The laughter, Priad. That's what...' She jammed the heel of her hand onto her forehead and ground her teeth. 'They eat away the order that we make like maggots. They *piss* on the beauty we create like sneering infants. They see faith, such lovely, moving faith, loyalty and sacrifice, and they, he, he *laughed*. He murders my flock, taunts me, laughs to see me instead of cowering as he ought. Did you hear what he said to me?'

'Every word, my lady.' *Even if I don't know how* you *heard it*, he thought.

'This can't stand,' she said. 'This can't be allowed to stand. Every moment the magister sits in that city laughing at me is a moment that my Emperor sits on His throne on Terra waiting for me to silence that laughter forever. I can't... I can't betray His trust in me by doing nothing. I have to hit back.'

'Is that what the visions meant, then?' he asked her, and she whirled on him.

'I–' she got out, then bit down hard on the words and closed her eyes. Her hands were gripping the islumbine garland so hard they were shaking.

'I have thought about those visions enough,' she said. 'Before we even came to Rhole Cliffs I had omens, shadows. The same before the Eotine Walk, and before I took my faithful over the Peshelid Sea.'

'But we did not leave Rhole Cliffs until you had certainty. That certainty had a hard price, my lady. I remember it well, I was one of the ones who had to exact it. But still. You defied command and came to Ghereppan because you *knew*. Do you *know* now?'

She stared into his eyes. Her face was pale, wounded, looking far older than its years.

'I know this has gone far enough,' she said softly. 'Too far. No one, nothing can slight the aquila like that and live. We are going to Oureppan, Priad. And I am going to kill him.'

She turned on her heel and walked away, Natus and Aekon walking in from the sides of the landing and falling in on each side of her. Priad remained there on one knee, watching her walk away.

And he noticed the trail she left behind her, scattered flecks of white that were flecked in turn with red. With his fingers thickened by the gauntlet it took him a few seconds to pick one up.

They were petals, fallen from her garland, dead and wilting.

Damocles and the Saint
Landing shelf South-East Two-Gamma,
Keshriy Clade-House, Ghereppan

'Are we getting any kind of fighting escort from the Militarum air wing?' Crethon asked from the Thunderhawk's co-pilot seat.

'We are not,' Cepheas said.

'Have we arranged any kind of co-ordinated action with the ground forces we're going to fly over to disrupt anything that might want to shoot at us?'

'We have not.'

They sat in silence. Crethon pulled the maps of their route from the Thunderhawk's cogitator and flicked them past his helmet display. Again.

'But we're flying into a warzone,' he said eventually. 'The hottest one on the planet?'

'I think there's some competition for that title at present,' Cepheas said. 'The fighting between Zarakppan and Eltath has turned brutal. The air war over the Eltath approaches is why there's not much of an air wing left to support us here. Although it's also why there's no real enemy air wing left at all.'

'The enemy can take to the air when it counts,' Crethon said darkly. Cepheas twisted around as much as the pilot's socket would let him, and looked at his new crew member.

'My apologies, brother,' he said. 'I didn't mean that.'

'Not necessary, but thank you. I got brought down. I cost the Phratry a ship. No credit to be had in hiding from it. But…'

'But?'

'But did you review my report of the things that killed my 'hawk? Because if the Archenemy put one flock of those things in the air…'

'We all did.'

'All?'

'Phaethon!' Cepheas called over the shipboard vox. 'Mathos! You've reviewed those ugly damn things your brothers took down to avenge Crethon here?' There was a double shout of affirmation from where the two brothers of Kalliopi Squad were locked into berths behind them.

'They're each by a side-lock,' Cepheas went on. 'If that flock has cousins in the air over Oureppan we have our brothers back there to take point, and I have your hands at my weapon controls ready to avenge your ship with. We'll make them wish they'd never spread their wings, brother.'

Cepheas held out a hand. Crethon reached out to take it and ceramite chinked as they gripped gauntlets.

'I think–' the Damocles pilot began, but then a flurry of hails burst out of the vox. With haptic commands quicker than blinking, both pilots grabbed the gunship's optic feeds into their helmet vision.

Brother-Captain Priad stood at the base of the Thunderhawk's ramp. He had mounted the banner-stave onto his reactor pack and the colours of Damocles Squad now flew over the crest of his helm. A second pennant depicting a sword and a stylised islumbine bloom fluttered from the pole's very top. In his left hand he held a sea-lance, in his right a bronze vial. Khiron and Pyrakmon stood at his sides, and from there Damocles assembled around him in a loose circle with five spaces empty. The two pilots and the two Kalliopi Space Marines joined them a moment later. With one final gap in the circle, directly across from Priad, they waited as impassive as temple carvings, the only sound the snap of Priad's banners in the rising breeze.

The Saint found them before their final brother did. She was in armour now, plates of blaze-bright gold over black body-fitting chain. She held a slim sword in her bare right hand, and her left gauntlet was a stylised eagle's claw, its talons silver blades like scalpels. Purity seals fluttered back from her shoulders and hips, the lettering on them somehow hypnotic, more intense than life. Kassine walked at her side, dressed in scarlet silks and part-shell armour in the livery of her order. She had dismounted the lantern from the head of her staff and fixed a fighting piece in place instead, an adamantium-toothed chainpike head bracketed by the nozzles of incinerator jets. Colonel Mazho was at her other shoulder, in his grey camo and full battle harness, flanked in turn by two troopers wearing the red-and-yellow shoulder patches of the Cinder Storm, their faces invisible under ash-visors. Behind them came Ghelon and two of his fellow devotees, a man and a woman, grim-faced, weapons in their hands and blue ayatani sashes pinned over their flak armour. Aekon and Natus brought up the rear of the little procession. Between them moved an oddity, a blur and shift in the air that parted and resolved into Trooper Milo. His pale face and black fatigues appeared in odd patches and flickers as his camo-cloak shifted about him and took his shape away.

And finally, a few paces behind Milo, came Brother Xander of Damocles. At last.

'Please board the gunship, madam,' Priad rumbled. 'This will be quick, and then we will secure you and be on our way.' Natus and Aekon moved into the circle.

'Perhaps we can join you,' Sabbat said, standing just outside the last gap. None of the Snakes around her moved to widen the space. 'I think it would be good for us to pray together before we go out to battle again.'

'This is not a prayer,' Priad said, and left it at that. She met the gaze of his faceplate, nodded, stepped back and led her followers around the outside of the circle and up the Thunderhawk's ramp. Xander stepped forward, and the assembly of Iron Snakes was complete.

The Sharing of Water was as wordless as the wait had been. Each brother's helm tilted to watch the droplets fall from Priad's flask into their armoured palm. Most of Damocles simply stared at the little gleam of water until it had run through their hand or evaporated in the breeze. The two brothers from Kalliopi put their hands to their plastrons and anointed the armour over their primary hearts. Holofurnace snapped his hand closed as soon as the water was in his palm and stood with his fist raised in front of him. He was the only one who turned to watch Priad as he left the circle, walked to the edge of the landing shelf and let the final trickle of water run from the flask, out into the breeze where it was caught up and carried away. It was only after Priad had pushed the stopper back into the empty vial and replaced it at his waist that Holofurnace turned and, fist still closed, walked up the ramp amid the rising skirl of the engines.

Less than a minute later the Thunderhawk was making a graceful curve down from the edge of the landing shelf into a low run out over the causeway, towards Oureppan.

Priad and the Saint
Contested airspace, Ghereppan Strait

Priad was watching Holofurnace and Trooper Milo when the Saint came and sat next to him. The Thunderhawk's troop emplacements were more like sockets than seats, designed to lock a fully armoured Adeptus Astartes in place. They were so big that she was able to climb completely into one and curl up in it, her back braced against one side and her feet against the other. Wedged in place, she stared up at him.

Holofurnace, helmet off, had been sitting with his left gauntlet raised to his face as though to hide his expression. He had lowered it now, and turned his head to the young trooper. Priad saw Milo touch the place by his side where his pipes usually hung, and then the stock of his lasrifle, which was cut from a deep, lustrous wood Priad didn't recognise. They were talking together, but their words were lost in the rumble of the gunship's engines and the distant song of the air over its hull. Priad didn't bother to tune his auto-senses in on them, or watch their lips for words. He was curious, he admitted to himself, but curiosity could defer to politeness for now.

His left ear tingled and a blue rune flashed into the lower left corner of his vision. He opened the message packet with an eye motion and quasi-haptic command and listened to Crethon's voice, then the tinny and crackling human one that came after it. Then he turned his eyes back to the Saint.

She was still staring at him. Now, her eyes were large and solemn over the top of a face mask she had not been wearing a moment ago. Looking past her, Priad saw she had requisitioned it from one of Colonel Mazho's guards, who was now looking around the compartment barefaced and uncomfortable. Priad almost chuckled.

'How did you know?' he asked her.

'Know, brother-captain?'

'I just got a message that I had to discuss with you, directly with you alone, and when I turn to you you've got yourself a mask with a vox-pickup.'

'Channel?'

He gave her one. She shifted forward, kneeling in the socket-seat with her forearms along its edge. Priad, who was locked into his own socket and filled it from edge to edge, found himself almost envying her. She was not a young woman any more but her movements had such a childlike unselfconsciousness that they acquired an odd kind of grace.

'I didn't know you had had a message,' she said. 'I wanted to apologise to you. Make peace.'

'For what, my lady? I was not aware of anything between us.'

'Your ceremony at the ramp. The one that was not a prayer. It was disrespectful of me to interrupt it.'

'It doesn't matter,' Priad said, splaying and tilting his hand to make the point. 'The Sharing of Water is a battlefield ritual. Of necessity, it's... robust. There's no offence there to amend.'

She considered that.

'Your brother there,' she said, indicating Holofurnace with a tiny inclination of her head. 'He might not agree. He was far angrier than you at the intrusion.'

'Every squad in the Phratry interprets the sharing in its own way,' Priad said. 'But I think for Brother Holofurnace it was the fact of the ritual, not the detail of it. It has been a long time since he was able to share water. Touch the sea of Ithaka again. There isn't much water left to us now.'

'No water at all,' she said quietly, looking across the compartment. The conversation appeared to be over. Milo had moved to another socket-seat; Holofurnace had replaced his helm and sat motionless. 'He didn't have so much as a drop of Ithaka's sea to carry with him when he stepped into Salvation's Reach. The vial at his belt had been empty for months.'

Priad didn't bother to ask how she knew. She was right, he was sure of it. And if she were right, then perhaps that meant that whatever connection she carried to – he absently touched the aquila emblem on his plastron – to a power that sat enthroned on a world whose sun was invisible from Urdesh and Ithaka alike, perhaps that connection was strengthening again. Perhaps that hunted, haunted look, so unfamiliar on her features, would leave her.

Perhaps this day would see Anakwanar Sek dead at her hand after all.

* * *

Priad and the Saint
Contested airspace, Oureppan approaches

'What was the message?' she asked him after the first engagement alert had sounded for them to secure themselves in place. Priad had been watching a display from the machine pulpit, watching over Pyrakmon's virtual shoulder as the Techmarine ran final checks on Damocles' armour systems. He let the feed fall away and looked over at her, sitting cross-legged inside a cargo harness that was the best they could do to secure human-sized passengers against combat manoeuvres. She didn't seem concerned.

'You said you had a message,' she went on. 'One that no one else on board could know about.'

'Ah. That.' Priad chuckled into the vox-link. 'It's rather less urgent now than it was, madam, but yes, you probably should know. When we were about halfway across the strait we had a tight-beam hail bounced here from the command echelon at Eltath.'

'The Warmaster.'

'It carries Macaroth's code-seal, yes.'

'It passed to you? You've seen it?'

'I had no way to pass it to you, mamzel, so the message stopped with me. It unpacks to a short vox-recording.'

'Saying?'

'I can't pass the transmission directly on,' Priad said. 'Code-locked. I'll recite. Begins. "When you get this, well, you're not going to answer, of course, you'll be most of the way to Oureppan if I'm right about how a Thunderhawk can fly, and of course I am. So I know you'll be too far forward to risk a transmission with either of our names in it, even coded, even if you did have the inclination to explain to me why. Why you decided to follow up launching yourself out of hiding into the most infernal warzone on Urdesh by launching yourself out of one of the only truly secure Imperial holds on the planet into one of the only truly secure Archenemy holds. While I wait to hear word of your success I shall count my blessings that you at least saw fit to send an envoy to tell Grawe-Ash you were leaving. And perhaps if I ask for a blessing for you as well, the Throne shall hear me and see fit to pass it on. You are as mercurial as this war, madam. I trust that that will prove kind to us."'

Her eyes were crinkled above the line of the mask – she was laughing.

'Your voice is no more like his than mine is,' she said, 'but the words... I could hear him in the words as though he were talking over your shoulder.'

'I wish more battlefield transmissions could bring that sort of merriment,' Priad said. 'I think your next conversation with the Warmaster is going to be a little more incendiary than the last one.'

'He'll come round,' she said, the laughter leaving her eyes. 'When we next speak it will be after I have thrown the Anarch's banner down between us. We'll rest our feet on it while we talk, and burn it together once we've finished. So, incendiary indeed.'

'That's the way you still see ahead?' he asked her as the gunship began to weave in the air, rocking the compartment back and forth. 'That that's the purpose you've been assigned? That you're being drawn towards?'

'What do you think?' she asked him. 'Do you feel it yourself? If the sharing of water wasn't a prayer, then have you prayed since we lifted off? I know your Phratry is not given to mysticism but you cannot be servants of the Throne without understanding what kind of being sits on it.'

'You're right, my lady,' Priad said. The compartment jolted hard around them as Cepheas dodged around something outside, and Sabbat had to clutch the strapping around her to stay steady. 'We aren't mystics. We are given a very clear purpose when we are remade into what we are. Other Chapters have their prayers, I know. Vision trances. Sacred mysteries. Those traditions aren't ours. We express our devotion through deeds. You've seen us at war, madam, so you've seen us at our devotions.'

'"To slay is to pray",' she quoted, with a smile in her voice. 'Hagia's style of faith was never the most militant but still, that was one of the first axioms I remember learning. And I know, I know,' she went on, as they veered, climbed and then banked and dropped so hard that for a moment she was airborne inside her nest of straps, 'that that should be enough for me as well. Perhaps I should be learning your style of devotion instead of trying to teach–' A shockwave slammed against the hull and rang the Thunderhawk's fuselage like a gong. '–teach you mine.'

'You're still not certain, are you?' he asked her as the compartment tilted and they climbed again. 'That's why you wanted to talk. You wanted certainty from me.'

'I know that you've put yourself and Damocles totally at my service,' she said, 'but you've commanded your squad in so many wars.' Her voice was getting faster and more urgent. 'More than any of my soldiers could ever live to witness. You've been the final authority in the field, you've had the lives of your brothers and the name of Damocles itself dependent on your command.' Priad found himself glancing over at Holofurnace at those words, but his newest battle-brother was still as motionless and impassive as the rest of the squad. 'I trust you, brother-captain. You have wisdom and judgement. I want to hear your counsel.'

'Second engagement!' Crethon called from the co-pilot's position. 'Look to weapons!' Reflexively, Priad ran through his ammunition count and put his hand on his bolter. White runes appeared, changed and vanished in his vision as the Thunderhawk's feeds began to uncouple themselves from his armour and retract. The lights in the compartment dimmed and turned to red.

Saint Sabbat wasn't looking at him any longer. She killed the vox-connection, pulled the mask loose and handed it back to the trooper she had taken it from. The man began fumbling mask and helmet back into place as they accelerated, swerved and jinked.

There was a double slam of metal, a blast of daylight and a scream of rushing air, then another slam and the dully roaring redness of the compartment again. Phaethon and Mathos had punched out through the side ports, starting their long power dive through the open sky ahead of the Thunderhawk's insertion run. The instant the hatch was closed the gunship wrenched and rolled in the air again. There was a shrieking detonation somewhere close to them and the compartment filled with acrid, sizzling air that vanished as suddenly as it had appeared. Somewhere off to Priad's right, one of the humans cursed.

The Beati's eyes were closed, her head down. Priad thought he could see the faintest movement of her lips.

My counsel is no good to you, he would have told her if there had been time. *Not now. My certainty that we should be here comes from you. You led us onto this ship believing that your newly ordained purpose was to hurl yourself straight at the Anarch and destroy him, and that everything around you would bend to that purpose the way it bent around you when you set foot in Ghereppan. I am no mystic, but I know what I witnessed in that city, and if your faith is true now then I believe we are saved. But if it's your doubt that is true, and all that led you here was your own rage, your need to polish up your dignity by avenging an insult thrown down at your own feet? Then, my lady and Saint, then we are not the agents of divinity. We are flying into the Archenemy's maw for no reason than one mortal's anger, with no power watching over us. And then? Then we are lost.*

Then the temperature in the compartment jumped as the laser destructor in the dorsal mount fired a salvo, and the humans looked around in alarm as the hammering of the cannon mounts echoed through the hull. Air began to whip around them as the rear seals cracked and the ramp readied itself to lower.

Then Cepheas was calling third engagement, and it was time.

Erasmos
Personnel core, upper silo complex, Old Ourezhad

First the laughter, then the monsters.

The pressure-hatches from the silo chamber had been sealed but a melta charge and half a dozen deft thrusts of Akanthe had broken them open. The lower hab levels had been pitch dark and empty, the lights broken or so grimed with ash they might as well have been, the air intolerably hot and reeking of volcanic gases. Twice as Erasmos climbed up through the crew hive they thought they heard human voices sobbing somewhere out there in the gloom, but they did not slow.

The higher, airier levels where the cramped dormitories gave way to individual rooms and apartments were blessedly cool by contrast, the air merely stifling, some of the recirculation scrubbers still working. They found their first corpses in the communal halls and galleries, some laid out in apparent reverence on dining tables or arranged in significant patterns on the engraved floors of the processionals, but more, so many more as they kept on, were piled unceremoniously in doorways, left to rot in the middle of rooms, scattered in pieces along passageways.

And not all of them were human. In the main cloister of the upper habs they passed a trio of multi-utility servitors crushed into a mad tangle of lifter-limbs and dendrites, their organics lacerated and ruptured. Two were encrusted with long-dried human gore; the third had bled the same neon-yellow blood they had seen in the lashed-together monsters below. At the top of a sweeping stair a figure in ragged magos' garb was lying in a pool of the same stuff.

'One of the power shrine magi?' Iacchos wondered over the squad vox as they passed on either side of it.

'Look at it,' Symeon said without looking back. 'I could see four different ways that gown and hood were being misworn. Stolen, all of it.'

'And the blood…' Laukas said. 'Look ahead.'

A figure was hanging over the stair landing, suspended by long dendrites of dark grey steel that had been crudely grafted into its shoulders. Dribbles of dried yellow blood ran down from where the metal met the red stumps of arms. More of the stuff ran from its mouth and the stump of its left ankle was clotted dark red and yellow. Its face was a torn ruin; a mouthless copper mask lay on the floor below its feet. The body twitched in the rhythm of laughter, but made no sound.

'Unsuccessful tests?' Anysios wondered. 'But… the wounds are too fresh. That couldn't have been older than the things we were seeing down in the silos. There's no sense to this.'

'Then stop looking for sense,' Demetios told him, 'and start looking for enemies.'

'I think,' Anysios replied, 'that the enemies are looking for... No, scrap that. I think the enemy knows exactly where we are, and has for some time. And it still makes no sense.'

'We knew that would happen,' Symeon said. 'There's a point in every mission like this when guile is abandoned for speed. We know we've passed it. The lance is cast. Enough talk.'

Erasmos Squad followed their sergeant's wishes and ran on in silence, picking up speed as the halls widened, even as the corpses thickened around them, the mutilations ever more extravagant, the remakings ever crueller and more bizarre, the death-postures ever more tortured and wretched. They were past the silos and refineries now, angling upward and inward, into the core of the complex and the Mechanicus temple-hub. Erasmos started to notice ragged sockets in the walls where the Omnissiah's shrine-stations had been torn from their alcoves, and the arched side chapels where the altars had been broken open and the machines inside them stripped away. The leering chrome gargoyles at the point of each archway chortled out scratchy bursts of static.

The hall below Old Ourezhad's alpha-shrine, on the other hand, was filled with new machines. There was nothing ramshackle about these, although their designs were odd, unsettling, with an organic flow of line that cut against the angular Mechanicus aesthetic. Control pulpits sat amongst what looked to Spiridon like strange reflections of his Apothecarion machines, and tubes and sluices connected serried ranks of glass coffins, crusted with dried yellow fluid, rising up like the seats of a theatre. Sixty-four bio-modification pods.

But they were inert now, abandoned, whatever use they had

been put to long complete, and the Iron Snakes did not slow. Only when their boots were ringing on the steel ramp up to the temple's narthex did they break stride, spread out and fall into a more cautious advancing pattern. Galleries swept around the walls high above the ramp, their columns more gargoyles swathed in cast-copper robes, barking out static. With a sour lack of surprise, Anysios recognised a rhythm in the noise. It was laughter.

Something scratched against Agenor's armour, offering brief resistance to his movements before he bulled through it. He looked down at himself. Something had draped him in a loop of fine, flexible wire studded with metal and glass burrs. It would have lacerated an unarmed human, and there was a stink from the yellow mucus coating the whole thing that made the Snake's nerves twitch.

'Enemy overhead,' he voxed, 'dropping wire.' Another loop landed neatly over his head and tried to tighten on him. More fronds of it fell about his shoulders and arms. Agenor reached up blur-fast, grabbed a fistful of wire and pulled, dropping into a half-crouch to add all his armoured weight to the motion. There was a tear of flesh and a shriek, and something wet and many-legged dropped onto his head and started scrabbling for a foothold.

In the arched galleries a chorus of flaring shotcannon blasts shattered the gloom. The ceramic balls crackled against the Snakes' steel-grey plate, one fracturing Iacchos' eyepiece and a tight chain of blasts triggering haptic feedback stings in Demetios' skull as splinters flew from his pauldron and helm.

Their answering shots were already in the air, aimed and fired without conscious thought, and when they heard the heavy sounds of their shells detonating inside flesh they fired outward, then inward, bracketing the hits they had just made, the exploding bolts joining the muzzle-flares and silencing them.

The air was filling with scrabblings and scuttlings as distorted things leapt from their hiding places in the galleries or clinging to ceiling, running down the walls and columns on mismatched legs or leaping into the air to glide down on suspensors and stretched-skin membranes. Their patchwork bodies were studded with blades and gun muzzles.

Erasmos advanced, implacable, in a bounding, interweaving pattern that kept them moving across one another, covering every angle. Demetios was in the lead, his sights on a four-winged, three-armed thing with a rack of lasguns grafted to the exposed bones of its ribcage, when his vision cut out. A lascannon beam had passed so close in front of his face that the flare had overloaded his helm's eyes for a split second. In the time it took him to recover Anysios had drawn a bead on the source, a twisted thing like a backwards centaur, its vertical torso jutting up at the rear of the main body, which crawled on two scrawny human legs, one muscular human arm and one creaking many-jointed metal dendrite. The lascannon was mounted on a pintle fixed to that body's spine and the creature was aiming it like an emplacement gunner. It had no eyes but a broad mouth that guffawed at them through glistening, toothless gums that wept yellow blood. It fired again as the Snakes advanced on it, the beam too slow to catch them as they leapt from its path; their bolt-shells hit it and tore at it but couldn't quite break through the carbon cables woven over and through its flesh. Two cousin-creatures, made to the same concept but jarringly mismatched in their construction, came waddling past aiming melta barrels and rocket tubes.

The gargoyles' speaker-mouths screamed and giggled.

Agenor was spinning in circles, swinging his flamer up to bludgeon the thing that was clinging to the top of his reactor pack as it kept trying to wrap its secretion-sticky wire around his neck. The beating was slowing it enough that Serapion got a clear look at it as he aimed his bolter: it looked like a plump human torso piggybacking a child-sized body on its back, stitched and grafted together at the seams, each set of arms and legs replaced with clicking metal armatures. Where the head of the child-body would have been there was a spooling device paying out the creature's garrotting wire, turning by muscle spasms rather than motors. Serapion's bolt-shell hit it square in the main torso but it went through it without slowing, as if the thing's flesh were no more substantial than foam. Before he had time for a second shot Agenor bashed the thing with his flamer barrel, found the angle by touch and intuition and triggered a white-hot burst that sent the creature toppling onto the ramp, lying on its back with its legs scrabbling like an overturned beetle for the few moments it took for the flames to do their work and still it. In the instant it took Agenor to turn and raise his flamer, a lascannon bolt from the centaur burned into his plastron and downward, piercing the armour at his sternum, drilling a cauterised tunnel through his body. Agenor fell to his knees and a rocket blew a gouge into the side of his helmet, sending him to the floor. Spiridon was at his side in an instant, protecting him with his own body, narthecium unfolding from its mount. And the rest of Erasmos was charging.

Iacchos took the lead, torching the air with great sweeps of flame to glare into the enemy's sights. Grenades from Symeon and Anysios arced over his head, their detonations setting the pack of creatures to squealing and cringing. Demetios kept the pace halfway up the ramp and then dropped to one knee and began a calm succession of viciously well-placed shells that painted the narthex with yellow blood. He avenged Agenor with a shot that amputated the centaur's foreleg and a second that punched the lascannon off its mounting, and then Erasmos was in among the enemy. The brilliant yellow plumes from Iacchos' flamer turned the narthex into a shadow-play, a war of silhouettes, looming Space Marines and their capering, misshapen enemies. The power-flares from Akanthe glittered blue-white in counterpoint.

In a flame-burst, Demetios saw the remains of the guncentaur staggering and howling, then saw its packmate come apart at the waist and totter away in a welter of fraying armour cables and bright yellow spray. His own shot blew apart a thing with a bundle of eye-dendrites for a head and buzzing suspensors bulging out of its back that was swooping on Symeon's back with a lit melta torch. His sergeant shouted with rage as the sputtering torch seared the side of his helmet and sent his right eyepiece dark.

Spiridon ran past him carrying Agenor's flamer. Demetios shot a hunchbacked thing that leapt at the Apothecary with sawblade hands outstretched, then ran after him. Flame-jets criss-crossed and a quadruped made of stapled-together corpses convulsed in the flames until its rocket magazine cooked off and the explosion engulfed the brawl in a cough of red flame and acrid black smoke. The gargoyles chorused laughter as Akanthe beheaded another monstrosity. A point-blank double rocket shot exploded Serapion's faceplate inward before a point-blank double bolter shot felled the creature that had fired it.

But now the cobbled-together creatures around them had started to shy away from the fight, ducking their heads like defeated dogs and scrabbling backward for the shadows. Those with voices to do it let out panicked gurgles and despairing wails. Muddy, creamy tears wept from their neon-yellow eyes.

The Iron Snakes sped them on their way with shell and plasma-shot but they did not pursue.

'Forward,' Symeon said. 'Through the outer temple to the high shrine. At all costs. Forward.'

Erasmos
The Power Shrine, Old Ourezhad

The high shrine was a perfect sphere of etched and filigreed silver, positioned in the centre of the volcano's inner chamber over the domed top of the colossal thermovoltaic spike that the Adeptus Mechanicus had driven into the volcano's core all those millennia ago. It stood out from the chamber wall on the end of a long, slender buttress whose top was a path paved with white steel tiles and lined with lanterns glowing blue-white on delicate carbon-glass armatures. The shrine itself was a single space, the circular control pulpit hanging in its centre big enough for a dozen-strong cabal of magi to couple themselves into it, the silver caryatids mounted around its outer edge ready to intone the data-flows to the shrine controllers in binharic or sing them through the manifold. A gallery ran around the shrine's equator, lined with its own lamps and decorated with glass-and-pewter sculptures mimicking arcs of electricity.

Sometimes the Adeptus Mechanicus claimed to be creatures of reason, their minds frictionless and unencumbered by untidy concepts such as beauty and grandeur. No one who saw the artistry of a creation like this believed that.

The lamps of the shrine and the bridge to it were still unbroken and lit. Out beyond them the chamber was in pitch blackness. Occasionally a brilliant discharge of power would arc through the great space, illuminating for an instant the mad three-dimensional maze of pylons, cables, junctions and machinery clusters that surrounded the shrine and filled the chamber from wall to wall. This was where the raw power drawn up from Old Ourezhad's molten belly was marshalled and fed down the fulgeduct tunnels into the Oureppan grid.

Not a single Militarum tactician had considered this a viable, accessible target. Every analysis had assumed no Imperial eyes would see this chamber again without a long and brutal siege once Oureppan itself was taken. Sýmeon, not given to false pride, allowed himself a smile and a murmured Ithakan blessing as he led Erasmos Squad to the doors.

It did not look like the brightly polished tribute to the Omnissiah's grace that the briefing picts had shown him. The silver ball of the shrine was scarred and tarnished almost black, draped and disfigured by growths and blotches like fungus growing on a dead rainforest log. The illuminated blue glass of the double doors was still glowing, but almost obscured by dark stains and splatters. Symeon had a grim premonition of what that might be.

Erasmos Squad rushed the doors in storm formation, fast and silent, auto-senses tuned tight. Nothing responded as they sped down the pathway, no shots came, no cries sounded. Behind the blue glow of the glass doors, nothing moved.

The final steps up to the doors were littered with corpses. Except that not all of them were corpses. Symeon and Demetios both saw the movement at the same time. Neither opened fire. Even their combat-hot nerves saw no threat.

The woman was emaciated, filthy-haired, the grubby remains of her clerk's gown clinging to her with sour sweat. Her face was slack and lifeless, but her eyes rolled around to watch the Iron Snakes approach. The movement they had seen was her right arm, which jittered up and down in the air beside her. It did not seem to be by choice. A little motor crudely embedded in her bicep was repeatedly winding in and dropping out a length of carbon fibre strung across her elbow, pulling her arm up in a curl and letting it flop back down. That, the roll of her eyes and the shallow rise and fall of her chest were the only motions.

'Multiple survivors,' Demetios said. A portly man lay face-down across the shrine steps. His skin was deathly pallid and marked with cuts and punctures. More than a dozen neuro-connector plugs had been driven into him up the length of his back, but in a random, brutal scatter totally unlike the carefully placed augmetics of the Mechanicus, the Legio or the Astartes themselves. Most of the man's plugs were nowhere near his spine and were pushing through into flesh and organs; the handful that were connected to vertebrae were jammed in at angles where they would simply sever nerves rather than tap them. The man was flopping slowly up and down like a fish, trying to move. As his face came clear of the steps they could hear him panting for breath before it smacked back down onto the metal.

There were a handful more still alive ahead of them, their uniforms and markings as various as their mutilations. None of them would live even if an intensive medicae ward lay on the other side of those doors ready to treat them. They were certainly no threat, and so Symeon shrugged the sight away and brushed living and dead aside as he walked up the stairs. He drove Akanthe's blade through the gap between the double doors in a note-perfect fencer's lunge, the power discharge severing the lock and scorching the surrounding armaglass, then kicked the doors in and was inside, blade crackling over his head, ready to do battle with whatever final enemy stood between Erasmos and their mission.

There was no battle.

Symeon turned this way and that, Akanthe still raised. His squad had already filled the space around him, taking up firing points, covering the pulpit, the other exits, the gallery outside. In the cold light of the lanterns and from the power-flashes outside they looked like a second set of statues brought in to adorn the shrine.

But the shrine was already fully, and foully, adorned.

Nine of the stations around the circular silver pulpit were still occupied. Six of the magi in them were dead, most slumped over and only held up by their couplings, one whose augmetic frame had locked rigid in his final spasm and held his corpse there like a felon in a gibbet, one just a pair of silvered-steel arms attached to a stripped human skeleton, the flesh and the rest of the augmetics nowhere to be seen. The living ones were barely in better shape, wasted bodies swaying and shivering, infected blood running from their cable couplings, eyelights cloudy and dim. None of them seemed to register the Snakes' arrival.

Sprawled inside the pulpit's ring were more bodies, the same mix of ugly death and wretched life, these in the garb and tattoos of Sekkite ingeniants. Blood saturated their robes and tunics and glued their bodies to the floor, and the wounds of the still-living ones wept a bright yellow fluid whose sharp reek jabbed at Symeon's senses. Every one of the ingeniants' skulls had been laid open. Many of them had been emptied. From the rest, thick black cables snaked up to the base of the shrine's cathedra, where the high magos should have been sitting enthroned.

There was no high magos any more, and no exalted seat for one to preside in. A seamless crystal capsule like a distended egg, half again as tall as the Iron Snakes surrounding it, rested in its place on a cobbled-together metal stand. It was full of fluid, streaked off-white, brown and yellow like excrement-tainted water that had stagnated into layers, and in the lower third of the tank floated human brains. Many intact ones, some divided into beautifully precise slices like anatomical specimens or artworks, others roughly pulled apart into gobbets. The broken-up ones were strung back together with delicate webs of wire, and larger and more complex laceworks joined the brains and linked them to the bottom of the egg where the cables came in. Every floating brain and every part of one appeared to be alive.

And above the brains floated a shoal of torn-out human eyes.

Tac-tac-tac.

Symeon looked down. A slim metal dendrite was tapping against his ankle. As soon as he looked down, before he could lift his foot to stamp it flat, it recoiled and nipped its pincers into the puffy dead flesh of an ingeniant. It pulled up the dead woman's arm and swayed it back and forth. Symeon stared at it despite himself, not willing to pull the trigger, trying to understand what it wanted.

One of the ingeniants, whose empty skull was stuffed with cable-plugs, suddenly convulsed. The husk's lips pulled back from its teeth. It tried to smile at them. In front of Anysios an eight-fingered mechanical hand attached to an eight-jointed arm attached to a half-alive magos grabbed the foot of a disintegrating corpse, tore it loose, tossed it in the air, picked it up and tossed it again. Anysios looked over at the tank. Many of the eyes were dead, some leaking or collapsed, but some had repositioned themselves somehow to look at him.

'Was this some kind of trap for us?' Demetios said. 'What's it trying to do?'

'It's the controller,' Symeon said. The little dendrite was tapping at his ankle again and he stepped away, leaving the metal tip to scratch at the floor where he'd been. 'Those cables don't just go into the corpses. They go into the pulpit and the floor. There's enough capacity there to be directing the power sluices and the forge levels too.'

'Nothing much is controlling any of those,' Agenor said. 'The forge levels had been working like bastards, but that stopped long before we left. Everything was running down.'

'So I wonder,' Anysios said. Looking down, he flicked his boot forward and kicked the dead foot that the machine-arm was tossing in the air. It hit the pulpit and plopped wetly onto the floor. The hand went after it, the arm dragging it until it got its fingers under it to scuttle to its prize. With a little difficulty it got a grip and tossed the foot back towards Anysios again.

'There it is,' he said. 'It's playing.' He looked at the eyes, at the cabled-together carrion around him. 'I wonder how many more people got built into this thing? Maybe some of these magi refused to turn their coats, or the Archenemy thought they could do better without them. They must have thought they were putting something together that could keep the whole of Old Ourezhad running. A single intelligence running everything inside the mountain as its own body.'

'It failed,' Symeon growled, stepping towards the tank with Akanthe spitting blue sparks in his hand.

'You're right,' Anysios said. 'It might have run the forges for a while, something certainly did. Maybe it degenerated, or went mad.' He looked down at the metal fingers waggling the torn-off foot at him. 'Or it got bored.'

'It got what?' Iacchos asked disbelievingly.

'The things we fought on the way up here didn't really work, did they? Most of them,' Anysios said. 'They were strung together like toys. I think it made potent weapons for a while, and then it just got more interested in having fun with its raw materials – those pitiful things outside the doors, let's say – than doing what it was supposed to. There was nothing to threaten it, after all. It was bored and it started playing.' He kicked the foot out of the air again and once again the metal arm lunged after it. 'It wants us to play with it.'

The lights in the shrine flickered and static squealed from the maws of the silver gargoyles. It had the rhythm of laughter.

'This is not what I expected to find,' Anysios said. 'Did you?'

'Enough,' Symeon answered him. 'Talk later. Capture picts if you want to, but we do what we came to do. You can't seriously tell me you have qualms about killing this thing, brother?'

'I was just ready for a fight, that's all,' Anysios said with a shrug. 'Not euthanasia.'

'Iacchos. Spiridon. Will this pet of the Archenemy's burn?'

'Aye!' the two Snakes shot back in unison.

'Then be about it,' Symeon said. 'And the rest of you, follow me out to the gallery. Get your charges ready and look to my markers. It's time we cut Oureppan's sinews.'

* * *

MATTHEW FARRER

The Enemy
Eastern door, Pinnacle Spire, Oureppan

No one in the crews spoke. Speech was almost forbidden down at their rank anyway, a dangerously rebellious act in a cult that fetishised the act of self-silencing, and since their positions had been stiffened by squads of the massive, silent, brutally indoctrinated Sons of Sek they were less willing to talk than ever. Some hours ago the Sons had caught one of the ingeniants maintaining the auspexes on the laser battery at the core of the fortification, caught him passing on rumours. They were saying that the maggots who came crawling out from under the Throne had managed to cross the strait, had broken through what was supposed to be the impregnable defensive lines at the causeway and around the bay. They were grinding forward through Oureppan almost unopposed and the Anarch was giving no order to mobilise and stop them. They said that the Anarch had fallen silent. That the Imperials were raising their voices and there was no Voice to drown them out. That was only the start of what they were saying. So the ingeniant claimed. The distant sounds they were starting to hear from around the far side of Pinnacle Spire – the grunting thuds of overpressure from explosions, the supersonic cracks and booms from the discharge of engine-scale weapons – seemed to bear him out. Not that anyone else dared say so.

The ingeniant had thought his rank and role would protect him. In response to the shouted accusations, he'd fitted his own hand over the silver-tattooed silhouette of a hand that surrounded his mouth and pointed his other hand at the auspexes he'd been tending. One of the Sons had stepped forward and lopped off his pointing finger with a neat downstroke of an exquisitely sharpened skzerret. Now they had dragged him out past the front line of the fortifications, out into the vast expanse of breeze-swept open roadway, to make an example of him. From the serried rows of sandbag parapets and gun nests that blocked the grand northern doors of Pinnacle Spire, cowed and sullen faces watched. Every mouth was obscured by a bandana with a hand printed on it, or pinned shut by a hand-shaped brooch.

The Sons' overseer still had his skzerret drawn. The punishment would be the same as it had been for the militia commander who'd made the mistake of thinking she could give orders to the Sons when they had first come to this emplacement. Cut the lips to shreds with the bayonet point, then over the edge of the orbital. They were twelve hundred metres above the rest of Oureppan. They would never hear the body land.

Blood was already slicking the moaning ingeniant's chin when the shouting started. The Sons' masked heads turned, black-tinted goggles glinting in the afternoon sun. It was the ingeniant's second, the chief to the slave-gang shackled to the anti-air lasers' aiming machinery. She was up on the sandbag parapet, arms waving, shouting something that the wind took away.

The Sons looked up at her, at each other, and guffawed. That even one person in this pathetic little garrison thought they could stop the consequences of failing the Voice That Drowned Out All Others just showed why they needed the Sons of Sek to stiffen their crumbling spines. The overseer grunted, pointed with his skzerret. The Son nearest him, the bone fetish at the side of his helmet marking him as a sharpshooter, swung his weapon up. It was an Urdeshi PA-7 stub rifle, powerful and accurate. The shouts from above them rose to a panicked shriek and then the report of the gun cut them off. The Sons laughed again. The rifleman stayed where he was, gun raised, daring any of the rest of them to move.

He saw one, then more of them gawping upward. One raised a hand to point. The Son of Sek had a moment to make the connection – the woman had been pointing at the auspex and the sky, not at them – but he didn't quite get there. He saw two militiamen raising lasguns, and took aim at them.

'Ithaka!'

A quarter-ton of armoured Space Marine crumpled the Son against the roadway like a burst waterbag. Kicking his suspensors in again, Mathos stepped and spun and his chainsword sheared two more Sons in half. The stroke turned him fully around to the Sons' little execution squad, and brought the bolt pistol in his right hand to bear. One shell detonated inside the overseer and knocked the Sons on either side of him to their knees. A figure-of-eight stroke with the snarling chainblade left the rest of the detail scattered in pieces across the pavement.

Las-fire speckled the rockcrete behind him and Mathos felt hot pockmarks open up on his leg and hip. A burst of hard rounds spattered off his reactor pack. Roaring, he rose up and spun, his jets on full, brandishing his sword.

'Ithaka! Ithakaaa!' His helmet grille turned his battle cry into a battering ram. He flew at them on a tail of flame. He drew every eye and every gunsight to himself.

So none of them saw Phaethon dropping in above them.

He came down behind the laser battery, so close to the corpse of the luckless second-in-command that the exhaust from his jump jets set her uniform smouldering. Two bolt-shells, fired so close together that the shots sounded like one, blew the auspex and traversing motors to pieces. A few heartbeats' worth of butchery with his chainblade and the rest of the crew was gone.

The Thunderhawk was still high above him, corkscrewing down around the tip of the spire. Many seconds to go yet. Time enough for any Astartes. Phaethon vaulted the parapet in front of him, beheading two Sekkite riflemen as he tossed a grenade down into a heavy stubber nest. By the time it exploded and took the stubber's ammo cache with it he had jetted into the air again, sighting in on the heavy weapons that looked like they were getting a solid bead on Mathos, and taking them out. A single shell was all he needed to leave one gun crew gone and the rest staggering, eyes and nostrils full of gore and heads ringing from the bolt-shell detonation. Small-arms started to crackle back and forth as the regular militia in between the weapon nests panicked and started wildly pulling triggers.

'Missile nest six metres to your right and up one tier,' he voxed as he jinked the other way. His flank and shoulder crashed into a tripod-mounted autocannon and he stomped the weapon to scrap under his boots. He flared his exhaust jets as he lifted off again and the screams of the crew, knocked sprawling and now blinded and scorched, followed him into the air.

'No, there isn't,' came Mathos' answer over the sound of a screeching chainblade and a brief cry that ended in a gurgle. 'What's left that can threaten a Thunderhawk?'

'Those two sandbag ziggurats flanking the doors. Lot of heat seeping out of the left one.' Phaethon was already in flight again as he spoke, hanging in mid-air then leaning into the leap and firing himself forward on a hard flat trajectory towards the ziggurat's base. Las-fire struck puffs of smoke from his pauldron and helmet, and high-calibre hard rounds thwacked into the sandbags behind him as he landed.

'I've got the heat source,' Mathos said. 'You kill whatever just shot at you. Sounds big enough to wing us if it hits lucky.'

Phaethon's first jump took him to the first step of the ziggurat, a ledge set behind a thigh-high parapet. A startled Sekkite militiaman goggled at Phaethon as he rose up; he crippled the man with the same kick he used to redirect his momentum, twisting into his second leap as another stub salvo struck ceramite chips from his pauldron and arm. His jets spun him like a pinwheel as he hurtled in front of the spire's great ceremonial doors, and a second before he made contact he thrust his pistol upward and fired blind over his head.

Blind, but not unaimed. Phaethon had only taken the briefest upward glance but his mental map of the two ziggurats and his own position between them was perfect. He arrived at the top of the right-hand ziggurat and tore his way through the flakboard and wire into a gun nest already full of smoking debris and vaporised blood. His bolt-shells had smashed the heavy stubber emplacement and blown the gunner backward into the nest. The loader and spotter were still trying to wipe their comrade's gore off their faces when Phaethon's chainsword went through both their necks with one stroke. The return stroke caught another gunner with the flat of the sword and sent him toppling out of the tower with a smashed sternum. The next five kill-strokes were too fast for the eye to follow.

'Well spotted, brother,' Mathos voxed as Phaethon tore the other two stubbers from their mounts and crushed them into unusability in his hands. 'Another two laser barrels like the ones in that battery down there. Definite threat.'

Phaethon looked over to see the peak of the other ziggurat sprout a plume of dirty smoke shot through with dark orange flames. Mathos stepped out of the conflagration, his cloud-grey armour now black with soot, and pointed out over the roadway and the great flat plain of northern Oureppan beyond it.

'And behold, Phaethon! The Beati for whom we are the heralds!'

His helmet grille was on full amplification and the words boomed out from the fire. Below them the surviving Archenemy defenders seemed to understand the words. They shouted and wailed, throwing themselves down into their gun nests and defilades, trying to crawl from sight as their voices were drowned out, not by the voice of the thing they called their master, but by the scream of jets.

Nautakah
Pinnacle Spire approaches, central Oureppan

Helm tilted back, eyepieces reflecting the majestic shape of Pinnacle Spire, Nautakah watched the Thunderhawk go in. Its descent had been a fine display of art, spiralling down out of the sky above the spire's peak, hugging tight to its sides, using the lines of the spire itself to foul lines of fire from below. As he watched, it made a tight half-roll and curved in towards the base of the tower, flared its braking jets and speared straight into the spire's side. He had seen – had been part of – plenty of aerial and orbital assaults that had been carried off with less skill.

It was good that he was on his way to an enemy he could respect. It pleased Nautakah when missions overlapped, fitted their contours together like this. It did not particularly trouble him that his bloody march to the centre of the city had begun out of simple revenge. What more ancient and honourable reason for war was there than that? But it was satisfying to know that his rage for the betrayal at Ghereppan fitted seamlessly with his oath to punish slights against the Blood Pact and the rule of the Gaur. And now a third satisfaction: this path would once again cross that of his loyalist cousins. All of these satisfactions meshed and spun like the whirling links around the head of a chainaxe, fitting themselves flawlessly around the most profound duty of all – the duty to do butchery in the name of the Lord of Blood and Skulls.

The central belts of Oureppan were a ghost town of windswept rockcrete, empty windows and blowing ash. There was no one there to see the arnogaur break into a run.

Damocles and the Saint
Pinnacle Spire, Oureppan

For generations of Urdeshi the Pinnacle Spire of Oureppan was the grandest place they would ever stand in. The soaring vaulted space held whole microclimates, the four grand colonnades that met at the chamber's edges broad enough for thousands-strong congregations to file past and watch the cascades of daylight falling on the plinth of basalt and adamant at the top of a ziggurat of inlaid stairs.

The great octagonal block at the heart of the spire was what made it the symbolic heart of Oureppan. It was carved from the sinking-site of First Javal, the greatest and most venerable of Urdesh's seismic spikes, built when the Mechanicus first started to bring the world's volcanoes to heel. Four statues had stood guard around the plinth since the spire's construction: the Soldier, the Labourer, the Pilgrim and the Magos, each eighty-metre steel colossus gazing down at the tiny figures toiling up the steps at their feet.

This day, all the spire's majesty was buried in silence and gloom. The grand storm-doors at the end of each colonnade were closed and the spire's thousands of lamps doused or broken. The hundred-metre-high diamond-glass windows around the spire's upper tiers had lost their brilliant shine and were now bleared with ash and grime; what light managed to fall down from the great windows in the vault itself did little more than brush out hints of texture and shape in the dark. Not even the gunfire and death cries beyond the western doors penetrated the stillness.

A flash. A streak of heat raced up the join where the double doors met and the frames burst into lethal sprays of white-hot metal vapour. The heat blast blew the door slabs loose, but there was no time for them to topple before a blizzard of missiles and shells stove them inward and scattered their debris down the colonnade like leaves in a gale. For a split second the Thunderhawk made an angular silhouette in the ragged hole where the doors had been, and then it was inside, its engine wash and braking jets filling the colonnade with scorching air and shattering noise.

The gunship slammed down onto the mosaic floor and skidded forward, slewing and spraying showers of splintered tile and gouged rockcrete ahead of it as it came to rest. The barrage of heavy bolter fire from under its wings was all but lost in the glare and din of its arrival until lines of explosions burst up from the floor ahead of it almost to the great stairs, choking the inner parts of the colonnade with stinging clouds of smoke and pulverised masonry. Its turbolaser fired a single shot that carved a glowing trench into the stairs, cooking the air and whipping the dust clouds further into frenzy, sending a scouring hot shockwave over the top into the chamber beyond.

The boots of Damocles Squad landed on the floor of the colonnade before most of the debris did. Aekon and Natus in the lead, Xander and Kules behind them, Dyognes, Andromak and Holofurnace racing forward as the others spread wide, Khiron anchoring their rear. They had cleared the Thunderhawk while the humans were still recovering their wits from the bruising final descent, moving through the scorching rubble-dust so fast that it hissed against their warplate like rain. Broken rock crunched and scattered beneath their feet.

'I hear no movement,' Natus said. 'Empty?'

'It wasn't,' Xander replied. 'Watch your step.' He was weaving among the columns that divided off the left-hand cloister, and in the shadows the neon-yellow splatters were clearly visible against the columns and smeared across the floor. Even through the clogging dust he could smell something acrid and biological about them.

'Living traces.' Aekon had spotted them too. 'And scraps of metal and ceramite. Might have been weapons, armour, augmetics, hard to tell. But the pattern doesn't match splatter from the barrage.'

'I can tell you,' Crethon snarled into the vox. *'I can tell you where I've seen that blood before.'*

Damocles
Pinnacle Spire, Oureppan

Dyognes and Holofurnace were first up the stairs, one on each side of the smoking wound the Thunderhawk's turbolaser had left. They moved cautiously by their own measure but still as fast as a running human, auto-senses tuned sharp and bolters questing for targets. Andromak came behind them, plasma gun to his shoulder ready to blaze. The rest of Damocles advanced behind them, with Mathos and Phaethon in the centre of the formation ready to launch themselves at the first enemy to show itself. They were climbing out of the Thunderhawk's sight-line now; whatever waited for them in the vault would be out of reach of the gunship's firepower.

The filth-smeared window-walls high above them smothered the daylight down to a listless gloaming. The Snakes had no problem seeing in that gloom, but nothing moved in their enhanced vision except for the gusts and swirls of air still welling up the stairs around them from the landing and the turbolaser shot.

The statues were gone. The Pilgrim should have been watching over the Space Marines as they finally gained the vault floor, the Labourer and the Magos should have been visible as they gazed down the east and west cloisters. Where those colossi had gone there was no telling. All that remained were craters on a rhyolite dais where each pair of feet had stood, and a strange circular curtain of even greater proportions than the statues had been, which hung down the very centre of the chamber and masked the plinth from sight. It looked like a shower enclosure or an insect-veil about a gentle-born's bed, hanging from a clumsily welded metal ring that in turn swung from cables that disappeared in the gloom overhead.

Damocles was fully deployed in the vault now, spreading out from the stairs. The vox chatter had fallen away, but to Xander the silence rang with unspoken questions. They were here to break open the Beati's path to Anakwanar Sek – had they reached the end of that path already? Was he here? Was this his fastness? Was he inside that curtained enclosure, readying himself for battle or cowering from his killer? Xander was used to his battle-conditioning making his thoughts clean and frictionless but now these thoughts kept nagging at the edge of his mind like a dangling and baited hook in the corner of the eye. Like – the thought slid into place with a slick, ugly ease – the dangling and baited hooks that hung in the centre of the chamber.

Xander suddenly realised what it was he was looking at.

The Saint
Western colonnade, Pinnacle Spire, Oureppan

There was a wail and whoosh of jets below the Thunderhawk, and a brief double flare of light. The little coterie of humans in the gunship's transport bay shifted warily and hefted their weapons. The Beati looked up from where she was kneeling by the dazed Sister Kassine, to the two Iron Snakes standing guard at the top of the ramp.

'Our brothers from Kalliopi,' Priad said, sensing her question. 'They were our vanguard for the final descent. Rejoining us for the advance.'

'No fighting yet,' the Beati said. 'I hear no gunfire. Do you, Priad? Brother Scyllon?' Both shook their heads.

'The fighting will be ahead of us,' Priad said. 'Such a light guard on the outer doors should mean the teeth of the enemy's defence is still in front of us.'

'An entry like that will have caught them off guard, surely?' Mazho put in. 'Did we really just wreck our way through what was supposed to be a siege-line, straight into the fastness? Are more of your brothers making up a second wave, captain, or does that fall to us in here?' Despite the querulous words the colonel's tone was hearty. Years seemed to have fallen away from him once the full combat harness had gone on. He even found a comradely nod and smile for Ghelon and his two warrior ayatani.

'Damocles will clear the way through the defences,' Priad said a trifle curtly. 'Penetrate as deep into this stronghold as it takes. If the…' He glanced at the Beati, who was helping Kassine sit up. 'When they locate the Anarch we'll move straight in on their location, if it pleases her to do so.'

'And this time maybe the brother here will be slow enough for the rest of us to keep up with,' Mazho said, nodding towards the bright steel strut that had been clamped to the stump of Scyllon's leg. It had only been fitted for a couple of hours. Scyllon could already move on it with fair assurance but his exquisite, inhuman balance and body control were still out of tune with the crude new limb. He did not dignify Mazho's joke with a response.

Damocles
Central chamber, Pinnacle Spire, Oureppan

The curtain was made of human bones, pierced through or wrapped in long barbed cords hung less than an arm's length apart, all around the great metal ring. The cords punched through skulls and tangled around ribcages; they looped around femurs and threaded long collections of vertebrae. Here and there they were knotted into strange patterns that somehow seemed to distort the shapes of the objects around them, as though the knots were tied in cloth that the scene were merely painted onto. Elsewhere they held scrawled parchments, machine-parts defaced with hammers and meltas and excrement, or censers giving off dim yellow light and filthy, fatty smoke. Each cord must have weighed a ton or more with all the foulness strung upon them but still they stirred as though they were nothing more than hanging fronds of grass caught in a breeze.

That was it. The movement. Xander kept glancing around to look at the way the charnel curtain twitched. The way that the trails of light from the moving lanterns seemed to echo the after-images that had hung in his helmet display ever since the wirewolf fight. The way the sway of the cables triggered queasy synaesthesic memories of murder-screams bursting from wire-cage throats with no living tongue to shape them. The way that the click of bone on bone as the cables swung together somehow evoked the clitter of metal hooks running across stone.

Xander slowed. His hand drifted from his bolter up towards his faceplate. He shivered inside his armour. He needed to see. He needed to see what would happen.

He steadied himself, locked his legs in place and invoked the movement and sensing routines his armour used to sharpen his marksmanship to its keenest. Carefully, he sighted in.

The Saint
Western colonnade, Pinnacle Spire, Oureppan

'I want to move soon,' said Sabbat. 'This place is unclean. Can you sense it? Smell it? I have a promise to fulfil. I won't fail it.'

'I'm hearing that there is something in the centre of the spire, ma'am,' Priad replied. 'If you have insights into what it is, please tell us. I counsel waiting for Xander's word if not.'

'I smell bone and charnel,' the Beati said, 'and I can hear the creak of cables. Something... something *hiding*.'

'In fear?' Priad asked her. 'Or in ambush?'

Her eyes closed and her face grew tight, and she did not answer him.

Damocles
Central chamber, Pinnacle Spire, Oureppan

Xander's aim was perfect. The shell connected precisely with a cable-splice, severing the join, bringing half the hanging cord down amid a foul, fleshy rain as it shed its own cargo and tore pieces loose from the cables to either side of it. The flickering after-images in Xander's vision went berserk, swarming like the black blooms of oncoming unconsciousness. They flashed and darted in time to the flashing and darting of the light that was starting to arc up and down the cords hanging above them. The cords that held up such a weight of obscene symbols and human remains, the cords that suddenly lashed and curled as though they were alive.

Xander keyed a pulsing vermilion alert rune into every one of Damocles' helm displays and they formed up on him now, following his gaze up to the new threat.

Long, glistening fingers pushed the carrion curtain apart. A gleaming face three metres across looked down, saw them, and smiled.

The Saint
Western colonnade, Pinnacle Spire, Oureppan

There was barely any sound in the halls of Pinnacle Spire, and everyone in the Thunderhawk heard the shot. The Beati was on her feet before the echoes had died away. The other humans surged forward to surround her. Priad did not need to be told that there would be no stopping her now.

'Cepheas,' he said, 'close the ramp once we're down. Stay ready.'

'Affirm.'

'All of you, fix rebreathers and eye coverings. You'll be moving through dust and smoke. I'm the vanguard. Scyllon, you're the tail.'

'Affirm.'

'Sister Kassine.' Priad stepped forward and bent over her. 'The landing took a toll on all of you, but you in particular. No one will condemn you if you remain here.'

In reply the little woman struggled to her feet, using her staff as support.

'What is the terror of death?' she demanded, turning to the other humans. They all knew the answer, but they gave it mostly in clumsy mumbles. *'What is the terror of death?'* she repeated, the strength seeping back into her voice.

'To die with our work incomplete,' they answered.

'And what is the *joy* of *life?*' Kassine demanded, clanging the foot of her staff on the deck for emphasis.

'To die, knowing our work is done!'

'To slay is to pray,' the Sister said, and looked back around at the Snakes and the Saint.

'Then let us all pray,' said Saint Sabbat.

Damocles
Central chamber, Pinnacle Spire, Oureppan

Damocles needed no order to fire. They unleashed a firestorm at the blistered moon of a face that smirked down at them, their fire as smooth and surgical as if they were at a range rather than on a daemon-haunted battlefield.

But nothing was connecting. Their shots shivered and

corkscrewed in the air, tumbling away well before impact with all their force abruptly spent. Mathos blasted himself vertically into the air and flung a grenade on a perfectly judged downward arc, but it coasted to a stop metres from the creature's sloping forehead and exploded in mid-air with an exhausted pop and barely a puff of smoke. The flechettes simply dropped rather than exploding out, tinkling on the stone floor. The last couple of falling fragments were vaporised in mid-air by a yowling red plasma shot from Andromak aimed at the creature's chest, but the lethal blast unravelled, puffed apart, cooled and faded into nothing.

The thing moved forward through the curtain. Its body bowed and blurred as though it were an image projected onto choppy water, and then suddenly it was standing over them, swaying, looking down over its cavity of a nose and its simpering idiot smile. Although it had taken no visible step, the Iron Snakes clearly heard the heavy *slap* of a flat, soft-fleshed foot hitting stone. Something about the sound made their skin crawl and their guts squirm. Holofurnace clamped his bolter to his pack and in the return movement grabbed his lance, wound up and cast. His form was masterful, good enough to skewer the heart of any normal beast, but the lance never got close. The clank as it hit the floor was weirdly flat and muted, as if heard through water.

The monster's smile did not change. The chains of the curtain swung back and forth behind it and it swayed on its feet in rhythm with them, its eyes drifting half-closed.

'See its movement,' Xander called, his voice doubling up on itself in eerie, reedy vox-band interference. 'Target those cords it was hiding among. Maybe it's bound to them somehow.' He was already matching action to words, swinging his aim up and right. His bolt exploded a limbless torso transfixed by chain and jarred half a dozen more bones loose from their mountings. Khiron's shot went high, struck the ring that supported the cords but skated off and detonated in the air. Two shells from Kules hit a rusted steel plate to which a pattern of bones was wired, punching through it, shattering it, and sending the chain that hung from it crashing to the stone floor.

There was a sigh and a slick sound of wet meat as the daemon sank to one knee. Its eyes were open again and its smile had brightened a little, become an expression of mild wonder. It looked over at Kules, and when its full attention fell on him he could feel a hateful, buzzing vibration filling his senses, seeming to soak in through his skin. Gritting his teeth he back-pedalled, trying to keep his distance, picking his next target in the carrion curtain.

A pallid, glistening hand reached for him, jerkily, like pict footage run by someone with an unsteady hand on the forward spool. One moment the arm was bent by the creature's side, then in a blink it was opening at him, and then it slowed to a crawl through the air. The last bolt-shell in Kules' magazine went inert on its way to the hand, dimpled the middle of the palm and fell away. A shell from Dyognes aimed at its wrist lost all its force two-thirds of the way to its target, curved down and bounced across the floor.

'Spread back!' Kules shouted. 'It moves–' Then the hand blinked down again, too fast to follow, and three long fingernails plucked his helm from its collar and his head from his neck. The daemon's smile brightened from one of faint bafflement to amiable cheer. It tightened its grip, but its flesh was too gelid and slack, and Kules' head squirted out from the bottom of its fist. It landed on the stairs in front of his body as the rest of the corpse sank to its armoured knees.

Below him on the stairs, Andromak felt his teeth grind and a sour taste fill his mouth: his Betcher's Gland was secreting venom, a rage reflex, cousin to a flushed face or wordless shout. The urge to point the plasma gun into the enormous vacant smile and blaze it until the flask was empty was almost irresistible – and then it was gone, short-circuited by his training and conditioning. Instead he aimed high over the thing's stooped and bony shoulders, replaying his squad's last shots in his head, calculating how far away from the creature the dead zone extended. He ignored the way the broad flat face was swinging back and forth, looking for another Iron Snake to focus on, ignored the way one vast and ugly hand seemed to be stealing through the air towards him almost of its own volition. He coughed a quick burst from the gun, watched the infrared trail pass over the daemon's bent back without dimming, and flushed a third of the flask's charge out in a sizzling arc of yellow-white. It cooked a trail through the air above the thing, the lank black hair plastered to the tapering top of its head curling and steaming from the passing heat, and scythed half a dozen chains down out of the curtain.

Pallid, knob-knuckled hands slapped down flat against the floor. When it turned its face around to Andromak its smile had turned sly, malicious. Its body began to shift as it prepared to move on him, each piece of it out of phase with the others. The slick skin bulged and stretched as if the thing's bones and the flesh that wrapped them were trying to perform two different manoeuvres at two different speeds.

Andromak back-pedalled, reading his distance off peripheral vision and motor memory, trying to make sure he was out of its reach without looking directly at its blighted form. Bolt-shells were streaking past his shoulder, to lose their force and drop from the air. Both his hearts were drumming as his body responded to the daemon's proximity by pushing itself to its peak. The telltale runes for the plasma gun were shifting colours, as though the thing simply turning its attention to him were enough to make its superheated fuel gutter out. Andromak aimed at the creature's forehead. However little good it did, better to die with his plasma cooling in the air rather than in the flask.

'Firing!' he called, but the vox was full of scraping, buzzing feedback that echoed his own words back to him, drained into a pale echo of his voice. There was no way to know if anyone else in the squad was trying to speak to him. He raised the gun, and then with an ungainly jitter in the air the splay-fingered hand, as wide across the palm as Andromak was tall, was in front of him. The runic displays in his visor began to fade and he felt his armour growing heavy and sluggish on him. He sent the firing instruction down his armour coupling at the same time as he squeezed the trigger, but he felt a familiar and horrible sensation, a tingling in his palm and forearm like gooseflesh, a sign that the magnetic relays in the gun were churning on a cold and empty flask. It shouldn't have been possible, but there was no shot, no heat splash or muzzle flare. The flabby white hand closed around him and the gun's snout wasn't even hot enough to sizzle as the wet flesh pressed against it. Like a candle flame underneath a snuffer hood, Andromak began to die.

For Xander, time seemed to stretch out. Like Andromak, he had felt the flush of rage at Kules' death, a bright blaze he could sense at the back of his mind like flames behind a windowed furnace door. The light of it flickered across the thoughts he was trying to pull into formation. He wanted to shoot, strike, rip with a blade, pound with his fists, stamp that drooling smile into a meaningless spatter of ichor across the floor. The leg actuators in his armour were pre-tensed to leap and rush. The decision was his. Damocles would follow him in an avenging charge as soon as the order passed his lips.

He slammed the furnace door shut, slowed his run, sent curt barks of battle-cant over the squad band as his brothers fired again, trying to blow the arm that held Andromak free from its shoulder. Against any mortal beast it would have been the right move, but still their shells found no purchase, falling and clattering lifelessly on the steps, even their infrared trails fading out.

'Don't waste your shells!' he shouted. 'Hurt those chains, that shrine. If we can't hurt it, do what you can to goad it. Keep its attention switching between us.'

'It killed Kules! It has Andromak!' Aekon's voice was tight with rage.

'And we're not feeding it the rest of Damocles as well,' Xander snapped back. 'Goad the filth. Now we know how. We'll...' He felt actuators across his torso armour tense and whine as his interface layer sensed the teeth-grinding tension in his neck and shoulders, and tried to interpret it as a command. 'We'll lure it after us. If even the Thunderhawk's weapons can't hurt it, the laser destructor can bring the colonnade roof down on it. Distract it at least. Hit the stairs with missiles and catch those chains in the explosion. But we will not squander our lives standing here trying to fight it out.'

The daemon's enormous flat face had swung around to regard him and Xander had the crawlingly repulsive certainty that the thing knew he was talking about it. The fingers of the great misshapen hand that held Andromak were working as though they were kneading dough. As the rest of Damocles started to reluctantly fall back down the stairs, Xander sighted his bolter on one colourless eye. He tried to work out how few shells it would take to keep the thing's attention, how they would need to move, how likely it was to follow them. The eye he was aiming at, slimed over like raw egg, rolled towards him and Xander sneered in disgust, taking another step back out of reflex, telling himself not to fire yet, not just yet, wait and see.

Then, he realised the eye was not focused on him, but past him, behind him.

The Saint
Central chamber, Pinnacle Spire, Oureppan

'Mockery.'

Despite himself, Xander looked around.

'Miserable, misbegotten joke of a creation. Bow your head. You are unworthy to raise it here.'

The daemon's brow undulated and knitted and its smile seemed to strain on its slack face. It looked down at the fist that enclosed Andromak like a child caught with a stolen treat as Saint Sabbat came walking up the stairs towards it. Her sword was out and she kept it pointed unwaveringly at the drooling smile in front of her.

'One life lost to you is one too many,' she told it. 'No more.' The flat-faced head bobbed and shied, eyes shifting back and forth, unwilling to meet hers. The smile had not slipped but now it was forced and rueful, the expression of one who was trying to bear up brightly under some terrible adversity. It tried to back away, tucking Andromak protectively against its chest. Its feet skidded in the frothy white sludge that had started to sweat through its skin.

'No,' she said, walking up the stairs to the line of Snakes

without slowing or looking at them. 'No hiding, no fleeing. Bow your head and surrender the existence you had no right to.'

Her cloak blew back from her shoulders in a wind that no one else around her could hear or feel. The thing reached out its free hand again, once again with that evil, sense-warping speed, but the hand came to a shivering halt barely an arm's length from the sword's point.

The tips of its fingers split open, peeled back and shrivelled like spent seed-pods. The rest of its flesh rippled and flapped like loose clothing in a high wind. Its eyelids drooped. It swayed towards Sabbat, not in an attack but like an unwilling dog dragged forward on a leash.

'Brothers of the Snake,' she said, not taking her eyes from the daemon's disintegrating hand. 'Do your work.'

Andromak
Central chamber, Pinnacle Spire, Oureppan

Andromak became conscious with a jolt and a spasm. He was trapped in a thick, gluey darkness that stopped his senses dead. There was only blackness in his vision and a filthy, sludgy churning sound in his ears. He could hear his own breathing inside the helmet. The vox-band was silent.

Something was restraining him. Not like hard bonds or water, more like thick mud or the weird, lingering drag of a misaligned ship's gravity field. His recent memories were a blank. He did not know where he was. He flexed his arms, kicked his feet and found points of harder resistance in the muddy nothingness. Encircling bands, like, like... like the bones in fingers. The fingers of a fist that was gripping him. He started to remember. Gelid white flesh, fingers stretching and reaching for him fast, too fast. He fought down the urge to thrash wildly for his freedom, fought to awaken his armour although the memory was coming back with despairing clarity, the memory of the power in his systems ebbing away, dying and leaving him alone.

Except that his vision was alive again, with spiralling orientation readouts and query runes. He could feel the thrum of his reactor pack. Barely daring to hope, he directed his readouts to his weapon feeds. The flask of his plasma gun was burning crisp and clean, full to capacity. The bright green ignition rune spun briskly at the bottom of his vision.

While Andromak's conscious mind was still registering the fact of his salvation, his hand was working the trigger.

The Saint
Central chamber, Pinnacle Spire, Oureppan

The fist the daemon was cupping against its chest burst into vapour that boiled away in an instant in the glare of the plasma shot. It looked down at the disintegrating wreck of its limb as Andromak tumbled out of the splattering mess and crashed to the floor. Its smile turned triumphant. A colourless tongue slid out through its lips, the dripping tip questing towards Andromak as he kicked himself over onto his side to bring the plasma gun to bear again.

Bolter shots stippled its face, bursting one eye and sending ripples through its sludgy flesh. A second salvo compounded the damage, and Andromak cratered its chest and throat with another burst of plasma. It was helpless to stop them now, dragged out of the dead hollow in existence it had made for itself, pinned to reality like an insect against a collector's board. Pinned by the point of a slender sword that glinted with green light, and by a calm and quiet voice.

'The Emperor protects,' she told it as it slumped down onto all fours, flesh hanging from its bones. 'Your masters should have warned you of that.'

She took a step up, another, and by the third she was running. She sprinted through the Iron Snakes' firing line, her feet no longer touching the floor. Green firelight played across the walls around them, lit the Space Marines' armour, coalesced around her shoulders as her cloak fell away and the flames burst free. They fanned out into wings that lifted her and sped her forward, the daemon finally collapsing into rags and scraps and then into non-existence as she blazed through the space its remains had occupied. She turned in the air, face serene, sword still raised, spiralling upward as an eagle would ride a thermal. The charnel chains that had curtained the daemon's lair burst loose from their mountings and fell, their foul ornaments burned to nothing in seconds, the cables collapsing unheeded into a heap far beneath her. In the green blaze the four mighty statues that had stood beneath the spire were there once more: the Soldier, the Labourer, the Magos and the Pilgrim, sketched in cool emerald light. The clean scent of islumbine dissolved the daemon-stink from the air.

'Anakwanar Sek! Show yourself!'

The Enemy
Oureppan

She is there.

That knowledge lit up the minds of the lekts who crouched in their nests around the base of Pinnacle Spire. From there, like a beacon fire bringing answering flame from mountaintop after mountaintop, it sprang up in mind after mind out across Oureppan. The knowledge, the sense-memory of that spark of green light high in the spire, the cold touch of mountain air, the scent of red-and-white flowers.

She is there. It is her.

In an orbital delivery silo to the north of Pinnacle Spire, a lekt convulsed in the web of ropes that held him in the centre of the cavernous driver shaft. The void shield generator that hung directly over his head crackled into life, supercharged by the ingeniants' re-engineering and the massive power cables rerouted from the mass driver's accelerator coils. The generator threw out its void field not in a curtain or a dome but a pillar that went crackling up through the fake silo roof and into the sky. The lekt had been hung here as the container for a single word, spoken by a single voice that drowned out all others. He spoke it now. The voice that had been placed in him tore the air in front of his mouth. It slammed against the hazy, rippling energy of the void shield. Entered it, harmonised with it, built to a deadly waveform that radiated off the column of force and bathed the surrounding city with that single, malefic voice.

Her light, her words. The sound and scent of her.

The lekt sat cross-legged in a locked chamber in the keep of a monetariat tower in the Adeptus precinct south of Pinnacle Spire. Her wrists were shackled to her ankles and her collar to the floor. She had made no attempt to fight the restraints. They had been her idea. Around her were a dozen data-looms that had once run the Imperial tithing cycle for Oureppan's transport nexus and for most of Urdesh's northern hemisphere. Now they were interwoven with contraptions of stripped bone and remade flesh merged with salvage scrap and servitor controls, contraptions that

Erasmos Squad or Brother Crethon would have found familiar. They were running the looms to a different end now, using them to perfectly sync three Titan-scale void shield generators mounted in this tower and the two adjoining it. The lekt and the constructs had been waiting for the same thing, and here it was.

Stitched-together limbs flexed and slices of half-alive brain matter channelled stimuli, responses and commands. With a precision that would have made a tech-priest gasp the three voids threw fan-shaped fields into the sky, intersecting them to form one perfectly tuned membrane of energy, filling more than a square kilometre of air with eye-twisting distortions and ear-stabbing discharge flares.

In the chamber below, the lekt added her voice to it. It rippled up through the ether and through the void field, emerging into physical reality in a flare of golden light across the tripartite field. All the way back to the bay soldiers turned to look at the horizon, wondering if that strange second dawn meant an atomic atrocity had been unleashed to their north.

Green fire in the tower. She was called and she came.

In the streets upon streets of freight-houses that made up a great plain of rooftops to the north-west. In the generatoria hubs that ridged the shielded launching complexes above the north-eastern arm of the bay. In burned-out convict dormitories and the abandoned mansions of merchant grandees, in temple complexes and sewage stations, in auspex towers and drinking holes. Every one a makeshift nest, hiding a plundered void shield and a waiting lekt. One after another, they answered the inaudible call.

We know her sound, we know her sight. This is the one for whom the Anarch has had us wait.

The magister's servants had completed his design to perfection. They had hollowed out their precious, unassailable fortress, sacrificed it to make his trap, but the Anarch had decreed that the sacrifice would be made, that Oureppan could fall as Ghereppan had fallen, as Eltath and the Eotine Walk and the Ghentethi citadels had fallen before it, as all of Urdesh could fall if that was what it took for Anakwanar Sek to claim this one life.

What was done in the spire could only have been done by her. There can be no doubt. She is here. She is here.

Oureppan's sublevels, built to house the great web of fulgeducts that had once fed the power-greedy mass driver wells, thrummed with purpose. Invaders and occupiers alike felt it around the substations and capacitor stacks, and wherever the hidden roads of power crossed battle lines or troop columns. Compasses went wild, magnetic locators returned impossible readings or became unmoored completely. Vox transmissions fought their way through a rising fog of interference.

Great tracts of outer Oureppan had started to crumble where the ingeniants and work crews had not bothered to maintain districts that their army did not properly occupy. Now momentary flashes dotted the city's dead zones as neglected systems overloaded, and thin pencil-scribbles of smoke began to drift up over the flat skyline.

None of that mattered to the Anarch's plan. The conduits that it needed, the ones that fed the carefully positioned void shield emplacements, had all been scrupulously maintained. Now that system within a system had come fully to life, flooding itself with a city's worth of energy pulled down from Old Ourezhad and pouring it all into the voids.

* * *

The Enemy
Low orbit, Oureppan airspace

From directly above, the blooms of energy and the echoing psychic shouts made a pattern that shifted and evolved as each new emplacement lit up. A pentagon became a pentagram that became a circle and then a spiral, and then a darker and more complex design that sent rumbles and churns up into the atmosphere and magnetosphere even before it was fully formed. Fully ignited, the sign interlocked with a point above it in high planetary orbit, perfectly aligned with the centre of the pattern, a point simultaneously empty and packed with psychic mass.

A ripple passed through the patterns of stars. The sunlight pouring down onto the planet buckled and parted. A ball of strange electromagnetic echoes manifested out of the empty dot of space, expanded at the speed of light and was gone. All around Urdesh's dayside, astropaths and Navigators flinched under sudden stabs of migraine.

A blister that had been pushed into space and time vanished. The tract of space it had enclosed rejoined the physical universe. The flagship of Anakwanar Sek hung silently over Urdesh.

It was barely bigger than Pinnacle Spire itself, of grand scale to a human eye but a swift little yacht compared to the monstrous crenellated fortresses of the Imperial battlefleets. Its surface was a mottled, tarnished grey-black, its texture blending the rigid lines of machined parts with gnarls and whorls that cast unnatural, eye-trapping shadows in the sunlight.

The ship basked at the focus of a cone of energy whose base spread across the city of Oureppan. It rode the glare of power. Scented it, tasted it.

It is true. It is certain. She is here.

Now it answered. It inhaled the power beaming up to it and exhaled it again, in a tight rail that shimmered into existence beneath the circular black window in its prow. Cleanly and perfectly focused on its target. On Pinnacle Spire.

Nautakah
Pinnacle Spire, Oureppan

Nautakah looked up as the psychic thunderclap split the sky apart. Colourless lightning was radiating out through the Oureppan sky from a point dead overhead, like cracks spreading from a bullet-hole shot in reality. The lightning-cracks did not flare but they seemed to sink into the air, turning from cracks to scars. At their point of origin, the cloud, the air, the light itself was bending and curling. The Nails crawled and squealed in Nautakah's skull as he watched the vortex form and tighten, dipping down towards the city like a mouth descending on a morsel, a supercell storm made of the winds of the immaterium. The eye-blanching non-light filled the sky.

Nautakah smiled with satisfaction. It appeared he would be just in time.

The psychic vortex kissed the tip of Pinnacle Spire, and then engulfed it.

Damocles
Central chamber, Pinnacle Spire, Oureppan

A noise came echoing down the hollow column of force like water crashing down a well shaft, smashed and rolled and echoed through the chamber in a tsunami of sound and thought. Human and Astartes alike dropped to their knees or sprawled headlong as it smashed down on them.

There were no words to it, not at first. It was a singularity, an instant of utter sensory obliteration. Then, over the stretched, endless seconds after the hammer blow, the whirl and ricochet of echoes teased themselves together into words.

NO MORE. ENDED. ENDED, YOU ARE, LITTLE SAINT. UPSTART. END FOR YOU. ENDING NOW.

Priad's vision swam back into focus. He realised he had toppled forward, the joints in his armour locked up. His lightning claw had driven a hand's length into the stone steps. Teeth gritted, he directed a flash of power through the tines and yanked it free. His head was still full of echoes: *ending now nding now ing now now now now.*

There was a splintering crash off to his right as Phaethon hit the floor of the western colonnade. Holofurnace was sagging against the steps to his left, using his lance as a staff to prop himself up. Priad tried to speak to the squad vox-band but his tongue was dry and his throat could do nothing more than click and gag. He reached for the ancillary symbol-code instead, trying to send the runes for *stand your ground* and *look to the wounded* and *rally on me* into Damocles' helmet displays. It took him two false starts to focus his mental grip on his armour interface enough to get the transmission off. As his brothers started to drag themselves up, Priad forced himself up the stairs and looked for his charge.

She was still hanging in the centre of the chamber, her fiery wings spread but motionless, her face upturned. She was utterly still, her flesh barely even giving off heat. Below her, Ghelon and Milo were both on their knees retching. Mazho and Kassine were supporting one another, managing to half-stand between the two of them.

There was a half-formed choking sound in the vox that Priad's flickering display said was Khiron. After a moment his Apothecary tried again.

'Th... the Beati. H-how do we protect her? From th-that?'

'You see to our brothers,' Priad said, his voice a creaking wreck. 'Identify the worst hit, try and find something you can do to counteract whatever that did to us. Rally on Xander. We're getting her out of the spire.' His throat was loosening up. Words were getting easier to form, both in his head and on his tongue. 'We'll drag her down from there and carry her if we have to. Andromak, incinerate anything that tries to stop us.' Affirmation runes lit up. 'Cepheas?'

'Engines turning. Ministering to the machine-spirit now in the wake of whatever that was. Ramp is–'

And then words and thoughts were gone again as that stunning force smashed down on them. If the voice Priad had heard through Tschemherr's mouth in the Psykana roost had been a blow from a fist, then this was a meteor impact. If the voice there had been the striking of a match, then now it was an atomic fireball. If that voice had been the touch of a snowflake, this was the relentless force of a glacier that could grind a mountain range beneath it.

This time it was Andromak he saw in front of him when his vision swam back out of the yellow-white haze, half-collapsed into the scar in the floor at his feet from the plasma burst he had fired in his convulsions. Above them, the Beati had stretched out in the air as if standing on tiptoe. She had lowered her sword and was reaching up with her free hand. Her outstretched fingers were shaking. He tried to call out but couldn't make a sound. His head was still full of echoes from the voice that had dropped on them like a warhead.

ENEMY MY ENEMY END OF YOU ANSWERED MY WILL MY VOICE SEE YOU SEE–

He forced himself forward again, not bothering to try and verbalise. He projected more wordless directive-symbols instead: *press on, reiterate, mission objective, press on.* Holofurnace had reached the plinth and was sagging against its carved side. Dyognes was trying to aim his bolter straight up. The weapon swayed drunkenly in his grip until his arms shivered and froze. Priad recognised the signs: his brother's body was not obeying him, and he had sent the order to his armour joints to lock and brace for him. Inside his skull, that maelstrom of echoes gradually weakened until the words were discernible: *It was my will that you answered this call, my voice that commanded you, do you see that this is the end of you?*

An alert rang in his ear; the signifier icon in the right side of his vision was for Crethon. The chime rang three more times then cut out. If his brother had managed to say anything into the vox, Priad couldn't make it out.

Ahead of him Holofurnace was on the plinth, pushing himself to his feet to reach upward, but the Saint was ignoring him. The green fire of her wings was just a misty glow. She hung in a column of sickly yellow light, unable to drag her gaze from whatever she was staring at beyond the spire's ceiling. Her face shone with tears.

Nautakah
Pinnacle Spire, Oureppan

Nautakah had walked up to the western doors of Pinnacle Spire with perfect poise, his breathing easy, his axe motor at idle. The fortifications rose up in front of him in tiers and parapets, already breached and gutted, their defenders a scatter of corpses in drab Sekkite militia uniforms. For some reason, a knot of dead Sons of Sek were scattered in front of the foremost wall. Nautakah paid them little attention – his focus was on what was in front of him – but a corner of his millennia-old warrior's mind noted the marks of their deaths, the print of bolt-shells and chainblades. He glanded a trickle of combat drugs into his blood, and the metal lace in the back of his skull began to throb a little faster.

Movement stirred around him as he cleared the rear barricade line and walked between the two sandbag ziggurats that flanked the ascent to the doors. He stopped and looked about him. Faces began to appear over the parapets, wide eyes staring at him over the Sekkite bandanas that held the handprint over their mouths. It was a shabby, slipshod look compared to the sneering metal grotesques the Blood Pact wore over their lower faces. Nautakah was pleased by the contrast.

'The Pact would have fought better than you,' he told them. Several faces vanished. The ones that remained just stared at him, mute. Nobody spoke to him, or shot at him. Nobody picked up a weapon and climbed down to follow him, either. They hid in their holes and vanished from Nautakah's thoughts when they vanished from his sight. He stared past the fortifications now, out over the city, watching the power flying skyward from the Anarch's grand work, then turned to look at where that power had been sent.

Beyond the ruin of the mighty spire doors there was just yellow-grey nothingness. A fog of it, a wall of it, filling the archway, passing through the walls and floor as if they were void as it enveloped the chamber at the heart of the spire. It breathed and shone and mocked the eye: it was hard and glossy-smooth as diamond-glass, insubstantial as water-haze, at once depthless and colourless and yet swirling with rich bands of ochre and ashy grey like a gas giant's cloud bands, at once motionless and whirling past him like a tornado's funnel cloud. Like an optical puzzle, it presented every aspect and none of them, letting the brain slide between images, trying to reconcile them until it went mad.

Nautakah shared his Legion's loathing of witch-trickery, and this sight filled his mouth with bile. This was not the work of a gore-mage, who took the fundamental human truth of shed blood and revealed truths more fundamental still. This fed lies into the simple stuff of reality, made the plain and solid universe betray itself, and so they convinced one's tools, one's thoughts, one's very senses to lie too. Treachery begetting treachery.

The rage was back, and it was total. His poise vanished, his careful serenity was burned to nothing in the furnace of his skull. The world fell away as every sense blurred into one hungry funnel of perception pointed at the insult in front of him. The Butcher's Nails filled him with their urgent, wordless raving. The brass collar about his neck and chest sizzled with heat and crimson droplets oozed from the visage of the Blood God worked into its front. The chainaxe teeth became a screaming blur as he brought it over and down.

Damocles
Central chamber, Pinnacle Spire, Oureppan

The concussion cracked the air open inside the spire, sending shockwaves down the North Colonnade.

'Crethon! Cepheas! Thunderhawk auspex!' For an instant Priad thought he heard one of them start to acknowledge, but then their voice shredded away into more howling, chortling interference. He set his armour to pulse a signal up and down the band to try and find a way through. That last shock had been something different, he was sure of it. Not one of the psychic blast waves crashing in from all sides. It had been directional, and physical, some kind of detonation from the same way they had come in. Somewhere behind their gunship.

Ahead of him, Xander vaulted onto the plinth, braced himself on Holofurnace's shoulder and reached upward. The Saint showed no sign of knowing either of them was there. Xander's hand seemed to be split and doubled, the way the surface of water breaks an object's outline, and then he was pinwheeling backward through the air, tossed like a doll, his right arm ending in a sizzling stump an inch above where the wrist would have been. The pool of light that had fallen onto the Saint was brightening and flaring around her. She rose even further into the air but now she was not flying. She looked more like she was being dragged upward by a noose. Her grey cloak was burning, her mouth open and twisting. Her sword fell from her hand and then hung motionless. Loose fragments of cable and stone started to rise up into the air around her.

Stentorian echoes bounced and slammed around the spire like swarms of bats, coalesced into another crushing psychic impact and broke apart again, leaving the throbbing memory of words trodden into the brains of the mortals below.

ABANDON ABANDON YOU WILL KNOW ABANDONMENT NOTHING WITHOUT SUFFER–

And from the end of the colonnade another thunderclap impact on the psychic wall with which the magister had trapped them.

* * *

Nautakah
Western colonnade, Pinnacle Spire, Oureppan

It was not the cut of the axe, although the teeth were sharp enough to carve the armour off a battle tank. It was not the impact of the axe, although the force of the arnogaur's swing could split a Space Marine's helm even with the chain at a standstill. It was what the axe represented. The power that came behind it, that the blood-weeping collar symbolised, invoked and drew to a head.

Nautakah struck again. The brass collar thrummed like an organ reed, in unholy anti-harmony with the keening of the pain machine. Both halves of that harmony rose to a shriek as the axe-teeth tore the curtain of force. It retreated, parted like fog before a jet of air, contracted away from the axe-stroke like flayed skin stretched on a frame and sliced. Nautakah wound up and struck again, walked into the wound he had opened and struck again. The axe chain wailed like a grieving beast. A spray of blood burst from the eyes and mouth of the visage on the front of the collar, and where the scarlet droplets contacted the psychic barricade they bleached it out and melted it away, as if the curtain were ice and the blood were boiling. He pushed through the tear, the barrier shattering like plaster and evaporating like mist and parting like thorn-scrub, its touch numbing his mind and scraping his body raw as though his warplate were not even there.

And then... then he saw...

...he saw that the shimmering ahead of him was not warp-trick but heat-haze, the strange shapes the wall had tried to weave in his senses resolving into the outline of a Thunderhawk gunship silhouetted against a bilious yellow glow from the far end of the colonnade.

Half a dozen steps into the dimness he felt something wrong, a foreboding that he could not describe, and a second later it hit him. The cascade, the avalanche of dust and ice and roaring noise crashed down on the hot whirl of his thoughts, almost extinguishing them. The furious answering shriek of the pain engine was the only thing that kept him conscious; the automatic reactions of his armour were the only thing that kept him upright. Swaying in place, Nautakah tried desperately to hold on to the white-hot trails that the machine in his skull had carved through his thoughts, clung to them amid the tsunami of words that were not his own.

I MYSELF THIS I DO MYSELF DOOM YOU MYSELF MY WILL YOU WILL KNOW THIS I DO–

There was more, he thought, more to it than that. With senses and intuitions schooled by long ages in the madness of the Eye he sensed deeper patterns and meanings, a grander declamation by a powerful mind that his physical nerves could only perceive in this simple jumble. But he knew all he needed to know. He was in the right place. This was where he would unmake the Anarch's plans.

Sounds and scents enveloped him as the psychic shock wore off. The thick fumes of the Thunderhawk exhaust and the sharper notes of Astartes jump-pack propellant. Fyceline, ozone and stub-cartridge propellant. A sweet, astringent floral scent. And blood. Human blood, Space Marine blood. Splashed and clotted and scorched blood. All down the colonnade ahead of him, blood. Whose it was didn't matter.

Blood for the Blood God.

Nautakah walked towards the light.

* * *

The Enemy
Oureppan

From high above, the whole of Oureppan pulsed like a melanoma sore on Urdesh's ashen skin. From their lairs among the Anarch's unclean ley lines the lekts screamed ever louder, lighting the great and foul design steadily brighter, dragging ever more power down from Old Ourezhad's sides. The vortex forced into being over Pinnacle Spire by their master's will kept tightening, relentless as a strangling noose.

The miniscule breach Nautakah had opened in the vortex was less than a speck, too small to sense, lost to the lekts in their joyous agonies, invisible to the magister as he bent every thought and word to the final destruction of the Saint. The cries of the lekts and the will of the Anarch drove the great design forward, unstoppable, the wound the arnogaur had left barely even a flea bite on an ogryn.

And yet, this flea bite did not heal. The cascade of raw energy and psychic might failed to erase it. The violence of the act, the furious essence of it, set up its own imperceptible ripple in the great construct, festering around it like corrosion, like scrapcode. Like the single tiny out-of-balance vibration that could build, and ramify, and shudder an enormous, perfectly tuned engine into pieces.

Nautakah
Western colonnade, Pinnacle Spire, Oureppan

Nautakah ran as close in to the Thunderhawk's engines as he could, using the miasma of heat to mask his approach. The ramp was closed and the running lights flaring – the thing was still crewed. Nautakah hissed at the thought of all the time it would take to hack his way in, already scouting the hull for open side-hatches, vents, battle damage he could add to to goad the crew out of their cockpit. A blind rush onward in search of easier enemies would take him right into the sights of the gunship's weapons. There would barely be any remains for the Snakes to gloat over.

Then he realised the engines were cycling up. He saw the landing gear lift free of the gouge it had made in the floor. The gunship was rising into the air, leaving him exposed in the middle of the colonnade. At the base of the steps ahead, silhouetted in unholy yellow glow, an Iron Snake propped on one leg and one ungainly metal stump was aiming a bolter at him. He must have turned, seen the World Eater coming, and signalled or voxed the Thunderhawk crew. He had made a mistake.

The pain engine blew white heat into his skull, trying to drive out doubt and thought, trying to launch him into a charge, and this time he let it. *And my blood too is welcome*, he thought, the only coherent thought he could frame as he built up a killing speed. Perhaps he could make it to the injured loyalist before the Thunderhawk's guns came to bear. Perhaps there would be one more skull for the throne before his own skull joined it, one axe-stroke to find its mark and consecrate the ground, just one more kill to offer up and then Khorne could have him.

And another hammer blow of psychic force dropped on them all out of the sky.

Nautakah and Damocles
Pinnacle Spire, Oureppan

For the Iron Snakes and their human companions this was the most brutal assault yet, a seismic mental shock which took an age to fade down into word-echoes in their reeling brains.

LAST WORTHY WORTHY FITTING END YOU TAKEN YOU ME NOW THIS DOOM DOOM DOOM–

For Nautakah it was a grinding, maddening wasp-hum that went to war in his head with the scorpion-scrabble of the Nails. If the voice booming down on them from the heavens had been aimed at him then not even the brass collar could have protected him, but it had not been. The collar could not stop that voice dead but it could part it like a ship's prow slicing into a wave, just enough to spare Nautakah's mind the punishment of those around him.

At last we are at a worthy end, was what he heard, *a fitting end for you. If you have taken any instruction from me now then pass it on to the one who you thought sent you. You sought this doom. You alone.*

The one-legged loyalist crashed down on his side as his balance went and the crude prosthetic skidded out from under him. His bolter sprayed out half its magazine, ploughing up mosaic tiles and scattering explosions. Above and behind Nautakah the Thunderhawk lurched in the air, slid sideways to bring down one of the high galleries in a scream and crash of stone on armour, and landed askew on the floor only metres forward of where it had been sitting. And Nautakah's charge did not falter.

Scyllon died before he had regained his senses. A great arcing overhead stroke of the axe drove straight through the crest of his helmet and hacked helmet and skull in half down to his gorget. At the top of the steps, Aekon had made it halfway to his feet when Nautakah smashed into him and sent him staggering backwards. Reflexively Aekon let his legs buckle and raised his arms to protect his head but his body was still sluggish from the psychic blow and Nautakah was moving with the blaze of his Nails. He took Aekon's right arm at the elbow with one stroke, swatted the bolter aside as the Snake took aim, and set his shoulders for a lateral backhand cut that would carve off Aekon's skull at the eyeline.

It never connected. A foot away from Aekon's exposed head it crashed into the casing of Khiron's bolter, shearing the weapon almost in two before Khiron yanked the ruined halves sideways, trying to sandwich the axe-head and trap it in the twisted metal and splintered ceramite. Nautakah let out a snarl of frustration and dragged his axe back savagely towards him, and Khiron let himself be pulled with it, releasing his grip on the remains of his bolter as he was pulled inside the chainaxe's range and thrusting his arm forward. Nautakah let him come, his reflexive reaction to get the empty-handed Snake into even closer quarters, but the arnogaur's reflexes hadn't accounted for the fact that Khiron was not empty-handed.

With a whine of accelerating motors the reductor on the old Apothecary's forearm extended its drillspike. Nautakah realised there was still a weapon in play when the tip of the drill came through the right lens of his helmet and next instant was spinning and scraping against the back of his eye socket. The arnogaur howled and slammed his elbow into Khiron's chest, knocking the other Space Marine away, feeling a foul grating sensation as the spinning spike extracted itself from his eye and out through his helmet. He kicked Khiron back further, used a dainty twist of the axe to shred the short sword the Apothecary had drawn, and stepped in, eyes locked on the spot on the neck where his next strike would land.

'*Ithaka!* The Phratry lives!'

Phaethon came in on Nautakah's newly blinded side, chainsword out ahead of him to slash across the arnogaur's face along the crease that Iapetos' lance had struck into it, and then smashed him bodily off his feet. His ammunition was gone but his voice was strong and clear as he shouted the name of his home world again, and he smashed his sword's thick adamantine handguard into Nautakah's skull over and over, every strike landing with a force that would have made a shapeless nonsense of a human head, jump jets roaring and suspensors whining in protest as he dragged the World Eater across the rubble-littered floor, away from the staggering Apothecary.

Nautakah bared his iron teeth, swung his body up, kicked his legs out, hauling Phaethon's arm down and forcing him to break his attack and redirect himself in the air. They slewed, tacked and rolled, now with Nautakah running along the ground half-dragging Phaethon with him, now with Phaethon yanking the arnogaur off his feet, swinging him through the air and smashing more blows into Nautakah's cracked faceplate, which had finally begun to buckle and fold inward. They slammed into the curving wall between the north and west colonnades and began to skid along it, still brawling. The screech of Nautakah's chainaxe blended with the cry of Phaethon's jets and suspensors until there was no separating them. Finally the axe struck true and blood fountained from under Phaethon's ribs, falling in sprays of flash-clotted flakes, the young Space Marine's control deserting him for the brief moment that was all Nautakah needed. Long enough for him to strike off the sword-arm, carve a bloody trench through the belly armour, flay open the faceplate and drop to one knee on the chamber floor, holding Phaethon's chainsword in his left hand as his latest enemy spiralled away to crash in an empty colonnade somewhere beyond the light.

The light. The dirty, craw-clogging golden light.

It filled Nautakah's remaining eye as the machine in his skull burned away the pain of his injury and scraped his nerves and senses sharp. A human form hung motionless in the centre of it, head wrenched back, alive or dead he could not tell. The arnogaur cawed laughter when he realised who it was. He wondered how she liked being trapped in this light as he had been trapped in hers.

And this sourceless, depthless yellow light, Nautakah recognised that too, knew it from the days when the Blood Pact and the followers of Sek had marched and fought together. He had seen their witch-rituals and the lekts calling down manifestations of their Anarch master. Never remotely as powerful as this, but he didn't care. That was what he was to destroy. His duty to his gaur commanded it; the rage of the Blood God demanded it. His god would piss on the Anarch's light, extinguish it along with whatever rat-cunning trickery the traitor magister was trying to engineer. Then for good measure he would stamp the girl's body into red mash, and then when that was done he would turn on the rest of the lackeys around him and pour their hot, rich blood out onto the steps.

Buoyed by the pulse of the pain machine and his own ululating battle cry, Nautakah felt himself almost float forward. Inside his helmet his face was lit up in the ecstasy of the bloodletting to come.

And then he was lying on his back, pinned in place by a long-hafted Ithakan sea-lance. Hissing in furious frustration, he looked up and met Priad's eyes.

* * *

Erasmos
The Power Shrine, Old Ourezhad

And that was the moment that Erasmos Squad, ranged around the burning wreckage of the thing that had controlled the silver shrine, detonated their charges.

The Enemy
Oureppan

In the vast mass of the volcano and the machinery that nestled inside it, the explosions were barely pinpricks – but they were pinpricks inflicted with the precision of acupuncture points. The mechanical heart of the spike continued to beat, but its monstrous piezoelectric pulse no longer reached the arterial channels that ran through the volcanic cone and outward into Oureppan. The city's systems began to flicker, falter and fail.

The first collapse came in a chemical pipeline terminal not far north of Pinnacle Spire. The giant pumping and refining station had furnished the heavy-duty power connections, and the tops of the catalytic processing towers had been the perfect vantage points. Each housed a nest with a lekt and a rebuilt void projector. The interleaved sheets of screaming energy they were raising to the sky were thick with their warp-tuned harmonics.

And then there was the thump of a failing power connection somewhere below them, and each void shield quietly died.

The lekts were too immersed in their psychic cries to silence themselves now. They would have killed themselves trying. But without the void resonators they were no longer anywhere near strong enough to send their power up to their master's ship. Nor to focus it. Nor to control it.

The fields were gone but the power that had saturated them was left behind, a frozen etheric cascade hanging over the city. A smaller event might have played itself out with less harm. It could have soaked back through the veil of the real and vanished, or collapsed from warp energy into more mundane forces and flared off as light, heat, a concussive shockwave. But there was too much of it, an overdose of a lethal drug dumped into the metabolism of reality at an unbearable concentration and purity.

The air tore. Light and gravity twisted and squalled. The lekts both vanished in an instant, the psychic blowback obliterating their physical bodies without trace and sending booming, mocking echoes of their voices racing away through pipes and tanks, shouting blasphemies. Blue-yellow lightning stroked the surrounding streets, tearing gouges in the buildings and raising plumes of pulverised dust. The psychic blast front radiated out and around the chain of lekt stations…

…to a distribution house where a lekt lounged on bolts of musty cloth looted from broken containers until the void projector on the brass tripod over his head blew out and suddenly he was thrashing and screaming as a tornado of flame flew up from him, forming words and faces and sending the shockwave leaping along…

…to the loading crane over a railhead where the lekt laminated the inside of the crane cabin with her remains before she ever knew anything was wrong and the void projector at the end of the crane arm exploded in an eye-skewering point of blue-white light under the strain of the blast…

…which swept through the north-east driver silos and filled

them with smoke and screams whose echoes came alive and laughed and tore the voices from the screamers forever...

...and around through the commercia clusters in the city's east and south-east where the great beams of etheric power fell back from heaven as if the sky itself had been shattered and was bleeding its fragments down to trample the unworthy earth beneath it...

...and in the south, in the south where the mortal soldiers still fought one another for the fate of Oureppan, it came upon them like artillery, like Titan footfalls, like orbital bombardment, as the Anarch's great design shook itself apart.

Damocles
Central chamber, Pinnacle Spire, Oureppan

Priad stared down the haft of Holofurnace's sea-lance at the mockery of himself pinned to the ground. He took in the blood-crusted red armour, the brass baubles worked with hellish designs, the notched iron spikes. The blood welling out of the drilled-out eyepiece. The heraldry of the World Eaters on the pauldron, barely discernible under the gore and filth.

Then the World Eater bellowed in defiance and went to kick himself out from under the pinning lance. He couldn't get quite enough purchase, bellowed again, tried to grip the shaft and force it back from his chest. They stayed that way for several long breaths, their battle silent but for the faint whine of armour actuators and the creak of the lance-haft under monstrous strain, before the beast switched tack and grabbed for the chainaxe bound to its arm by a leather cord. The axe teeth yelped to life as the beast swung.

Priad had been expecting that move. The chainaxe carved

only air as the Iron Snake whipped the lance away, whirled it over his head and drove it back in, this time past the edge of the pauldron and into the front of the World Eater's right shoulder. It bellowed again as it found it couldn't raise the axe at an angle to strike at the lance-haft.

'Holofurnace,' Priad said, voice tight. Something felt different, something in the air that his auto-senses seemed to pick up as well but couldn't quite pass on to him. He had the sense that perhaps no more of those crushing mental roars would descend on them, but he couldn't afford to act as though that were already fact.

'I've almost got her!' Holofurnace called back. 'Whatever was keeping us from reaching her is gone, she's still held but she's alive.'

The World Eater had grabbed the lance-head with its left hand. It didn't have the traction to bend or break the weapon one-handed, but Priad could feel the scrape of metal on ceramite as it worked to drag it clear. Its bloodied gaze had not so much as twitched from Priad's.

'Get her to the Thunderhawk. Her retinue. Our wounded brothers. Then the dead.'

'Affirm.'

Priad jerked the lance back as the World Eater kicked up, trying to jolt his grip loose. Once more he spun it whooping through the air and drove it down into the top of the World Eater's plastron, catching the head under the helmet-join, pinning the enemy in place again.

'Mathos, scout the Thunderhawk's path back down the colonnade. Xander, to me. Dyognes, Andromak...' He whipped the lance out of the path of another chainaxe swipe that came close enough for the adamantine teeth to skitter along the haft, whirled it again in a blur of steel, rang a stunning blow off the enemy's helm and then pinned its shoulder once more. 'To me as well. Come here and let's kill this bastard.'

But outside the spire, a roar was rising.

The warp
Central chamber, Pinnacle Spire, Oureppan

The chain reaction of psychic collapse had finally reached all the way inward. The break Nautakah had made in the warp-work would have been trivial had the Anarch and his psykers still been in control of the structure, but now, like a flesh wound to a body too sick and exhausted to spare the energy to heal, it was festering and spreading. And the shockwaves from the dying psykers and collapsing voids all around the spire would not stop coming.

The column swayed, at first still stolid and stately like a high tower in a fierce gale, then twisting on itself like a crumpling paper tube, sweating corposant flares, ectoplasmic fog and screams. The sides bowed in, puffed out, burst into tatters and reformed. High in the atmosphere the Anarch's flagship was dragged into a corkscrewing spin, the compartments and corridors filling with the cries of the crew and the bone-shuddering groans of superstructure under insane stresses.

Ghostly aurorae and thunderclaps that almost made words surrounded the peak of Pinnacle Spire. Warp-lightning leapt back and forth across the vortex, growing faster and wilder until one bolt brushed the side of the spire and sent a shower of stone chips spraying out into the eldritch storm-funnel whirling around it.

Perhaps that somehow earthed the storm's power, short-circuiting it and hastening its collapse. Perhaps the storm decided it liked the taste of solid matter. Whatever the reason, the walls of the storm collapsed inward and the psychic maelstrom fell upon the spire.

Nautakah
Central chamber, Pinnacle Spire, Oureppan

Nautakah's vision had narrowed to a predator's tunnel, and the walls of the tunnel were a dark swimming red like an after-image on which the pain machine left white scribbles of rage. It had not fallen silent while he was killing (and it never would, not until either or both of them were unmade) but it had acquiesced, added itself into the smooth choreography of body and armour, muscle and mechanism, thought and reflex and breathing, instead of screaming over them. Now it was angry again. He had to fight not to let its hooks any deeper into his thoughts. He could not afford to slide down into mindless thrashing fury while this upstart child kept him so carefully pinned like a specimen on a dissecting board.

He kicked again, connected with the lance-haft and gave a convulsive heave of his body to surge upright and swing his axe, but then the head of the axe was knocked aside and the lance-head was driving down again, catching under his chin and clanking the back of his helmet against the floor. He could feel the grind as the lance-head twisted, the enemy trying to work it into a weak point, pierce an armour-join or pop the helmet clear of its seal. He swung the axe and once again its teeth managed to gnaw off a few bright metal shavings before the other Space Marine whipped the lance away, whirled it, whacked the axe aside again and slammed the lance-head back down into Nautakah's gorget.

They could do this all day, they could do this until doomsday. The lance couldn't hurt him, but the bastard Snake was fast and cunning. Every hit and pin was another few seconds drained away. Every one of those seconds was a chance lost, his options strangled a little tighter, but worse, every one of those seconds was an insult. A humiliation.

The keening of the pain machine rose up and up, sharper and hotter until it seemed to rise out of his hearing completely, passing into his thoughts and merging with them instead of clawing at them. In the silence that it left behind, the sounds of the scene around him sat with a dreamlike clarity, separate and perfect as though they were exhibits in some elegant museum-hall, each on its own pedestal under its own light. The rising cry of the Thunderhawk's engines. The sound of ceramite boots on stone and tile. The distant throb of the psychic storm outside. The almost imperceptible rising whine of a plasma gun field.

Nautakah swung his axe.

Priad
Central chamber, Pinnacle Spire, Oureppan

Time ran out. There was a change in the World Eater's movements, a shift in its body language so subtle beneath its warplate that even Priad, who had fastened his attention so totally on his enemy that he could almost feel its movements in his own limbs, barely perceived it. It whipped the axe around once again with a speed it had kept hidden until now, and as Priad once again swung the lance-head out of the way of the blow the monster came up off the tile. This time it pushed itself up onto its side with that eerie speed, and when the lance came back around the axe was ready to meet it. Priad couldn't quite arrest the swing of the lance-haft, and a burst of sparks and chewed metal fragments sprayed from the impact.

With an elegance born of a century and more of relentless drilling and forms, Priad reversed the spin of the lance and snatched the haft away before the axe could hew all the way through it. He sized up the enemy warrior's movements and reach, so fast and instinctively he was barely aware of the process, found a weak point, the angle it would be hardest to swing the axe around to, sidestepped and whirled the lance around and up into the creature's knee. The lance came whooping through the air with a force that would have smashed a human clean in two even without the cleaving head, a force that could destroy even a power-armoured joint.

But instead it met the head of the chainaxe, perfectly positioned and angled to catch the blow, timed so that Priad could not arrest the motion of the lance. There was a quick yelp of metal and then the warrior had surged back to its feet as Priad pulled the headless steel haft back.

'Andromak! Kill-shot, *now!*'

But there was no reply.

Nautakah
Central chamber, Pinnacle Spire, Oureppan

The Nails were a storm of pain and rage right through Nautakah's being, and his mind floated in that storm like a kite on the wind.

He had foreseen the Snake's final strike; there could be no question of the best point of attack, and his enemy had never fought a World Eater before, was unprepared for the speed and focus that the Nails' pain-trance brought with it. His body felt weightless, his movements effortless. The axe-head was there to meet the lance without conscious thought and as soon as he felt the haft judder in his hand as the teeth bit, he knew the counter had been perfect. He was on his feet in a dreamlike moment. The lovely pain – the clean, white pain of the Nails – was carrying him forward. All he had to do was ride the wave.

The Snake was flanked by two of his brothers now. One had taken the wide-legged Adeptus Astartes firing stance, bringing a bolter to bear. The other was on one knee, a plasma gun resting muzzle down on the step beside him. Broken grey-black rockcrete was bouncing and scattering about him. A chunk of the spire's roof had been broken free by the psychic storm outside and plummeted who knew how far to crash into the Space Marine's head and shoulders. A strange, crawling light clung to some of the fragments like mucus, piercing the vision as though they were brighter than they actually were, deforming the masonry, flaring into bright bubbles or flashing into crystals. The storm outside had lost its last traces of structure and control and now the raw stuff of the warp was precipitating out of the air, eating away at the spire to the point of collapse.

None of that mattered to Arnogaur Nautakah while his enemies remained unbled. A criss-cross of vicious axe-cuts carved the air between him and the Snake commander, too fast to counter, actually forcing his enemy back up a step, then another. The Snake on Nautakah's right made ready to fire and the tiny shifts and locks in posture as his armour actuators prepared for the recoil went off like a klaxon in the World Eater's Nails-sharpened senses. He ducked his head and tilted his shoulders, and the first bolt-shell was fouled and broken in among the unnaturally hardened spikes that curved up from his pauldron. The second clipped the pauldron's corner and exploded against his waist before it could drive into his armour. The pain engine screamed at the insult, Nautakah barely more than a passenger in his body as he pivoted, lunged, forced the Space Marine back with a sweep of the axe and tore a gouge across his torso with the return sweep, then stepped forward and raised the axe two-handed over his head for the beautiful kill. The thin web of thought stretched over the furnace of pain began shouting in alarm, agonisingly aware of the two Snakes to his left and more coming down the stairs now, but the weight of the axe was so delicious, the triumphant note of the pain-song so hypnotic, so true. He let it carry him.

The headless lance-haft slammed into his armpit, driven by all the power of the Snake captain's augmented strength and armoured weight. The impact cracked Nautakah's armour, the quasi-organic carapace beneath it and the bone beneath that, and sent him staggering away. The cries in his head were an ugly cacophony once more. The machine screamed at him to kill.

He turned to the captain, held himself in place. Revved the axe in his left hand, pointed with his right.

'You,' he said.

Priad
Central chamber, Pinnacle Spire, Oureppan

The World Eater pointed at him, spoke. Priad didn't bother trying to understand what it said.

'Andromak! Dyognes!' His brothers were alive, a thought and an eye-twitch bringing their markers to the edge of his vision, winking to show damage but not death. But there were no seconds to spare. He had heard the Archenemy had World Eaters Space Marines scattered through the Sabbat Worlds but Priad had never confronted one directly until now, never fully understood the hellish puissance that battle-frenzy brought out in them. The briefest respite, a fraction of a move out of place, and it would have him.

Perhaps it would have him anyway. But Damocles would go on, and the brother-sergeant who had defended Saint Sabbat at Pinnacle Spire would be named in the declaration of deeds, from the clifftops over the crashing waves. A sudden, vivid sense-memory struck Priad, the crisp, clean tang of Ithakan sea air, as he lunged, driving the headless lance forward.

The monster already had its chainaxe raised to counter the stroke, but before either weapon could bridge the gap between them there was a skull-splitting crack of fracturing masonry and tiles flew up around them like landmine shrapnel. Stone ground on stone as the steps and the colonnade floor gave convulsive tilts in opposite directions, tipping each warrior to their right, and an eye-watering tendril of warp-lightning whipcracked along the new fault line. Strange echoes bounced in its wake and rock chips hung drifting in the air as if they had forgotten to fall.

'Andromak!' Priad shouted again, but the vox was full of howling interference. He hazarded a look over to his gunner but Andromak had been struck by a second chunk of masonry that had driven his helmet down into his collar, giving his head a sunken, twisted look. He was moving, but sluggishly. The muzzle of the plasma gun quested up and down. Priad knew that motion. Andromak's sight-through targeting vision had been damaged by the hits. He was trying to see what he was shooting at.

'Andromak! Round fifteen, decline five, now!' Andromak was half-blind and still woozy but Priad's words hit the combat-conditioned pathways of his brain and his body jolted into action, dragging his battered mind along behind it. His gun gave out a shout of blazing energy.

Nautakah was already moving again, with that terrifying, deceptive speed. The leading edge of the plasma burst scoured his side but by the time the core of the blast caught up he was out of that space and it burned the air behind him. Growling wordlessly, ignoring the wound, Nautakah charged.

Priad
Central chamber, Pinnacle Spire, Oureppan

Priad drove the lance-haft at the World Eater's face, only to lose another half-metre of it as a chainaxe stroke went through the steel with barely a twitch of resistance. He back-pedalled up the steps, whirling the lance in front of him and from hand to hand in forms honed by centuries of Phratry warriors, made to hide an arsenal of possible attacks in a few simple movements, foiling an enemy's ability to predict when the spinning blur would turn into a skewering lunge or a pulverising strike. He let the haft roll and slip in his gauntlets to change its angle and speed, going on the attack again now, using the lance's reach advantage to feint strikes at the Traitor Space Marine's weapon, his wrists and hands, knees, helmet. The appetite of the Blood God's slaves for hand-to-hand battle was infamous and so Priad fed that appetite, forgoing the obvious trick of sidestepping into the creature's blind side and shifting the other way instead, keeping himself in the centre of its vision, goading it up the steps after him so it could present its back to Dyognes and

Andromak, for a bolt-shell or plasma shot to make Urdesh just that little bit cleaner.

But the psychic storm was not done with them yet.

Andromak
Central chamber, Pinnacle Spire, Oureppan

Gouged and bludgeoned and dragged apart by the brawling torrents of force still spilling into existence around it, the top of Pinnacle Spire ceased to exist. Rockcrete and stone sang a chorus of funeral groans as the structure beneath it was wrenched out of true. The last of the unbroken windows exploded from the strain and filled the air with vicious shrapnel that sparkled in strange colours from the unnatural lightning that followed the thunder of demolition.

Andromak was catapulted into the air as a squealing streamer of unreality earthed itself in the steps between him and Nautakah. The jagged wound it left in its wake parted light and gravity, and Andromak tumbled high above the steps, his battered senses trying frantically to find something to orient themselves on, leaving a bright corkscrew of plasma trailing behind him as the magnetic seals on his weapon's flask began to leak. Warning runes crowded his vision. He could hear the hiss and crackle as the leak accelerated and feel the heat starting to spray across his torso, first as feedback through his armour and then a real and raw burning as the plasma found the seams and joins in his warplate and came seeping through. He triggered the jettison command through his armour link and slammed the manual release, but the distorted magnetic fields and the damage to the gun itself had jammed the leaking flask in place. He struck the flask mounting with the heel of his hand, then with a fist, and the flask finally came loose and was snatched away. The seals on the damaged flask were too weak to hold on their own and overloaded an instant later, just as the vortex tossed Andromak aside. The white flash of energy enveloped him and then he plummeted back towards the colonnade floor, leaving a trail of dark smoke through the air.

Holofurnace
Central chamber, Pinnacle Spire, Oureppan

Fragments of reinforced glass fell across the steps like sheets of hail. Holofurnace registered them striking his armour but gave them no thought. They could have shredded a human but to him they were gravel hitting a roof, nothing more, until the ripple of an immaterial shockwave fell from the storm, struck the plinth and flowed over it, moving like both fog and water, turning the tile to slurry and the glass to frost. Holofurnace's hand closed on thin air just below the Saint's ankle before he skidded away and crashed down onto one knee. An errant twirl of vapour wrapped around his leg and then suddenly was solid, carbon-hard, anchoring him in place.

Holofurnace pivoted on his trapped hip, aimed and fired, but the shell detonated barely centimetres from the muzzle of his bolter. He dropped his gun to his side and fired at the floor, trying to uproot the unnatural grip on him, and when the shell struck the floor by his ankle it drove deep and exploded the warp-weakened stone. The floor of the entire chamber began to crumble and subside, dust and chuckling shadows oozing out of the spreading cracks. Kicking his way free, Holofurnace felt his balance shift and then his feet lose touch with the floor. He was drifting upwards through the air.

* * *

Priad
Central chamber, Pinnacle Spire, Oureppan

The sudden crumbling of the floor took both Priad and Nautakah's footing: if their weapons had not been between them they would have tumbled into one another's arms and ridden the avalanche down together. As it was, Priad felt his balance go first, and aimed a vicious stroke at Nautakah's axe-head, trying to smash the motor before he fell into its striking arc. Nautakah, who had spent millennia in fighting pits and battlefields countering just that move, simply pivoted the axe away, but before he could turn it back to attack he had overbalanced too. The Nails screamed in anger at being denied battle and Nautakah gave voice to the scream. The rubble-fall had shoved them apart and blocked the Snake commander from view, and the vision in his remaining eyepiece was starting to stutter and wash out as the damage to the faceplate caught up with it. With a grunt and a shrug, Nautakah severed his collar seals, pulled the helmet from his head and sniffed the air. The Butcher's Nails yelped their eagerness along his nerves.

Holofurnace and the Saint
Pinnacle Spire, Oureppan

The warp vortex was raging beyond all possibility of control now, the ship high above the planet caught in it as helplessly as the handful of warriors in the disintegrating spire at its foot. It dragged the Anarch's voice from his throat and drowned it as surely as it dragged the green fire from the Saint's shoulders and swallowed that. It unravelled the prow of the Anarch's ship and opened it to the void, and its touch trailed along the floor of the Pinnacle Spire vault, plucking up smoke, and dust, and rubble, and bodies both dead and alive.

Colonel Mazho shouted the names of his men as they tried to push him to safety and the warp-tide snatched them up. One dissolved in moments, just a boot and a few scraps of cloth and skin fluttering away, the other thrashing for footing that was no longer there. Mazho grabbed the man's hand, was dragged along the floor and then the upward tide had him.

As the wreckage of the spire was sucked up past her, the Saint hung motionless, pinned in the air. Holofurnace reached out as he rose past, but couldn't touch her. He tried to shelter her with his arms in case he could interfere with whatever force was holding her but he couldn't get close enough. Kassine could, the little woman catching one arm around the Saint's waist and thrusting her staff upward. She sang as she triggered a long blast of flame up into the vortex, but then a river of torn-up masonry and tiles swirled past them, battering them, knocking both weapon and Saint out of Kassine's grip. Semi-conscious, she spun up past Holofurnace and was lost to view. He thought he heard Milo's voice but could not see him, saw an ayatani sash swirl up past him and then catch fire and burn to ash but could not see Ghelon or his soldiers. The waste of the humans' bravery infuriated him and he tried to swim forward through the air, get to her and break her free, break them all free…

Holofurnace was turned over in the air and facing downward. The humans still alive were too blinded by shock and dust and light to see. It was only Saint Sabbat who looked up through the vortex, straight into the face of the Anarch.

They stared at one another, those two, across the thousands of kilometres of distance that the warp-funnel folded down into mere metres of simple empty air. Neither one said a word.

Priad
Pinnacle Spire, Oureppan

Rubble and dust cascaded off Priad as he clawed his way onto his hands and knees, pushing his way up out of the collapse as if he were fording a river. His armour was a mass of tiny mechanical twitches and pneumatic coughs as it expelled dust from sensory pickups, seam-joins, intakes and vents. He let it carry him up to a standing position as he scoured his display for a glimpse of spiked armour like old blood, or the sound of a chainaxe. In the edge of his vision there were nothing but blue-grey placeholders where the ammo counter and status runes should have been – the avalanche had torn his bolter away. Well, it would be his pleasure to make this kill by hand. He felt as much as heard the thrum and click as the tines of his lightning claw extended. There was the briefest shift in the movement of his armour as it recalibrated its energy needs around the now ignited claws and adjusted the pull from the reactor pack accordingly.

He stopped himself. The mission. Not pride or vengeance. The mission.

'Priad to Damocles. Cepheas.'

'Engines up, ready to dust,' came Cepheas' voice. *'Four aboard.'*

'Moving,' came Xander's voice. *'Got Andromak.'*

'Priad to Kalliopi,' Priad called, scrabbling across the face of the rubble-fall as the air crackled and light and sound bent and tangled. 'Priad to Kalliopi. Status! Show your markers!'

A bright FOE rune flashed into his vision but danced and

skittered as the scry-sprites in his armour called to their siblings, trying to fix a location to show him.

'Brother-captain, the upper spire is almost eaten away,' Cepheas told him over the vox. *'If the colonnade roof comes down there's no chance of taking off, further casualties certain.'*

'Get ready to fly,' Priad told him. 'Get out from under the colonnade then circle and find a way to break back in. Who has eyes on the Saint? Xander, respond!'

But it was the World Eater who answered him.

Damocles
Central chamber, Pinnacle Spire, Oureppan

'This is fitting,' Nautakah told the Iron Snakes captain. 'Fitting that you bleed now as you have watched your brothers bleed. Bleed for him, Snake. The true divinity. Blood for the Blood God.'

Gobbets of yellow-green flame rained down across them, screaming when they spattered against the stone and leaving trails in the air like spiderwebs.

'Skulls for the Skull Throne.'

The spire walls were peeling away and the four great colonnades were shuddering and caving in. The arnogaur clashed the revving axe-head against his chest.

'Blood and skulls. *Blood and skulls!*'

The air moaned and twisted. Cracks zigzagged through the floor beneath them, spewing corposant flares and writhing plumes of psychoplasm. A churning red haze formed around the axe-head as though the speeding teeth were cutting a wound out of nothing. Priad thought he heard a brief shout from Xander in his vox before the markers for his Damocles brothers flickered and vanished.

There was no time to think of what that meant. The enemy's axe was screaming, Priad's lightning claw blazing in reply.

They charged.

Priad and Nautakah
Central chamber, Pinnacle Spire, Oureppan

At a level so ingrained it needed no conscious thought, Priad knew this: his enemy outreached him. If he could not close inside the kill-zone that marked the chainaxe's reach then he would be hacked apart, but inside that deadly circle the axe-strokes would be cramped and smothered while his claw would be perfectly placed for the kill.

At that same level of effortless reflex, Nautakah knew this: that the Iron Snake would have to rush through the striking circle of his axe to have a chance of fighting him. There would be one moment when he was at the perfect distance for the killing stroke. But the Snake would know this too, and now he knew Nautakah's reach and speed. Every scrap of his skill would be bent towards spoiling that one crucial moment.

He might hunch down just before he came in reach, hoping to force Nautakah to readjust a decapitating swing and putting extra armoured surfaces in the path of the axe: more obstacles, more chances of it skating away instead of cutting. He could leap, forcing the swing to readjust in the other direction, but his footwork the instant before he closed would give that away, give Nautakah the chance to adjust his counter-attack, and once he was in the air there would be no way to arrest or change his movement once the axe came in. He could turn into the axe-stroke, if this Snake were fool enough to put his very life on such a coin-toss: it would present his chest, neck and face to the swing of the axe while winning his claw that fragment of extra reach. If he did that he was dead. Nautakah could feel his muscles and nerves straining to move under the pain engine's lash. He would cut faster than the Snake would know, and once that turning lunge was begun there was no halting it.

Or perhaps he would simply ward off the axe-head with his arm, take the cut, sacrifice the limb for the chance to transfix Nautakah's hearts. Their corpses would collapse into one another's arms and their blood would paint one another's armour. And even though it would mean his end – no more bloodshed to flow before the throne, no more skulls taken to pile in front of it, no more service to his Pact and his Legion – still the thought of that lit Nautakah up with excitement.

Priad saw the grin split the enemy's face as he closed the last of the distance, propelling himself towards the axe's killing arc with incredible momentum. He saw the monster raise its axe, preparing the swing, a movement he could read as effortlessly as a tactical map, or ocean waves, or his brothers' markers inside his helmet display. The precise position of its grip on the haft, the angle of the axe-head. The way it placed its feet and the tiny adjustments as it got ready to put the full torsion of its body behind the strike.

With every tiny movement of the weapon, with every one of Priad's rushing strides, every second in which the gap to their meeting narrowed, options and choices fell away. Priad was moving too fast to drop into a crouch and so the monster adjusted its weapon to better make a flat swing at neck height, which meant it was now too late to change and prepare for a lower strike at Priad's weapon hand, but now it was also too late for Priad to begin an overhand slash; he would have to lunge, which meant that the World Eater would have no choice but to strike into Priad's helmet, and now he was two strides from the axe's killing arc and in less than an eye-blink that was one stride and there was no more time...

...and in a movement faster than Priad had realised he could make, Nautakah shifted his grip on his axe, pivoted on the toes of his armoured boots to reverse the angle of his body and swung a quick, brutal stroke into the base of the lightning claw, on an arc perfectly calculated to cleave the mounting and leave the blades half-severed, inert and dead...

...and in the last instant before his weapon was destroyed Priad gave the briefest twist of his arm, and instead of carving into the claw's power circuits the chainaxe squealed as its teeth sunk into the chunk of reinforced rockcrete Priad was gripping in his gauntlet, concealed by the crackling incandescence of the blades. It was softer than ceramite, not stopping the chainteeth but clogging them with pulverised masonry and dragging them, stalling the axe for just barely the time Priad needed to shove his arm straight, twisting the axe-head just enough to force the strike out of true...

...and in the instant it took for Nautakah to register what had happened, Priad was inside the range of his axe, smashing his other fist into the arnogaur's face.

Nautakah actually staggered a step, unable to stop the frustrated howl of the Nails from bursting out of his own throat. He twisted the axe and a blow from the pommel rocked Priad's head sideways, but there was no hope of deflecting the Snake's momentum. He crashed headlong into Nautakah and both warriors sprawled in the rubble.

Priad grabbed for the axe-head as they fell but Nautakah had already pulled it away, and now he shifted his grip and slashed sideways without bothering to rise. The strike was aimed into Priad's reactor pack, hard for him to counter without throwing his whole body into a turning block, but Priad was already inside the swing again, driving his claw forward. Nautakah got his other hand out, caught and gripped the claw mounting around Priad's forearm, and they froze like that, locked like tectonic plates, the apparent stillness masking the tremendous build up of force. There was the smallest of quakes where gauntlet met gauntlet. A scorched, acrid smell rose from Nautakah's plastron where two of Priad's claws had managed to pierce it. For one breath's worth of still time, the only movement from the two was Priad's back banner flapping and snapping in the tortured air.

Nautakah fought against the urge to thrash and roar against the indignity of his position. He knew the Snake's mind would be focused sharper than a laser, every tiny shift and tic of his body picked apart for the hint it would give about how his own focus and balance had changed, where the opening was to drive those sheaths of energy just that little further down, and just that little further again. His empty eye socket throbbed and his nostrils filled with the smell of his own armour burning.

And then – at last! – the blare of agony in his eye found harmony with the nerve-scraping pain of the Butcher's Nails, as old and beloved as the feel of his axe revving in his hand. Nautakah's eye fixed on the Snake's impassive faceplate and his tongue uncurled from his mouth as the acid-hot pull of the machine in his skull trickled out through the wires in his scalp, filling his mind and overflowing into his body. There was the feeling of being in a gunship as it climbed, of being buoyed up in a grav-lift. The weight of his armour, even his own body, felt airy and light. His hand began to move.

Priad's first thought was alarm that his armour was rebelling on him, that he could not trust the feedback it was sending into him like the extra layer of his body it was supposed to be. What other explanation could there be for his hand being forced up, up, the tips of the lightning claw pulling free of the enemy's blood-crusted armour, and up still, all his weight and the power of his mechanically augmented Adeptus Astartes brawn pushing it down, but still, impossibly, the enemy was forcing him up.

Its remaining eye, bright green and cat-slitted, was alight with something that could have been agony or could have been joy. Its teeth glistened and its tongue was tasting the air. It was smiling up at him.

Stress indicators were starting to fade into view in the corner of Priad's eye, and he could feel the strain of plate and mechanism as the World Eater forced his claw back. The tremor in their joined fists was stronger now as Priad's own muscles and bones began to creak. His feet started to skid on the shattered tiles as the World Eater pushed its arm straight and then started to rise from the floor.

Nautakah had misjudged the Iron Snake. He had expected stubbornness, the kind of mulish, childish pride that he had managed to goad out of so many fresh-faced little loyalists over the centuries, driving this brother-captain to show off his strength and his faith and push himself even harder into a losing position. But the Snake ended the contest the instant he realised it was hopeless, pulling the claw back, letting Nautakah's built-up force throw him off-balance while he was still halfway to his feet. His other fist was already raised to batter Nautakah's skull into shapelessness in the moment it would take the arnogaur to rebalance himself...

...but the pain machine changed all the rules.

Nautakah's elbow crashed into the dead centre of Priad's

faceplate. A hairline crack appeared across his vision as the left eyepiece fractured from the impact, and his breathing took on an odd sibilant note from the distortions in the mouth grille. The blow was not enough to hurt Priad and barely enough to disorient him, but that *barely* was all the opening Nautakah needed. Another elbow smash toppled Priad backward as Nautakah gained his feet. A shove sent him a pace back, a kick sent him another as the chainaxe came screaming over and down.

The tines of the claw batted it aside, leaving cauterised weals along the side of the axe-head, but Nautakah yanked the axe out of its arc before they could properly cut it. It crashed down into Priad's pauldron instead but found no purchase. Adeptus Astartes power armour had been built for millennia to present smooth curves to the enemy, perfectly designed to send a chainblade skating away instead of biting in. Combat drills had developed a sophisticated set of body movements to capitalise on that, always shifting, never allowing an enemy to strike the same plate twice. Priad took the strike on the top of his pauldron, twisted his body and shrugged it down onto his arm, and once again Nautakah had to pull the axe away before Priad could slash or grab at the haft. The World Eater shifted his grip again, parried a swipe of the lightning claw that would have scraped his face from his skull and swung at Priad's hip with a tilt of the axe that would let him redirect in a split second and hack apart the Snake's knee. But Priad had read the move and was already lunging inside the axe's reach again, filling Nautakah's nostrils with the stink of ozone as a near miss from the claw sliced the air in front of his face.

The floor tilted and cracked under them, and a vortex of howling wind foaming with warp power formed around them. Fragments of glass and stone began to spang off their warplate. The glass-hard scab that filled Nautakah's empty eye socket cracked in half and a fresh welling of red spread out from the ruined eye in eight directions, before it too hardened.

Nautakah and Priad
Central chamber, Pinnacle Spire, Oureppan

Nautakah wasn't going to get his mighty duel-ending axe-stroke. He knew that now. The Snake was too skilled to let him create the opportunity, the precise alignment of space and time to rev and swing. So if he wasn't going to be able to stay distant, Nautakah had no choice but to close the distance in turn, pushing in chest to chest and nose to nose, denying the Snake the room to use his claw the way he had been denied the use of his axe. Even here the claw would still be deadly, more so than a chainblade at that range, the powered tines able to sink into his armour with no need for angle and purchase. A single mischance would see him carved open. Unacceptable. He needed the Snake's claw arm across his body, where the only strike available to him was an easily countered backhand instead of the armoury of moves the forehand offered. But the only way to get it there was to have him committing into a killing stroke, present him with a chance to end this that he could not pass up.

Not so much as a hundredth of a heartbeat separated insight and action. Nautakah stopped matching his movements to Priad's in the intricate step/counterstep by which they had both tried to control the distance between them. He readdressed his axe in a grip that was unworkable for such close quarters and quarter-turned his body, letting the

Snake circle for a clear strike at his right side and exposed head. Despite the brutal, astonishing speed of the duel this moment felt to Nautakah like aeons passing, bright adrenaline flickering through him like firelight as he offered himself to the blue-blazing blades.

Priad took the chance without thinking. In an eye-blink his arm had hooked around and aimed the claw, and then he was pivoting to drive the blades across with the torque of his entire body into the strike, so fast that the monster would never have time to register the mistake it had made to give him the opening...

But then the creature shrugged up its pauldron and the tines of the claw were in among the thicket of spikes that curved up from it, flashing and sparking as they cut and blasted their way through the alchemically hardened iron, but the way the Traitor Space Marine rolled its shoulder the spikes fouled the claw for just enough of an instant to slow it. And then against all sanity the creature was leaning into his blow, letting the claw skewer into its pauldron and then twisting forward to push Priad's arm back, the tines of the claw jittering and screeching as they tore through ceramite and scrawled three new smoking gouges across the traitor's chest. The clumsiness it had affected for its feint was gone and it bore in on him now, leering in triumph, using its whole body to pin Priad's arm between them. It gripped the chainaxe high on the haft, right up beneath the weapon's chin, punching the screaming blade forward at Priad's face.

Blood.

The pain engine was no longer screaming, it was roaring in Nautakah's ears as though he were wading through surf. His body was barely under his control. What was left of his conscious mind watched the chain teeth shrieking against the Snake's gorget and faceplate, leaving an insane cuneiform of ragged gouges criss-crossing the ceramite.

Blood.

The teeth screeched across one eyepiece and shattered it, tore out the mouth grille, ripped through the gorget and the articulated pieces beneath it until Nautakah's bare face was being sprayed with tiny particles of the black carapace bonded to the Snake's own skin, the axe-head burrowing deeper into the gouge, ready to open the side of the throat.

Blood for the Blood God.

Priad was cut off in the dark of his helm. One eyepiece was a flickering mess of feedback that did not respond to his commands to deactivate back to clear glass, the other was smashed to opacity. The air inside the helm was acrid with shredded metal and pulverised ceramite that its systems were too damaged to scrub out. His ears were full of the mad chorus of the World Eater's chainaxe and its baying voice. The connection to the helm's locks was broken and he couldn't command them to uncouple. He would be dead in the moment he tried to pull the helm free by hand.

Running blind, on memory and the balance and movement he could read through his armour, Priad let himself go, give way, and once more his yielding caught Nautakah by surprise. If the arnogaur had still had possession of himself the trick might not have got the better of him a second time, but too much of him was gone in the red furnace of the Nails, traded away for the speed that had outmanoeuvred Priad and the brute force that pushed the axe-head relentlessly forward.

Priad felt the split-second falter of the chainaxe as they crashed to the ground and he was finally able to throw the traitor off him and tear the broken helm away.

Sensations crashed in again, less acute without the helmet's auto-senses to filter and refine the stimuli but richer, rawer, more immediate. The change from auto-senses to innate ones could be jarring enough to disorient, but Priad had drilled himself and Damocles rigorously in just that transition and now he did not miss a beat as he feinted wide with the claw, drew out the beginning of a chainaxe swing and lunged at the enemy with his free hand, driving into the Chaos Space Marine's raddled and unlovely face.

Nautakah shied away from the blow, not quite fast enough but still he barely felt the crumpling of his cheekbone under the corrosive yowl of the pain engine. He was back-pedalling now, trying to create better distance and cut at the Snake's right side where catching his axe on the claw would need a clumsy cross-body parry that would expose him to a switch of grip and a decapitation stroke – but that meant swinging on Nautakah's newly blinded side, the side the Snake kept circling into, forcing Nautakah to fight by instinct and feel. He felt the scrape of metal as his teeth ground with the effort of clawing back the control the Nails were trying to abrade away.

He managed a high, flat forehand that came in aimed at the Snake's elbow joint, axe-head at a subtle angle so when the enemy ducked to catch the strike on his pauldron it would skitter up and into the side of his now bare head instead of stalling. An old and cunning move that had won loyalist skulls for his god on many a battlefield, but the Snake somehow read it in time and got his hand up and under the flat of the axe-head, punching it upward and ducking under the hit, turning the movement into a lunge with the lightning claw. Nautakah spun and blocked in turn, reaching out so that when the lunge inevitably became a crosswise slash into his side he could grab the Snake's forearm, get his fingers around the vambrace and start crushing the lightning claw's casing. But the bastard bluffed him, forewent the lateral cut and pulled the claw back, the central blade leaving a smoking welt across Nautakah's palm and fingers before his gauntlet closed on empty air. There was no time for anger or frustration, the fight was moving too fast for emotion to keep up with. Duelling at a speed that would have confounded a human observer, the two Space Marines were taxing one another's nerves, senses and brains to the limit.

Priad fended off a screaming series of half-wild blows meant to stop his constant circling into the World Eater's blind side. He held his nerve, made use of the onslaught to study the exact range and motion of the axe, mapping it onto what he knew about his own reach and speed. His reward came a second later when the traitor lost the last dregs of its patience and half-leapt into a murderous full swing that would have split Priad from shoulder to hip had it connected. But Priad slid forward, met it halfway and caught the axe-haft with perfect precision. The shock of it travelled through his wrist and up his arm, and he felt his armour's mechanisms shudder with the strain of stopping the movement. Once again they were locked motionless together, the World Eater so deep in fury at the denial of its killing strike that it took several seconds more to realise Priad's lightning claw was buried in its belly.

The Traitor Space Marine's remaining eye widened. It took in a short breath and then barked it out. Priad sent more power through the claws, trying to cauterise more of the traitor's innards and blur it with pain, but the thing seemed to ignore the claws and only tightened its grip on the axe-haft, ignoring the sizzling wounds in its gut, once more pushing the squealing blur of chain-teeth towards Priad's face.

Now it had two arms to commit against Priad's one, and the powerblades lodged in its body were not sapping its strength – they seemed to be goading it. Their feet scraped dust and rockcrete chips from the floor, and the air churned around them. Tendrils of warp-plasm condensed out of lightning flickers and writhed and cackled or burst into flames. The ragged roofless walls of the spire roiled around them as if they were no more than projections thrown onto billowing cloth. Somewhere Priad thought he heard a scream that might have been the wind, or Thunderhawk jets, but it was lost in the tumult that was now pressing in on them. His left arm was wedged against his body and he could not pull the claws free from the World Eater's gut, or twist or drag them. He tried to give way but the monster moved with him, finally wise to the trick, smiling with a hideous kind of serenity as it pressed the chainaxe forward. He could feel the breeze from the rushing teeth on his skin now.

Priad's jaw tightened and his lips pulled back from his teeth in a last snarl.

Nautakah
Central chamber, Pinnacle Spire, Oureppan

It was happening. Not fast enough for the yammering Nails sunk into his hindbrain but nevertheless here was another one, another champion fallen, another grub crawled from beneath the Golden Throne whose Emperor would watch as a true Space Marine's weapon split his face and then opened his skull. Nautakah smiled as the pain from the machine mixed with the agony from his wounds, drew it up like fuel and fired his muscles with even greater strength. The Saint's pennant would make a wrapping for his axe-handle and he would wear the Snake's banner as a half-cape, hanging from his pauldron spikes with the brother-captain's skull mounted atop it. He would make sure every other grey-armoured Ithakan saw it before his axe bit them in turn. He watched the loyalist's face, so ugly in its soft, infantile smoothness, contort as the teeth of the axe closed in. Gloated at the working of the jaw, the bulging of the neck muscles, the parting of the teeth.

And then he realised too late what that meant.

The jet of bio-acid from the Betcher's Gland at the back of Priad's palate splattered among the axe teeth and onto the chain, instantly drawn back into the motor and spreading through the axe-head assembly, eating it from the inside.

The acid was not powerful enough to damage the adamantine teeth, nor even enough to destroy the machinery on its own, but it didn't need to be. The chainaxe looked barbarically crude but it had been made to run at incredible speeds and temperatures through the battering that the weapon of a World Eaters Space Marine would have to endure. In moments Priad's venomous acid corroded the machinery just enough that the metal could no longer meet the superfine tolerances it had been built to. It stripped away lubricant and contaminated coolant. It weakened, just infinitesimally, the chain links and tooth mountings. The speed and heat and sudden degradation of the machine did the rest.

The axe spasmed and sparked as the chain broke. Unmoored teeth went whickering through the air, clicking off the two Space Marines' armour. Three of them buried themselves in Priad's cheek and brow. A scrap of toothed chain whirled backward and laid open the side of Nautakah's face down to the bone. The wailing note of the axe's motor rose to a higher, thinner scream and then choked into nothing as the mechanism shook itself apart, leaving an inert and smoking corpse in the arnogaur's hands.

Nautakah could hear himself speaking to the Snake now, a stew of ancient and ugly words from the formative dialects of the old Legions, from the chants they had learned in the warp and the Eye and the Maelstrom, from the glottal butcher-cant of the Blood Pact. He took his hands off his axe for the last time, let the husk of his old weapon clatter to the floor at his feet. Still barking threats and oaths and curses, barking out the words in time to the pain-pulses that clutched at his heart and bulged his eye, he beat the Snake's response by a fraction of a second, reaching down to where the lightning claw was still in him and grabbing the armoured forearm mounting in both hands. His grip began to tighten on the armoured casing around the power coils and field generators. He felt the grate of ceramite on ceramite conducted up through his bones.

His grip was too much for Pyrakmon's field repairs. The lightning claw's housing began to deform, the joins to break apart. Grotesquely, Nautakah could feel the effects inside his own body as one of the blades buried in his flesh had its energy field flicker and vanish. His breath hissing through his metal grin, he tightened his grip again. He thought he might still be speaking, his lips seemed to be moving, but the Nails had rejoined their strength to his and all he could hear was a single high, drilling note filling his ears and his skull. He dimly felt the Snake's other fist battering at him, but he felt, too, the claw's casing crumple further. By now the damage to the systems that sheathed the tines in lethal matter-disrupting energy would be feeding back into the

Snake's armour, filling its artificial nerves with static, sending the power draw from the reactor pack into spikes and lulls, burning out the circuits to the gauntlet actuators. Groaning, Nautakah managed to shove the loyalist's arm backward, pushing a hand's length of claw back out of himself. The smell of his own burnt blood stung his nose.

Nautakah opened his jaws wide to bellow his war cry, to teach this child how a true son of the Legions gave voice to triumph, but his voice was lost as another clap of warp-thunder shook the collapsing spire and scattered them apart.

Priad landed, skidded, used his momentum to bring himself up to one knee. His armour was coated in swirls of frost that suddenly exploded into steam. He covered his exposed head with his forearms as the chunks of masonry around him suddenly burst like cannon shells, the fragments beating a calligraphy of cracks and pits into his warplate. His adversary was already on his feet again. Its mouth was open but the inhuman, metallic scream in Priad's ears seemed muffled, as though it were coming from the back of the World Eater's skull rather than its throat. Its fists were invisible inside impossible cascades of blood that welled into existence around them then trailed behind like comet tails, hanging in the air instead of falling.

Nautakah knew this was the end. He had fought on more battlefields like this than he could count, in the ever-changing, unchanging fever dream of the Eye. The psychic storm around them had worn reality so thin that the violence of their duel, the collision of their spirits, was manifesting around them. Once again he had been blessed. This was like a homecoming. He laughed to see the Snake raise his lightning claw, the casing crushed and smoking, the tines inert.

Face grim, Priad readied the dead claw. The machine was dead, two of its tines sagging loose, but perhaps he could ask it to serve one final thrust into the monster's bare face. He doubled up his other fist tight enough that actuators creaked in his vambrace and wrist, and the squeak of ceramite came from his fingers. The floor underneath him was vibrating so fast it was almost a musical note, and webs of glowing cracks were spreading out from his feet. A piece of masonry bigger than he was glided by overhead, turning lazily end over end.

The last moments of their duel mirrored their first: a warrior charging, a warrior waiting to receive him. Nautakah rushed Priad, fists ready to shatter bone, brass-taloned fingertips ready to tear the stripling's face from its moorings and show his bleeding skull to the Blood God. In the same instant, Priad stepped forward and sideways, holding out the remains of the lightning claw for the arnogaur's charge to impale its face on the points, deepening his stance, dropping his centre of gravity into the collision. Metal tore as the claw blades severed the World Eater's brass collar and then broke against its armour. Skin split and bone cracked as Nautakah's blows struck Priad's scalp. And then they broke apart again, Nautakah spinning away as the brutal momentum of his charge sent him caroming off Priad, losing his balance as his talons snagged inside the Iron Snake's collar and yanked his arm back before they pulled free of his fingertips. He reeled, and Priad drew himself up and planted a kick into his side that connected with wrecking-ball force, the arnogaur's feet actually lifting clear of the quaking floor before he crashed face-down.

Priad was a pace closer as Nautakah pushed himself up into a simian crouch, hand reaching up and over his shoulders. A step closer. There was a snick as the socket that held his banner pole disengaged. A step closer. The pole in his hand, grip effortlessly adjusted, his arm winding back in the classic ready pose of an Ithakan sea-hunter, waiting for the snake to show itself in the water beneath him. Nautakah was still moving with that scrabbling, feverish speed, but Priad had his measure now. The arnogaur was only halfway to his feet when Priad cast.

The throw could not have been more perfect if Priad had been beneath his native sun, gripping an heirloom harpoon. The banner of Damocles and the Saint's pennant snapped out behind the pole as it flew. Its spiked foot struck home just as Nautakah was starting to turn his head.

Everything changed.

Nautakah could not process what had happened. He felt a spasm in his body, something like a stumble or a heavy cough, and his armour seemed to weigh just a little heavier on him. He felt his movements become clumsy and pushed himself away as he turned, thinking his armour had been damaged. Just another thing to compensate for but the heat of the engine would bear him through...

But there was no heat.

Nautakah's winched-tight nerves had gone slack. In place of the fever the Nails had fed into his nerves for as long as he could remember there was a sweet, cool numbness. He felt his muscles slowing and slumping. His thoughts suddenly seemed to be floundering through mud.

The banner pole did not have the weight of a harpoon. The spike was to fit an armour socket, not made to be weapon-sharp. It had splintered against Nautakah's reinforced skull, not transfixed it. But it had struck the pain engine squarely, smashed the heart of the millennia-old neural circuitry into a nonsense, turning the tendrils and Nails that inlaid Nautakah's head into so much lifeless metal.

The arnogaur turned. His eye was wide in shock. The banner pole still jutted up from the back of his neck but he barely felt it. He barely felt anything. The pain engine was gone, and the simple and unadorned input of his nerves felt like icy, alien numbness. He had no memories left of what his body had been like to live in before the Butcher's Nails had sunk into his skull. Nothing to help make this familiar, nothing to navigate by. He was a desperate spirit locked into a body it suddenly could not recognise or understand.

His feet moved sleepy-slow and when he tried to make fists his hands felt hollow and strengthless. His voice, when he found it, was hoarse and reedy in his ears.

'What did you do?' He wasn't even sure what language he had used, but the Snake didn't bother answering. Nautakah tried again, reached for all the gravitas and savage majesty that he had carried as an arnogaur of the Blood Pact. He tried to demand again, but the words that came out were:

'Give it back.'

Priad
Pinnacle Spire, Oureppan

The pronunciation was antiquated and the accent barbaric but Priad understood the words perfectly well.

'Give. It. Back.'

He didn't waste time trying to understand what the creature meant; it was enough to know he had clearly injured it. It was moving clumsily, sluggishly, its mouth open and panting in distress. The banner and pennant swung and flapped but it was making no move to try and pull the pole loose from its neck.

'Give it back!'

A bright golden bellow of energy roared over them and left sizzling sparks crawling over their armour and skin. Priad cursed, scrubbing at his face, trying to clear his eyes. Something had happened to the new systems in the hip of his armour. He could feel it clicking and tugging with each step. His balance went as the distance around him distorted, his armour proprioceptors trying to tilt him one way and his own instinctual balance the other. Quasi-human voices were barking and chortling out of the fissures that were opening in ground and air alike.

'Give it back! Give it *back!* GIVE IT BACK!'

His skin felt as though it was burning. The air around him was filled with flying stone and his feet could barely find purchase on the floor. He thrashed his way forward, swimming in the tumult as much as running, shouting the names of the brothers he was about to avenge. His voice ricocheted around him in distorted echoes until it was whipped away by the wind, but he could still hear the traitor screaming at him.

'GIVE IT BACK! GIVE IT BACK! GIVE IT BAAA–'

And the light and the dark and the bellow of the warp all became one, and became everything, and the world was gone.

Damocles
Spire ruins, Oureppan

When the towering funnel of the warp storm finally abated, Pinnacle Spire was gone from the skyline that it had defined for centuries. In its place, in the centre of the ring of torn and blasted buildings that had once housed the Anarch's psychic trap, was a sunken pit into which the last of the spire's foundations had crumbled. The towering upper steeple was not collapsed but simply gone, unravelled out of reality itself.

There was not even enough of it to form a dust-pall to mark where the spire had died.

The Thunderhawk that had burst free of the storm in its final extremity remained to bear witness. There were many dead brothers to carry home, but not a soul on board ever entertained a thought of pulling away. They circled the gunship inwards and outwards over the socket that had been gouged in the city, grimly raking their auspex over the ruins again and again.

And even so, they only found him on the fifth pass because he had finally managed to claw his way upward and break through into the air like some giant of myth birthing itself from the earth of a battlefield. Xander came down the gunship's ramp to see Priad kneeling in the rubble, face a mask of shattered rock and dust lacquered in place by flash-clotted blood. Saint Sabbat lay unconscious in the crook of his arm. In his other hand was Damocles' banner pole, the base shattered and stained with red. Of the warrior who had left his blood on the staff there was no sign.

With the Saint and her captain aboard, the Thunderhawk rose slowly from the wreckage and turned its nose south, for Ghereppan.

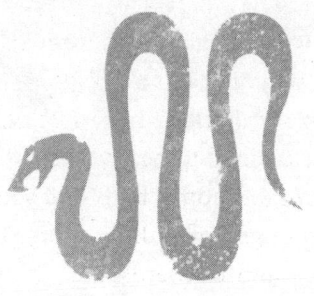

EPILOGUE

EPILOGUE

Urdesh had no moon to give it tides. He didn't think that would ever stop feeling wrong. An ocean should have tides to stir it. It was as natural as a living thing's sides moving as it breathed. Not that these were oceans, he remembered Holofurnace saying. Just weedy, ashy puddles to splash in, an insult as well as a disappointment from this smoky, reeking wreck of a world...

That's enough, Xander told himself. *None of that. Centre yourself.* He looked out over the water instead, the grey sea under the yellow sky, and listened to the waves lapping the black rock under his feet. That at least was familiar. Nothing could spoil that sound for him. He imagined the waves washing the rancour from his thoughts, leaving his mind clear.

The shore he stood on belonged to the northernmost of Ghereppan's little collection of islands, too small to hold more than a handful of steeples and domes. Battered and scarred by the night of the Miracle, they still stood proud behind him. Across the water before him, the Ghereppan foreshore swarmed with activity. Xander could have force-focused his eyes and attuned his ears to watch it closely but for now he was content to see it unfold at its natural distance. Mechanicus lifters were ranged along the foreshore and the Great Ascent, squat slope-shouldered quadrupedal walkers each as big as a Baneblade super-heavy, wearing the red-and-blue livery of the Ghereppan alpha-shrines. They had braced their thick steel legs against the seawall and were hauling on enormous chains and cables that ran down into the water. The waves were already parting around *Lupus Noctem*'s carapace as lifters dragged the Titan up and in to shore.

And there were footsteps behind him.

Brother-Captain Priad and Saint Sabbat were walking down to join him, she picking her way among the ridges and pools, he ignoring them and treading them underfoot. His armour still bore the scars of the battle beneath the spire and the Chapter colours had not yet been repainted; only the faintest ghost of colour on his pauldron suggested where the mighty Ithakan snake had once writhed across it. Priad's face was sombre and stern, the puzzlework of wounds that had covered it now healed almost to invisibility. Only the pockmarks where they had pulled the chainaxe teeth out of his flesh were still conspicuous.

They joined Xander at the water's edge and the three of them watched the reclamation work in silence until *Lupus Noctem*'s head, distorted by the hellish heat of the plasmapults but still snarling in defiance, rose clear of the water.

'It'll be a strange day for the Legio,' Priad said. 'An engine and comrades to mourn even while they celebrate their commander returning to them. I've never met the princeps maximus myself. I will have to be sure to before we leave the city. Diplomacy, remember?' he added as he caught Xander looking over at him.

'No.' They both looked down. 'They are alive,' the Beati said as conversationally as if she were mentioning the weather. 'It will be a hard path back for them, but *Lupus Noctem* and its crew will walk again.'

That seemed to be enough for Priad, but the casual certainty in her voice set Xander's thoughts spinning away, his equilibrium gone. He caught himself, tried to find his calmness in the sound of the water again, but finally the question burst out of him.

'Were we wrong to go to Oureppan?'

Her expression grew guarded and she lowered her eyes. Priad said nothing, but he turned to watch Xander as he spoke.

'All these things you know. These... these insights, these decisions that just come upon you. We stand here and suddenly you tell us that Mereschel's alive. Because you just *know*. But did you *know* what would happen in Oureppan? Did you know Sek was never there? Did you know you were spending Damocles' lives chasing a phantom? I can't not ask, my lady. I need to know that it meant something.'

She accepted his words without demur, as if she had been expecting them. It would occur to Xander later that he couldn't have said anything to her there that she hadn't already heard from her own conscience after she had regained her senses aboard the Thunderhawk. Now, though, she sighed and spoke without raising her eyes to his.

'You have a right to be angry, Xander. I stumbled. There was a moment where the Archenemy had its way with us. The Anarch did just what he boasts that he does. He drowned out the voices of faith and duty with his own. I lost sight of what He-on-Terra wanted for me, and only thought about what I wanted for myself. And once again, I still stand here while others have paid for my faults in blood. Every time I let my will weaken...' She let the sentence tail off.

'But even then,' she went on after a breath, 'His design unfolded as it should have. Do you understand that? If not, will you try to? Even when I was defeated by my own imperfections, I was His instrument. We revealed Sek's trap and we forced his hand. Between us we set the pieces in place for the Archenemy's own nature to play itself out and when we gave them the chance they overreached and betrayed and destroyed one another. Destroyed themselves. And so we find ourselves back in His design, back where He meant us to be. It is a lovely thing to know.'

'Sek is not destroyed, my lady,' Priad said quietly. 'I'm sorry, you speak some beautiful words, but you're speaking them too soon. We hurt him. We cost him his greatest stronghold on Urdesh and uncountable numbers of his soldiers, but wherever he is, wherever he confronted us from, he's still alive. The mission is not over.'

'That was my pride, you see,' she said. 'I killed one magister and could kill another, do you remember me saying that to you? He knew just how to goad me. Prick my pride. Make me so gloriously sure that I was anointed for the task, the weapon in His hand to strike Sek down.' She shook her head. 'Never was. I heard my own pride and anger talking and thought I was hearing Him. I so wanted to believe that I would be the one. But not this time.'

Off in the distance, *Lupus Noctem*'s head and shoulders were clear of the water. The faint sound of sirens and horns reached them on the breeze.

'It wasn't futile to go to Oureppan, Xander,' she said. 'The whole city had been made into a trap, for me. Sek opened the way from his lair into Pinnacle Spire to get to me. And that was my part to play. To walk into his trap for him.' She shrugged. 'Perhaps if I had known that that was all I was doing I might have baulked, failed somehow. Perhaps I needed to believe that I was on my way to kill him. I doubt I'll ever know.'

'But he did not catch you,' Xander said. 'And so we're back where we started.'

'No. We are finished. Finished with him. We did our part.'

'But–'

'My part was to walk into his trap,' she said again. 'He would never have shown himself like that for anyone else. It had to be me.'

'But you didn't kill him,' Xander said.

'Four souls,' she answered. 'There are four souls who'll form the weapon the Emperor will use. When Sek reached for me, he took up that weapon instead and pointed it at his own heart. He doesn't realise it yet, but that doesn't matter. It won't be long now.'

'This is hard to hear,' Xander said. 'Even if my head understands it, my hearts are still in the war against the Anarch. And now I'm being told that war has been taken out of my hands and finished.'

'Endings and beginnings,' she said. 'For all of us. The war is about to change.' She took a breath to speak, then stopped. The two Snakes waited. The waves sighed and slapped at the rock behind them.

'I am travelling to Eltath tonight,' she said finally. 'General Grawe-Ash has arranged my transportation.'

'It will be a day or so before our Thunderhawk–' Xander

began, and then caught Priad's expression. 'All right then. Tell me. What's happened? I've had no word that our orders have changed.'

'*Damocles*' official orders have not changed,' Priad said, his tone carefully neutral. 'The Warmaster's appointment stands.'

'Then we go where you go, mamzel,' Xander said, with a salute that the Beati returned with a smile and a shake of her head.

'Wait,' Xander said. 'Priad, you just said–'

'I did.'

'Ah,' Xander said after a moment. '*Damocles*' official orders have not changed. The *Warmaster's* appointment stands.'

'I am absolving Damocles Squad of your office,' the Beati said. 'I think there is work ahead at Eltath, bad and bloody work, but it's work for me, not you. It's no longer right to keep the brothers of Ithaka apart. Urdesh still needs you. The crusade still needs you, and it will need you shoulder to shoulder.'

Xander mulled that over for a time. A brief chorus of alarms came floating across the water: one of the cables had come whipping loose from the rim of *Lupus Noctem*'s carapace and the Mechanicus crews were scrambling to stop the Titan's tilting dead weight dragging the other haulers over the seawall.

'Let me guess,' Priad said after a while. 'You're wondering how to explain this to Damocles.'

'You mean you're not going to?' Xander asked, then forced a laugh to show he hadn't meant it. 'Don't worry, I know it's my job. But… did I ever mention that "Brother-Sergeant Xander" never stopped feeling strange to me? Especially not when you're standing here, but even when you were gone on Koram Mote for a decade and a half, it never seemed to sit quite right.'

'I'd like to say you get used to it,' Priad said, 'but in all candour "Brother-Captain Priad" still feels strange to me most of the time.'

'No hope for me, then,' Xander said ruefully, and shook his head. 'But actually, I was wondering how to explain it to Macaroth. I know I've been impatient about rear-echelon politics in the past, Priad, but I find myself almost wanting to be within earshot when he asks why we're not there and our lady tells him.'

'Changes ahead,' Sabbat said. 'The Warmaster has many troubles on his shoulders and he'll soon have more. I doubt he'll let this bother him. It's not as if we won't have plenty else to talk about.'

'So what are we to do, then?' Xander asked. 'Brother-captain?'

'We'll talk with Grawe-Ash,' Priad said. 'I'm minded to put the fighting elements of Platonos and Kalliopi into the Thunderhawk and send them north. The Militarum threw back a major Archenemy push on Eltath at the same time as we were breaking into Oureppan, and that means a major troop migration back towards Zarakppan that needs some terror struck into it.'

'And the sea,' the Saint put in, without looking at them, and fell silent again.

'The sea, mamzel?' Xander said eventually.

'The sea needs cleaning,' she said. Priad and Xander looked at each other.

'Well,' Xander said eventually, 'it's not that I disagree, but…'

'Erasmos Squad will be back soon,' the Saint said, and the two Snakes exchanged another look, of startlement this time. 'And they will have news. The loxatl aren't gone. If we aren't to let Andreos Squad's sacrifice go to waste then you will have to take to the water again.' She smiled. 'This is why He wanted the Iron Snakes with me on Urdesh. You are born sea-hunters. Who better to bring their old ways to a new world?'

'As if there's any comparison,' Xander said before he could stop himself. 'Apologies, my lady, that was impolite.'

'"Brackish slop full of ash and sulphur",' she said. 'I may have overheard Brother Holofurnace expressing his opinion of Urdesh's seas.'

'Look at this,' Xander said, unclipping a bronze water-vial from his waist and holding it out. 'Look at what they gave me. Someone in the Ministorum – that's them, isn't it, Priad, the ones in the red and white who preach for the Militarum and the rest? He heard some mangled tale that the Iron Snakes perform a rite with seawater and somehow got his hands on one of our empty vials. He was very pleased with himself when he gave it to me.'

'What…' Priad began, then shook his head. 'Ah, no, I can guess.'

'I was polite, brother-captain,' Xander said. 'You would have been proud of me. But…' He stared down at the vial.

'It's Ithakan ocean,' Priad said. 'We performed the rites after the Ghentethi planetfall and poured our waters into Urdesh's, so the two are joined. And every sea on Urdesh touches every other, so this water…' Priad gestured at the little waves pawing at the rock in front of them. His tone was noticeably more dutiful than sincere.

'That's a custom of your Chapter that I admire very much,' the Beati said. 'The water-sharing rites, and the thinking behind them. Carrying your ocean with you across the stars, using it to make fellows out of battle-brothers, humans and planets alike.'

'Not much left to carry, now,' Xander said. 'Each Apothecarion has a little extra, and each of our ships has a reserve, but this crusade has been a long one. I don't know how much we have left to share.' He looked around at them. 'I mean, Priad's not wrong. Now the seas are joined we can take water from Urdesh and share it just as we did with water from Ithaka. They're the same thing now. Except. Well.'

The Beati nodded.

'It's not just symbolism, is it? It's something more profound. A scent or a touch can conjure memories or create bonds that hours of ritual can't equal. The songs and prayers I brought with me from Hagia are beautiful, but when I want to think of my home they're not the equal of a single breath of islumbine on a crisp mountain breeze. Those little touches, those little blessings, can be so powerful. Losing them can weigh on the heart.' She looked at the vial.

'I suppose he was trying to help,' she said. 'Show comradeship. I'm sure he had no idea he was doing wrong.' She stepped up to Xander and rested the tip of her finger on the vial.

'Be of good spirits, Brother-Sergeant Xander. Have faith. I hope perhaps I've been able to help you do that. I would be proud to think so. If He should will it then we'll meet again.'

With that she stepped back from them, bowed deeply to each Iron Snake in turn, and turned to pick her way back towards the cliffs. She had not gone more than a few paces before a great clamour of horns and sirens came to them once more from the Ghereppan shore. Priad and Xander had both tensed, hands going to weapons, but the notes were different now. They were sounding in celebration, in jubilation. Priad realised what it meant. Just as the Saint had told them, the crews had found *Lupus Noctem*'s crew alive.

She turned back to them then. The stricken expression that had haunted her face since Sek had spoken to her had fully lifted at last, and she was smiling broadly with her arms spread as if to say, *You see?* And then she was walking away again. Priad reflexively scanned ahead of her, picking out the guards and sentries waiting for her above them at the edge of the rocks, and searched the sky and the water for hostiles. When he turned back he saw that Xander had unstoppered the vial and was staring into it.

'I...' was all he said when he looked up. His eyes were wide. Priad walked over as the other Space Marine held out the vial, and breathed it in. The beautiful, stinging-clean scent of the water of Ithaka's oceans. He closed his eyes, hearing the crash of the great waves in his mind, feeling the memories break and cascade onto him as if one of those waves had just fallen on him as he stood on the heads below the Phratry's battlements. When he opened his eyes and looked out at the flat grey Urdeshi sea it was like farewelling his home world all over again.

'It's even cold,' Xander said, and he was right. Condensation was forming on the side of the vial as he hastily stoppered it again. 'It will be cold there now, you know,' he went on. 'The great wakes will be skin-numbing. It will be sleeting on the water from the Phratry house all the way out to the horizon.'

'Cold enough to see your breath in the cloisters,' Priad replied. 'And the fog will be so thick in the balneary, your own hand looks like a ghost when you put your arm all the way out.'

Their eyes turned to the receding figure of the Saint.

'What *is* she?' Xander asked as the little cloaked figure picked her way up the steep rocks to where her new retinue waited.

'You know, I don't think even she could quite tell us,' Priad said. 'I find myself wondering if she wonders. Or if she has enough faith to just carry her on past the questions.'

'Faith again,' Xander mused. 'Do you ever find yourself thinking of faith as a human thing, something we left behind with all the rest of it? I understand why they need it. What do you think we need it for? We have the strength, the speed, the skill. We have the biology and the machines. Faith is for stopping up gaps. We're made to be seamless.'

Priad considered that for a time.

'I think,' he said finally, 'that what we might learn from Oureppan is that once we start to fancy ourselves seamless we set a course for a hard lesson to the contrary. I don't claim to understand her any better than you, let alone what she represents, but I do believe she's more than just the simple mechanical weapon that the Warmaster insists on seeing her as.' Priad held up a finger as if he were marking a spot in the sky. 'She's a fixed point. A star to steer by. I believe the crusade needs one of those. I believe Damocles has been honoured by being able to help her stay in the sky.' A shadow passed through his expression. 'We need that star as much as anyone, brother. There was a time once when whole orders of us decided they had left their humanity behind, and that that was something to embrace. We met one of them in Pinnacle. There was nothing about that creature that I want for myself.'

They watched the grey waves roll in. A matted mass of seaweed, yellow and glossy-slick, undulated in the shallows. It had been freshly cut, but within a day or two the tendrils would have grown back out of the water and halfway to the cliff.

Eventually, Xander cleared his throat.

'Ah. Yes. You were out here to declaim,' Priad said. 'I saw you getting ready. I apologise for the interruption.'

'I've been reframing my declaration of deeds in my head

ever since we touched back down,' Xander said, 'but it hasn't passed my lips yet. I need to see how it sounds out in the air. And over the sounds of the sea is even better. Yes, even this one.' Priad chuckled and nodded.

'I'll hear it in full one day, back among the Phratry. I don't doubt it. I'll be proud to salute you for it.'

'Thank you, brother-captain. I'll do my best to make it worthy.'

Priad turned and started up the path the Saint had taken, back to the rocks and the island. Behind him, over the waves, he could hear the scrape of footsteps and the faint sound of joints and actuators as Xander turned to the sea and spread his arms. Priad slowed his steps, set his feet down more carefully, the better to hear.

'*Listen!*' Xander's voice rang out over the waves and the incoming wind. 'Listen to words carried home to you from Urdesh, the world of two faces, Urdesh of the mighty forges and the teeming seas, Urdesh of bloodshed and mourning! Listen, Ithaka, and hear of a world that bore the tread of the Warmaster and the Saint, that heard the voices of the Gaur and the Anarch! Urdesh who bore the banners of Damocles and Andreos, Kalliopi, Erasmos and Platonos, and who received the blood of their brothers as her seas received the waters of Ithaka! Silence your voices, warriors of the Phratry, and learn how frailty and humility give birth to might. Hear of the arrogance of the enemy, and how that arrogance brought itself undone! Hear me, warriors, hear me, Iron Snakes, hear the deeds of your brothers among the fires of Urdesh!'

Priad smiled as he walked away.

ABOUT THE AUTHOR

Matthew Farrer is the author of the acclaimed Warhammer 40,000 novels *Crossfire*, *Legacy* and *Blind*. He has also penned many tales set in the Sabbat Worlds, including the Urdesh duology *The Serpent and the Saint* and *The Magister and the Martyr*, the novella 'The Inheritor King' in the *Sabbat Crusade* anthology, 'The Headstone and the Hammerstone Kings' in *Sabbat Worlds* and 'Nineteen-Three Coreward, Resolved' in *Sabbat War*. For the Horus Heresy he has written the short stories 'After Desh'ea' and 'Vorax'. He lives and works in Australia.

YOUR NEXT READ

SABBAT WAR
by various authors

As the forces of Chaos are thrown back from a dozen worlds, the forces of the Imperium forge ever deeper into the Sabbat Worlds in a savage campaign of reconquest.

For these stories and more, go to blacklibrary.com, games-workshop.com, Games Workshop and Warhammer stores, all good book stores or visit one of the thousands of independent retailers worldwide, which can be found at games-workshop.com/storefinder